A HANDSOME MAN

SHAKUN
FOR
HER IMMENSE PATIENCE

A HANDSOME MAN

A NOVEL

P.C.K. PREM

abhinav publications

First published in India 2001

© P.C.K. PREM

All rights reserved. No part of this book may be reproduced or transmitted in any form or by any means, electronic or mechanical, including photocopying, recording or any information storage and retrieval system, without permission in writing from the publishers.

Publishers
Shakti Malik
Abhinav Publications
E-37, Hauz Khas
New Delhi-110016 (INDIA)
Phones: 6566387, 6562784, 6524658
Fax: 91-11-6857009
e-mail: shakti@nde.vsnl.net.in
Website: http//www.abhinavexports.com

ISBN 81-7017-396-5

Lasertypeset by
S.R. Enterprises
Lajpat Nagar-IV
New Delhi-110024

Printed at
D.K. Fine Art Press Pvt. Ltd.
Ashok Vihar, Delhi

1

Those were nostalgic moments. I was lost in thoughts of fantasy. I was thinking of the shadows. The beautiful face of Suraiya. Her words and movements. Sparkling eyes. Her compassion and sincere concerns. The way she warmly escorted rather dragged him to his room. He was speechless and still. Jaycee, a strong man, becoming an innocent lamb.

I was quiet. For a while, there was a feeling of genuine affection for him.

"A man of substance," he used to address himself, probably a borrowed expression. Today, at the threshold of crisis, there was no redemption. His words had association with a girl, half, almost half his age. His eldest son was now thirty-one years old, a daughter having one son and a third son running business with an investment worth five crores with contracts in several fields and in many countries.

I was reminded of his wife Romi. Immediately after joining civil services in early sixties, he got married to Romi, who had just passed out her graduation. Extremely intelligent and well-behaved. At that time, she was hardly nineteen years old but was a girl of mature emotions and intellect.

Her grace, beauty and intellect impressed everyone.

"He is a master." I had once said.

"Yes, but remains glued to the chair," she had told him, as one morning, we were sitting over breakfast. Those were the days of Indo-Pak War.

"You know, the country is experiencing a disastrous breakdown of relations. A collapse unparalleled by any international standards. It is sheer treachery. No one believed. First that country stabbed us, killed feelings of brotherhood. China gave us, what we never thought of. It threw away relation...that bond of Panchsheel."

Jaycee was carried away by emotions. He was talking in detail about the nature of job importance, politics and what not. I was not much interested. In business I was facing countless constraints, challenges, competitions and threats. I was fond of a few sweet words, natural warmth and comfortable stay.

He has stopped, "Hey, you've lost."

"Nothing...I was thinking of...?"

"Arrey, don't think, I shall help you. You plunge into business without fears. I am there."

"Yes I know."

"You know, we are presently passing through a difficult period. At a very young age, this country got terrible shocks and wounds..."

I had thrown an unwilling smile.

"You know, Bhai Sahib, he is becoming a politician also."

Romi had added laughingly, "Meets big people. Always involved in big decisions. Lengthy notings, Figures, Arguments...you know, he talks of economy and trends in politics." She with a firm and confident voice had added, "He is associated with..."

Jaycee had suddenly burst into a crescendo of loud laughter.

"Romi, now don't befool me, my dear. The usual epithet he used for me without using the name." "She is now very clever. yes, very smart. You don't know her impeccable and tacit style. She moves voicelessly with words and yet without voice. Vicky is hardly four years old...you know I am a junior officer...with less than a decade...and it is surprising that Romi is known in official circles. In fact, I am being known..." Jayanta had looked into her eyes filled with loving anger and pride, "Yes, I am telling you. She is...your sister-in-law is a famous personality. Whenever, we go to meet our military friends, they, as is their wont, encircle her and start using flowery words and sometimes poetry flows down their lips."

"Now, Mr. Chauhan, don't brag." Romi returned to me and said, "He passed on the buck to me."

"All right I am responsible. But you know, my dear, she is learning from the mother, 'why and how' are her words now. If this continues, my existence will be threatened."

He gave a hearty laugh.

"Now have mercy and stop this politics at home. Here relations and mutual understanding are important. An assuring feeling. Small words of love and warmth."

"Where is Vicky?" He had asked.

"He is growing into a handsome man." I joined to continue the conversation.

"He is playing out..."

"Like father...," Romi was meaningful, "he is running very fast. He plans, each day. Lost in dreams. New ideas, modern free thinking. He thinks and speaks about those men and matters which don't concern us. Vicky, I believe, will definitely make a name without much fuss or drama. His mental attitude is positive. And then at home he listens to...Chauhan Sahib always advising him...to carve out a niche, a deep impression. But I doubt, Bhai Sahib, your friend will think of human beings."

Romi was now serious and from her eyes, I could observe that she was full of complaints and possibly suppressing herself.

Her lips quivered for a minute.

"What do you mean?" Jayanta showed a slight anger and expressed disapproval— "He is a little child and you say..."

"Why should you do...how about...?" She was going to utter something, but controlled— "I want, before children at least, we should stress family ties. How he has become rich? How has he grown great? Why he wanted to amass..." She wanted to be sarcastic but did not know how to put her thoughts in words.

"I want Vicky, Ashy and Rahul...these kids should grow into godly...a mother wants..." There was a tinge of arrogance.

"I know, I know what you want!"

"Mr. Chauhan," she said teasingly— "A clerk...you must know how to get out of the jungle of files and...any way humanistic approach is required. An ethical...It looks, we are drifting apart. This has to be stopped. That is why mama asks you, why have you done so...or how the things deteriorated? Living within the four-walls of the house does not give you the correct picture of the world. By moving about in parties and clubs does not mean that you know the world and its conspiracies."

"It is monstrous to think so," she laughed.

"Romi, I admire you. I like your frankness. I am not unaware of the shortcomings. You are not prohibited to say either, but I am restricted. You have the prerogative to be critical. You can inform yourself with a sense of respectability, can talk of social, moral, economic and intellectual pursuits. You can call us stupid and dull. You too, my dear friend..." He also addressed me in a calm and extremely composed manner— "We must do what is asked. Now why, how and what? It is only, yes, perhaps that is the experience constantly dished out to us. Romi, no moralising. It is enough. You are bright and brilliant, I know but..."

"Look, Bhai Sahib, you have listened to his thesis. There is no point in arguing. He is making up...I don't know why we cannot do small good things..."

Romi had spoken at length and we listened to her as if under a magic spell.

It was a voice of a triumphant person.

"Romi, this ego..."

She smiled — "No, not that, Be fair. I just speak out what I feel. You see those concrete structures...consisting of many flats..., you officers, who run or claim to manage..."

She had not said a word but had got up to bring a few eatables from the kitchen.

"She is a terrible woman. Like a mother...she is didactic."

Jaycee was spreading butter on the slice.

I had not responded.

Again, he had started telling me about the impact of war on the political and economic life of India. I was only giving a nod in helplessness. But he was not bothered at all that I was uninterested. Jayanta was deeply involved, that for a while, I too was concerned and was convincing myself that a woman never sees beyond her nose. Jayanta whom I never considered more than a person above others had made an impact on me.

'No, ambition was secondary with him. It is service to the nation that remains uppermost.'

I had heard a voice from within.

"In this world of white collared, one cannot exist on truth."

"So early a conclusion!"

"It is not mine. But senior colleagues say. If you want to live life, live it, don't complicate it by confusing it with morals and..."

He had tried to peer into my eyes.

Was he withdrawing? A question inside me had started taking birth. Romi could not be wrong. Those were not irrational or disingenuous comments.

"You are a businessmen," Jaycee had begun with his eyes still on the table, "Do you think, you can go along the way of your choice. No, you have to make suitable adjustments with people working around. It may not affect your position but the higher you go, the problems also increase proportionately. I think there is a slow and covert acceptance, though silent yet forming words and these laxities shall become parts of the system. I am hinting at the possibilities. A few heads have already rolled down..., but no, it is an initial embarrassment. When many join a crowd, there is only one voice and a weird pall of mystique wraps them up."

"You are justifying a wrong approach to..."

"No, I am looking at a convention which is taking shape. A modern tradition that ignores norms. There is no strict adherence to...anyway. If I don't do 'Sirring', bending and licking..., though these are dehumanising and against your...what then, who is concerned about...I am to ensure that I have a rich, fruitful and well-known public life. I cannot make enemies. No, this is unwise. You cannot sit in a corner table and scribble words."

"I want recognition, and today you have to join the horde of people who are noticed, talked about and accepted."

"I want you to live in this home among your children..." Romi had said in a cool and appeasing voice, "I understand, you want to be in the frontline, the same design and fashion suits you, I know you want parties, clubs, discotheques and...Bhai Sahib." Romi's voice had the aura of an eerie influence, "I don't say, he should...no, I simply want that he should concentrate on parents... children. A few hours...sitting together, taking tea, eating and exchanging pleasantries or just relaxing. You can be part of the house, while...it is sufficient, you are present in the house. This is then a feeling, you can call yours. A possession that is invaluable."

"What do you want?"

"No, not demanding. I only want that you should not expend yourself too much. These whispers and whimpers of your files, pins, paper weights and phones will not add glamour to your person. They are the means not the ends, living amidst dead makes you..."

"Look yaar, she is both temporal and appalling."

"No, I am not. By the way, Bhai Sahib, I must tell you he rarely turns up before ten. Does he come to sleep? What is all about? And we at home with fluttering familiarity go around in the evenings or at any vacant hour." She controlled her emotional tilt of the voice and said, "We too, I mean these officers' wives...imbibe a vicious relationship for one another, talking about frivolities and pranks of others maliciously in the absence of...I am sure, you understand, pick up stones..." She laughed, "It is a continuous belittling of soul."

"What do you want!"

"Your...nothing, I wanted to tell Bhai Sahib that we are forgetting to live, losing threads of co-relations...I have a firm belief that when we speak of relations in the contemporary context, there is a latent, unspoken and unconscious acquiescence of a functional way of living. I mean, man has started measuring utility in terms of mutual benefits and that is the..."

"And what you expect, my friend?" Jayanta said in a slightly irritated voice — "They are also busy. This life is not very long. How can you live in isolation? One ought to be practical."

There was an unending conversation on the life patterns, unexpressed desires and secret wishes.

I wanted to get out. I had an important work with my suppliers. It was a business trip to Delhi and I had come to pay a visit. At that time, I thought my friends in the lucrative govt. positions were not satisfied and contented. They had their own doubts, hesitations, uncertainties and ambivalences and they also felt humiliations. A social world for them was a ladder to fame.

His father had once commented.

The words even that day echoed. His father a highly sophisticated man with a taste for finer elements was not unaware of the ground realities of life.

He had once observed, "These people do not know how dearly this nation has achieved freedom. It was a war. Any way forget but I must tell, these people are growing greedy, cold and egoistic. They talk of nation but it looks false and stupid. There is no depth that is why it is ridiculous. These officials are creating social distortions with no clear-cut thinking." Jai Bhadra was very emphatic.

They were landlords, no doubt, but not very rich, for most of the land had gone to the cultivators. It went to his credit that Jai Bhadra did not ever make a complaint or had any grudges against anyone.

"I have advised Jaycee to serve people. I am reminded of an English officer, who was faithful to the Govt. and yet at his personal level, was humane. He developed personal relationship with the local people. Mingled with them, studied their customs, traditions and culture. Spoke of the everlasting spirit of sympathy, love and compassion of Indians, as a whole. My son, he was a noble soul. Like him, there were many. I had a warm equation with them. But they were rulers, foreigners, they knew that harsh truth and they also had an inkling that no one can stay in a foreign land for a long time.

"They had a unique sense of history. That English officer had a kind and gentle nature. Perfectly docile. He was intelligent and knew the unreasonableness of his countrymen, in spite of their reformatory cliches that were occasionally used to impress. I am not claiming that all was good. There were faults. And we had numberless ailments. Cantakerous diseases. No one could ever think. Contempt and banter constituted our psyche."

Jai Bhadra was down to earth in his approach. I knew his sense of fun and seriousness. His virtues were his own. Jai Bhadra knew history and traditions. The fast flood of changes was not new to him. The great movement had nursed him and standing on the bank of the movement he listened to great words, sermons, slogans and songs, and at the same time he was conscious of limited options. A thorough man he was. Never boasted that he was concerned about the country.

Jai Bhadra knew he had committed no sin. He also had known the spirit of sacrifice, the nervousness of the countrymen and the delayed action of the British Government.

"I know their affectation and fear. I don't deny that some were exceptions but in my case, I could not divide myself between the nation and the rulers. I sincerely say I did not contribute much but I never sabotaged the freedom movement. I had sympathies but I never made them public. And then my foreign friends were doing good by engaging themselves in social welfare programmes. I never found fault with them."

Jai Bhadra's words were true and spoken out of depths. He had carried out his work with gusto and a spirited fervour. He was perfectly conventional and yet modern. When in free India, they lost some of the brilliance, Jai Bhadra was the first to admit failure of the clan of landlords and others. He readily agreed and propagated social reforms. That was the age of Jai Bhadra.

"Arrey, my dear darling." Jaycee's words disturbed my chain of memories.

In a splitsecond moment, Jai Bhadra's face had disappeared in the musical tunes of air. I looked up and saw Jayanta consciously waiting for my reaction.

"I don't say...it is all my doing. But an officer with hardly a few years service should think of work. If at this age, one becomes lethargic, then...I know it is disconcerting to stay out, but it is an inthing. An officer is noticed when he overstays. You don't sit in the chair during office hours, with a couple of files under arms, you go about with a manipulated time-table, manufactured words of worries for the work, visit corridors of power and behave as if you were the only trustworthy public servant and at the same time, show to the other fellows that you are only his admirer...laugh at every word...throw praise at the slightest available opportunity, and then..."

It was a violating and provoking proposition to which I was being introduced. My sensibilities were hurt, I realised. "Wasn't crude and ludicrous?"

Romi was mild, sprightly happy, affectionate, wise, lovingly graceful and Jayanta over the years had grown loathsome and selfish though he had a tremendous control. I had not allowed my desperation to take over me. It was a testing time without a conclusion, for it had a smashing regularity without a break.

"He is justifying," she had laughed.

"I am practical."

"Jayanta, is it happening everywhere?"

"It has become a fashion. The more you run about..."Jaycee said in defending posture — "I shall be a drop out, left out all alone to fight my ways."

"..."

"In a contemporary world, it is the collective wisdom that will be all-pervasive and that is the spirit of democratic set-up. Do you think, Romi...you my dear friend..., you do everything, according to what you plan or do you determine the 'how' and 'why', 'what' and 'where' of actions?"

"I can see what you want to say?"

"Precisely. I am not alone. If I go alone without caring for others, I shall invite their wrath. It is also a relationship that brings us closer, allows us an opportunity to know and understand one another. All are demanding and wanting. I am one of them. I need them. I cannot live alone. Even if they reject me. I have to face rejection and yet try to be near them. It is also a relationship. Here relations have various meanings and all of us accept them without reluctance...it is demolishing the four-walls and search for new relations."

"He is right."

I said in a resigned spirit, for I was not willing to continue with the heavy conversation.

"I have to go to big suppliers...lately there have been despatches of poor quality."

"Should I speak to..."

"No, it is alright, I shall manage."

"Bhai Sahib, have some more..."

"No...he is becoming a big bore."

I had thrown an exhausted laughter.

"I do have a tender bosom."

"Jaycee!"

"Arrey, I am a servant."
"That is your standard answer."
"It is the only reply I know, for it defines my limits."
"It is easy to say but how?"
"Jaycee, relations have a sacred fragrance."
"Romi, my friend, is in business but has become a philosopher. What does he know about the pangs of a civil servant?"
"Jaycee, you are not a servant. You are a public benefactor. I would request you to banish all sickening thoughts that belittle and bring disgrace. It is a democratic country."
"Alright, now I think you should..."
"Yes, I am getting late."
"I shall drop you."
"No, it is okay."
"Anyone, you want me to ring up?"
"No, thanks."
"Romi, my friend is angry with me. Whatever I am doing, it is not without good connections."
"Yes, I know."
"They have a function in the School. You should go...at 3 p.m. today. I shall wait for you. Vicky will feel happy. I shall be keeping Ashey and Rahul ready...Bhai Sahib, you will also join us if you can manage to come soon."
"No, I have to do lot of things. Sorry, I shall be late..."
"No Romi, I too shall be attending a meeting. This boss always calls for meetings after three and then chitchat...gossips..."
With disdain the words of Jaycee had brought rumples on her face but sill she said in a calm and quiet tone.
"Please make it possible. You know, this is the third function and you have not been...children get disheartened. Now the principal and others also enquire about Mr. Jayanta..." She tried to inflate his ego.
"I can't say for certain."
She was slightly sadder and disappointed but without any further exchange of words, we had left. It was a beginning of a contemptible chapter in relations I thought after many years.

*** *** ***

● 2 ●

When I had returned in the evening after doing odd jobs relating to market and supply, Romi and the three children had been playing in the courtyard of the ground floor. They were engaged in the game of hide and seek. There were other women too who were sitting on concrete benches or cane chairs beside the fence and were involved in a spirited conversation. A hurried but observant look explained the scene to me. They all seemed to belong to well-to-do families. All women were putting up an air of superciliousness, extra care in the use of words and a few haughty frowns on their faces when in disagreement.

I had stood there not knowing what to do and how to disturb the children.

But Romi had seen me, so without wasting a minute, she was calling back children. And in a couple of minutes she was standing before me.

"It appears all the worries are over."

"Yes. I have almost..."

"How are you, uncle?" Vicky was with the other two— "We were playing. You didn't come. Our function was a grand success. I was waiting for you...you know, I got a prize..."

"I am sorry, my son..." I had taken Ashey and Rahul in my arms.

"Do you want to play?"

"No, now we shall...play at home...Chess...or..."

I was feeling a sense of guilt within. When I had entered the drawing room I had asked about Jayanta but a cold and dry response had discouraged me to enquire further. Romi's words, "He has to attend to the country," had quietened me.

When I had looked at the children, there looked a lava of simmering anger and disappointment. I had settled down myself comfortably on the sofa and the children also had seated themselves in front of me.

"So how was the function?"

"Thrilling. The hall was packed. Noisy and very many clappings. It was difficult to sit through, you know uncle, we missed you."

"I was...I am really sorry."

The taxi-driver had brought some packets inside which contained a few ready-made garments, a couple of woollens, a pair of parker's pen and sweets. The children first hesitated, looked rather detachedly at the packets and wanted to slip away but at that moment, Romi had come with glasses of cold drinks.

"Bhai Sahib, this is not fair."

"I have brought for the children."

Vicky had made a beginning by stretching his hands and then they had engaged themselves with me in sweet prattle. After about ten minutes, they had disappeared for a wash.

"Uncle, let us go to the community centre."

I was surprised.

"We shall play either table-tennis or badminton or anything you like..."

I was, in fact, not interested in the proposal, being very much tired.

"Uncle, don't say that you won't."

I was defenceless before the children. Anyway, after extracting a promise, three of them had gone to their rooms.

"Very lovely."

"Bhai Saab, why should you bring all these? You shall be spoiling them. And every time...?"

"Yes, but with tiny kids, it is difficult."

"What would you have? Coffee or...some snacks or a toast."

"Anything!"

I had entered my room for a change. After ten minutes, I was in the drawing room, sipping coffee.

"At what time Jaycee comes home?"

"No fixed hour." She was sad. "In fact, in this building, it is the women who..." She had thought better to keep quiet, perhaps.

"All of them are busy."

She had said in a spirit of resignation.

"You know, file work and meetings..." I had justified him — "All these things keep you busy."

But disapproving my mild contentions she had said, "I know, many foreign delegates do come. Parleys and discussions. Those marathon seminars. But I find something has gone seriously wrong with them. This chain of lunches, dinners and drinks and...how long...you know, he is playing with his health."

She had made a complaint but I knew it was not health that worried her, for Jayanta was energetic and vibrant, as fit as a fiddle, but it was her concerns and anxieties on a different plane which had created fears.

"I shall speak to him."

"I also know officers who are punctual, disciplined and affectionate. Now, when you'll go to the recreation centre, you will find children with their..."

"Bhabhi Jaan, you are unnecessarily upset. You very well understand that Jayanta's seat is of immense significance and he has to keep himself aware of matters relating to defence, policy affairs and economic conditions keeping in view the international background. Not only this, he is also keenly observant of the people's aspirations for whom all welfare programmes, plans and policies are framed. It is democratic socialism, I mean whatever that term indicates. So Jayanta has to be excused."

"..."

"And now the experience of the two wars, thrust upon, has awakened us to new realities. It has made our leaders redraft and replan priorities."

Possibly, I had used arguments which did not appeal to her, for she abruptly got up and said, "You ought to be fair."

"Bhabhi Sahiba..." It was a soft and gentle address, "I understand. I fully agree, he should devote some time..." I was looking at my watch.

"He'll not turn up before eleven...but today it might be different. We shall be lucky in any case." She had given a doubtful smile. I was looking at her, making an attempt to follow the meaning she wanted to convey.

"I think dignified clerks have to obey. You know our political set-up. In a rule of people...a common man's welfare is of supreme consideration."

"..." She laughed, "Well, Bhai Sahib, you are giving justification... I agree and you must defend your friend. But I tell you, my parents and his...all right why..."

The three kids had appeared, fresh and well dressed. Vicky had said entreatingly, "Now, uncle, come on...we shall take you around the community centre."

Those two hours were truly enjoyable. That evening when Jaycee failed to return in time, the children took their dinner and retired to their rooms but I had politely told Romi that I would take my meals when her husband comes back.

"The children were in good spirits today."

"Yes, they are lively and I almost had gone to my childhood days with uncritical mind and innocence. Delightful flashing memories struck me and I forgot that I had business worries."

"What do you do at home?"

"It is the same inflexible routine, very tough and monotonous. But I must tell you, I am the lord of my own time. I am not to seek anybody's permission. I enjoy myself...though not always."

" ..." Romi had remained mum.

"Where are the parents?"

"My mother-in-law is very dominating. For every little work, the 'how' and 'why' are continuous and tiring. These two words virtually irritate you but I think with such an experience of human affairs, she is tolerable and I worship her as a guide—a kind of teacher—to which Mr. Jayanta is not reconciled, so there are minor quarrels and misunderstandings and lately, I too have developed a bad habit of how and why." She had put up a calm posture.

"She is a well-wisher."

"But you know, much fault-finding to the extent of condemning is an unhealthy habit. She is always right, she claims and this has to be admitted without reasons. You can't speak out your mind and with an educated background, you feel hard to digest. But then, I think, with the passage of time, elderly relations become overprotective and zealous. Though absurd she may be many times, I wordlessly nod and move out. She contributes a lot to the business operations of her husband, does various philanthropistic duties, participates in different welfare programmes and thus her awful schedule of socialising exhausts her. But she still snatches out some moments to meet us. Whenever she stays here, she spends at least four hours with the kids and further..." Romi was visibly satisfied, "She ensures that both of them lunch and dine with us."

"You should be grateful to her!"

"Yes, I am. Do you know, when she is here, she gets up at five in the morning and straightway goes to the kitchen. Prepares breakfast for us...who does such things? But it is she, who gets a sort of fulfilment, she tells me."

"But Jaycee tells me she is a very strong-willed woman, harder and tougher than her father."

"Yes, Jaycee is right. But she also does not like his habits. She does not take offence to his drinking, but too much..."

"I understand."

"They were contemplating to shift...but..."

"But, what happened?"

"In fact, the problems should have been from my side. It was the other way...I just ignored her admonitions but the son and mother never see eye to eye. They are victims of shared prejudices."

There was a long pause.

Romi's face exhibited disappointment.

"She decided to...she comes once in a week from Chandigarh, conducts herself without expectations, meets us and plays with the kids."

Romi's recriminations were carefully worded and I could imagine, she had a deep regard for her mother-in-law, which raised her in my estimation.

To whom should I give the credit, I was unable to decide.

"She is a remarkable woman."

"Yes, she is great, worldly-wise and practical." Romi heaved a deep sigh and added, "My mother-in-law is not an ordinary woman. If she has social responsibilities to share and obligations to discharge, she also has an unlimited capacity to nurse relationships."

"It is a tribute to her sagacity."

"She is a noble soul but then with such a tough exterior, she is not acceptable to Jaycee."

"There must be some other reasons."

"Once she told me to respect relations. Family warmth and conviviality are source of strength and inspiration. She has all along held that a few words of care and love are sufficient to lessen bitterness and enmity."

"..."

"Bhai Saab, perhaps we may not understand the sanctity of tender feelings and emotions, at our age, but as we grow and find that..."

"I agree, you know...that is exactly I have been feeling," I had not allowed her to complete.

At that time, Jaycee had entered with a bang. He was in extremely happy and jovial disposition.

"Oh, you are...I am sorry, they spoiled my evening but then I have achieved something which my seniors would envy."

"It is, I supposed relating to..."

"Top secret but you must know that it was a proposal conceived and initiated by me. An indigenous project."

Jaycee had settled on the sofa with his arms at the back of his neck.

"Have you taken your food?" He enquired leisurely while yawning.

A servant had brought a glass of water.

"Thanks."

He had taken water and felt relieved.

"I am feeling hungry. Have you..."

"No, we were waiting for you."

"I am very sorry, I should have rung you up."

"No, it is all right."

"You may have a wash." Romi said while getting up, "I shall go to the kitchen."

"Romi, he has come after a long time,..." He had tried to look into her eyes and said rather demurely, "We shall have drinks. If you allow us to...."

"Okay, I shall bring..."

She had left.

Jayanta had closed his eyes as if he wanted to take rest. I took a cigarette and offered him one, "Why don't you wash yourself? Do you want to have a few puffs?"

"No, it is all right."

He had got up with a tremendous effort, "You get tired when you come back."

"..."

"No, not in a position to enjoy."

I had penetrated into his eyes and also stood up, "I shall also come in a moment." I was standing near him and as a gesture of assurance, put my arms on his stout shoulders.

"You come very late."

A whiff of foul-smelling air had entered my nostrils. I just intentionally had not bothered. Jaycee had grown into a strong individual, I found, though inwardly, I had seen in him a person of gentle nature and then Romi's worries! Jaycee could not be so audacious as to humiliate his mother or pick a quarrel. In office, he was not an advocate of consensus, compromise and submission. He had to my mind a formidable sense of impending dangers.

"You should not...go against the wishes of your boss. Even if you underrate him, try to..." Jaycee had once told me, "I have watched them intimately. Their facial expressions belie courage. I am a weakling in this ruthless system. I am filled with a feeling of scorn, but even then put up a brave face. A sense of contempt and disdain overtakes you but you don't accept. A callousness creeps in silently. I am afraid, I may not be a victim. You know, have you have a wrong notion of working independently and with authority, but in fact, it is never so. You work according to the degree of selfishness. It might seem mysterious but it is a fact. You know, I have seen them from close quarters. Those were initial years. So many factors worked. There..." Jaycee had not spoken ill of them and also was positive.

"But, that is life. Why to claim that you are a great man. Remain a simple human being. There are men who just work, faithfully accomplish their duties, attend to obligations and keep a bright face in tough conditions. The problem arises when you want to overstep your brief."

I was remembering his words. Jaycee was showing courage and helplessness at the same time. After about ten minutes we had made ourselves cozy in a small room adjacent to their bedroom.

"You are looking bright."

Romi had brought eatables, veg and non-veg, in two plates and Jaycee was pouring whisky into the glasses.

"You are changing."

"You know Dhawan, my senior by one year...bloody crook, a rascal. I never knew, he could be a dangerous man. At his age, he has learnt the art of sycophancy thoroughly. In order to usurp my seat, he was regularly paying courtesy-calls with gifts to the secretary and the minister. Also roped in a few public figures and outwardly he maintains those ideals and honesty. It is a cut-throat competition to exist. You know, if a person forgets even the basic human values, and those too at our age, what will remain after a decade? Nothing. The deterioration is rapid and that is the misfortune. Dhawan, a mild man with a gentle tongue, has surpassed all.

"He says, all goes well, when you place your head on the feet of these people without a question. You should be like a devotee, an unquestionable prostration. So I am a Bhakta, a sincere devotee. They are Gods, our godmen, I tell you."

"Jaycee, these people die unknown, Godmen live...though notoriously many times."

"But I am also not interested to make a name if you have to remain under tension."

"Jaycee, you know,...but..."

"I know, yes..." He looked at Romi with a questioning glance, "Nobody wants it. It is my desire to live happily...I have seen the fate of certain officers..., leaders and other prominent figures who dared to go against the collective wishes, and...." He took a long whispering puff and said, "All relegated to the background."

"That is no consideration for hiding weakness."

"I am not weak. No. When I look up, I find, we are lacking in warmth and passion for one another. I don't know why our big brothers try to find happiness and joy in parties, clubs and... anywhere. It is an outside world that attracts them. It is a running away — a thought out plan. Or it happens just without any sign or predetermined line of thought. I don't know but people are spitefully indifferent. It is all cold. Like Dhawan, there are many who have shortened their stature. Nothing graceful if you assess them. And Dhawan, when you ask him, he gives out a list of names, who have bothered only about their professional growth. A nasty failing. It is not service to the people, they often proclaim, it is indirectly your own service, which ultimately helps others. Enough is enough. No more hollow description of an ideal life. No shallow rhetoric. Rendering of noble thoughts does not land you anywhere. Everybody says. That fellow, you know, T.K. Mukherjee, he explained to us one day in a seminar that ground realities should determine man's future course of action. Such a big man, but when you go back to probe into their past, you'll be shocked. They did nothing but pursued all those little and unimportant matters which were promoting their career prospects. There, no principles obstructed their path. A mutual give and take. You know Malkhan Dave is a person whom I admire. That black-faced short-structured man is a public figure, frank, cruel and blunt, without any reservations."

Jayanta was specific and accurate. At the mention of Malkhan Dave, he became more excited and outspoken.

"Malkhan Dave and a horde of such people always dictate. It is not their fault. It is the quality, a unique characteristic about which we have made them aware of. Malkhan Dave knows my ability. He feels and predicts the pulse of age. I don't know how many Swamy Ratnams face the consequences, but all remain happy. It is a collective degradation."

I had finished my glass and did not want to have more. It was already midnight and there was no end visible of early dinner.

*** *** ***

3

It was a sustained attempt to revive past. We were silent at times but in constant dialogue within.

"What happened to Ratnam?"

I could not resist the temptation.

"Nothing. He was faithfully involved in official matters. And you know the system. Malkhan Dave is not a person who would forget. He had to bear the brunt of his adamancy. He had to suffer. In the end, he had to submit. Ratnam no doubt was interested in socialising and public relations, but what happened later on is a well-known fact. For full one year, he was continuously shifted from one place to another. So many enquiries. He was insulted. Demoralised. Hated. His colleagues wanted to avoid him. Everyone sympathised but none really helped to boost his sagging morale.

Swamy Ratnam, who was unbiasedly vocal, severe and also sweet-tongued, who, not for a moment, annoyed anyone and made noiseless efforts to help, was disheartened when Dave took revenge. Swamy had links with seniors and leaders and to a tolerable extent, he followed their dictates which were patently wrong and immoral and for these things, he was rewarded off and on with money and gifts. At that time, he didn't know that he was being imperceptibly initiated to harmless corrupt practices, which shall..."

Jayanta with a small morsel in his hand had been saying as if delivering a sermon.

I was chewing and beholding him like an obedient follower. "All clerks are serious over drinks." I had been ironical.

"For full one year, Ratnam was a rolling stone. Nothing substantial came out of the enquiries which had been started at the behest of Dave. You know these people. Ratnam, despite the fact that he was not very clean in his worldly outlook and was lax in financial matters but to my mind, he was not a corrupt man by any standards. Yes, I mean it, he was not a man of...You know, what a petty officer can do. He lives under constant strain."

Jayanta was serious and distressed. I had found a strong current of aversion to life-style in his voice, "What do we get? All nonsense...for this stomach and...this living."

He was rolling his eyeballs on all sides, "For these small comforts, we do all..."

He had pushed away his plate, "No I don't want." His voice had started faltering. There were signs of growing disillusionment with life. But he had mustered up smiles, "I feel perturbed when I think of him. It is simply unbelievable. I think of all these babus. Matters material and moral. What do you extract out of these values? Nothing. I am practical. In abstract thoughts, there is no meaning. Very much down-to-earth. This is life. You require comforts. One cannot live on morals...no, don't misunderstand. I am visualising the inevitable that will befall without notice. You are in business. Now tell me what is the truth? Where is the reality? What is the criterion of profit?"

"I find no answer to these questions. But no, it is a fruitless exercise."

He was silent.

"Romi, tell me..." He resumed his argument, "I know she wants me to live among...where I am...what is the use of all this?

"Jayanta, you came home quite late! Children were disappointed and down. They eagerly wanted you in the school. You should find a few warm moments for your home."

"..."

"It would divert your attention. Make you happy. If you occupy yourself and think of rut, you will be vacant...Jayanta, think of something pleasant. It is not the end. I am not against babus...no, you have wrongly interpreted me. I never said I am upright...in business if I am making myself dear. I no doubt give weight to profit, because without gains I cannot survive. I am not telling lies...but one thing I want to share with you...I am dishonest to a certain degree and perhaps a man is..."

"And then your..."

"I don't say, in worldly affairs, anybody can maintain himself for a long time. Nobody is above board, when it comes to facing facts of life. I am also not an exception."

Romi and Jayanta were looking into my eyes with a questioning expression, totally wonderstruck.

"Bhai Sahib...you are...?"

"Madam Romi, Babu Jaycee has a strong analytical sense. He has been accurate in matters of life and human affairs. I don't know but he has persuaded me to assess whether what I have been doing was right or it was my misplaced conception."

"I know the comparison was unfair."

He had laughed rather assumingly.

*** *** ***

I was unable to understand what exactly he wished to convey for he stood for a long time without a word.

"It looks odd when you are the culprit and still trying to defend yourself. I know, it is bad but people at our level cannot perform better, if you have grasped the meaning. These petty favours in the beginning prove suicidal. You know the implication. You keep roaming about among the big and the unimportant people. Your spheres are varied and wide. You have the requisite clout. But where do we stand? It does not give peace. I am also getting disturbed these days. Swamy Ratnam, while he was on forced leave, wrote a perturbing letter from Bombay where he had gone to live with his sister. Just wait. I shall show you."

We had all come out.

He had again added with a touch of intimacy, "It is after years that you desire to talk and share thoughts. It happens after a gap of couple of years and so many events and non-events are there to be discussed. I...I had a good measure of spirit you know." He had again spread out eyes and lips in a sem lance of smile, "After many days, it has given the desired stimulation. A nice sitting."

We had entered the drawing room. "Now it is comparatively tranquil outside. This metro is crowding itself. No planning. Barely three hours rest otherwise all are rushing out and running in. We are also not an exception. Late evening sittings, dinners and drinks outside and you call yourself very busy."

He had stretched himself on the sofa, "Don't mind my remarks but don't you feel the difference? Otherwise intolerable noise appears to haunt you. Files continue to stare at you. You fear. There is a kind of restlessness, I feel at office and home...a terrific lack of will."

His voice was low and slightly inaudible. He picked up the cigarette pack and lit out one and threw the matchbox and the packet at me not meaning to hurt.

"Romi, in the drawer of the table, there is a serious letter from Swamy Ratnam received months back. Would you kindly bring? We'll all read. How outlandish, frank and naked he is? I think, we shall not be able to wriggle out. No, we babus talk only but a few comforts and unfounded fears restrict us, suffocate us many times but we are, I suppose, accustomed to walled living and unfortunately refuse to open our hearts."

She had disappeared to fetch the letter. A moment of curiosity filled me.

"Madam...Jaycee she is an asset."

"Yes I know, if she stops calling for us, we shall be in a difficult situation." He had taken a long puff and closed his eyes in an extremely contemplative mood. "My dear friend, I don't know if I were a brilliant fellow but luckily I was selected and you...you are fortunate to have an independence. I am repenting. I feel pensive. I want to fight out but I fear these people may not eliminate me. Inspite of the influence of my father...that strong lady, my mother, you know Rajshri...It is killing yourself. I am not living my life. It is in fact a lease given to me. The way I had behaved in the past nobody would have endured for long but wisdom dawned upon me. My dictating mother Rajshri once told me in a haughty and despotic voice that if I wanted to exist, I had to know realities, understand the posers of life properly. You know, she was loving, dominating and proud — all together when it came to commanding a situation, but she was a mother...gentle and loving, affectionate and copiously warm...You should be honest. Analyse the situation. Know the 'how, what and why' of a given situation. These were words of that woman. My mother." There was an under-current of humiliation in the words he was uttering. Jayanta, it seemed, was coming face to face with realities.

I felt he was deeply aggrieved within and sincerely wanted to express his inner pains.

Another dissonance and cause of disliking me was that I was not having emotions of pity for him. But there was a sudden antipathy and coldness for him. My patience was exhausting and this babu — a tiny influence — had given no inkling of tiredness.

"I had slowly, despite her love, developed contempt. An unexpressed disliking. She was invariably commanding, domineering and..."

"Was it from the childhood?"

"No, that is strange...the moment I joined civil services, she became...I don't know...whether it was a feeling of possession or otherwise. With Romi and kids, she is playful, kind and generous. When she comes here, to attend political and social gatherings, she is vocal and loving. Vicky, Ashey and Rahul become immensely..."

He was forgetful and quiet, "I don't mean; I disliked her. No, I cann't. But there is something lurking within which instils fear and insecurity. Does she want to deprive me of...no this thought is horrible. She is a prominent social worker possibly greater than my father...She has many listeners. I am not a...my mental make-up is getting averse to her, each day. That is an inconsistency, no peace. At office, it is a total romance with surrender and here at home, you are miserably lost. I fail to understand the present imbroglio...within and without, it is a scenario of stark darkness."

Romi had come out with the letter and she handed it over to Jaycee. He had opened it and appeared to read, and after a minute folded it back.

"Yes, it is darkness. A passion for negative life-style."

"What?" Romi asked with a surprised voice.

"I was telling him, there is darkness..., a vast sea of confusion and uncertainty encircles me from all sides. I try to fathom deep with a detached mind. I am conscious of my limited options. Either it is open acceptance and submission to the present system or torturing bowing down. I don't know to what extent I shall sustain my belief but we should, I believe, live it magnificently. Here I feel stumbled, knocked down and discouraged. Nobody comes to rescue." I was swallowed by his philosophic strain and I wondered he could have been obsessed, thoughtful and pensive.

I had not disturbed him, for I thought, his needs were more genuine and immediate. I was not pitying him earlier but now I realised, I was ungenerous.

"She speaks of..." He diverted his attention to Romi. "She says I care little for relations. She wants to confine me to these four walls. Romi, without hesitation, blossoms into a passion for all. But among our class, who is concerned! It is a feeling of total un-relation I would say. Nobody is happy. All seek peace and fun outside."

Romi remained silent.

She had been patient and dignified.

"Don't you cherish the deep silence. It is calm and quiet." He was in a ruminative frame of mind.

"You are tense?"

"No, I am pained to think about the environs. Inside and outside. Can't say with certainty but a feeling continues to make rounds of the corridors...You know, those cigar-smoking squinting babus, tobacco-chewing white collared big clerks...I watch them...are they beetle-eyed, one can't say with confidence. They sniffle about, talk and titter, pen pushers they remain blubbering and whimpering but I tell you, they know not what they write. It is just a mechanical movement of hands. A well-rehearsed use of words, highly cultivated show of manners. They chuckle wildly and suddenly get excited. They plan and boast of brain. I tell you I hear lot of things. I also participate in interminable dialogue. Any person or place and the conversation starts. It is drab and at times 'savoir vivre' is the creed. I don't know how we get started but it is moving. I fail this minute and reach my goal the next moment.

"You know, I try to understand them. Their words convey vacuity, confusions in meanings. Impregnated with passions but after a short while one feels an inherent barrenness. Outwardly I find everybody is happy and satisfied but there is an utter vacuity within. I come across faces who have strange nay dreadful expressions. I don't know why this occurs? A crazy confrontation to look courageous and spirited. I call it an encounter of egoes. Yes, false notion about self. Here clash of egoes takes precedence over all other activities but there is no action. In the corridors of power they are viciously engaged in pursuits of aggrandisement. I am frank with you because you don't know the inner pangs.

"Romi is worried about me. My father, the kind Jai Bhadra, a big landlord, once upon a time...and that strong-willed mother Rajshri—no doubt proving right or I must correct myself. She is egoistic and vain...I really can't make my views clear. At this age, I must form opinion about them but then I don't want. She is concerned because I do not reach home on time. How can I come? Why should I come on time and then what is the purpose behind all this? I shall move from one question to another. Perhaps her pertinent questions will find some basis to sustain a plausible answer. Yes, I am a little unclear. I want to be. I enjoy myself speaking in terms of non-issues. That gives me solace, a kind of impetus...it is difficult to express. It is with Ratnam, Rajput, Mukherjee and...all."

He had stretched his arms, opened lips in a sarcastic manner. A few lines had appeared on his smooth face, showing disdain, and helplessness. In a slightly loud voice, he had resumed, "I cannot incur wrath of my boss. He is sitting in his office. He sits after five because he is awfully busy during the day. He runs frantically after connections, powerful connections. He makes friends, attends meetings which never finish, dictates, redictates minutes, writes, rewrites suggestions and notings and then asks me on intercom to come. I don't want to go. I curse him but still I go willingly and laugh. I have to admire him for duty and honesty. He must understand that I am faithful though I want to kill the bastard. He is a scum, bloody shit. He wants praise. I go to him. I cannot escape. Earlier I thought, there is no room to go at the close of the office but he administered me a piece of advice. I stay back but I don't tell my staff to overstay. There are good, efficient and faceless clerks and leaders who never show off but majority of them... Romi insists, I should return. Nobody does so. All are servile. They entreat and fawn with a demeaning conduct. How can I remain blind? I am to exist. I did it once or twice and I had met with humiliation of a life-time. At home, too, I was treated with contempt and scorn. My parents disapproved of my behaviour."

"You are not the custodian of duty and faith. And remember, you are not the Constitution."

The old Jai Bhadra had roared. And on the top of it my mother, the undisputed champion of women's cause had said, "You have a long way to go. In this modern age, power and wealth are gods, collect these vices and virtues then issue sermons and directions. In this set-up of democracy, when a corrupt and powerful man speaks he is listened to and bear in mind that unscrupulous persons getting wealth and power are only exceptions, of course." She had, as was expected, propounded her thesis, and last when I had not looked at, she had finished with a conclusion that looking up and around means more than that appears on the surface. Man cannot survive in isolation. And there had started the unwanted war of attrition between the son and the mother. "But no, I avoided. I had seen very closely the plight of colleagues. Masters. I realised that a public servant has to behave. Those earlier days were not enjoyable. Coming on time, ordering others to turn up on time,...commanding to work, I found out, was not acceptable to many. I was creating enemies...yes a very bitter situation. What do we achieve by making foes. No one is serious, I found. It was not a question of ethics or morals but it was the convenience that ruled supreme. You ought to speak of principles. Right. A very good thing but too much indulgence costs. You have no choice. This is what I observed. It is a four-track race and you are running on all and it may be a mechanistic operation but you have to run fast. In such situations what can I do?

I am an individual, without a name in that...many faces move about but what do we achieve ultimately. Here we live happily without telling out what is within and that to my mind appears to be the right choice. After the war, relations, equations and thinking have changed immensely. I cannot be strong, obdurate...or upright...these words are outdated and meaningless. When I used them, yes morals...virtues...I soon found out that I shall be kicked out in case I did not carry out errands." He again laughed rather remorsefully. "In such circumstances, I cannot come out. I have to live my life, in my own way, and if I show intransigence, this concrete monster of numerous corridors will devour me. I cannot resist. There, we babus have relations. Yes, relations of selfish co-existence. I know, Romi resents my coming late but that kind of life also has its charm. You come to know about the secrets. The real purpose behind all the facade. No true words come out. It is all concocted. People enjoy such a living in a vacuum which they don't know. Here relations are cultivated with a motive and you hesitate to disclose the untruth."

Romi speaks of personal relations!

I know what she speaks about. When you went up to play with the children, I knew their feelings but I could not afford to come."

I had kept looking into his eyes. He was uncertain, I knew. His arguments were specious but lacked sincerity. It was a matter of comfort. "You know. We have to do it. It is at the personal level that we perform varied and difficult functions. In meetings, nothing definite emerges. I think, a time will come when nothing shall remain impersonal. All files move with a purpose. I don't know who has what connections and if you create a hurdle, you may be thrown out. That is the reason, I return to old pastures. Only those who hold on to their places will reach the top without ever concentrating on what they are doing. My time is important. The time that I spend there. Following, obeying, praising and...licking. It is a total subjugation, negating soul. No question. No suspicions. I am learning to surrender. An evil process has started. When I put up a brave face, a few colleagues..., public men appreciated but then most of them began weaving stories...casting shadows on my functioning...I had to get out of it. When I did nothing..."

Jaycee was emotionally perturbed.

His voice was clear though trembling. :His words were appropriate. There was a tinge of diffidence. He was candid yet weak-willed.

"I don't come."

"Jaycee, you are..."

"Romi will continue to carp and coerce but she must know that truth is nowhere."

"Jaycee, it is too early to deteriorate."

"May be, but the colour and shade are their attainments. A process. I hinted earlier will...you know, nothing materialised immediately. It takes over him."

"It is not all bad. You are unnecessarily deriving meanings which are not there. It is unbecoming of a man, who has sound and strong background."

Jayanta had laughed again, but this time the roar showed anger and contempt for both of us. We were feeling uncomfortable. Romi's sober and graceful looks still indicated a tremendous sense of patience. Without a word. I thought, she was preparing to go to sleep.

Jayanta had said, "My mom...that great mother...I don't know, Romi says she...any way..." Again, he had drifted away from the reality. He had wished to say but restrained himself with a good deal of pressure.

"There is something going on within? You said many things. There is truth in what you said but that is...Jayanta, you have to..."

"No, it is too early to speak of..." He again retreated, it seemed. "I told you, I cannot come. And when there are many enjoyable moments, why should I? There is a purpose, if you think. There is no idea also to look back, I can prove. There are personal reasons. One can always find sufficient cause. So I fall back upon them. They have a purpose in those evenings' jaunts, rendezvous, dances and dinners and I also have a purpose, without a purpose. I live here without a question and still questions haunt. It is a contradiction and yet a plain fact."

There was a dead silence.

I was reminded of his words, uttered ten years back, "In free India, we need an ideal and a principled system and in this direction I shall always endeavour. We must strengthen the cultural treasure which we have inherited."

He had spoken of great teachers, who were parts of history. Then it was Gita, politics and religion—for him. And now, a transformed man was sitting before me.

"I am part of it. I shall move with the..."

"Jaycee, we missed you."

"Romi can never change. But she can also like her mother-in-law devote her time to welfare activities."

"No, I want you to...at least some day...this change will not lead you anywhere. Mr. Jayanta Chauhan, if an individual is strong, nobody can damage him. Or is it that you want to live a life of...?"

"Even I have been unable to understand."

"Jaycee?"

"Yes, whether I want or not?"

"This is obnoxious."

I have got up in a hurry.

"Yes, I am telling you what I have in mind. I don't want to hide anything."

"This kind of attitude will bring miseries and..."

"Who is afraid of truth? There is no such thing...a new truth is making its presence felt...there is no soul. Yes, we servants try to think deep and analyse. Where is the soul?" He laughed again, "That is why I say, I am going deep into the system."

"But you are making it so."

"May be, may be not."

We had started moving towards the bedrooms.

"It was a nice time..."

"Yes, you can't dishearten me. You are my friend."

"No, I felt."

"Romi, you feel some consolation somewhere. Yes, I know your dilemma. You want to save me from a dangerous fall. I know, but the fact remains, there is no such situation. There are merely internal fears. Have faith."

Jayanta had said goodnight to me and moved to his bedroom along with Romi.

I had not said a word but felt myself relieved as if a heavy load were off my head.

*** *** ***

4

I had gone to my room not aware of Jaycee and Romi who were still following me like shadows. It was an eerie and dreadful feeling. I was still experiencing their presence.

"No one can shake off his past."

The words were thrown at me from somewhere. I looked around. The room was neatly furnished and tastefully decorated. On the wall, just in front, were fixed two life-sized photographs of Jai Bhadra and Rajshri as if smiling and blessing. Yes, I remembered those were Jai Bhadra's words. His voice always created echoes and those resounding sounds charmed me immensely with a kind of unimaginable fulfilment.

"No, you are bound to the past."

Jai's authentic approach had an unreasonable impression. It used to bestir me. His words were deeply engraved. I tried to recollect hours of association with him. A thoroughly practical man who loved the world and its inhabitants and also kept his reservations. He was unusually realistic. And Rajshri, that graceful woman with an ear for melodious notes and tunes, had an exterior which was far more tougher than one could visualise. Her words had unique rhythm, an enchanting symphony like the whispering birds in a sleeping jungle. She loved the dancing waves of silent streamlets. Always in joyous spirits, she had met me freshly, richly and elegantly dressed. I was beholding those two photographs with deep reverence.

"You are good and kind-hearted boys. I love you. We want you to achieve something in life. All are not fortunate to have a shelter."

"I have a feeling that he is tearing himself apart. You cannot snap ties. There is sufficient resilience in human affection, pure and chaste. Why pollute a sacred thought? The soul with its beauty opens up panoramic vistas which are simply bewitching. You are his friend. I find he is facing many paradoxes. He justifies frivolous actions and at times speaks against. To be practical does not mean that one should be dishonest. Agreed that he is a busy man but he should know that he has a family."

She was expressing in a low and calm voice. I had seen no signs of contretemps on her face. But twisting lips showed numerous riddles.

"You too have a wife. Small children. Don't you feel that you should speak out in depth about your heart-felt sentiments. Words that come out...spring out like a bubble, then there is the warmth, a deep passion. You are in harmony with everything around when innocent eyes sparkle."

Rajshri's voice was soft and gentle. I had thought for a while that a mother could not be harsh.

"I agree Mamma."

"You are his friend, also a businessman. We do not want that a man should not be attached to interests, one should be. You know, a man cannot contain his emotion while living alone. I remain in an impasse...no time...yet even then I make it a point to find some private moments. But he is going on his own, along with a troubled heart."

"I agree with her. He is obsessed." Jai Bhadra had said briefly.

"I know, in this fast-growing society, there is a tempting thirst for the outside world. I wanted to be financially sound with a very comfortable position. Raji stood by me. Consciously and carefully we nursed each minute. We found a sort of strength from all those who met us."

He had taken out his pipe and stubbed it, perhaps pegging on something invisible as a habit. Once my father, in his emotional upsurge, told us, "Ours was a society when it was passing through uncertain times. No one knew what will happen? Various social influences were operating. The English here trying secretly to precipitate communal disharmony by inciting the communities. Imperceptibly seeds of discontentment were being sown. Nobody knew anything. I had good friends among Muslims. Even missionaries visited our bungalows. Those bright and warm festivals, solemn occasions. It was pure friendship, yes, it was an exchange of warmth, love and little sweet words notwithstanding imbroglios. Good happy days of Easter, Good Friday, Christmas, Id-ul-fitar and Moharram are still very fresh and alive and those people regularly visited us without prior intimation. That was the depth. An understanding among men who loved and respected one another."

The old man had continued.

"You will not believe but majority of the people are humble and submissive, have no suspicions, no wickedness. We never mixed up on the basis of what you call..."

He had talked of prevailing circumstances which had driven a wedge between man and man.

"Good, everybody agrees. I too don't find reasons to find shortcomings. No harm if we have thousands of religions, castes and classes."

At his words, I was thrilled.

Jai Bhadra sniffed and added, "Yes, it would look odd but then the elders felt the pulse of the people." When I had told him that the age is different, he had shot back, "What do you know? You have a name. I was also given a name. All of us have names. There is no controversy. I feel, we have different religions to identify communities. Then why quarrel? Our origin was never different. We meet warmly, but when collectively think, we become Satans, Kafirs and ungodly. I say, Hindu is the son of God. He has the right to live and none other should be allowed to live... and then there is a rejection. And so my Muslim, Christian and Parsi friends would pray. An utter nonsense. There is much religious talk. Numerous discourses, mammoth congregations and rituals. I, a modern man, must change myself.

"You know those old men, my grandfather and father, were terrific talkers. They would go on speaking for hours without listening to anyone. My father too had imbibed this habit. My grandfather was a deeply religious man but with awakened social outlook. He knew what he wanted to do. Social and political changes were not unknown to him. He understood the evil design of the rulers. There were drastic changes in English thinking after the First World War and so...without aligning with anyone he had his own way of life...quite independent and assertive. May be..."

"My father had become deeply morose and depressed." But after a second had slowly said, putting pressure on his memory, "The thought had an everlasting influence on my father also."

Jai Bhadra looked at his wife Raji, "Jayanta has not come?"

"He will take his time."

It was a state of helplessness.

"Let me talk to him. Lately, he has started coming late, very late. It is not good." Her subdued tone had calmed down Jai Bhadra.

"No, no, let him stay in the ministry. The burden of the nation is on him." Jai Bhadra's words showed anger but without envy or rancour.

I had found it quite astonishing.

"My son, you are of different nature—very plain and unassuming. In business, a man is more practical and less idealistic—and now..."

I without interruption was trying to comprehend the hidden meaning. He was extremely incommunicable and yet I was obviously witnessing a bridge between us, in the air, transporting realities and dreams.

"Yes, I was remembering my old and dead relations. The recapitulation is sweet and satisfying. Memories infuse unity and oneness. I often think of those noble souls because it is peace-giving. You know, I am fond of old people. I think each of us derives strength, guidance and pride. In the background these souls continue to haunt...these expand and teach us. Console and bless. A slow revelation of inner harmony and bliss overwhelms, it sweeps and pacifies the violence within."

Again, he was lost in his own world. I was inwardly cursing myself. "This babu...Jayanta should have turned up."

Beyond this I was unable to think. Jayanta's parents were hurt somewhere, and it was a moral obligation. Not wanting to show off, I had to listen and agree.

To this extent, I was covering distance between sincerity and casualness. They were neither absurd nor unreasonable but, I thought, demanding too much and in a way, it was an encroachment on my privacy. Then I would correct myself the next minute and aver "I am unloving and insincere."

These words would often put me on the right path. I was forgetting myself in the continuous onslaught of moral obligations. It was not a question of faith but a crisis, surpassing all mundane considerations. In a world, full of comforts and happiness, as Jai Bhadra would often say, a man, if not at peace with himself, should better make a march towards another world.

I was shaken with a tremendous force, I thought. Jai Bhadra asked me with a sharp tongue, "Are you listening to me?"

"Yeah, I am...should I ring up? He should have returned by now."

There was no reaction.

I had gathered strength to make a reasonable defence, "Jayanta understands his duties to the nation unlike other officers."

I had used words which apparently expressed lack of realism. The bookish sentence had unnerved me.

There was utter silence. Nobody had spoken for a couple of minutes.

Jai Bhadra's facial expressions showed that he had disapproved of my words.

"I know your sentiments. When a man is empty within, he often speaks of nation and society and now-a-days, when one is allergic to good things in life, one considers it a social duty to make...any way...I was telling you about our ancestors who lived not long ago. They did not participate actively in any national movement but tacitly and perhaps indirectly those souls were engaged in...I don't know but it was 'man as material' that was important. For them, names assigned by man to things, emotions, actions, ideas and...what is there? You give me a Muslim name...and...they always wanted to expand man and his mental horizon. It should be something like the limitless sky where planets and stars...are in abundance and there is no...like the vast sea...ocean...where all rivers merge in sea and become one. Not a new thing, it has been said many times...My grandfather was a pious individual. It is not rare. Even now there are men who live away from dreadful feelings of isolation. They live in such a shelter, indifferently and detached as to give an impression of a saintly and secluded existence where people from all sections visit, sit and find themselves immune to earthly enticements. That old man was a pure worldly man, interested in trivial and close-to-heart noble deeds.

"Those were golden days. Such small islands of human milk were always existing. Sacred and saintly souls were persistently overlooking man and his sufferings. So did our old men. A few drops of love impelled them to live better. It was an oasis of love, sympathy and compassion. For my grandfather was a source of grace and goodness...you know, he used to say so many things. The one thing, which even today surprises us, is that in the big house, family of about sixty souls would sit together for meals, the old man would talk to all. Listen to whatever they said. Agreed and advised them to do better. Little matters pertaining to man attracted his attention. We are told, during his days, all kinds of people had a common sitting place in the courtyard of the big house. He only said, if a man can keep his soul happy and free from worries, that would be...I mean, these ideas and feelings were not nascent, were explained in a typical style, imbued with the spirit of love and compassion.

"I don't know, but, in the evening, if not daily at least twice a week, he, along with the old lady, a goddess status she had, among children, would visit us in our rooms to find out what exactly we were doing. It used to be a great moment of celebration for us. Yes, a kind of festival, because we would often...find our demands accepted. Games, picnics, festivals and feasts were animatedly approved. There was discipline and still we found we were free.

"You know, unique and lively were the methods of those old guys. When they visited the rooms of children, they talked at random. Small toys attracted their attention. They would examine books, clothes and beds.

"All children would sit cross-legged on the floor with eyes wide and inquisitive. Sometimes, mischievous words greeted the old fellows. The old people would unintentionally ask about the village. Through children they would learn how we behave and live...and then the grand old men would inform them how they could be helped. The old men were kind and gentle. It is said that the grand old fellows spent hours together with the children and outflowed fairy tales in copious measures. They also chatted with men and women of the house in groups."

"It is a big family."

"People of the area proudly commented. It is said that our grandparents inherited that quality of a well-knit family from their ancestors."

Jai Bhadra, it had become clear to me, would not stop. His words were slow and confident but those were becoming unbearable. On the other hand, there was no indication of Jayanta returning home. I was simply helpless. I had to listen and also show that I was eagerly interested in whatever he said.

And then, I had heard Jai Bhadra, "Listen, I know you are getting bored. Your face clearly shows signs of...any way, but you must understand old man's mental make-up. I am not a person who would sit. After all, we have to give and share talk and listen. But first talk only. I like talking. Raji is also fond of giving sermons. We want to keep that tradition alive. And we find it quite healthy and strong. It keeps us warm."

He was filled with thrills, I found. His eyes were making rapid survey of the room.

"Now Raji, you tell me...Isn't it a fact."

"Yes, it is really remarkable. You find fountains of love, an everlasting spring of togetherness. There is no loneliness. It is a crowd...which never disturbs you. Here relations grow and strengthen you."

Rajshri, the strong-willed lady of 'how and why' had started saying, "You men...never understand, what it is that brings us closer."

"Our elders had a marvellous sense of history. They knew the distortions, the birth and the synthesis." Rajshri in her own grand demeanour had started saying, "We wanted to find out the origin. After all, it is not in isolation that we grow."

"Raji, the questions are different."

"Nothing has changed."

"But we are not the same."

"Do you know to what extent we have changed? How? It was not an abrupt movement."

"It is difficult to argue with you."

"Your attitudes have remained static."

"One can't..." Jai Bhadra had laughed.

"Now the world is undergoing a metamorphosis. You know what happened to those who refused to move with the times."

"Raji, ours is an age, when we want peace."

"How about our children? There must be something radically wrong in our behaviour."

"What do you mean? It was an open..."

"No, otherwise this kind of..."

"He must be..."

"Now, this..." She had tried to control her voice, "No, I am not to hurt their feelings. Somewhere, we are cracking up. You know some crevices...in relations. I don't know if I am correct? What has happened all of a sudden? You talked of man. A single man's asset? What I think our old men...great-grandfathers' intentions were clear, unblemished. They intended to do good. There was nothing bad. Even we are not opposing. But, what to do when such situations arise? There was warmth."

She was silent. In a reminiscent mood she had added, "May be right, we cannot shake off..."

"Yes Raji," Jai Bhadra had exclaimed for a while. We were both amazed at his sense of apparent joy.

"Yes, that is my view. When there is something dead within, I mean a state of dormancy or it could be vegetative living or when you feel you are moving around in grooves of darkness and depth, with no end in sight, you wish to gather shreds of inner happiness. In such circumstances, what really happens is that you presume, you are protecting yourself and helping others."

She without letting him know that she was interrupting had made a polite presence.

"That is why the problems remain alive. Nobody really wants to extricate himself from such deplorable mental reservations. I had an opinion, verging on self-projection but possibly we fail each time. We don't know our mental puzzles that raise their sharp fangs every now and then. I had a feeling in the beginning that I was right. But it was not so. My mother-in-law thought that she had inherited a great tradition or I would say, she constantly thought herself as the repository of family's values, heritage and culture."

"Using strong words."

"No, it is through these mills of petty experiences that one can construct one's thesis. I had been doing so." She had pulled out her corner of sari to one side and said, "If I had refused, there would have been utter chaos. I had been feeling, I am not moving. As you said earlier, there is something dead within. Those strong women of this family had certain well-defined duties for themselves and those they wanted us to continue."

He was just listening to his wife without any movement of the eyelids. But gathering a meaningful smile he had said, "Now, a leader speaks."

She had become serious but then getting up, said, "Yes, one has to..."

And had burst into a surprise laughter.

"I understand there is no alternative." She had looked at the wall with vacant eyes and said, "He has not come."

She was depressed and uncomfortable.

"This makes you unsure and weak. Why?"

"Romi..."

She had called Romi in a loud but affectionate voice.

"A cup of coffee!"

There was an inconvenient silence.

"Why we adhere ourselves to...?" Jai Bhadra wanted to lessen a mother's worries, "I find there are a few drops of water...could these be of sadness? Some inner unknown agony or a hidden desire not yet fulfilled?"

She with the palm of her hands had experienced her eyes cautiously and bringing in a disarming smile said, "No, you have not got me. I was thinking about him."

After a pause, she had said, "Do you know what goes on in Romi's mind? Why she restrains? It is a difficult exercise to explain to children."

"Explain what?"

"Unwanted and too frequent absence of Jaycee."

"You have..."

"You tell me..." She had asked me, "You tell us, can you afford to...or were your parents away..., your father or mother?"

It was a straight question. I had hesitated and chosen not to answer.

She had repeated again, "I was asking this question because it has bearing on our future. We, no doubt, form a tiny part of human ocean but we must know that in case we live indifferently as a new thinking has crept into our lives. We shall be unable to put our heads and hearts together. I think we are shattered within and we know not. There are uncertainties and indecisions the degree and extent of which is not known to us. This I know out of harsh experience.

She was in her most poised state of mind. Rajshri by her demeanour looked an impressive woman impregnating her words with gist and traditions of a great heritage. As a businessman belonging to a bania community always weighing the pros and cons, I was examining the elderly lady with awe and respect. She was an ideal woman. There was no end of discussion. She was probing into my mind. But it was a blissful moment and she was really commanding.

*** *** ***

5

I was delighted within and felt like sitting by her side. There was no time-sense and I had felt a revigorating thought within.

I had heard her but the beginning was not disturbing or meaningful.

"I asked you..."

I had fumbled for appropriate words for hers was a question which needed careful answer.

I had said briefly, "I try to remain as much as I can at home, but in business matters one cannot be unstable and careless."

"..."

"I have to go out. Arrange raw material, supplies and collection. The fluctuation in financial dealings is often a headache."

"But then in commercial dealings too you require a great acumen, understanding and sympathy. You don't operate in an unfavourable situation."

"We can't help."

"That was a different question."

"I am aware of..."

"Tell me how many days in a month..." The left out words were more incisive and clear. It was not a dead shot. I wantingly rather helplessly looked at Jai Bhadra to avoid a reply.

She had understood my dilemma.

"One seeks happiness at home."

"...."

"You may stay out. Have lavish dinners and gorgeous dances but that is no substitute for..."

I had not contradicted her but I knew her sharp perception of environment and also the mind of an itinerant shopkeeper. A lovely name given to me, she often had said. Once in the beginning of career, when Jaycee had joined the Civil Services and I had preferred to become a business magnate, she had called me a shopkeeper. I still remembered those cutting observations.

"Jaycee is a poor...I don't know, why a sense of detachment is taking roots?"

She had again asked me.

"I hinted at late night excursions and...don't you ever do..."

"No."

"How do you run this business?"

" ... "

"What are the tactics you adopt?"

"No tricks. I am straight, plain speaking. I am at very small position. It is just a comfortable living. No hassles and I can't imagine myself at a...the business world is violent and crook. I thought at the start but with each shock of loss and unemotional negotiations, I found that to cry for a moon would push me into depths of a crisis."

"You are unnecessarily giving a moral outfit to your weakness."

"No, mamma, we have lost many things. I think the old generation...is no more. It is dead. We are surrounded by monsters, invisible and terrific. I realised very soon that it was of no use to...I found human element gradually disappearing...my father had high hopes but when I saw the hideous face of business, I resigned myself to a state of non-resistance. My own friends in business attempted to cheat me of my rightful profit. And that made me conclude a..."

"It means..."

"Mamma, I am not different. I know, it is good to live with your own people but exigencies of services mean a lot."

"Where are your parents?"

"In the village."

"Do you go to meet them?"

"I go."

"When and why? Are they dependent upon you? And what about your that Pandit friend?"

"No time is fixed. I don't know how to specify the urge. I can't fix up a particular moment. No, it is difficult. I had visions of a sensitive relationship...yes, for those benign four eyes, I have a deep respect. It was the moral force..."

I thought of them. Their mild soothing smiles, wrinkles, quivering lips and comforting words, mild voice and blissful hands unite me. It is an unobtrusive thinking. They are always kind. I go without ever making a plan.

"I go because I have to meet them. There is no escape, Mamma. Yes, I don't call you..."

I had suddenly become conscious.

"Yes..."

"No, I inadvertently don't call aunty...Anty...Aomty. I still recollect those words. But as the years rolled by, I was aware that you were..."

"You are coming to my point of view, but the question has not been answered."

There were silent callings. In the innermost recesses of my heart many voices arose and awakened. It was ringing of bells. There were trumpets. Blowing of bugles. Those piercing sounds recalling childhood memories. Kidding, playing and singing. Cajoling and stealing. Little words of warning and scolding. Roaring and jumping among the mangoes' trees. Shepherding of cows and animals in the mountainous terrains and river banks. The lovely grasslands and the singing rivulets. Those windy and dark cloudy days and hailstorming in rainy season. Roaming about in the village pebbled paths and puffing off bidis in secret.

"Mamma, I have been pushed back into those heavenly good times."

I was unknowingly walking swiftly into the winding stony ways of villages' sweetness. Refreshing and moral dimensions had entered into present.

I was feeling a kind of suffocation. The present was turning into a sordid drama.

At once a question raised its ugly and terrifying paws to scare me out of my dizzy stupor and romanticising the good old days of past had been soporific and vapid.

There was a long pause.

"Why do we love past?" It was an exciting question.

"My dear son," she had put her hands on my head, "It is always I too had a wonderful past. For that matter, all of us cherish memories of past for we remember it in order to relate and re-relate it with a telling force. It was with us and it is with everybody."

"Yes, aunty, I go back to my parents. It is here that I get a feeling of oneness and unity. At home while talking and playing with children, I realise that we have a world full of joy and sharing. Small agonies just do not matter. A sense of closeness and intimacy gives energy to live more. I don't know how it happens but it does occur."

"In solitude he can expand within but it is loneliness that squeezes him out of life."

Jai Bhadra had taken out his cigarette pack now and was fiddling with cigarettes and matchbox. It was at that moment that Romi had entered with a tray.

"You could have told the servant. Where is he?"

"No, we have dispensed with him."

"Why?"

"Now, it is an official peon." She had said facetiously, hiding a great truth.

"But..."

"Everybody makes use of..." Romi had left her sentence incomplete.

Jai Bhadra and Rajshri were looking at each other with a flat expression. Romi with her hands had handed over two cups to them.

"I did not want him. But he...and, Mr. Jayanta once told me, when all his colleagues...do it." Perhaps she had wished to say that she no longer required him at this hour. Sensing this, Romi had not felt it necessary to give a long justification "if you do as other officers and leaders, social workers and philanthropists do, you will be appreciated." Romi propounded her husband's thought rather reluctantly.

"You agree with him?"

"No."

"Romi, why this...?"

"Mamma, you have seen the world in a..." She had not spoken further but kept mum.

"Romi, it is an easy way to live life but it does not create a man in the real terms. You ought to look different." Mamma Rajshri took a few sips and heaved a deep sigh, "I think we have gone too far."

Romi had sat quietly by her side. I was trying to understand the hidden meaning of her words. She was putting up a smile in her melancholic disposition. But I knew her compulsions. She always showed utmost patience, the courage to fight back in her own stoic manner.

"Romi, I think we are selfish."

Jai Bhadra said rather uninterestedly and after a second or two had corrected himself, "She has her own fads. A woman of convictions."

"Papa, you're too smart."

"Romi, thanks for the comments. I am proud of, at this age."

"My son has not answered."

I had become conscious.

"He is our second Jayanta." Jai Bhadra was sipping his coffee.

"Mamma ..." I had said quietly without dragging the argument further, "I want to go. I simply cannot keep living in the crowded city but at the same time I have a feeling of love and passion for nature. You know natural environment gives inner peace and strength. I get solace and you know, this way, you meet relations, simple and rustic in those green fields. The cool morning breeze hums divine tunes in the ears.

"..."

"The visit kills boredom."

"I knew it."

"You know relations give you warmth. It is an association with your birth place..."

"..." Jai Bhadra laughed, "It is good."

"Don't you feel?"

"It is not my...or yours...nobody is seriously worried about the movement of time. It happens with us many a time. I am running against time. I don't know how long I shall be able to sustain my interests and extra work."

"You are forthright and that is expected of a person like you," she had said.

"I don't know but in business...if you are independent you are also...I can understand the compulsions of Jayanta. He has to obey. No questions...where."

I had contemplated to convince them that Jaycee was working under immense pressure.

After a little deliberation, I had said, "It is not different with Pandit, Yadav and Rajput."

"I would visit your native place." Raji had said excitedly, "I would see the landscape. Hills are not that big but largely different in contours, accessibility'and climatically. A little difficult living. But anyway, whenever I went around, I enjoyed myself bountifully and the warmth with which I was greeted and listened to, cannot be erased from my memories. I agree it was not social work always but some other motifs drove us to them."

She was minutely concentrating her gaze at her husband, "You know these people are always approached by vote-hunters."

She had been blunt and ironical.

"All roads lead to villages." She was relaxed now, "You want to exhaust your love, humanitarian sympathies pour tremendous compassion and then shed tears on..."

She was endlessly saying words not out of heart but from her intellect.

Jai Bhadra, as if reminded her, "We have to manage ourselves."

"I don't know...how one tries to disconnect himself from..." Rajshri was looking into my eyes, "How about that Pandit and Yadav? You had been very close."

"Yes mamma, they had been very intimate. Those days when we returned to the villages during vacations are still fresh. In our free time, we used to pay visits to one another's villages. Yes, it was enlivening and emotional. A life in the midst of your own people, related in one way or the other. It was a cozy, thrilling and deep association with no strings. Open arms and beaming faces. Those sparkling eyes among wrinkles, trembling words in soft voice and weak and passionate hands rising to bless you, are still our tidily kept treasures. I feel I should go back to re-surcharge those little experiences. Ordinary people with simple loving relations. You, I think, are right. But then vagaries and uncertain conditions of today's life do not permit a man to...one has to live and pull through an unemotional state. After all one cannot tie up with the dead and drive to future. We have to accept. Pandit, you know very well. Mamma, now my parents don't want to come. I don't know why? They want us there every now and then, this they don't say but their eyes convey. It is a voiceless language of some old affinity.

"I think those moments, when a message is thrown without words, are terrible. It is deep and agonising to accept the bonds.

"You feel, you are disintegrating into pieces. I am talking of small experiences. I don't know. I reason with for a long time and try to bail myself out...but fail miserably."

It was a painful exposition of small emotions having no relevance to practical life but then I had enjoyed the opening up of heart without caring for, whether I was true or not.

"I was sentimental today." I had given a small timid smile, "I know in spite of my wanting to do all these things I shall never be in a position to do. I have to run away from what I feel restricts me."

The last words were harsh, I understood, for all of them sat benumbed and emotionless.

"You are unguarded in your words, I suppose. Not in a position to stick to...or is it the fear of intense feeling." Rajshri was mildly loud.

I had understood the intent.

"I cannot hide but I want it. There is an unspecified will somewhere in everybody's heart. I desired to give language, I defaulted. I am sure of one thing that I am unable to shake off what has happened."

"I think, we know and still..."

"Yes, mamma, it is with everyone. I am frank. I don't know the depths and intensity. There is definitely some force concealing itself in the unconscious mind which encourages every now and then to get up and...Yes, I have a burning desire to go back. And you know what happens." I had attracted her attention with a question, "When you meet villagers...relations; young and old, you find genuine feelings in their words. They are warm, true and very near the heart. Always undemanding but listing a few problems without ever caring whether you solve them or not."

I had stopped suddenly. I found a tepid expression on their faces.

"I am listening. Carry on. I was just trying to co-relate my experiences with yours. People seldom speak what they feel or try to hide what they should not and project an image which is untrue, affected and devoid of any semblance of reality. You are sincerely and constantly unfolding a scenario which is rooted in facts. When you go to your native land you find a spiritual grandeur around you. I mean a hidden joy and peace, if the word spiritual appears too lofty."

She was correcting herself.

"I am reminded of my friend, a true social worker who always devoted her time for the upliftment of the downtrodden and weak. She was Soma Gandhi, who wrote and thought about the poor and deprived sections of society. It was listless and stale. In private conversation too, she expressed her anxieties about the poor. I had full knowledge about her background. She was a rich and sophisticated woman fond of night-clubs, dances and drinking parties. She was an uninhibited woman. Frank and sensuous, she was proud of fine tastes in eating and fashion. No room for others. Her temperament of gay-abandon was marvellous. I could never place her in my scheme of things though my association with her was close."

She had fallen into a dead silence.

"Soma was a very rich woman. Both the families had strong business ties yet slowly and imperceptibly she started feeling a kind of vacuity. A queer sense of loneliness began to creep into her thinking. The fame was constant and lasting. Money attracted powerful connections. All kinds of people used to come and posed their problems. There was no time for them to look within. She was well-educated and thought long over human miseries. A sensitive heart she had. But it did not take much time to understand the direction in which her family was moving. At their level, she found out whatever her parents and relations were doing, it was to enhance and expand the business empire. To the outside world, they were kind-hearted and benevolent, but, in fact, they feverishly wanted to keep their commercial activities partially in secret. She soon discovered that her marriage to Vimal was also a deal. Vimal was, and perhaps even now-a-days, is a man of vices and sins, not gentle to her. He mostly spent his time in hotels or on foreign tours. Extra-marital relations was a disease with him, an obsession he could never get rid of."

"I want to expand horizons."

"I often had heard him saying so. Soma, a woman of taste and sensitivity, could not contain the disgrace for a long time as she came to know that it would be futile to restrict Vimal. At the personal level, he scarcely cared for values or virtues, she soon realised. He was a worldly man. In business too, he was tough, calculative and unforgiving. And above all, shady transactions also hardened her attitude. If some money was donated and distributed or community lunches and dinners were arranged, beggars and the poor were helped, it was a meticulous affair with a purpose. To build up an image of a great soul."

Rajshri had laughed rather angrily. I had observed a deep sense of hatred and agony in her eyes. "There were no relations." She had said after a few seconds, "No emotions. It was a living purely on the basis of business. When she could no longer withstand an ignominious living, Soma thought to sever her ties. There were quarrels and fights, and fist-wielding became an ordinary affair. Perhaps it was much more than that. She never told me, but I could guess that there was a wilful separation. Vimal offered her a small house, good amount of money and..." Her voice was muffled and disquieting, "You can never imagine. It happened. Slowly, she recovered. Dedicated her energies to the service of the poor."

She had heaved a deep rueful sigh, "But could not disconnect herself from her family. Whenever there is somebody sick or unwell, she invariably visits them. Vimal and her in-laws had numerous problems from the government with regard to sales-tax, income-tax and permits. A number of enquiries were initiated against them when there was a change in...His young son was murdered by a friend for...his old mother committed suicide and elder brother forgot everything in drinks when he discovered that his wife, belonging to an erstwhile family of rulers, had illicit relations with...any way that is how misfortunes come. You cannot know the mind of your wife?"

Her statement was sharp.

Jai Bhadra taking a long grumbling puff had said, "Why do you stick to the selfish. Always thinking..."

"..."

"Why does Soma go back to the sick husband? Vimal dissipated his energies. A bunch of renowned doctors attend to him and others, but...ailments do not lessen. The other day, when I had gone, Vimal was emotional as he made a frank admission, 'What do we get? Nothing. Those strong men who once ruled are vegetating in hospital's bed. One-line bulletin is their fate.'"

"We have rid ourselves from a corrupt..."

"All these words come to our notice. I think, you can hide nothing. Nothing, I mean. People know your ins and outs. May be for a certain period, out of fear, they do not speak, but slowly the dark side overshadows you. It is a fact of life. Those babus, social workers...and...you cannot write history of the future. Your offspring has to suffer. Jai Bhadra's deeds will be known after twenty years. Who knows the social work in which we are engaged will prove our undoing. It may be turned out as selfish so as to engrave our names."

"Mamma, you are..."

"That is what I am afraid of. I do feel that our small welfare activities are after all a step towards recognition. I am selfish but still I feel happy when he is around, these children...Romi... Jaycee..."

Rajshri was dismayed and upset.

"Raji, man must know that fundamentally it is the self-interest that matters in life. It is a source of inspiration. Yes, you get a feeling that you ought to do something. The spirit to excel, to do better..."

"I understand your intentions."

Rajshri had responded rather disenchantingly.

"I am advising you to compromise with reality. You are pretty realistic and there should not be any difficulty in..."

"I know...I know..."

She had said interrupting him.

"It is the question of age."

"..." I was sitting like a statue. Expressionless.

I had been caught in an unintentional web of relations, known and unknown.

"If Soma Gandhi is concentrating on poor, it is to find an escape, a meaning in the process to attain inner peace. Her personal life was not..."

With those blank eyes, Jai Bhadra had conveyed his message.

"Raji, this will happen. You have to accept. When your near relations go away, it is better to concentrate on...and...Raji what do you do exactly? We should be prepared for eventualities Jaycee is throwing. It is not even in the hands of Romi."

"..."

"Should I explain to you what happened to Som Dawra? He served all. A godman among the politicians. Offered important positions in the government but refused and truthfully thought about the society and nation. He was a revered man. People visited him from far-off places to pay obeisance, touched his feet, sought guidance and blessings. Ministers stayed because of him. He was active and agile still he felt much detached. He wanted to live with his grandchildren and...but his political life...when Dawra became ineffective, no one came to him and finally the poor man became mad. He is in the asylum among the lunatics.

"His own sons and grandsons ignored him. He had said, "I knew about the culture of my party. They worship those who have money and muscles. They squeezed the last drop of blood out of me. I am not disillusioned. I had not hoped for a better treatment. This age is cursed." He had added further, "But the most unfortunate part is that my own family...you feel cut up when your blood...refuses to recognise." When he had been in the hospital, very few people enquired after him. The white-clad leaders slowly stopped going to him...it was a visible trend, Dawra noticed."

"I was appalled to see his fortitude. But what struck him hard was the indifference of his sons and...this attitude of dear ones drove him to mental imbalance. Filial ingratitude was the last thing he could have tolerated. Raji, things don't move always according to your plans. Dawra is in Ranchi...May God save his soul. And then Samanta, that textile man, is a forlorn soul. When business touched a profit of twenty crores a year, his sons usurped the operations and forced him to take rest. Now what is his position? A wretched man lives on medicines. Eats very little. I have been told that lately he has started spending time in the temples. Just sits cross-legged with eyes closed. That is the ugly fate of the man who once donated lacs of rupees to hospitals, orphanages and missionary schools. I don't say that they had no personal axe to grind. They had a killing instinct to govern in a different way. However when age defeated them, even their relations decided to behave otherwise."

Jai Bhadra's voice had immense prowess and all of us were just watching minutely his facial expressions. The distorted and harsh truth had possibly shattered us badly. There was something known, yes, quite intimate to us and still indefinite. Rajshri was serious yet was keeping her dignified postures. Romi was a bit flustered.

*** *** ***

• 6 •

Time was running fast and we were now restive.

"He has not come!"

"..." Romi had composed herself, "I have made beds for you."

"No, we shall wait for him. He seems to be so cool and unaware of our worries. Have you told him we have come?"

"..."

"Aey Raji, why are you perturbed over him? Imagine the fate of Soma, Samanta, Dawra and Sonali."

"Everything she had. All comforts of the world. But on the death of her husband that well-known family disowned Sonali. Condemned her for the death of her husband. She was cursed, abused and kicked. They dubbed her a witch — and, you know the amount of odium Sonali had confronted. It was obnoxious. She was finally compelled to...and then a Sadhvi...and there the big...priest, the Dharam Guru tried..."

"I know them all."

"If you have known them, you would not have regretted."

"But it is our own..."

"In relations nothing is different."

"You are so..."

"We should know, we are different. As human beings we should accept our fate."

"I agree."

Raji had said in order to conclude a savoury argument. I had noticed another beginning of an unpleasant debate in the offing still had brought a smile on my parched lips.

"Mamma, you are too gentle."

"No, I was just reminded of them."

"In all earnestness one should perform one's duties. You have been doing your assigned work as if it were a religion not mere rituals. It is fine and deserves compliments. In social sphere also, it is not that you win people and have your way. No. In noble work, too, you encounter problems. In right spirit, you espouse a cause. To reach your goal becomes the target. And remember Raji, you are not a saint. You are a commoner because you are in social service where you do not expect anything in return."

Jai Bhadra addressed her in a mild, loving and assuring voice, "One should realise one's position in life. Dreams have no relevance. I have not found a terror-free day. There had been selfishness around. We talk of our ancestors to derive inner strength. It is a tradition. You are doing your work, expanding your activities, that is sufficient. I have found out that...any way forget about it. I know Jaycee's friends. Ramanathan who thinks for hours and then Ratnam who is deeply involved in the present system. He is practical as far as social affairs are concerned and I know his undiminishing warmth."

"Raji, we think differently. Why should you want them to pay special attention to you? Don't you realise that they also have their own areas of duties, love and passion?"

He had been too incisive.

She laughed without the earlier streaks of anger and then added, "You are right. When did I want any reward in return?"

"May be you are not considering all aspects."

"I feel sorry for them."

"No. I even admire Malkhan Dave. He is without grudge, happy and throbbing with life. He is engaged in social work but it is with a purpose. And you know those two cunning officers — Arif Khan and Patel. I tell you they are highly successful. They will achieve enviable position in the years to come. They have twinkles in their eyes, strange kind of sparkles, I observed them while uttering words. A forceful way of utterance. Their lips contain thousands of words."

"It is terribly disconcerting and..."

"I am reminding you of certain facts. It is not always that things happen according to our...as we walk ahead new people come across. A fresh thinking. Twisted ways and involved relations. We too had them."

"Yes, what I wanted, was a straight living."

"It depends upon you."

Jaycee had not turned up on time. Being tired and mentally exhausted, we thought at last to retire to our rooms.

*** *** ***

I was measuring the immensity of love with which Rajshri and Jai Bhadra approached us. I was making efforts to fathom the depth of feelings. I found somewhere that Jayanta was drifting away casually but in a designed pattern. The faces of Soma Gandhi, Dawra, Samanta and Sonali appeared vividly before my eyes. They were real individuals with failings and human love, but somewhere there was radically wrong in relations which drove them away.

I had been too occupied. And then my friends. There was nothing unheard of or unusual with them. Swamy was making himself effective and comfortable. So was Ramanathan. There were no inconsistencies. I was thinking about all probabilities but was finding it difficult to arrive at a decision. In the cobweb of relations, everything looked hazy and befuddled.

Pandit had said once when we were travelling together a few years back, "I took upon myself the work of educating people about the rampant loss of values. Yes, I tell my juniors and seniors to be honest. That is a simple conscious attempt to go close to a man. There are no roundabouts in this. I do my official job but keep telling whosoever comes to me. Not a restraining job. They dislike me but then I get the praise. All is not lost. I feel happy and content. No hanky-panky. Why to be worried about others? I am concerned about what damage will be done to me."

At that time Yadav had joined us, "Pandit is a dreamer. Useless words, he speaks. In day-to-day dealings, it is entirely a different story. You have to live. What is this he says about? No, I don't agree with Pandit. I do what others do. I don't want to cut off myself from the mainstream."

"I know, you don't like me."

"Pandit, I love you."

"Then you should..."

"Pandit, we go to a temple to pray. He listens to us or not that is not the question. The consolation is that we have offered prayers — and that mute...brilliant and benevolent God or Goddess does not say anything, but you feel, you are getting blessed. An aroma spreads around. A bunch of flowers soothes and alleviates you."

Yadav was so correct, I had been thinking.

Pandit had laughed away, "I don't agree."

"Pandit, it is not necessary."

"Forget about it." I had avoided to be involved in their wordy duels. It was a subject close to Pandit's heart, I knew, but I also understood Yadav's growing love for a luxurious living. He was urbane outwardly but lewd at moments of assault.

"How do you manage?"

Pandit had become peevish and angry.

"And you know that mad man, Rajput?" Yadav's words had rung in our ears.

"He does not need anything. But he does not know that the world would not bother about him. He may be a selfless worker, honest and upright...my experiences tell me that such persons inspire respect but do not cut much ice with practical men. I know my father had such qualities but what became of him?

"When he died, he left nothing for us."

Yadav's face was showing signs of disillusionment. It appears he had gone back to his past.

Soon he had recovered and said, "I don't repent. Also, I do not condemn him. I admire him. He used to speak of great men. Much influenced by Gandhi though such persons are out of date. I had regular fights with him. I remember those days when we had to go without a...meal. Our pecuniary condition was deplorable. When enough harm had been done, he sold his property...and spent on me. So I am here. I am not unaware of those days. Yes, truth, honesty and integrity are good words. I do not deny the sanctity but what do we get?"

"Yadav...you talk too much."

"No, it is a fact."

"..."

"A small time shopkeeper...sold unrestrictedly liquor and...in black, in connivance with the inspectors. He entertained people and do you know...he was furtively involved in kidnapping and...I become tense when I think of those dark days. When my father made a written complaint, the officers concerned did not have faith in him. He was also a party to the immoral traffic of women by organising fake marriages. Simultaneously he propagated no dowry, no entertainment and...when the truth was revealed, everybody's lips were sealed. My father again lodged a report. Police did not awake. On the other hand, my father was humiliated and abused. I remember that frightful night. My mother had not spoken a word. For the first time, I had seen my father weeping. Those tears, rolling down his wrinkled cheeks, I still see...fresh and hair-raising." He had been penetrating into the eyes of Pandit, "And you Pandit, you are suggesting me to...those who have known sufferings being inflicted at odd hours cannot forgive the perpetrators. I know that shopkeeper. He is bloody...a big fraud...so many factories and mills and on the top of it, district president of the party. The party moves as he directs. I know him. He is a respected man but a history-sheater. I think sometimes we deserve such leaders. And look at the impudence. That bastard does not miss an opportunity to shower praise on my father in public functions. In the village, he gives the example of our family. He fully knows that I have amassed wealth. He had turned his attention towards me; "I am waiting for the right time. No file moves till I charge commissions...nobody admits and yet everyone approves of it. Now I have created so much property...that three generations will live happily even if remain idle. And you know that shopkeeper...he is Mohan Khanna. You cannot say, tomorrow he may be lording over us. He is a killer. Killer. After that incident my father never recuperated. Mother became silent and lost the will to live. They lived for one year only. Pandit, I am the son...so unfortunate. I want to take revenge...but I know these people will..." Yadav's eyes were filled with tears. "So many Yadavs must be living..."

Pandit had not said anything.

"You know, it is nothing. When I am alone, I feel something is happening inside. I seethe with rage. The inner agony tears me apart. Yet I am helpless. Look what I have done to my father's value-system. These are lying dead. I have no one to console me."

I, with a cigarette in between lips, had been thinking of them.

That night was a terrible experience. His words continued to haunt me dauntingly. He wished to be among his own but could not spell out. I was extremely perturbed with no hope of sound sleep.

Those days of innocent childhood were no more. Everybody was grappling with the problem of existence. The issue of living a life fruitfully was much more important than anything else. It was a challenge and to me it had become a gravely serious matter.

Even if not wanting, I was thrown into the past. I was trying to fasten myself so that a clear picture emerges. But it was in tumult and dismay that life was to be witnessed. There were hopes and wishes. I was, without a knock, walking into all conceivable situations. I did not know why I was going back and back to my friends. They had never bothered to ask me questions about me. A few words about family and that ended the story. Contemporary life was irresistible, full of hopes and uncertain in many fields. They confronted the hazards and endured the sufferings. They were all tough, I knew there were unknown wounds somewhere near their hearts, a delicate thought disturbing the mind which combined to tease them, and they had always put up courageous thought. It was during vacant hours that there arose a compelling necessity to fill the empty mind and heart.

"All my friends who were now in government service holding high positions, had felt that something was missing."

"Don't you feel...?"

"No, in business you are occupied."

I had said.

"You don't have time when you think..."

"Yes, we think. There is a kind of togetherness. I sit at home. I discuss my problems with my wife, parents and sometimes with the kids. I share my little business matters perhaps to bridge this gap."

"Don't talk..."

Rajput's voice was resounding.

"You speak to children? Really..."

"Yes, Yadav, I do talk. And when I sit with them there is no thought of time. They, returning from the school, just drop in at the three agencies offices, look around, chatter a bit, ask questions without waiting for answers and disappear. I would rebuke or scold them for intruding into my busy schedule, yet they won't stop. After a day or two, three of them again come with an excuse. You know, it is time, when you do nothing."

"And how do you ask questions?"

Pandit had enquired.

"I don't ask. It is they who annoy and perplex me with small harmless questions. I am given full account of what happened in the school from teaching rooms to the playground. Those irritating yet bearable little acts of mischief, quarrels and pranks! Friskiness and impishness. It is all told vividly. I get tense when they don't stop. They obstinately adhere to innocent prattle and ask questions in order to tire me out. I like their questioning but sometimes they are difficult. I am busy. You know, we people are businessmen. I daily earn my bread and it is a planning, even then I find sometimes to get out of the rut. You cannot answer all their questions but you can join them in asking questions without the answers. It is like Yaksha, one has to ask questions without getting correct answers."

"You are fantastic." Rajput had admired my words, "So you enjoy yourself. But who'll answer?"

"None. I am not a Yudhishtra."

We had all laughed.

"You must spend some time on..."
"Swamy says, your business is growing."
"Yes I am working hard. I don't have fixed income."
"You are free."
"How do you know Malkhan Dave?"
"He is a social worker. I contribute some time to avoid a major trouble."
"But he is..."
"I know all of you are there!"
"You are impressed!"
"I have to be careful about my business. In case, I do not care for these people, I shall be in crisis. That black monster Dave is spreading his fangs..."
I had said thoughtfully.
"He is close to Jaycee!"
"Yes, Swamy and Jaycee are known to Jacob and Dave...a slight difference in age can easily be called men of connections. Jacob...is a smart conduit...and I am slowly...They are always dreaming high."
"You want to keep everyone in good humour."
I had not responded.
"At least I don't need anything...I shall try to maintain on whatever I get. I know there is no end to greed and lust."
Rajput had declared emphatically.
"One has to be practical!" Pandit had said, "I like him."
Those days were enjoyable and stimulating. Pandit, Yadav and Rajput had treaded a long, arduous and difficult path to the corridors of power. Yadav was fast and unkind in his approach and was probably the most successful. He also knew the ways of the world. They were also aware of the hard-hearted world.
There was a darkness around and I had realised the limitations.

*** *** ***

7

All those old faces were fresh. And I had found out that each one of them was in search of peace and happiness, something very close to his heart. I knew that Pandit was not happy. There were some teething problems at home. Numerous relations from his village visited him and sought assistance for they considered Pandit to be a big and influential officer. In a remote backward village, with majority of people illiterate and rooted in traditions worn-out and dead, Pandit's joining civil services was of immense importance. They admired, loved and respected him. But he had not changed. Simple and without pretensions, he in a low and rustic language, under a peepal tree, gave minute details of training, academic life, tours and then the grandeur of civil servants, the amount of respect they elicited and the halo of prestige and honour they have. He told them how he was being introduced to the practice of passing orders and ensuring compliance. "To serve your own people is a matter of great satisfaction. Such an opportunity comes in a life-time."

Pandit used to relate his experiences in detail. He would talk of great Indian cultural history. Values and morals. All of them listened to him with pin-drop silence. Pandit was really a noble soul. His elders blessed him and prayed for his long life. But Pandit's style never changed. A few young boys who joined as clerks in the offices soon transformed themselves into different individuals. They had started living a luxurious life. But Pandit could only live ungrudgingly with moderate comforts. Whereas his relations among clerks began to come in cars and taxis, Pandit would travel to the village by bus with an attach in hand and a small bag slinging on his shoulders. While walking along the green fields he would talk reverentially to his elders and enquire about everyone's welfare.

The villagers understood the difference yet kept their mouths shut and thus the image of Pandit grew stronger day by day. That was a poor Pandit and often in my solitary hours, whenever I went back to initial struggling years I had praised him.

And Yadav! I had been driven to past. Those faces young and old were dancing before my eyes. Their words, harsh and sweet, were creating a frightening scenario.

*** *** ***

I was cursing myself within with a cigarette pressed in between my fingers. I was reminded of Yadav. A man from a humble beginning in the social set-up and now wanting a definite place in the hierarchy with the power of muscle and money. He had never claimed for himself a place among those who could be called men of substance. No. It was a simple relation. He knows each one in the society. He had seen eyes of those who always spoke a different language. Injustice made an indelible scar on his sensitive heart and he burnt inside with a spirit of vendetta. He started thinking dangerously and I had seen those eyes blazing menacingly. Now it was buried deep so that other could not see.

One thing uncommonly linked them. I liked their bonds of affection. Whereas Pandit had a simple living with down-to-earth philosophy of life and won the hearts of people, Yadav, too, remained tied-up to his own people and occasionaly helped them in kind and cash. He had the devastating instinct to exploit his position. He not only fed himself fat and filled his coffers but also managed to set up secret links with persons of doubtful integrity. Though he disliked Mohan Khanna and covertly nursed a dreadful wish to eliminate him yet his desperation grew manifold, when he thought differently. Khanna's public showering of praise rendered him confused and bewildered.

"When I watch those two helpless souls, my heart writhes in pain and I become mad. That bastard is responsible...but then, I being a...I am disgusted. He has satanic connections. A murderous instinct. But I tell you, I shall..."

I had seen those red eyes in flames with all-consuming rage.

But still an unannounced niche had been established between the two. Tacit and self-destructive association took birth between Yadav and Khanna. And there those two good friends Pandit and Rajput played a sobering role with a sense of chastisement. The sweep and distance looked limited but somewhere restraint had taken roots with the result that the fiery and vehement feeling of revenge had been mollified to a great degree. Yadav's imperceptible inclination brought him closer to people who had suspicious and fraudulent dealings. Their operations had areas of violence and disgrace and without a voice expressing agitation he had entered into those prohibited lanes. The outrage was tremendous and it was a march towards comforts, money and muscle.

At this stage, Rajput stood by him. A dozen other officials were included in the list of clandestine activities and thus the journey to material prosperity began. Yet Rajput had a different approach. Curiously enough, he had no wish to mint money and...and so I had a kind of attachment towards him.

"Why do you require all this?"

This used to be his standard question.

There had been long and arduous discussions. Rajput quite often spoke of society and nation but pushed himself to the background and took a humble position. He never claimed that people could do nothing unethical who were engaged in having both ends meet.

"I am not interested in all such matters. I want to concentrate on my work. I like to be among my friends. You know, I don't hate files. No, not at all. Why should I? When I was a child, I had a habit to listen to stories of bravery of ancestors. I felt proud of it. Strange, it is that all of us belong to different places with slightly different family background and cultures but I find there is a tacitly agreed platform that binds us. Pandit is a noble soul. I love him. Then he had directed his words towards me, "I don't know why I am attracted towards you. Old friendly words and those college days. Roaming about in the corridors of Govt. offices. On the roads and India Gate. I can vividly recapture all those small incidents. Those thoughtless and a little hurried looks about uncertain future. The silence of Ghats. The fearful and shocking noise on the roads. Those celebrations. Violence and bloodshed. Funeral processions."

He would invariably relate the same thought rather oft-repeated banal opinion on Delhi.

"You know, you are a businessman. You loved good, true and honest men and views. I like your nature. Yet now in business you can't be honest. No. And you should not. Why should you be? Time is fast coming when..."

Rajput had been sharp and blunt. He never hesitated to ventilate emotions in a vociferous manner.

"Pandit!"

He would peer into the eyes of Pandit and Yadav and then return to me.

"I would go on recalling words. I don't have a strong vocabulary. Neither I am fond of words in high flown language. I love you all and when an element of cunningness takes over I hate you. You know, do not understand what happens to me."

Rajput's face and eyes reflected an eery and unbearable brilliance which, to this day, I have not been able to see anywhere else.

I was thinking. It was a torturing experience.

*** *** ***

It was a long journey without a movement.

"I don't know what they would be thinking, Rajshri, Jai Bhadra, Romi and..."

I had stretched myself on the bed but undoubtedly I had been fascinated by the memories of past. Those faces, warm and loving, appearing in quick succession before the eyes created an aura of joy and pleasure and I, without loss, wished to protect that sentiment.

Again words of Rajput had rankled in my ears and I had failed to make out the meaning.

"Here nothing happens. No man does anything himself. He just moves with others. All these people are happy and yet...they hardly know what they do and still profess they do everything. It is the thought of misery and helplessness consistently plaguing and irking. We are all good. Or am I right...this stirs me out of sense. I don't know why people require crores. My necessities are limited. I don't feel the itch. I know my friends...they have unlimited wealth. Unsatisfied still and hunger for everything on earth. Why do we want to grab? I have seen the surfeit and the dissatisfaction. You have fatty bank balances and still want to have more. I too had the intense desire...but I developed a feeling of hatred...I know all. I cannot express myself possibly. The world is fast growing. Those three wars. All kinds of people...persons had eagle eyes on money and..." Rajput had described the craze and madness, race and recklessness of the age. "I saw those persons...in authority and with connections exploiting the situation. It was an ugly vocalising of..." When I had seriously pierced into the eyes, he had stopped for a while and I realised he had forgotten to say what he ardently wanted.

After a few minutes, he had added, "I am watching the progress. I am not growing but you are going up. Pandit is somewhere in old grooves...good and noble. There are scintillating patches in his eyes.

You know this face. A glow is maintained. Yadav, you have a made-up look. Yet I like you. I have no complaint against anyone. But I admire, love and then think."

"You cannot afford to forget yourself in a crowd. Yet you cannot live in a desert. You feel a dry land is spreading within you. I want to avoid that possibility. It is an awful situation. You are all going on your respective paths. Sound and strong. Jayanta Chandra Chauhan basking in the glory of his illustrious ancestors. All carry history. Don't we ever take pride in the past. Everyone does it. Ramanathan and Ratnam at this young age are learning the art of living. Look at those senior officers...Mahapatra and T.K. Mukherjee...they have a glib tongue, a docile and yielding nature, who do not think yet do what others ask them to do, speak and think what their bosses want them to do. With sound and respectable family background they lick shoes. But nobody bothers. It is the...the way of the world. Such people are acceptable in the society. They are successful. I am envious. In a few years just before my eyes, all of you have become rich, men of sources and resources..." He had laughed in a roaring voice, "You are a businessman...you know how to feed. I don't know how and to what extent you will be able to achieve your goal but I consider it practicable that in business, you have...oblige and...I am sure you'll understand. Somehow, I have not been able to reconcile.

"I too want to become a wealthy man. Everybody wants. I am not fastidious. I can go to any extent. But then something restricts me. I see all of you. So many others also meet me. I exchange notes with them. It is always thrilling to convey good wishes on others' success. But then I have also observed that a kind of moroseness is all-pervasive...I realise they are not happy. There is sickening dullness at home. Some secrecy, a wordless failure to understand life. They say at times that comforts give happiness. It is a contradiction. Yadav has a burning desire to wreak vengeance though he is still indecisive. They are...all these happy people are in a real sense not happy. Asif Khan and Patel senior, very senior officers, all dance to the tune of...always cajoling and wheedling. Bending backwards and admit everything without a word. That is a technique to become rich and powerful. Yet I have found them emotionless people...probably they are away from their kith and kin. I have found them sparing little time for families. I have observed children silently and docilely looking at the sky with blank faces and sometimes naughty and..., they express aversion towards their fathers. A slow and voiceless transformation is taking place among these families. You are not an exception."

He had flirtingly told me, "If you stay away for long and without reason, you'll become cool and frigid." That was Rajput's cold judgement. I had been stunned at the way he had arrived at naked and obvious conclusions. "And you know Jaycee? His great mother Rajshri who would spell out her emotions even."

"Jayanta is coming close to reality...I don't know, if you'll agree. As far as their family tree is concerned, it grows to touch history. I find invisible crevices. Could it be a busy today? Contemporary life is hardly glamorous. It is not tied to a particular thought. I find people engaged in different fields at the same time. A ruler of the past is becoming a hotelier. A cobbler is...I mean everything is happening the other way round. Pandit knows the scarcities of his village and for that matter each one of us is not unaware of the hidden pangs. Rapid changes happening around are affecting our emotions and sentiments. There is some pollution. Foul smell. Unwanted corrupting influences spreading everywhere. Everyone is feeling the pinch, the assault and the consequent fall-out. There I remain a spectator. I want to do but then retrace my steps.

"I want to keep the flame of love and warmth alive. That is what Pandit is doing..."

I had not contradicted him.

*** *** ***

And at that moment, Rajshri's enquiries had awakened me to harsh realities.

Life was wide and bright.

Her words echoed.

"Look at these young men. How intimate and still far off. Jayanta must look back or else the devastating noisy today shall engulf him. He is going away."

It was an uneasy night for me. I was running at two parallel streams of thoughts. There was a quaint eruption of feelings of brotherhood. Ramblings and disconnected thoughts had created a wide gulf and I had been making sincere efforts to reconcile the opposing strands.

Rajput was one man who could hit you on the head. I was really at a loss to know what I wanted and where I intended to proceed.

Pandit, Yadav and Rajput had driven me mercilessly to the days of earlier years in the college.

We had then joined the intermediate classes. The college professors with deep passions related stories of freedom struggle. There were years of resurrection and reconstruction. Nehru's idealism was being given practical shape. It was a democratic set-up. A socialistic-democratic concept took birth. Inconclusive debates continued on planning. It was an age of learning in a free country.

"I shall join an army of selfless workers."

Jayanta's enthusiasm was noticeable.

"Yes."

"Our P.M. is young...it is a treat to hear him. In his eyes, one can see an unflinching faith."

"You are right, Jay."

"There is something..."

"..."

"India will be a strong nation."

"Yes, naturally."

"We shall have to work hard."

"I am with you."

"We shall take upon ourselves the hazardous task of getting rid of social evils."

"Yes."

"We young boys, as our teachers advise, should pledge to make India a better country to live."

"Yes, Jay...we should..."

I had wished to say many things but Jayanta's flow of words and thoughts was so torrential and vociferous that I could hardly muster up requisite strength to silence him...my answers were mostly telegraphic and sound-filled without conveying meaning.

"My mother is a social worker."

"She is great."

"Father Jai Bhadra has warm relations with rulers in Delhi also and many State lords are his personal friends."

"Yes, it is a fact."

"I shall also join movements that serve deprived segments of society."

"It is a sacred ideal. You must. You can afford. You have the means and..."

"Why do you say so? Do you think only persons with means can serve people?"

"Yes, Indians, excepting a few, for generations remained exploited and disunited and there were many important factors to enslave them. It is poor country. You know here a war among castes and classes continues...and...the white people wanted to perpetuate the gap. A divided community served their purpose in a more befitting manner."

"Yes, but you..."

"Jay, you are men of power and money. A large section of society is poor and weak."

"That is why I want to associate them. That is the political thinking. The idea of dramatic socialism cannot be translated into reality unless all of us join hands. Collective will and strength of countrymen will make it a mighty nation."

"You are right."

"Let us join social organisations. Before independence these were raised to create social awareness and political consciousness to free the country but today an entirely different war has to be fought on various fronts. A monstrous communal war!"

I had remained stupefied at the amount of zeal and idealism that Jayanta exhibited. And that too had encouraged me to think about the people and country at large. Then in my private conversation, I used to admit that even to speak of selfless service to the people and nation was a matter of heritage and great cultural traditions.

Jai Bhadra had his roots in a family that was, and perhaps is, intimate to the historical events and that was why, it had thought to serve the country. Rajshri was, in a way, part of that historical necessity and tradition. I remembered each and every word of Jayanta, Rajshri and Jai Bhadra. Jai Bhadra was close to Congress and inter alia an admirer of Gandhi, at the same time fond of reasonable status quo in a world of upheavals and revolutions. Jay had in late sixties discussed, debated and argued at length about the serious economic, social and political issues confronting the nation.

I had been graphically underlining all those important events and words.

There was intensity in emotions. I felt the need to meet them daily. Not only I but all of us were unconscious of this latest sentiment. Those were days of immense love, emotions and warmth.

"Love among relations, a feeling of togetherness and brotherhood, harmony and mutual understanding are our strength." My mother's words had infused renewed energy and vigour. I was simply wonderstruck. Thoughts had run wild and on the other hand Rajshri, Jay's mother, fortified my argument by saying that man's most consecrated and pure thought lies in his heart and the passions it sustains.

Those were days of idealism and lofty thoughts of ambitions and grand future of promises and pledges. We used to talk for hours.

There was an element of innocent love and affection.

"Don't you agree with me that we ought to..."

Jayanta had asked me pointedly.

"Now yes..." I had not allowed him to continue.

"Now first listen. When we cannot live...even for a day...without meeting..."

"..."

"We should maintain..."

"Yes."

"There is an inner joy...among..."

He had not completed the sentence but the meaning was clear to me. "No sublime search better than finding love and the necessity to prolong it."

*** *** ***

8

It was Jayanta who had said words about love and relationships so excitedly and with passion and conviction. And today after years when he had more than a dozen years put in service, the scenario had changed and widened. I had not totally anticipated the implications.

"Jayanta was the most consistent and determined among us." Rajput had said after the war with China was over.

"But today, I find him a different man."

"Those burning moments to tilt the whirlwinds are gone!"

"There is calmness."

"He is smiling and ironic in his facial expressions."

I had listened only.

"Yaar, you big baboos are difficult to understand."

"Baboos!" He had turned back.

"Yes, I mean, you people are experts in using words convincingly."

"Oh, don't tell me. I am flattered."

Rajput was examining his goggles closely, "Look out of fashion."

"You have not changed."

"With this packet, you can't."

"Where are others?"

" ..."

"I mean members of the family?"

"They come to stay. It is heart-warming. Father-mother growing old. Now that I have completed my field tenure, I hope to get absorbed in Delhi. It is just useless to go to the States. They are inconsistent and parochial. It is so restrictive. You are biased and ungenerous because regional sentiments are uppermost."

I was amazed at his comments.

"Rajput, you are..."

"Yes, I am telling you. I did try to put my thoughts in black and white but encountered stiff opposition. I thought I should persist but constant disapproval and naggings had pushed me to the wall."

"It could happen with you?"

I had shown surprise.

"Yes, I think, we are fools."

" ... "

I am carrying on with the old goggles for years because these are silent spectators of my rotten state."

"You are repentant."

"No, I am sorry for those, you follow me...?"

"One should not feel disgusted so soon."

"No, but even our close friends did not..."

"When a fight for existence starts you have to be alone."

"There is a marked difference in what you say."

"Yes."

"Pandit and Yadav!"

"Pandit is happy. The same glow and shine. You simply cannot see for long the twinkle and sparkle of his eyes. He is unaffected by the changes. Do you know he is in charge of the in-coming and out-going dispatches. Virtually no work. And Yadav! He is a remarkable chap. He has built up a strong economic base, purchased shares, running two textile firms in the name of his wife and his sons are getting training right for now...he obliges all...Mohan Khanna is his godfather."

"Rajput!"

"He is his enemy also."

"You are...!"

"Don't ask about me? I am happy like Pandit. Perhaps my small relations...emotionally rich parents, children and wife are a source of inspiration and happiness. You know we spend maximum time together. Many like us also feel happy. The inexhaustible fountain of love keeps us alive in the cosy embrace of one another."

I had not reacted.

"But I find our friends are slowly drifting away from the warmth of relations."

We had discussed everything on earth. Many names had appeared on our lips. Rajput had also taken me to Yadav who in turn had asked us to have dinner at Taj. And I had known the glamorous side of these big baboos who, I thought, were still not in the conspiratorial dangerous game. But the next five or six years had introduced me to the behind-the-curtains kind of life. There was full exhibition of sex, scandals, business, jealousy, enmity and politics. It was a violent and sizzling passion, hot and scathing wordy duels.

What amazed me was the all bright and smiling faces of those big people. In business affairs, I had ignored that aspect. Whenever big officials and influential leaders visited Delhi for physical or political rendezvous, it was my responsibility to look after them in Delhi...and that was how...my success was to follow me.

I had told Rajput who was astonished though not convinced. At that moment, Yadav had told him, "Rajput, look you don't aspire, so it is not with us. We want to move ahead. Doesn't matter who meets us with what intentions? It is a common approach."

"Yadav, are you happy?"

"Have you asked from him?" His questioning shot alerted me, "What about Jaycee, Rama, Raghu, Ratnam, Harry Singh, Samanta, Dawra..." He had released a long list of acquaintances and I was just fiddling with my cigarette pack to gather courage to confront him.

"Jaycee had called our thinking as a product of proletarian intellectual born out of inferiority complex, false pride...and what not?"

"He always spoke of strong nation, hard work, honesty and faith. He was one who spoke of social ills for hours." I was trying to defend Jaycee.

Rajput and Yadav had in a threatening tone disallowed to say anything and to that I had retaliated, "And I am small clerk!"

"We know you entertain many in Delhi."

Suddenly they were relaxed and spoken at length about the power-brokers and politics. The files and corridors of ministries seemed stinking when their version of life was given.

"You see all those...you are also disappointed? You do it and condemn. You don't agitate and become indivisible part of the monolithic system and then speak violently against it. I must call you courageous."

I had taken a number of long puffs.

"But to maintain oneself it is not easy to cut off yourself."

"What do you suggest?"

"Nothing!"

"Yadav! I will not argue."

"Thank God, you have put an end to the debate." Rajput had blurted out, "Have pity on them. They carry the burden of the nation."

He had laughed and pushed the pack to Yadav. The words of Rajput, Pandit and Yadav were depressing and grieving. When we had assembled at a common friend's house, I had asked Jay to come to me.

"Yaar, we don't get time. But I shall fix up some meeting."

"Romi was telling you..."

"Yes, it is correct. Nature of my duties is tedious and it is impossible to..."

"You talked of those noble and high sounding ideals."

He had given a faint smile.

"Don't change the subject. I am your old friend. In fact many of you have taken different directions. Those youthful exuberations have been crushed."

"Those were mental aberrations."

"Jayanta, you cannot be rude." I had insisted on the earlier line of argument, "Mamma and Papa too are worried over this change."

"They want me to be tied down to their aprons?" He was harsh and loveless.

"Those dreams...you wanted to join an army of social workers ...who could make India strong, united and prosperous. Those long inconclusive discourses on social evils, inequality, communalism, casteism and violence were, I understand, not without meaning."

"..."

"Yadav, Pandit and..."

I had spoken out numerous names spontaneously to prove my point that they were going out of the man's bonds of love and togetherness.

He had loudly laughed and roared.

"Yes, I know. My mother a great social name. She is a big name. She has access to almost all the...but then, it is different. Swamy and I...we know how things move at the highest level. It is practical approach to life. There is nothing wrong."

"I was not interested in all that you do. What do you say when I find, you are not available at home? This is my fourth visit and you have opted out..."

"I was busy."

"They also need you."

"It is an old fashioned sentimental approach. It makes me sit up in anger."

"You are losing hold on..."

"No. Time waits for none."

"It is a simple suggestion."

"..."

"Jaycee, Vicky, Rahul and Ashey need a father. Romi Bhabhi requires some words of..."

"..." Jaycee had laughed, "You are strange. Mamma and Papa are..."

"She is a social worker. She comes to meet all of them. Jai Bhadra too wants you to..."

I had seen Jaycee's moving eyeballs and quivering lips gradually appearing on the wall. It was an offending and stinging experience. Memories were too pacifying to make me sleep. I was looking out of the window to release my tensions. I had visited Delhi many a time, knew its history, but that day's contortions were astounding and provoking.

I had to bear the pains inflicted by time. The past was not away and the present age was also not very fit to attract an analytical study. They were kind and gentle human beings worried and concerned about welfare of one another but then something intrinsically was compelling them to protect self-interests. They had found their respective destinations.

It would be futile to shift their individual stands. I was proud of the fact that they were sincere in their admissions.

"Yes they had changed immensely."

The conclusion was haunting me.

*** *** ***

The next morning was as fresh as ever. The crimson rays of the sun had entered my room when there was a knock. I had opened my eyes to look around. I felt, I had done my work properly, negotiated with them on many points and yet gained very little. In spite of this, a feeling of intense satisfaction had swept over me.

A servant with a cup of tea was entering the room.

"Saab!"

"He is getting up."

I had taken about fifteen minutes to get ready.

After half an hour, we were all sitting at the breakfast table, facing each other.

"I am pleased. Really, it is an honour to get a chance to have..."

"Papa, I am sorry, These people are...I had to go. You know the nature of my work."

Jaycee was fumbling for a convincing argument but I had found out a few twisted lines of diffidence on his face and his eyes were still carrying a hangover of last night.

"Jay, we have been intimately observing. It is objectionable. You ought to snatch some moments. You should stand on your own for a few seconds in which you could take care of your wife and children." Jai Bhadra's words were slow, authoritative and quite effective.

Jaycee's hands stopped near the cup of milk. It seemed the slices were fungus-covered, pale and stale. Suddenly, he had found out as if his cup of tea were containing poison. His entire body appeared to be contorting under some intense and unknown agony. The lavish, noisy and fun-making drab scenario appeared to be opening up before his eyes, for, I witnessed a few streaks of broken smiles on his lips and his eyes were filled with joy. He looked at us with half-closed eyes but remained mum.

The unerring observation of Jai Bhadra had awakened him, "You are exhausted, Don't go to the office."

"Oh, dad, I shall be alright. It is a daily routine. Nothing more. And I tell you nothing fresh really occurs. It is the rut, the common words...put up, speak, noted, draft...amended, as proposed, discuss...I mean these words constitute the diary of a table-loving big clerk. I enjoy myself. We don't do anything special. We are not there to innovate, no, it is not our creed. We smell an air of change. This is what I am taught. Yes, not beyond this. It is a smooth walk with no unevenness, no obstructions and odds."

"Jaycee, you are ignoring..." Raji mamma had interrupted him, "I don't say, you should not attend to your duties. You should. But never confine yourself to boring and monotonous files. It moves on. I have seen what is done at the...every man is supposed to spare something for himself. Your friend was complaining..."

He had looked at me.

"Mamma, you are right."

"Yes I understand..." Raji had said, "Where is the idea to stay back? How is it that only he..." She was neither angry nor disapproving but her voice contained feeble signs of pain, "I want, he should..."

"I am doing it in my own way. After all, ground realities cannot be disregarded." It was a voice of a disgruntled man.

"And what has happened to..."

"..." Jaycee was quietly fixing up his eyes on the plate.

"Malkhan Dave and Madhav Wadia are praising you."

Jaycee had looked up in sceptical amazement. His lips had squeezed and a layer of darkness had covered his face, it appeared to me.

The movements of eyeballs were suspicious and gloriously wicked. He had not answered her but munched a piece of bread while eyes counted the number of scattered eatables, though non-seriously. Everything looked dirty and rubbish. Dave and Wadia were turning into strong public figures with commercial vested interests all around. They were sickeningly rich and knew how to enter into the body-politic. Their brand of social work and altruistic thoughts had begun to seep down the innocent consciousness of people. I had been browsing articles lately in magazines and newspapers about their foolish excursions into all social, religious and reformatory areas. They, along with a host of friends, with the intentions to serve some ulterior motives hidden and at times visible, wanted to expand boundaries of their operations. They belonged to the new breed of crop of social enthusiasts who had taken birth to go beyond the assigned and natural limits. Such thoughts were giving genuine headache to me.

"Jaycee, Wadia and Dave..." Mamma Raji with utmost restraint over herself had said, "I know them."

"They are not only business magnates but also social workers. In our country these people are urgently needed."

"You should be careful. Dave's underhand methods to influence are known to me. And Khan...you should be watchful about Patel and Khan. Their mild and inoffensive approach can land you up in some grave situation. They are more clever and behave like politicians. It is not the end of their careers. And mind you, all these fellows...are..."

"Mamma, we are all friends. All of them know...I don't think they can..."

"Yes, in relations too, one has to examine all aspects."

"Mamma, you are..."

"I know, you had arranged your...very few do it."

"When you get indication from above..."

"Jay, don't shift..."

"Mamma, I would like to spend some time among...I am thinking to strengthen your hands. Yes, mamma, you are right. One cannot be sure of what one is doing."

It was an abrupt change. Jai Bhadra burst into a prolonged laughter.

"Bravo, my child..."

"Papa, I am trying to make out."

"No, my son..." Jai Bhadra looked meaningfully at his wife, "I think, he is right. These officials are caught up in moral issues unnecessarily and without intentions to do something...they do it just for the hack of it. It is luxury to engage themselves in baseless debates, for these build up their image. But I don't think, Jay wants to adopt these tactics."

"You are complimenting?"

Rajshri had questioned him.

"You are to change your methods and thinking."

"Mamma's social awareness is total and perfect. I know Papa... you cann't be sarcastic. Romi's words were directed to all with a clear purpose, Papa's judgement cannot be incorrect."

"Yes, he is never wrong."

"Jaycee, you are too smart."

"Mamma, you cannot find faults with any social organisation. To me, it is my opinion, all those who have ambitions to usurp power and pelf are indulging in such acts."

There was a long uncomfortable pause.

"Yes, that is right but we want you to stay away. It is a highly explosive game-plan."

"I know."

"Jaycee, if you'll ignore or avoid them, you shall be able to achieve."

"I have not done anything to...and why should I shirk duties which have come to me. I am morally bound to look after their interests. They are involved in the nation-building process. Everybody knows that these people are strengthening the economic foundations, contributing to the growth and development of the country."

"These are pious words?"

"..."

"These are oft-repeated goodwill gestures of social workers and..."

"Should I conclude...?"

"I would have appreciated your staying out of the fray. It is a dirty and unprincipled scramble for recognition. I find those are important in the society, need some renewed..., and so vested self-interests are taking deep roots."

"Mamma, a social worker should not be perturbed about them. You are running charitable institutions and...I will not go into that now and why. But I would only appreciate...that you allow us to live life as we want, not as your injunctions dictate."

Raji Mamma's eyes sprang concern and anguished worries. It seemed she was taking pity on him. But then she as a mother, no doubt, wished her son to rear up his opinions. Was she not contradicting herself? These suspicions had started haunting my mind. I was apprehending serious threat to their mutual faith and affection.

It was apparent that Raji and Romi were gathering and arranging threads of love out of a limitless vacuum.

"I don't think a clash would provide solace."

"No, I wanted an identity, an individual who contributes substantially to the society."

"Dave and Madhav and a horde of benefactors can prove self-destructive."

"You must be careful."

"You are occupying a very important seat and...through you they want to control..."

"I shall not permit them to make me an instrument."

"Do you think they'll subvert future?"

"It is an understanding."

"What?"

"To live and...?"

"I know those rogues." This time Jai Bhadra intercepted the conversation, "I know their hollowness. There is not even a morsel of ethics. It is a perfect plot to cheat. I know the hidden maliciousness and vulgarity in their commercial operations and social pretensions. Don't go by the impulses. Play cool. When a person gets lost in outside affairs, he is immune to..."

"Should I resign?"

"Jayanta...you should not ignore the gravity of the situation."

"Our interest is to save ourselves. We have to rescue ourselves from these sharks. Shouldn't we safeguard our souls."

I thought we were all involved in fortifying our weak positions. Perhaps we had become oblivious of the surroundings. It was a timeless experience. Abstract thoughts had invaded our minds.

*** *** ***

9

Raji's questions were converging in from all sides.

"Mamma, I have not forgotten my sense of discrimination. I am swayed away by emotive words. I am conscious of my limitations but then I know the inevitable. We have devised this system for our preservation."

Jaycee had tried to laugh, "We are the villains and the heroes. Now words flow through parallel currents of meanings. At one moment, I am a saviour and the next minute persuades me to act like an anti-hero. It is reliving your innerself in noble deeds to..."

"Mamma, I know..." He had diverted his attention to his wife, "She is angry. But I know..."

"I am fully informed..."

"I doubt."

"You know that I know not and she knows what I fail to know or all of you know and Romi explains to us that she knows."

"Mamma..."

"Jayanta, why do you take pride in knowing everything when nothing is clear."

"I wished to be truthful...Romi has joined a number of social forums to have responsibility of improving the deplorable...and all that...I mean all...I am talking of those..." He was hesitant and doubtful about what he wanted to say, "It is a common practice. Mamma, people watch us. Your juniors and seniors...leaders and lampoons...saints and...all follow us. It is the light that guides us to temples and mosques. I am performing yajnas and...and I can say that all are enamoured of...your son has a safe place near their hearts...look at that fellow. He is social and religious, a nobleman." He had in a deliberative mood closed his eyes. All of us were taking breakfast without an argument. I had considered the pricks and attacks inherent in those words rather inconveniently, for I thought myself to be an intruder in the family.

"Many good words are said about me."
"Not sincere."
"I don't agree."
"My son." Rajshri advised him in a calm and dignified voice, "I know the import of those words. You cannot move out...ethics and values...are outdated for all these..."
"I do not know how people react to...you are right. I am helpless. Not only I but these days no one can extricate oneself from the pulls and pushes of times. So many functions. Man is out of tune with himself. Mamma, I stumble into various types of...in Delhi these big multi-storeyed buildings house and suffocate silently people from all corners of India. Everything dissolves into a single soul. A consciousness. It is an ideal situation. It can be a blasphemy. You can't explain the sacrilege. It is destined. Three stingy, narrow corridors...black roads and concrete streets...all these lifeless patterns belong to humanity. It is a city where colour, caste and creed disappear and surface. It is the love for man and here he wants to stay and survive. It has been happening for a long time."
"Jayanta, you are assuring or..."
"No, I can't be untrue. I mean what I say. There is a bitter conflict continuing within. Papa, in this age, events are taking place violently. There is damning confusion. But in this fluid and unstable human affair there is definitely an evil design. Nothing is coming to mind without reason."
"Jaycee, you are giving justifications."
"Papa, man's emotions and relations need shelter, isn't it?"
"Mamma, I was hinting at a possible..." He had totally failed to convince them.

*** *** ***

I had followed tolerably Mamma's intentions behind her careful words. She had been perturbed over Jaycee's secret visits to Dave's and Wadia's places of business. She had also been informed about the terrific ambitions he was harbouring in connivance with Asif Khan and Patel.
It was, I remember faintly, during those years when she had a family gathering at home. If I recollect it was Vicky's birthday. Jaycee had not come to look after the family of Mahapatra. And she had obliquely told me that Mahapatra is an unscrupulous person who wanted to dupe Jaycee.
"Mamma, you should have admonished him."

"I had but he is emotionally involved with Radha...it is learnt yet I am..."

"No, Mamma, please don't suspect him. It is a question of doubting relation."

"But Mahapatra...!"

"A senior and elderly person he is, and she is a widow."

"Yes, I also curse myself. Jaycee is a man of strong morals but then his frequent absence from home, genuine however might be, does not rule out..."

"..."

"He is helping these dishonest people who in the mask of social well-wishers are exhorting to cut...they are dangerous and without pity. They are in collaboration with others and regularly making invisible efforts to earn profits by undermining interests. Contracts are given thus and they are exploiting relations."

"Mamma, I think these notorious tycoons are hanging merely on relations than..."

"Yes, those are the lurking fears. Jaycee's and his friends might not be waiting to...but I think that these young men are becoming partners with fictitious identities and nimbly shall walk into the deadly snare of Dave and...here I condemn my own judgement. Why should I doubt? I think it is through relations that... are engaged in sinful ventures."

Rajshri's misgivings had become apparent when I also repeated word for word her observations.

Before I could assure Raji Mamma, Jayanta had said, "We need sincere social workers and I too would be happy to join the movement. Romi..." He had called out his wife in a soft voice, "At present, you are merely helping out officers wives...who are either Rotarians or...I think you can float your own..."

The great argument was over. Romi wanted to smile yet with the sparkle of her eyes, lips refused to open.

"You cannot undermine the sanctity of relations by resorting to trivial tactics of popularity. It is measure of forbearance. These things do not afford lifelong happiness."

"I am..."

I had been inopportune and weltering to catch substance.

"Romi, it is a fashion now to start charitable institutions...help poor students in schools and in a fluctuating political situation, we must..."

"These children understand...and you have to cry a halt. Otherwise the portraits that their sensitive minds paint out, may influence them in future. Mr. Jayanta, you should..."

"Yes, you are right."

He had been looking at his mother Rajshri.

"You people are getting upset with your relations."

"No."

"Why should you arrive late? These innocent children do require Papa's presence."

"Yes, Mom, I shall ensure that..."

"Don't involve in...we have opened sufficient charitable institutions and trusts. You devote your energies to duties in an honest way. When time comes, we shall..." She was beseechingly looking at her husband, "You prepare yourself my dear son...and at an appropriate time we'll gladly hand over the reins to you. Till then Romi can get experience."

"..."

"You have to concentrate on...thus home is a temple...if you infuse love, affection, warmth and goodwill." She was speaking in an impassioned voice, "My son, your duties towards your home are more important."

I had seen divine grace and brilliance in those eyes, and for years I kept reviving that hour of family re-union. Jaycee was overwhelmed with respect and had made a feeble attempt to cheer up his parents.

That day celebrations had occupied all of us.

*** *** ***

It was not difficult to search for reasons of Jaycee's unstable attitude. He had been reserve and reticent with regard to matters close to his heart. He would say in incomplete sentences and then shut up. He was in the queer habit of keeping things half-done.

I had been seriously analysing his thoughts and reactions. It had been a change. Dangerous. Emotionally shattering. When I had awoken next day, I had not been able to meet him, for he had to leave early morning, on an urgent official errand. Romi was slowly becoming averse to such an uncertain behaviour.

"Yes, he has an important role to play. A definite contribution." She had brought forth an abhorring look, "The entire burden is on them. Great things. Men are not relevant. It is a cultural necessity to spend more and more time in the office...outside and..." She had smiled laconically.

"He didn't observe the courtesy to tell you."

"No, no, its...I admire his resilience."

"I knew him..."

Romi was showing suppressed indignation.

"Some consideration should be shown. He is over-conscious about official duties. A work-obsessed man."

"But he should also have regard for the emotions of children."

"Bhabhi Sahiba, you are sentimental."

"I know his nature. And...I fear, time is running fast. Vicky, Rahul and Ashey...after all growing to understand. Looking around. It is mom and papa who keep coming but can't stay for long because of Jay's continuous...I fail to understand...and then, it is fantastic you know, astonishing to hear when suggesting to us to devote more time to welfare."

"I think to serve people is an ingrained habit with the upper-class society. A sick unbanity. Bloody forky and funky they are. I also find these sentiments being poured out in copious quantity with all the sincerity."

The irony was apparent.

"Are you a patient of senility."

"Yes, I think, we ought to engage ourselves in kind, good and soul-filling little acts. Nothing is wasted. I believe you cannot restrain people from ridiculing and belittling the entire process."

She had put up an impotent and quivering smile.

"You'll have breakfast...?"

"Yes. I will and may be in the evening, I may go back to..."

"You were going to Calcutta...?"

"No, that person had agreed to come over. And today I want to keep my operations limited. This crazy passion for money. Yes, I am unceasingly asked and encouraged to expand but there I find it would be an impossibility."

"One of my friends in Punjab wanted to sell his factory to me and had also agreed to receive the price in instalments...but..." I had stopped and threw an inquisitive glance at the newspaper.

"..."

"Where are the kids? No noise."

"They had gone to the room to say hello but thought you are fast asleep...and..."

"Oh, God...they should have disturbed my sleep." I had expressed disappointment, and added, "You don't know, I was remembering each word. I too observed that things are not moving in the right direction. There is a missing link somewhere and nobody finds the chain, what will come about and when."

"You are right?"

"No, not exactly. It is an undisputed truth that new trends in thinking have taken birth. I see people doing things quickly and want no delayed results. Architects, builders, fashion-designers, artists and engineers are in great demand. Mills, factories and huge dams. Fatal and severe pressure on man and nature. Don't you think we are sprawling to a far-off distance. Without an inkling we are heading towards a breaking point."

"Yes, when I go around, those people simply want their hunger... a few needs. I find them happy and satisfied. They listen to you, talk to you and give much in terms of love and respect. They don't doubt our intentions yet something percolates down...in the depth of their hearts. You ask them with faith feelingly and they arouse your imagination. In case the concern reaches out to family...these people pour out their hearts. All relations become alive. You can see in their eyes, and those tiny drops twinkle with intense love. It is a thesis on human relations. I have seen them talking about relations. You know what I concluded? In relations, you get immense comforts. You quarrel, you tease, create obstacles and even then a gentle feeling of togetherness keeps you cosy. It is a blessing to them. Even if scarcity stares in the faces, these people laugh away little sufferings. They share grief and miseries. It is always thrilling. It gives me strength. I feel a joyous fulfilment. No, it is no exaggeration. No hyperbolic statement. It is simple...and contacts with them are sweet...in my frequent journeys to and from, always warming. The virtue of emotions is known when..."

I had controlled myself lest I should have been misconstrued.

"You were talking about the friend from Punjab."

"His dilemma was that the jat's friend eloped with his wife. This fact he kept to himself till his children grew up and married off. Whenever I visited him, he looked composed and quiet. Like children, he would jump and dance in the courtyard. I never thought he was suppressing a volcano within. That day, he told me all about. I found that he was grievously hurt by disloyalty of a relation and even then he got maximum consolation. But I don't know what happened that he ultimately decided to...but one thing is clear, that he was disgusted and unhappy with..."

We had discussed for too long and Romi was forthright and succinct in her observations and the shocking aspect was that she had not hidden her disenchantment against Jayanta, "If he does not make amends, I shall have to engage myself in Mamma's work. Look at those elders. I am sorry to note that your friend with all his good intentions fails to..." She had not expressed herself fully but arresting her emotions and words, had said, "I agree with you. Your counselling is in our interest and I rate your opinion very high and then who could have thought good of us?"

I had no words to assuage her agitated mind.

"It is not the question of a wife..." She was addressing herself, "Not getting enough attention. No. It is unjust.I know the pressing nature of Jayanta's duties. He lives under constant strain and has to listen to unpardonable words with sweetness, said by masters. However, he too is becoming an integral part of the system. No time for the kids and, on the other hand, parents are growing old with each rising sun. Don't they need his..."

It seemed something terrible was obstructing her to say. Romi's mental worries had really disturbed me. Her blank deep eyes spoke of unmitigating inner sufferings and a volcanic rage.

*** *** ***

● 10 ●

I had decided finally to come back to Chandigarh, but during the day I had to attend to certain urgent meetings with important businessmen. Also some formalities were to be got completed at the Government level. I had to visit a few ministries. To meet high level officers in the Government was not a problem for my own old friends had been occupying prominent and influence-wielding positions in the Government and indirectly I had made my own sphere of operation more variable and strong.

To be of value to them, I had to do calculated serious thinking and spadework at home so that I remain close to their temperament.

To get my work accomplished, I had been manoeuvring chicanery. I was ruthless. I was undoubtedly indulging in slightly corrupt practices to achieve my goal because after deliberation, I had thought that it was impossible to move ahead in a cruel world. I too enjoyed these malpractices with a sense of pleasure, of course to a tolerable extent. There were rather two streams of thoughts. To this view even Jai Bhadra had once subscribed, "I knew the intentions. So I had to submit. It did injure me yet for a greater cause, I agreed to ..." He had looked at me without conveying the full meaning.

At that time, Raji had advised, "You must know the elements of recognition."

I had been inexorably compelled to think of their words as I too had been a little unfaithful. That I considered an act of expediency.

"You'll be singled out."

Jai Bhadra's words, witty though, had conveyed full import.

And I had understood the warmth of relations and all those gently initiated talks helped me in the long run. And it had been once very kindly brought home to me, "You are sometimes a crook."

I had lengthened out my lips into tiny smiles.

*** *** ***

All these confusions had dragged me to the large office of Jaycee unwillingly to remind him of inadvertent failure in understanding relations. For about half an hour he remained occupied with grey, dead files and officials. He had been quick, decisive and precise in commandments while shuffling through the bulky files and eyeing with doubt and curiosity each page and in lazily moving fingers, expressing confidence in those who sat in front of him. In one corner, I had been smoking and listening to words which had meanings without the relevant context, for, my objective was to rush out as early as possible. I had finished two cigarettes, in the meantime, when I heard him, "Oh, yaar, I am sorry. These..."

"..."

"Here one has to do without doing."

"Yes, I could count words. You have not changed." I had commented coarsely.

"Yes, I think, I have not."

"..."

"This hurts me that I could not devote much time. This time we could share sensations and feelings...I remained itchy in these..."

"Yes, I know. You had been..."

"Now speak out, what are your plans?"

"No, it's all right, I shall be free today and going back in the evening."

"When should I expect you next time. You must...so that I am prepared on time."

"No, you need not. I understand nature of your duties."

"..." He had signalled me to have coffee, "Did you have lunch?"

"I am having with the Board of Directors...that Ashoka Group."

"What is your..."

"All done. My old acquaintances are looking after my interests. There is absolutely no difficulty."

"You are shrewd. They tell me you cater to their needs..." Jaycee had given a prolonged and meaningful smile.

I had observed a tinge of disapproval.

"You should visit us and have a break. Don't be glued to these lifeless files."

"Nothing stops. My wife was telling me..."

"I know my parents had gone to you. They are all praise for you."
"Is it a compliment?"
My lips had expanded to show joy, "Your coffee is warming up."
Jaycee had said, "I am also as sweet and soft as you are."
"Jaycee, now stop it."
"I don't have to..." Jaycee had lit a cigar and added, "I wish to join some...it is a total enslavement. I am supposed to say yes. There is no other answer and to be frank, it is an absolute submission that you get happiness. I thought many times but a watchful individual...I found, I was not practical. You can't afford to be otherwise. And don't you know the world? It is good to do independent..."

Jaycee had spoken for a couple of minutes without halting, about his precarious state of affairs. At last he had resignedly said, "I know my limitations but I feel imprisoned and tied up. It is surprising that you want to run about in a defending mood. Yes, I do it. When I do something, I think afterwards. It is not always that you commit a mistake. No. We help one another. This structure is standing on mutual understanding. It is a mix-up. If I say it is wrong and immoral, it would be suicidal. I do want some nice ideas to...it is good. We look into...within. And tell me frankly... are you..." He had not said those harsh inconvenient words.

I had felt relieved.
"Jaycee, you are not untrue."
"I am neither."
"What do you mean?"
"It is not an easy escape. You cannot afford to annoy. I know all those people. It is an acceptance without arguments."
"I don't get you."
"I want to leave. Possibly I may be able to protect myself."
"Is it happening with everyone?"
"I believe, it is."
"No. It cannot happen. It is in your hands."
"You are wrong. I believe all are struggling in a vacuum."
There was no further exchange of words. After a few minutes, he had added, "There is no peace, I feel. It is an inner defeat that keeps haunting you. I do not want, still I am forced to do. All those friends of my father..."
"..."
"We are living in a very competent world."
Jaycee had given a cynical expression.
"Capable world. Yes, I don't dispute the fact."

"Then what is the issue?"

I had looked deep into his eyes.

"It is with all of us. Those laughters are not genuine. You see plastic faces with manipulated expressions. It is not a happy age."

"Jaycee, you are..."

"I know, Ramanathan, Raghu, Swamy, Patel and Harry...they are nothing. Do you think they can achieve anything? No. They are symbols of rampant...it is a journey downhill. All these fellows are symbols of decadence."

"You are condemning in order to escape responsibility."

"No. It is a naked truth. Ramanathan belongs to a middle class family. Yes, he has all those sickening ideas of a good life. But he wants to be rich. And to become rich, certain compromises he was to make. All is fair in the game. You know, he had two of his sisters in that Public Undertaking...and Wadia played his godfather. Raghu, that great debater, has ultimately landed up in hobnobbing with the local toughs and small-time Khadi-clad goons, in a racket, where wives are swapped. And Swamy? Dave has pulled him up. Patel and Harry are rascals now. By working as private secretaries to the ministers they have misused authority. They can get anything from cash to gold and jewels. Brutes and killers. And you are asking me to...do you think, they bother about relations? No, they are least concerned. Relations for them are meaningless."

There was a lethargic and vapid air sweeping over us. With puffs, long and short, at regularly timed intervals, he appeared to be gathering courage.

"There is nothing wrong. I find them totally upright and honest."

These words had sent shocking current down my sinews and tender veins. He had stood up and pressed the call-bell. I had found that suppressed anger and rage were consuming him.

"What do you know about us?" He had said as if crying.

"No." After a few seconds, he had resumed, "I say no. You do not know."

A peon had appeared.

"Bring two cups of coffee...and mind you, don't permit anyone for half an hour."

With a mechanised bow, he had said "Yes Sir" and walked out.

"Is it not their willingness?"

He had stared into my eyes.

"No."

"Happy!"
"No?"
"Unhappy it means. Fed up with the..."
"No. It is a detached state of mind. I find them as if they had no interest left and suddenly I discover that all of them are intensely in love with life."
"How do you say?"
"We often meet at a dinner or evening booze at some posh hotel."
"Jaycee, I think life of glitter is wanted much more."
"Yes, in fact, it is precisely there that one understands life. There is no remedy. An escape is impossible."
"They are earning a lot."
"I think, yes. A number of farm houses and then flats in famous cities. I envy them."
"You have not been able to strike such a deal."
"..."
"Jaycee, you have not answered."
"You will not be able to believe."
"Why? We are old friends...and I take your words seriously."
"... " He had emitted a spiritless smile, "I too have earned. Yes, fat bank balance but can't disclose."
There was a dead silence.
"It is good. I don't think I have equalled others. All our friends want to touch a few crores. They are investing money here and there. And in numerous cases, they have joined as unknown sleeping partners. With fixed share out of income. If you want to expand business, I can give you as much as you want. Tell me how much...twenty, thirty...it can be in lacs or crores. I have to move a finger only."
"Jaycee!"
"Don't get disturbed."
He was calm. No specific expressions. He had spread his lips to convey his satisfaction.
"Does she know?"
"No."
"Mom and Papa? Or those who...Malkhan Dave...and crude individuals of his tribe."
"No. Nobody knows. They should not know."
"Jaycee, you are falling into a dead fall. How would you redeem?"
"I am not committing a sin."
"Then why hide?"

"It is not in their interest. And also, I don't want they should bring in all those sermons. I don't want to be reminded of a silly discourse."

He had relapsed into silence again. I could guess that Jaycee had steadily recovered from his earlier sense of guilt and diffidence.

*** *** ***

Exactly at that time, a waiter had entered with two cups of coffee. I felt as if I were limping through a dark long tunnel of mental agony.

"I can imagine the shuddering revulsion out of these expressions but then one is accustomed to such shocks. Nobody is serious and yet he moves in style. I do that. I want to live. I have a feeling that I am in love with life. It is joyful, enriching and beautiful. Just walk out and you realize the glamour. It is not in this room. It is all rubbish. Files and papers do not attach importance to life.. It is a cold calculation." I had found him out of instinctive control, "Jai Bhadra and Rajshri suffer from ego..." He had diverted his attention to the window, "I am insincere. They are not. It is the cultural burden they are carrying on their heads. The memories of great ancestors, those days of struggles, glory and fight. It is a matter of heritage. They are also right. But what treasure do we carry with us? It is a big question. I am not asking questions. I am just looking within."

"We also had dreams."

There was a thick layer of sullenness on his face. No words were sufficient to describe the gravity of the conflict.

"I had come to..."

"No, I have not finished." He smashed the half burnt cigar in the ashtray, "I don't get time. I am talking seriously. I try but an urgency assaults you. You must understand the system. In a democracy, it is the will of the people that governs. Will of those who have clout, money, wry sense of ruthlessness, mercy and... all qualities clubbed together. I tell you, it is not our duty to talk of ...what you are fond of. I had a long argument with Mom and Pop, those fast-growing old persons."

There was a deep feeling of rejection in the words when he had forified long winding reasoning, "They are right. Jai Bhadra moves about in high society. At his back, he has history. Those great family traditions and so forth. These Malkhans...Mom is a prominent social worker in her own right. But I told...No, forget about it, it will push all of us into an ugly situation. We run the affairs and I am proud of it. There is nothing unbecoming. You know, I was frank about the evening forays into those..." He was serious yet a little relaxed, "Many compromises are struck under dazzling lights. Informally, you can open up. It is solid and pure business. When should I get time? I am much stuck up. During day, I am to make arrangements and at night it is their turn. Money does not come easily and I am convinced there is nothing bad. After all who is not doing it. A rotten goulash of men and virtues."

"Everyone. Those who do not, they possibly don't understand the pulse of the people. We also think of people, go to villages where ruralites watch us if I refuse to bow down? You know what happened to Sharma and Ghosh. They are dumped in Eastern states, pushed into unimportant seats and facing enquiries. They had the audacity to challenge their seniors and...now without mincing words I am telling you, such people don't matter. You can't carry the chit...tagged with the shirt and claim affinity. I know these people. Living a difficult life. I am in the net in a burning jungle. It is a big hash. It is a hunger for more without caring a bit about man."

He had turned to me sharply, "Are you listening?"

"..."

I had merely twisted my lips.

"We do spill emotions all over. When we drink...booze...dance and sing, we swamp over...these are sizzling sentiments. And that moment is the real life for us. I am not in favour of...we come across different people. I am in tune with these persons. I don't want to be cut off. Sharmas and Ghoshes are misfits and so stand ostracised. I am living now. I want to pack up the essence of times." There were mischievous twinkles in eyes. I found he was describing everything with sprinkles of ill-humoured insinuations. He was going too far.

A mammoth transformation had struck between us.

"Jaycee, I am impressed. You have been moving ahead of times. That is the spirit."

"Yes. I have caught the spirit of age. You, you don't know... those who do not move with the times, are ultimately finished off ...they don't die...they are suffocated to death and then who looks after, what is left out?"

"I am sorry. I am not in the mad race."

"Don't misunderstand. I think, those who carry misplaced notions are the victims. I am busy you know. I am rich, I know, what was inherited property...I know he is a landlord, a man of resources...but I want to add. Now is the time when I can become strong and mighty and I have opportunities all around. Malkhan Dave, the mastermind, is not old as many think. Once he took me to a Bombay's starred hotel and there he had confided in. "Look Jaycee..." His tongue was moving over his whisky-wet lips, "It is here that we find meaning. If you think, you are noticed, forget and enjoy. No one is concerned about you. My boy, enjoy life and enrich it. Serve people. Serve the nation...but..." Two young girls, full blooded and ravishing had settled by his side, their white arms encircling him and he, getting awfully excited, had mildly though passionately said, "That is life. Everything follows a mighty man. Earn and enjoy my boy."

We had retired.

*** *** ***

11

That was the first encounter with destiny awaiting me for a long time which had shown its brightness for the first time.

He had dragged nauseatingly I thought and I was peevish and unnerved. He was bluntly true and harsh and I had been still fighting within. Jaycee's journey had been, no doubt, very swift with an all-consuming passion.

"Hey, what happened?"

I had been awakened by the loud words.

"It is nothing. Out of an ordinary incident, I derived a relevant meaning. This was an important event which persuaded me to go ahead. I was becoming familiar with the nasty tricks of the world. The moment I started behaving as a commoner with earthy and self-centred interest and began superficially to care for others' views which benefited them, I was being unknowingly catapulted to a position of prominence. Earlier even little happenings disturbed me which did not fit into the design but a realism dawned upon that if I do what others liked, I shall become important, notwithstanding whether I did it by killing conscience or...I wanted to maintain that level of getting advantages which were in a way not immoral though you can very well make out that if you extract gains of even a penny that also amounts to an unethical practice...you will mind it, curse me and you may condemn me...but these are just preliminaries going on underneath."

"That is the limit."

"I can't say. But in all fairness to well-off friends, it is a path to enjoyment and richness."

"But you are ignoring a very important aspect."

"To achieve something worthwhile you have to sacrifice. Those who attain a position of fame, have to lose alternately."

"Jaycee, I think, there is time to come back."

"From where to where?"

"Jaycee, you are callous."

"You talk of ignoring a vital issue. What is it that you are so passionately concerned about?"

"You know!"

"All of them are socially conscious people. They wield influence in a vast area and I feel pretty protected and certain. When you have strong links and godfathers moving around you, make sure, you earn astutely and I am sincere with you. If you agree, I shall suggest you to expand...get loans...incentives and subsidies. We have a clique. A bundle of people who can really be an asset to you."

He had not hesitated to advise me.

"You are a businessman and I don't think you are meticulous in..."

He had burst into a sinister laughter.

"Yes, I am not. Jaycee, you are not wrong. I am dishonest if that is what you think. It is my livelihood and I invent upright means to augment income and resources."

"Honesty in financial matters...?"

"Yes. In business, I have to adopt methods after all I am to live life which may not seem upright but that is how I am earning a livelihood. It is my Dharma, my religion and I do not proclaim that I am honest. Honesty has different meaning with you. It is different with me."

"Forget it. Let us not involve ourselves in fruitless discussions. It is agreed. Now decide, you have a big leeway."

"Still it will not be corruption. It is my duty and a sacred duty of course to make profit, but it does not suit you. It is against all canons of justice and fair play. I don't know what should I say. I feel hurt when I am alone. But in a crowd, I feel safe and happy. Lonely moments tease me, injure me and I bleed without blood and screaming is voiceless. This is my predicament and misfortune also." Jaycee's voice had started cracking up. His eyes brought in a few drops of water which had puzzled me.

In order to hide his inner pain and confusion, he demonstrated an unwilling gleam and the camouflage was very much visible.

"This pain should find a sanctuary."

I had said and retreated.

"But it is transient. These emotions are fragile and create an amnesia the next moment when realism glints and warms. I cannot live in shell-shocking pain. I want relief. Just ordinary way of searching for joy is the purpose. You may not believe but the fact remains that these corridors, tables and chairs, bars and hotels... all these constitute a life for us."

"Then, why twinkling bubbles of water, which appeared in the corners of eyes which you hid so cunningly but failed."

"No, it is incorrect. That is a temporary emotional weakness. After all I am a human being. Such an upsurge of feelings does give moments of introspection and one realises...anyway forget. It is disgorged and...over. These corridors are made of stones, bricks and men who inhabit them are also made of such stuff. I am not bothered about emotions. Perhaps nobody is."

He had handed over the pack of cigar to me. I had silently lit and said, "I am afraid, I shall be able to..."

"No one can do it if he wants."

"Jaycee, we shall not be able to hold..."

"There is no solution. We have to accept the facts. When one moves ahead, such things automatically take place."

"I think you are sick."

"Yes, I am."

"...I am feeling disconnected. Totally, out of place, the way I see things happening around us."

"One should not mind."

"You are a man of crowd." I had been disheartened.

"Yes I am. The world wants it to..."

"Jaycee, I would go now."

"Sorry, I could not look after you."

"..." I had laughed to assure him that there was no cause to nurse a feeling of guilt.

"You have developed a genuine regard for us."

"..."

"Mom and Pop, Romi and those children..."

"Yes, parents should be listened and revered. They are worried about and then Romi, Vicky, Ashey and Rahul..."

I had wanted to keep the teasing thoughts unsaid. Jaycee's contentions and arguments had made his position unassailable. There was no more withdrawal, shyness or going back.

"They are occupied with social work and evince interest in politics also and have strong grip over time and fame. Their position is unsurmountable and fills one with awe."

"They want you."

"I know. I have great regards for them. I am contemplating to admit them at Sanawar or Doon. They are in need of good schools. Too much care may spoil them. Romi's love will weaken them."

"Jaycee, you are not making a correct assessment."

"The ways of the world should be known."

"Jaycee, I wanted you...when you stay away without knowledge you get entrenched in real and vicarious pleasures so badly that you don't allow others to penetrate."

"I think you are mistaken...you know, how much labour, patience and skill you put in during the last ten-fifteen years. It is only now that you have been able to settle down. Now if you don't enlarge, you are going to stagnate."

I had not been able to retaliate.

"They want you at home. I have heard the unspoken wish. Those trembling lips...that function and picnic. Playing together does lighten the burden."

"I know, I shall spare some time."

He had said rather passively as if he were obliging me.

"I would take leave of you."

"How about Bhabhiji and children?"

"Happy."

"Stay for a night."

"But you'll not be here."

"My God! We shall spend the night together."

He had entreated now in a polite and low voice. His imploring posture jeopardised my plans for a while. He had looked gravely sincere even in his gibberish reactions.

"Believe me."

"It had been many times. I don't find reasons."

"I will ring up."

"Are you serious?"

"Presently, ther is no plan. I am free today. We shall sit and talk. It is possible Mom and Pop may turn up. I am told there is an All India Women's Conference and a seminar of Social Bodies. The Welfare Minister is to preside over. Mom Raji is going to be honoured."

"It is all right but when I shall come next, I'll halt for a night."

"Just, have pity. Romi is unhappy with me."

"Look Jaycee, such requests you had made earlier. I had also welcomed the idea. But look at the funny situation. I don't find you there. It is a complete seize. You tire us out. You have kept us waiting many times."

"Yaar, I am trying to rectify."

"How long..."

"We have to accept the dictates of system. Believe me, these buildings rear up pets."

He had fallen into a thoughtful mood.

"..." I had been experiencing a peculiar strain on my heart and with increasing impatience, I was looking at the wrist-watch.

"Won't you stay for a night?"

"You always fail to..."

"I shall make it up."

There was an air of supreme satisfaction.

*** *** ***

I had rung up my wife that I would be delayed by a day. She had told me that the kids were feeling the absence and further, she had dictated a list of renewed childish demands. It was Jaycee's ardent desire to make a last minute effort. That day I had completed all my engagements. It was a tortuous callisthenic exercise in keeping relations warm and fresh.

When I had entered his house in the evening, Romi and children were amazed and happy to see me.

"Oh uncle, we were sad...come on we'll..."

Vicky had elatedly said.

"Bhai Saab...you have..."

"Yes, I have brought a few choiced delicacies from Ashoka. Jaycee is coming."

Romi had smiled and said, "It means, he has..."

"Yes, he has regretted. He shall spend the evening with us."

I had looked at the watch, "He should have come."

"I shall ring up, Dad."

Vicky had run to the other room.

"Hey, uncle has come." Ashey was calling out Rahul.

We had been sitting in the drawing room. Romi had asked the servant to fetch two cups of tea.

"Mom, I am hopeful..., peon was telling me, Pop is not available. Probably he is on his way."

The children were cheerful.

"Pop Bhadra and Mom, Jaycee was telling, shall also come this evening."

"May not be possible. They will come tomorrow."

I had not given my observations.

Romi looked satisfied and was in joyous mood. Children and I played and played but Jaycee had not turned up.

At nine, he had rung up us to inform that the minister had called him for a meeting saying, "I shall be dining with the Hon'ble Minister."

All had made immense efforts to join one another with feigned and venal smiles.

*** *** ***

12

Those years were spent in neurotic experiences and audacious will power to retain relations. I had expanded my business operations to tolerable boundaries of management. Many events had taken place and nobody had any purgative control over the piquant movements of time. I had wanted to bring changes but I chose to adopt an unblemished route brushing aside controversial business deals.

"You won't take advantages."

Jaycee would often comment.

"I am perhaps not capable of..." I had shown inability to derive immoral financial benefits though all these friends in the government coaxed me to come out of my puritanical attitude. Rajput had opened a pandora's box by kicking up a quarrel with a politician and would have almost smashed his head, had a senior colleague not intervened. It was probably after two years. If I remember exactly, it was in 1976. Rajput had to bear the brunts for his pugnacity. He was physically assaulted by a few hired goondas, but had managed to run away unhurt. After that he had kept hidden a pistol loaded close to his chest.

He was adamant by nature. Once, after two months of the unsavoury scuffle, that fellow, you know, Padma Raju, had met him in the congested bazaar of Karolbag. Rajput, with all the courtesy, had shaken hand and had spoken mildly in the presence of everyone and then suddenly pushed him towards a racing car and dramatised the whole thing by rescuing him, pushing aside other non-descript politicians.

"I am happy, God saved you." He had said.

He had then murmured threateningly, "Bastard...I will kill you if and look..." He had abused him.

Raju had perspired profusely. It was a mysterious attack. Rajput was despatched to Bihar on deputation to Govt. undertaking, where he developed intimacy with Thakurs and Yadavs and created a big influential caucus. I could know about him only when he had already bid goodbye to Delhi. And those were the days of Emergency. It was discipline and sense of duty that was supreme.

I remember that period vividly. For a small-time businessman, it was a blessing in disguise. There was less fault-finding and no irrational requests for commissions. But, at the same time, I knew, certain officials and a new class of rustic politicians who were extracting money...and favours, overtly or covertly, by threatening. I also saw another face of bestiality in the eyes of those in power and was also remorseful that a time of growth, progress and discipline was being wasted. It was a period of growth and debacle. Years of discipline and anarchy. It was an age of social resurrection and moral degeneration. Those were years of revival and downfall—Jai Bhadra had once commented. I remember words of Rajshri, even now, vibrantly and unfaded and those words drove me to bright raptures when hopes increased incessantly.

These words are deeply engraved, "I am conscious. We are running on two parallel lines and it is not good. It is strange that we, who are at the helm of affairs, respect and reject in the same breath. Values...morals, principles are all mere instruments to promote self-interests."

Her comments though perfunctorily made, had contemporary relevance. Those were the days when I moved very close to Jai Bhadra and Rajshri. I was fascinated by their wonderful sense of social service and philanthropic nature. I found them persons of meaning. The unfortunate part was that they were not happy with Jaycee. He was polite but indifferent and this was affecting the bonds. Romi, Vicky, Ashey and Rahul were finding themselves at a loss. Jaycee was intimate, warm and loving, but was unable, as usual, to find sufficient time for them. Now, he, along with others, was getting an opportunity to visit different places and countries. The most shocking aspect was his getting close to youth leaders who had dubious characters.

It was not peace but a created aura of harmony hiding a lava of chaos and disaster. Jai Bhadra had said, " I love you my son. Keep it up, don't vitiate thoughts. I am happy to find that you are keeping relations alive. You meet friends...your affections are loving and deep. My son, I don't know what these young men are doing. They are not reforming...and look at the amount of violence."

And for hours together, we would pensively count steps to disgrace. This period was the most important to me. It was the winter of seventy-six if I recollect when both of them had stayed with us in Shimla. Then we had spent time together at Dehradoon. Romi too had come with the children. Jaycee had left on tour for the European countries for approximately six months. I had still been optimistic that Jaycee would improve. I had for long thought and persuaded him though he was a deeply involved man. There were inherent contradictions.

"Only God can save him."

Jai Bhadra would often observe disenchantingly.

"There are very few people who..." He would fall into long fearful silence and we would wait for him to give expression to his inner anguish.

I was going back and back into the past so lovely yet disturbing. All those faces moved with successive frequency and numerous words echoed.

"He is great man. Why should you pester him?" Yadav had scolded me with downright truth. It was a baffling stroke.

*** *** ***

At Upper Dharamshala, I had kept a small bungalow for my exclusive use. Whenever I was on business tour or otherwise, I would stay there. My wife and kids too used to accompany me when they considered it convenient. Those days were full of inner conflicts and mental tensions. Jai Bhadra and Rajshri would not say but the faint redness of their eyes exhibited a continuous displeasure and anger. So was the case with Romi and her children. However, they had taken upon themselves to keep company with the kids. Jai Bhadra and Raji had made it a regular feature. Ignoring all other worldly commitments, they quite often visited Romi and made themselves comfortable.

"He is a much wanted person. The masters confide in him. You know, my darling, so many youth Congress leaders are his chums. Earlier it was different. Now I think, he is meticulously charting out his own course of action."

Jai Bhadra had opined. I had come to know many secrets. Strong Rajput and Yadav had given me detailed account of happenings at the highest level. Yadav, for that matter, had no fixed principles. He was cruel, blunt and terrible in approach.

"I am gathering strength." He had once told me, "Yaar, take full advantage of us. There is nothing to worry in a decomposed body-politic."

He had once counselled, "What is left with us? Now I have learnt not to answer. I create questions."
He had filled words with riddles and evangelical contours.
"Yadav, you are... "
"I, without hiding, tell Pandit and Rajput to realise the truth and facts. Who is bothered about what is happening within? These are just useless questions. I try to do what I feel very close to my heart. I do not possess a very bright track record. No, it is unpretended and simple. I am as straight as this table. Nothing under the table. And now if your friend Jaycee...is making inroads into the hearts and minds of young people, he is not mistaken."

And I had come to know that all friends with ulterior motives had developed deep proximity with young men having political links irrespective of their ideologies. "You know, those young men are found everywhere with minor changes of faces and vocabulary. And they are used in processions and rallies."

I had often listened to them. They had the guts and grits to speak to me what they wished. Once Ramanathan had said, "I am emotionally attached to this room. I don't have to grudge. I keep options open. They will liquidate you if you don't relinquish."

Ramanathan had spelt out the document in detail. It was his misfortune that he had been caught in his own net. One of my rich friends had offered him a big house in Hyderabad as a gift for favours and services. When the deal was taking shape, I had forewarned him, "Beware of him. He has no..." A few complaints had originated and he had been ambushed. It was with the help of youth leaders that the case was hushed up.

"I am a confirmed..." And after the incident Ramanathan was more ruthless in day-to-day dealings. He created his own circle and the pressure group worked well.

"Ramanathan, too, moves with a happy mood."
I had found out that old relations were present, a sentiment undying, remotely realised warmth but the only thing lacking was time.

"It is a complicated life and it looks innocent and without restraints also. But when dejected and alone in the room you find enormous load crushing you."

Ratnam's opinion was not different either. Swamy Ratnam had come back from Canada, for he had been included in a high level delegation to negotiate with the Canadian Government on significant commercial issues and when I had met him, he was slightly jittery and different.

"What has happened? You are depressed."

"Yaar, you don't know, this time...you know, people are not with the Congress. Who comes to power, that is the big question?"

"You should not worry!"

"So many things have happened, right or wrong, and you very well know, much bitterness and enmity is around."

*** *** ***

The variable and erratic contemporary scenario was haunting not only Swamy Ratnam but others also. It amused me yet in solitude felt pity for my friends. They were rich and still very poor. I had in those volatile months thought long about the miseries and dilemmas of white-collared friends with Jai Bhadra and Rajshri.

"Why are you worried?"

"There is a visible change."

"I know. It is going to happen. They will look after themselves."

"Uncle, you have been like my...you have to use your contacts."

"My son." This time, it was Rajshri, "I think, you are right."

"What are you talking? These people have practical and self-centred convictions."

"..." I had not understood the words.

"Yes, fixed and firm when it comes to their convictions but timely when the question of future is raised."

"Papa, these people will..."

"They had been very fast."

"You are indifferent."

"No, Papa you have to extend hands of protection towards them. They do not know that..."

Romi's words had not carried the desired enthusiasm.

"Romi, powerful individuals with a fox-like instinct should not be advised. It is provoking them to perform more dangerously." Rajshri had said as if concluding, "Romi, we were not wrong. But I think, we should catch up with the times."

We had failed to understand the import.

"Raji, you are a social scientist and have a good tie-up with all types of..."

"I do not want to..."

"To save, one has to compromise."

"They don't require us."

"No mamma, I move about in higher echelons of society even..." I had not said, for I thought, I should not disturb them.

"You are sincerely worried about them. I know."

Jai Bhadra had said and taken out his box of cigars. At such moments he, we had known for years, never wanted to be interrupted. We had waited patiently for him to divulge or speak out what had been rankling his mind and heart.

"It is also kind of relation."

He had said and was backsliding into a deadening silence.

"Pop, what do you say?"

"Nothing. It is a conspicuous failure in keeping the relations alive. Now relations are surviving under strains."

"What kind of relations?"

"That keeps the life going."

That was the end of conversation.

*** *** ***

I had been amply confused. With the change of government there was immense political activity. New equations were coming up. Change in the set-up also affected relations. Social and political horoscope was undergoing unbelievable transformation. There was sophistication in violence and treachery. Instability was the hallmark. There was an unexpected revival of values which were not present even for a change. It was a tall talk. Everyone was involved, engaged and was taking pride. I had been just a spectator. Unable to make a dent. A complete invalid. I wanted to do something.

Those days were reminding me of old morals and values which once Gandhi had advocated. Yes, the grand old man who changed drastically the course of Indian history. Yes, I claim, not that others said but because whenever I adopted his small, simple and easy words in common and unassuming way in daily life, these brought about a pleasantness, a bubbling shine and freshness in heart. Something used to happen within. It was a sheer experience in purification. Those were lazy and weary days. Even today, I find him relevant but who is concerned. It is all sham and deceit. I often thought long but of no avail. I had not the courage to stand up against the movements of time. I had been sharing and dispelling my doubts and dilemmas with Pandit, Ramanathan and others whenever I visited Delhi.

The unfortunate part of it was that nothing was possible and it was wasting of words and breath. I was accustomed to listening to the sermons. But in spite of these noble thoughts and intentions nothing concrete was visible. It was an experiment in disagreement intended to bring about harmony. It was a period of visible light but there was darkness.

Pandit had pointed out pertinently, "I am trying to be honest. Yes. You have to publicise that you are honest. You have to blow trumpets to declare that you are great. I can see them." Pandit had looked at me, "I too believed. But Rajput? He has suffered."

"That boss told me to do. I could not open the file."

"..."

"He himself wrote a detailed note and the proposal was through."

"Pandit, you were full of hopes."

"Yes, I am still...there is nothing wrong. If I say now, you'll laugh at me but I knew, it would occur. These ten years. Full ten years..."

"Ten years!"

"Yes, I have known them all. This age has been...you know, those twenty years brought about catastrophic changes."

Pandit's eyes looked blank.

I was terrified.

"Why did you come to stay with me?" He had shaken me with full force.

"..." It had made me alert to the surroundings. Pandit could have been brutal. I had never enquired and hence I had not answered him.

"I asked an inconvenient question. But I wanted you to face the truth."

"Pandit, why should you..."

"Now listen, you are a man of money and economics. When we competed struggling like a hawker. Look back...it is a period slightly less than twenty years."

He was sad and disillusioned, it appeared as compared with attainments.

"What are these ranks?"

I had taken out a cigarette. He had taken his own brand of cigarette and said in a penitent voice, "I had come with many hopes about a bright future. I had heard an epic description about freedom, its grace, beauty, tenderness and softness."

He was slowly becoming serious and I had found that his voice too was sinking and losing its vitality and fervour.

"There is no use to talk about failures."

"Yes, I am not interested either."

"Then, why did you hurt me?"

"You had been coming to us since sixty-three. Those young days ...and out of that stupor, China had given us a new confidence to understand friends..., you follow what I mean!"

He was emotional.

"I am at the same place. No change. And I wanted not to opt and go for the worst. You had been talking of Gandhi...and I think that psychology determines your...and I, a student of Vivekananda, found solace in his words...that is my weakness. Nobody is here . All are high in ego and...I am happy to have you as my guest. For the first time perhaps it has happened. Jaycee has changed, I know."

"Yes, he is there but not changed. You babus have a fox-like smelling power and an eagle eye."

He had given a meaningful nod and then with a faint smile inched along with me to his drawing room, "Now, sit down. I have also been disturbed at the freezing of relations but without wishing them to endure."

"I do realise that much has happened. But it had to happen. There was no alternative left. It was admitted in the beginning. When the fine, sensitive and thin threads of...anyway forget...those were storms of emotions and passions."

A prelude to hair-raising explosive action. Swamy Raghunathan and Ratnam had possibly made feeble attempts but the politicians and their seniors were too mighty. Those drunkards and women of liberal thoughts doing the rounds of corridors and Raj Bhawans were calculatively introduced to a rich and colourful variety in life. It was the materialistic splendour that proved fatal.

He had closed his eyes for a while. It seemed years had passed in between.

*** *** ***

13

Pandit's wife, in the meantime, had arrived with two cups of tea. She had sat beside us for about twenty minutes. I had expressed silent willingness to have dinner only for I had already planned to stay in a hotel where I had booked a suite. Pandit, being simple and devoid of any tantrums of pretensions, had not insisted. The time sense was lost, it appeared, "It was Swamy's weakness that he, without letting us know, fell for a young woman who had intimate and illicit links with famous tycoons and probably a handful of ministers too.

"Babus are docile and meak." He had laughed, "and spineless also. I think everyone would vouchsafe my widely accepted conclusions. And you also...say...and Jayanta tells me. Swamy could not resist the tempting charms and then the girl had given vent to her love in no uncertain terms to a man who was already married and...there the sensuous ambush emasculated him and you know the rest. What is it after all? I had been telling these chaps. I did not disclose to anyone else but my trusted colleagues as they were, had spent really good happy days during training. But nothing happened. Who listens? I too suffered, but how long? Could they continue with the indignities? You don't find anything exceptional here, I am happy with my wife, three children and a couple of relations. No hassles. I am not worried if I am not given importance. I have learnt to hold ordinary and casual seats."

Pandit had become relaxed, "Ratnam, the other great Swamy, too, collapsed under the..." He paused, "Would you like to have a few drinks."

"You are..."

"But it is my home. No restrictions. When you indulge in excessive drinking in those parties, you simply become animal. And how can you swap your wife? It is a fashion and an accepted norm among a few. Others are just looked down upon. You are modern, if you..."

As I was not very enthusiastic about what he was saying, I had coldly said, "I have heard but I think..."

"No my dear sir, it is. When they drink, they drink like a fish and eat like pigs and then...mouth loud comments, abuse and advance lecherously towards women and it cannot be ruled out that these women may evince interest. A lascivious humdrum. Even if there is an open resistance, the end is a noisy submission."

He had got up, "We could shift to the other room."

We had moved to a small balcony, overlooking the spacious playground down below.

"It is a fashion. Modern times are unpredictable."

Pandit had opened a small almirah and placed a half-consumed bottle of whisky and a pack of cigarettes on the little table. He was continuously grumbling though his words were not audible. Suddenly he had gone to the other room and in a few minutes was back with a tray. There was water in a jug, two whisky glasses, ice cubes and dry fruits in a china plate with potato chips.

"I had to do this, for nobody else helps me. Here, in this room, I am the king."

"..." I had been quietly watching the man, "Pandit, you are great."

He had poured a peg, dropped a few ice cubes and told me, "No facade of a high-profile life. I can't maintain myself. I am living happily in the midst of days of distress and miseries keeping intact the warmth. This four-room flat is sufficient to give me peace."

"I know..."

"I asked an insipid question. I am sorry you could not save. Jaycee and others were not fond of a life of discipline. They could not bear the temptations and it is nothing new when the laxity percolates from above, it weakens the entire fibre. Slow but persistent efforts bring results."

He had given a detailed account.

From Ramanathan to Wadia, everybody had been brought into focus and Pandit had given incisively accurate description of their behaviour.

"These people are indifferent. In fact, it does not occur to them that there is a wound within. I don't know...it is in their nature to rush off to discotheques and cabarets, dances and dinners, may be to forget...forget what? No, they do not know or if they know, they can't tell for fears of humiliation."

"I don't believe."

"Yes, it is there. Man is busy. Frightfully alone, I suppose. How can they admit that swappings give tensions and pricks. It is a hidden guilt that haunts them. You can find out in the eyes, in the shivering hands while talking and then in the words that emerge. They live from moment to moment. It is they who feel the pain and in fact this scene completely shatters me."

He had finished his glass.

Pandit's words were coming out of his heart, it seemed.

"You had been faithfully concerned about relationship."

"Yes, I am, even now."

"But, what about your Jaycee? I have been informed that you are developing a sort of...well, I won't injure your feelings."

"It's all right, you can be frank."

"These people are regretting their destiny. They are articulate and yet cannot be unequivocal and confident that their words indicating misalliance are theirs. They live in obscurities and still they claim recognition."

"Panditji, you are attacking the deep bonds."

"No. Bonds are no longer relevant. Inscrutable are the methods of this world."

"I am doubtful..."

"I have studied them deeply. From Swamy to Malkhan Dave and Madhav Wadia. You can believe me what I say. These people are very strong individuals with no scruples. Ethics and morality are not their concern. They are practical. They spend money and speak of relations in terms of money. There is nothing which can't be purchased. I met all of them. But I was of no help to them. I don't know, yes, they were considerate and that is why they took pity on me. And I am here."

"Why pity? Did you kneel down? Or was there a secret pact?" I had asked him.

"No, I was not strong enough to fight with them. Moreover I told them that I am a weakling, a coward, who wants to live life in his own way. I am a man virtually of no ambitions for I cannot adopt unfair means to...you don't have to tell them about intentions. Wadia and Dave got me shifted to an insignificant position. Had I resisted I would have been harassed like Rajput and others...I am watching and standing away from their vigilant eyes and find that Asif Khan and Patel are gathering strength in their doddering bodies day by day. These bureaucrats are very clever but merciless. They can sacrifice anyone when their survival is threatened."

I had lost interest in the shaky talks.

It was after an interval of two hours after having dinner that I was taking leave of him, when he had cautioned, "You are a mature businessman not an upstart. Remember, you have many interests at stake. I...or people of this class don't have to lose."

The driver had opened the door. Before entering, I had looked back, "You are great."

"I am a poor man."

Pandit's words had made me self-conscious.

*** *** ***

Not that I was unaware of transformation going around, but I wanted to see for myself the perceptible changes time had brought on all. During the last decades many events had affected us. It was an age when social thoughts underwent a colossal change. It was felt that all those who wished to stick to their positions could not act as they desired, as there was a visible change in living patterns and standards. I had been meeting them even if they had no time. I would always make it a point to revive old memories. I would not rule out the inner emotional storms or unknown desires growing within that keep the acquaintance alive which would be beneficial to me. In my journey, when I had travelled alone, in trains or aeroplanes, I would often feel the necessity to meet them.

"Why was I unemotional?"

This question would usually pester me.

Right from the day I left the University, I thought I would not make it up to this fabulous government service, where now, observing power-wielding friends enjoying themselves and living a sickeningly luxurious life, I felt quite jealous. On the other hand people like Pandit gave me immense consolation. I had decided to take up a job where I could be the lord. I had made half-hearted attempts to join other services like Banking or Insurance Companies but finally I resolved to become a bania. And the journey from the late fifties and early sixties had begun which was without a fixed terminus.

But I kept old relations alive. I don't remember the details yet a few infrequent dialogues and incidents continued to occur and reoccur in the mind. Those were the days bright, full of joy and pleasantness. I had got started with a meagre investment. It was an experiment, for I had been thinking to embark upon this course of action. I was given lengthy lectures on political situation, the fluid and uncertain economic policy vacillating between socialistic thought and democratic concepts. Nehru's all-pervasive and colossal master-strokes and movements did not permit others to speak a word which could have added anything worthwhile, innovative or refreshing.

I had been coming into contact with a few upcoming tycoons from whom I wanted solid assistance and guidance. All friends, fresh from academy, had occupied chairs, neat and impressive tables with files and papers, moving and moving. Those were years of dedication and hard work. It had been my sincere wish to emerge as a highly professional man. My ambitions were soaring high with a secret wish to do something lasting, for those were the days when Gandhian thought had relevance in daily life.

"There is no looking back."

I had made a pledge when I realised that I had not achieved my target. Young boys of average intelligence with a little hard work had entered top services and I had failed...so many thoughts assailed and provoked my mind. But I had never budged an inch. I had not been credulous in commercial matters yet also not very doubtful. My natural propensities were believing and unsuspecting and at times slightest hints had made me sit up and dig into the entire background. I was fully prepared for the consequences. I had encounters with owners of companies, mill-owners, owners of textile-mills, proprietors of laboratories and numerous others. I had without special inner desire or aspiration come across a large segment of business community. It had been a wonderful experience.

They were sordid, generous and ruthless. But I had found out a strain of kindness, of humanism in all. In business matters, they were biased, calculative and dangerous. Sometimes these characteristics had disturbed me and I had thought to make an exit. However it was not destined to happen.

The second review had always restrained me to the place where I was. In the formative years, my father had advised me to take a fresh look at my decision and plan for a better future. When he found out that a period of four-five years had elapsed, he too gave strength to ventures and proved a turning point in my life.

"Relations must be inculcated."

Those words invariably enthused me. Whenever I had told him about friends, he felt jubilant. I had started meeting Jai Bhadra and Rajshri regularly. There, in their words and behaviour, I had found unique loving depth, intimacy and sincerity which inspired me to see them and thus the bonds continued to grow. It was during those days that Jayanta and I went much deeper in recognising each other's emotional reach. It was an indulgence in the area of gentle feelings and we would often analyse this with all the sweetness. We had found a wonderful relationship where objectivity, sublimation and reasons worked.

Jai Bhadra would often say, "Whatever you do, remember one thing, that it should elevate you." He and his strong-willed wife Rajshri had begun to show more eagerness in social welfare programmes. Slowly though hesitatingly, I had unknowingly started calling them papa and mamma. They also felt the softness and delicacy of words. That was the moment when Jayanta and I had become much more close.

"How about this!"

He was in a district during those years and had signalled the chauffeur of the car, the gunman and others who were standing to pay regards to him.

I was impressed and had inwardly realised that I had committed a mistake yet had recovered to throw a forced chuckle..

"It is grand."

"That is what fascinates young people."

He had said with a low pitched voice.

I had found a satisfying expression and I still recollect those glistening eyes. The exalted image projected outside by bureaucrats was reflective of ego and prestige. I had not given comments but simply placed my hands on his shoulders.

"I like it, it is exotic."

"What about business?"

"Picking up. It is a challenge. I have to defend myself."

"A man of your thinking can hardly remain satisfied."

"How do you say?"

"Because life requires constructive and practical approach."

"I am constructive."

"Don't you feel, you are lacking in something?"

"No."

Jayanta had thrown a broad hint.

"How is your wife, and the children?"

"Very well. Thank you. How about Romiji and the kids?"

"Yes, it is a kingly living."

"Exactly. How large and vast! You are expanding within. My mind ascends higher and higher and at a far-off distance I see a bright new horizon opening up a life, beatific and fulfilling."

"Yeah, to achieve contentment is the purpose of life."

I was looking at him soberly and meaningfully.

"Purpose and happiness?"
His words pierced my ears like poisonous arrows.
"Yes, if you are happy..."
We had settled down in the car.
"In the field, you are the king, they say. Those big...pigs... chickens..."
"..."
"Yes, we are efficient people. You visit those expansive corridors and they tell us all these things. In the field away from the immediate prying eyes of your seniors, you are the boss and the lord of the area. A true hukamran."
"Yes, that is right."
"Had you joined..." Jayanta had handed down a cigarette to me, "I tell you...it is singing and dancing...endless fun and merry-making. You enjoy and your family remains satisfied. Oh, you were right, you are always right..."
"..."
"Yes, uncle, papa and mamma. Yet what is the summum-bonum of all this? I find the gist lost somewhere amidst hectic life."
"I don't follow...what is the idea?"
"It is in the goodwill and welfare that you are mentally at peace. You know our people. It is a collective wisdom. No. Not like towns. It is all that simple and I find rural people are innocent."
"They are away from the glitter and glamour of city life. I suppose or else, may be that they have urgent problems."
"No, they are happy. They don't make life difficult. They know how to live with nature with all its vagaries. They are hard and yet I find them loving, passionate and simple."
He was calm and quiet.
I had found Jayanta always talking of rural environs with warmth and deep convictions. About the lives and times of villages with concern and with a resolution to uplift them.
I would whisperingly admire him. It was a determination of a young man who thought about people and the nation.
By and large, this pious spirit was found in abundance among other friends, too, who were posted in different states and holding important positions very near to the villagers.
"Yes, I like the enthusiasm."
These were in all sincerity and without doubt my concluding remarks whenever I had stayed with any one of them.

Being in business might be on a small scale yet I was attached to ground situation and I had also those sublime and gracious idealistic layers.

"You are so much excited that you want to forget in the crowd of these innocent people."

Jayanta had been emotionally expressive many a time.

He would go on describing vividly with a passionate zeal the enormous amount of love and respect that he had extracted from commoners. He would speak warmly and lovingly with a sense of genuine concern about villagers. I used to take interest in his pious words. I, at that time, actually did not know that Jayanta had immersed himself in books of philosophy and religion. He would talk of great thinkers and I was also impressed and amazed. I, too, in the heart, appreciated those exuberant outpourings of intense passions. He would talk of social inequality and the ills rampant in the society. He ardently wanted to reach to the common man with all the agrarian, economic and social reforms.

Today, I can remember why a young man like him was so anxious and enthused about social upliftment. It was a pure youthful exuberance and unlimited energy that impelled to do positive and noble. If I was too swept away by an innocent reformatory excitement, it was not because of inbuilt thought-structure but due to the recognition that was conferred without concerted endeavour.

"Romi has also enlisted herself as a member of numerous social bodies. She loves to serve people. She is grand and you know people hold her in high esteem."

"Mom, who..."

"Yes, that lady, my mother cannot take things for granted. She becomes sure and then begins her relentless enquiries. Oh, my God, her hows and whys are irritating. It squeezes you out of your patience. A great reformer and a social worker herself, I think she abhors the idea of someone close to her not working for social betterment..."

Jayanta was in the habit of using high sounding words to convey his message. I had felt humble before him. Those were the days when he would, if free, serve drinks in closed doors. Generously and lavishly, "People shouldn't know."

A few hush-hush words communicated a harmless impression that to keep a clean social image, one has to adopt such measures. Romi's participation was of an ornamental kind. She would go to various functions which were concerned with rural people and the urban people also who were considered a deprived section of society. If ever invited, Romi went with an awesome curiosity and thrill. I had on many occasions found her away, for meetings or functions.

"You know, these are the days of flowers and fragrance. It is really a kind of prayer, a worship, when you feel, you are doing something for them. The real man lives here. This is my country and..."

Jayanta's outbursts, both emotional and philosophic, would not stop. He would deliver long speeches to me over drinks or when taking coffee or tea or even smoking.

The lot of a common man was his top priority. In days of natural calamity he would start a campaign to collect food, clothing and medicines for the affected people. I simply heard him and was stunningly attracted.

His catchwords I never forgot in my later years. Those were stupendously quote-worthy but I found these too oft-repeated and hence as a businessman I had developed cold-feet, "Do something for them. A smile and sparkle on their faces would provide you joy of a life-time."

And suddenly, at times, he would confide, "These people are innocently clever, may be some of them..." He would correct himself and say. I had observed that he was forming and re-drafting his opinions and thoughts slowly with the support of practical experience.

At certain moments, he had looked self-satisfied, firm and reasonable. There were no pretensions. I, in fact, had an inkling of a more emphatic appreciation from him. His interest in rural life and people was undergoing changes also. He was not arbitrary and yet experiential conclusions intervened. The earlier sophisticated and surfacial sympathies of a city-bred boy were being diluted to a large extent. The surprising aspect of activities of seasoned babus was a revelation to him. They had a unique characteristic of counting and recounting each good deed performed by them.

"All of us have, as many as possible, justifications to conduct ourselves and prove right."

"Here nothing goes wrong with us."

He would pensively observe.

And at some lighter moments, he would say, "You know, we can never be wrong. We are servants only."

The years moved with small jerks and jolts. I had been watching all of them very closely, noticing their good and bad deeds. Their obvious predilections and hidden designs.

"We have also to exist. Exist here in this society. Yes. Live as others live. Part of a flowing stream."

It was a terrific jolt I had received. In the corridors of power he had been a name to be taken notice of. He had become Jaycee now. As Jaycee moved in higher circles, his conduct changed to convey authority and confidence.

Jaycee could, to my mind, I still believe in my loneliness, never understand the transformation that was taking place within him. He was without knowledge drifting away from earlier high ideals and thoughts. He was becoming more down-to-earth and practical. Once in early eighties, I had gone to meet him in the office.

I was greeted warmly. There I found Malkhan Dave in conversation with him. A masked man. A devil. A saint.

"You are welcome. Where do you live? Arey, businessmen must keep meeting."

I had not sat down properly when the mild questions were directed to me. That short-statured man with wide eyes never for a moment had appealed to me. I had definitely found something deep rootedly repulsive in him but apparently I had to show regard. Jaycee, I recollect, had always spoken very high of him. Dave was a Guru to him.

I had not responded to his warm question.

"Seeing you after a long time?"

"..." I had smiled and said, "How are you? All well?"

"Yaah, everybody fine and fit."

In the meantime, tea had come.

"This fellow does not want to expand business operations. He has friends like us and can take advantage of but I don't know what he thinks about?"

I had not paid attention to his observations but Dave had asked me, "You can become a partner in our business. Why don't you think? Jaycee has always been talking about your uprightness. We need honest people."

"I was fully satisfied with the present. No complaint."

"..."

"But persons like you must..."

"I wanted to accomplish something notable. Sufficient money is required for heavy investments and I don't have. Raising loans from banks or other sources would not be proper."

"There is no harm. You create assets, increase production. In this age when everyone wants to help you, you should take hold of the opportunity. I invite you to join Mineral and Shipping companies."

"Yes, why don't you..." Jaycee has fortified his argument, "In a developing economy, innovations always prove profitable. A new thrust is being given to growth and development, science and technology and now in the field of mass communication awe-inspiring progress is noticeable. New inventions have changed the style and standard of living. In a few years we may find old technology irrelevant. We have to catch up with the times. Invest with Mr. Dave."

"You know. I began my career with a meagre investment so to say and now it has increased manifold. That I have created assets worth lacs of rupees, I would not commit but I am satisfied. Then there is so much work and I doubt, I shall be able to devote more time to any additional enterprise."

"Many of my colleagues have shares in various business houses in the names of..."

Jaycee was excited and optimistic.

"Money is needed in almost all spheres of life. It is required to influence people."

Dave had said in a low yet emphatic tone.

"I fully agree with you." I had thought to concur with him, "I shall think over."

Jaycee had said commandingly.

I had looked askance at him.

"Sir," Jaycee had lit a cigar, "Mr. Dave..."

There was an uneasy quietness. After a second he had added, "He has always maintained a steady posture with regard to worldly affairs. When there is haphazard economic growth around, it is money that shall solve most of the problems."

"I endorse your views, Jaycee."

"And when you spend a little time on social-oriented welfare programmes, you win the hearts of people."

"That is right."

"I am the chairman of many charitable institutions, social bodies and educational trusts and that gives me enough vigour. It is my humane face."

I had understood the allusive remarks. But there were also subtle innuendoes.

"Those days were different. Now, all want to move ahead. I am not an exception. Old guards in various fields are dying out. Young people have to take over."

It had been an unfinished dialogue.

Dave, as was his wont, had not hesitated to count and re-count his acts of generosity. I knew, he had nursed a secret pride in listing out his large donations and help he had often extended to many such institutions. But it was to enhance his image in the eyes of people who mattered.

I had often listened to him without comments.

"These small goodwill acts give you strength."

He had often repeated.

I had never seriously thought to align myself with any big business tycoon in spite of persistent persuasion. Wealth, social position and ego seemed to have made immense impact all around on such occasions. I was also treated to sumptuous dinners outside. Not to hurt even remotely, I had been attending to these favours by cutting short other pressing engagements resulting in paying less frequent courtesy visits to Jai Bhadra and others. Members of my family had also developed cold-feet and in no uncertain words had conveyed their displeasure by not sitting on dining table.

Once my wife had observed in her usual unassuming style,"Your business tours are too frequent."

"..."

"We want you at home."

Those words had disturbed and alarmed me.

*** *** ***

• 14 •

My wife from the day of marriage was ever patient and worldly-wise and at the same time well-educated, widely read and had the will power to be available to those who suffered from lack of confidence. She never imposed her thoughts on anyone but imperceptibly communicated the implied essence of her convictions. She was a lover of books and till today her habit has remained unchanged and depending on time she lays hands on new books. She is not shy but likes to stay in the background and operate silently without vocalising her thoughts.

It was her relentless persuasiveness and amiable nature that was responsible for keeping me close to those who were known to me. She was also attracted towards Jai Bhadra and Rajshri and harboured special regards for both of them. It was very late that I had found out her interest in various fields. She never disclosed to me but sometimes I found her busy and serious in shuffling books, visiting libraries and the University. I felt a secret pride. She gave certain very down-to-earth proposals to strengthen my business interests.

"It should have the moral element."

Not a forceful argument but in simple, soft and indirect manner, she would communicate her concept. She always wanted me to be reasonable and morally sound, so far as my business was concerned. Not always, but in the evenings, on dining table she would speak about moral aspects. It looked annoying and unwelcome in the present context but I attentively listened to her. I didn't know even now that I have not been able to correctly assess but I would never decline the ameliorating influence she exercised on me.

Her association with Romi and other friends was brief, warm and worldly-wise and whenever she met them, it was her spontaneous expression of closeness and deep affection that endeared her to everyone. She was desirous of expanding her circle of acquaintances. Once or twice a year, she would organise us and visit places and persons. Many new relations were added by her in the family circle and sharing grief and sorrow with friends and relations was her forte. Her friendliness with them would cross the limits of relations and suddenly go beyond and far off, where emotions and passions mingle to create intimacy. Rajshri and Romi had developed special love and regard for her.

Once when I had been dining with Jai Bhadra and Rajshri, Jai Bhadra said, "Your wife...She is a great woman."

"Yes, but she does not disclose. However, her role in the background cannot be denied."

"Yeah, she is the brain behind...you don't know, how much positive contribution she is making towards these welfare...in fact it is she who comes forward with little good and gentle ideas. She strives to understand a man as deeply as possible."

"You should allow her to enter..."

I had looked up. Mom Raji had not said further.

"No, mom." It was Romi who had said, "She would not participate openly."

"Why?"

"In her own way, she extends her support to us through letters and telephones. Her major contribution is her moral encouragement to us."

"She knows the value of relations."

"Yes, in case we..."

That was the unusual hour of admiration and boosting up. I had an inkling of wife's role in all our functions but when these people spoke out, I had felt a sense of self-esteem.

"The mainstay is the..."

Mom Raji was mum and after a pause had said, "You can always feel her presence...somewhere inside, deep within and she stirs you passionately." It was the poignancy that touched us.

"Romi's words are like mountain streams. Soft, musical and brightly shining."

I was inclined to agree with the observation.

*** *** ***

There was an unprecedented change in the working habits of all of them, I often thought. Whenever I had some lonely moments, I had fallen in old memories. Their spoken words and the unintended meanings were fresh but could never really gauge the degree of changes taking place. All of them had, at one point of time or another, an emotional relationship with one another, spoken sweet and nice little words, moved about freely with natural smiles on their faces, and the intensity had continued unabated.

I even now remember the words vividly.

"Yes, whenever we gather, it is supremely satisfying." Swamy Ratnam had once commented.

"Jayanta, it is love and warmth, intense and true that ultimately determines relations. I think, it is rare when old classmates meet and enjoy."

Those were Raghunathan's words.

I don't remember exactly what was the occasion but a hazy idea tells me that it was some reception. There, we had met the most successful big babus, Mahapatra and Mukherjee, who were the cynosure of every eye.

I had been a very small businessman at that time and was slowly expanding and strengthening my financial base as I said earlier also, indirectly by attending such parties and functions. I had been cultivating new beneficial relations. Because of Jayanta, Swamy, Rajput and others, I had been familiar with those who were important and powerful individuals with unusual political connections. On certain occasions I had been out of context and cut-off but then a strange bond had kept me close to them.

It was not apparent and direct. I had known all of them since college days...the transformation in character was without notice.

"You are serving your own people. It is great privilege. We had been an exploited nation and the foreign masters have done as much harm...now that the reins have been passed on to us, we should show to the people..."

It was the youthful explosion of thoughts and emotions of Pandit who had been under the influence of Gandhi and Vivekananda. Those days were full of joy and happiness. No worry about what will happen next. Everyone had a limitless treasure of sympathies and commiseration. I often recall those days with graphic details. Pandit, Yadav and Rajput were men of independent thinking but revered everybody's sentiments and valued each word. I was proud of them. In spite of my humble placing in life, they extended full regards to me.

They were the epitome of an age still struggling to find recognition. New hopes and aspirations were raising a dreamland of happiness and prosperity. Post-independence period was not very comfortable. It required hard work and devotion. Everyone would speak in his own way about the plight of commoners. I had seen them taking pledges to concentrate energies on making a better country, a happy society, a complete man. They were concerned about the meaning and interpretation of their words. I too was a confused man. A total wreck, I thought.

"I feel satisfied. You do one good deed. Help someone who has no relation and it will give you an inner joy."

Pandit would often theorise.

"You know, it is not an exaggerated emotional outburst. That you think and speak of a rich society and country with happy men. It is a dream. It looks so at the outset but not in reality. All of us are doing our little duties. No abdication."

I had often found the discussion dragging on and on with no end in sight. At such times Yadav would speak out his mind, "I like your lofty words."

And suddenly he would walk out.

Pandit would rely on him, "He had been thinking of..."

Abruptly he too would stop and penetrate into our eyes. And partially parched lips would start trembling to frame questions though always failed to utter a word. "We are good so we want each and everyone to act for the welfare of all."

Pandit's words would irritate them.

"Yeah..." Rajput had always been suspect and cynical, "Yes, we are all...good and honest." His choice of words had puzzled and also disheartened and angered me.

The three had certain inherent contradictions. Yet they pulled on warmly with one another. The earlier inclination towards life and people had definitely created a permanent dent. They were all noble souls it appeared to me.

*** *** ***

• 15 •

Once Jai Bhadra had remarked rather inadvertently, "I am interested in a man. So is Romi now showing increasing interest. And then Raji the great woman always prepared to cajole and initiate us. I have lately become interested, yes, naturally fond of people and their lives free of inscrutables, conflicts and discursive strains and to this end, I am exerting...I don't know how far I am successful."

"Numerous events are crowding around. It did not take a lifetime. It is a story of many years. Those nascent days when we dreamt a full life of hopes and aspirations. There were dreams. We had passed through those years of early eighties...not only after forty-seven...but the continuous travails and trials of the past. So many years. Everyone was in high spirits. Even today one is impassioned and in love with the people. One is wonder-struck to know overwhelming sentiments of patriotism. It is an overview of life. An idealised set-up. A land of peace and harmony so to claim."

Jai Bhadra was emotional though his words conveyed a sense of utmost restraint. I often decided to allay fear by talking of bright future awaiting all. In spite of brave confidence, the doubts remained strong about the possible fall-out. But how long, I could have killed my pain without resorting to remedial measures which were impossible for a single man.

Rajshri, the beloved, a sweetie-pie of downtrodden, had said, "These are transient phenomena. One has to take matters in a light view outwardly but seriously. No unwarranted pressure. No sneering response to the efforts we are making in the social edifice. What we say we must stick to. Unique and beneficial transformations have taken place in people's behaviour, attitude and culture. Everybody today is in a hurry. Very fast and somewhere deep down we are desirous of peace. A kind of symphony or harmony fascinates us. It is our inner wish but does not find expression. I am in the thick of people. I see into their eyes. Listen to the wordless prayers which emanate from their deep eyes. I listen to the voice of hearts. Yes, experience their emotions when in their midst. I smell these...in huts, dilapidated houses and skeleton bodies the essence of life scattered all over. When I roam about among them, I feel the pulse, the throbbings and the dreams which never find expression. I know the anxieties."

She had been tender, mild and quick in her assessment and we remained watching her face.

It was an incontrovertible analysis of great historical events from late fifties to early eighties. The indelible effect of those wars, the emotional setbacks, the deaths of those who carved out a place for the nation in History. The devastating agitations of mid seventies, the days of much-maligned emergency and the ferocious speed of reformation taking shape during those days. She was talking of great men and small minds. The how and why of every incident, event, relation and change however insignificant made her recollect and repeat.

At times, it was unbearable, but the truth was that an escape is a cowardly act. As it was said long back, perhaps in the thirties when uncertain and drastic turmoil had shaken the political and economic foundations all over the world that prosperity is just around the corner, a cliche extremely burdensome and without meaning. It was another slogan that changed the scenario. It was simple and emphatic, a catchy one, "Remove poverty" that provoked many hearts.

And to this date, the echo has not died down.

*** *** ***

I had been witnessing the advent of a new thinking among friends. Jaycee had become the rallying point of strength and political clout. He had always been humane and faithful. But this happened after he had suffered humiliation and defeat at the hands of politicians and businessmen who changed lives and loyalties like chameleons with each successive shift in policy.

I had felt shocked yet Jaycee had responded confidently, "I shall not be extravagant. No comments on incident around. Why? After all, are we not accountable? We are. I shall also not be stingy or frugal in self-condemnation. Mom Rajshri, the high-profile social worker and a philanthropist...is not wary of using strident words against us. Yes, we are assisting her in the formation of new class of workers who truthfully feel for those deprived poor people. It is an honourable escape."

Jaycee's words and voice communicated a mind full of inner conflicts.

The invisible change was discernible everywhere. It was an open declaration to serve the downtrodden. But on a second enquiry, I found out a dichotomy in statements. Their living style exhibited opulence and self-satisfaction. It showed that they were building up small, congested and dingy thinking tanks for themselves. Outwardly, it was love and no violence but within what went on, nobody understood. There were long, tiring and endless cavalcades of singing, dancing and partying. Late night merry-makings were inseparable daily routine. And they discussed without seriousness the phenomenal transformation taking place outside. Peace was a major casualty in day-to-day life. The more they talked about hunger, power, unemployment, social abuses and sufferings, the more frequent were the...Violence had been becoming an instrument to settle scores. Unity and integrity became the much condemned but overused words. It was a period of individual aspiration where class, caste and religion were raising heads to perpetuate an unethical system in which liberty and openness were the victims.

My thoughts were running around each individual who had come into contact with me. It was a languishing experience and I perhaps enjoyed myself in the vicarious exploits by refreshing lazy memories. Those were the days of violence and terrorism. Human life was becoming cheap and irrelevant. Conflicts within did not afford happiness. In my enthusiasm, I still nourished hopes that whatever I had been witnessing was a temporary phase and Jaycee and others would come out of the state of euphoria. However, the later events proved that my belief was misplaced.

They had become adamant and determined.

I had invited them for a lunch on that day to celebrate the honours my daughter had been conferred on by the University.

There was nothing fresh to talk about. It was stale, half-hearted and unwanted use of words which indicated how much concerned they were about the cult of violence taking birth in the country in one way or the other. The oft-repeated words of contempt were plenty for adroit politicians who were becoming unprincipled and greedy. It was a serious concern about exploitation of women. Indeed a sad commentary, I had heard from them.

*** *** ***

16

None of them had ever agreed to subscribe to the views of violence or communal riots. No they made faces as if weeping. Their moroseness had made me conscious. I was forcibly made to believe that the assemblage of my friends was superb. Was I waiting for some reincarnation of virtuous and godly people as Romi, Raji and Jai Bhadra had pointed out quite often? Or did I expect a miracle to happen as my wife often tried to dispel my fears about an unfortunate tomorrow. "Man is in a process of evolution."

Her sublime voice resounded in my ears.

"Togetherness is required to infuse will." Romi had once lamented.

Again words of Jai Bhadra flashed across my memory lanes.

"I think we are losing something. What was it? I was trying to read their faces. But failed to find the loss."

During lunch, they had talked to console themselves.

"To quell spreading acts of indiscipline, one has to be generally passionless. No emotions should play a role detrimental to our collective happiness."

"Collective happiness!"

I had raised my voice which made them aware of their sins, I thought. The word sin was too harsh I had realised soon.

"None is an apostle of truth. None, I say. I have seen this during the last two decades. You claim. Clamour for so-called values and morals yet in the..." Jaycee had felt a sense of deep guilt which I could observe in his wide and blank eyes.

"We were wrong."

"I take no offence for whatever you say." Yadav had said, "It is not a question of time. We have all slowly fallen into the trap of those who govern us. They were all kind, mild and generous."

Pandit had expressed strong opposition to this view, "When you commit an error or sin I would say you try to find justification."

"You will not rise above."

"And you have risen? Really?"

There was an inconvenient pause.

"Yes, you are at the top. Rich and famous."

"Pandit, you'll always remain poor..."·

"Yes, I know I make sincere efforts to become rich but fail. Even Yadav has risen quite high. And Rajput has suffered. I had been just appending initials without a word to contribute. Perhaps, nobody appreciated my pen and words."

He had laughed.

"Pandit..." Ramanathan had said while looking at Ratnam and Raghunathan, "No use to bemoan. A practical approach wants us to be...if you...I think barring a few hot-headed babus, we all wanted power, prestige and wealth. Yes, it is different to deliver a lecture in the classroom. Yes, quite a separate issue. When coming to ground realities...it is...I remember those days...priests...I mean those kind of people speak breathlessly at length on morals and virtues but ..."

He had not taken precautions to complete the argument and had directed his questioning glare at me, "Don't mind, if I say that you have been miserly...I know, you are, to some extent, an honest man and cannot spend money — it is neither lavish nor..."

"Rama..."

Jayanta had shown displeasure.

"We are in fact fond of..."

The meaning had been conveyed though the confusion persisted. I had after a thought asked Jaycee, "I am glad that all of you are rich and flourishing." The way he half-closed his eyes, made it clear that he was not convinced.

"What do you mean?" A caviling voice hit hard.

"I mean rich and happy."

"..."

"I want to invite you for an enthralling dinner tomorrow so that you don't call me a miser."

"You are slovenly and susceptible."

Rama's painful voice pierced me, "I never meant it." He had clarified, "I only wished to tell him that the world, I mean the whole system would live in spite of his wanting differently. You can distribute kindness, mercy and wealth indiscriminately. No. Not a wise approach. You are not infallible and so we are. It is not sixty-two when there was a sense of defeat, repentance and remorse among leaders for acts of...no, those were the days when you unquestioningly bowed heads. It was a flowing down of ethics and principles but then it was not to live for a long time. Slow and clear deterioration was visible. And now, I find such ancient sentiments outdated and unlaxative."

It was a long and discomforting laughter which made everyone present there conscious and alert.

There was no end to the descernibly innocuous exchange of words.

"Pandit...and...you must catch the spirit of times. You can still imbibe sweetness in life. Where is the harm if you too, like others, make yourself happy and wealthy. You have a status in the society. Your family lives happily with no financial stress. There is no bar. It is a world of shares, tenders and contracts and everything else is subservient to such acts."

"Yes, when...our families have no restrictions on them. And that is, briefly put, our moral duty towards them."

"But they miss you." I was curt and critical, "Have you ever thought what in fact they require?"

"What do you mean?"

Ratnam's voice was shrill, sharp and cutting.

"I think, it is all over. Enjoyments and pleasures do make a man forget the surroundings for a short period, yet..."

"Yaar, don't exhaust us. Let us not spoil the pleasantness of the lunch hours."

"I would not have invited you to a hotel had I been living in Delhi."

" ... "

"But with rare exceptions you often invite me to..."

"You'll not be treated with numerous dishes. Here you have somebody to attend to...ready to meet your demands from..." Yadav's eyes had a brilliance, "It is an unknown journey. There are plenty of pleasures..." He was looking at the young and beautiful receptionist.

"This world requires a kick on the bottoms." Swamy had said, "There were many kinds of tortures. I was subjected to humiliation. But when I decided otherwise...everybody submitted and followed.

"From this day onwards, I would take meals at your..."

"No problem. Our ladies will look after."

"Jaycee, you are...all of you going away, without knowing relations."

"No..."

"It is a fact. They crave for your company but you are forgetful. I think you are callous and hard. I often see a few sad wrinkles on their faces. They...your wives and children...search for words to hide intense agony and predicament."

"He is too smart."

"You are becoming rich, I know. All powerful... but I tell you, you are growing and expanding. Don't be apathetic and languid. Better halt this cankerous growth. It is not a recent prodigy. I have found a mute and dangerous change since seventy-two. You are degenerating. I don't know the exact words I should use but it is becoming intolerable. If I go back home, it is without doubt peace and consolation, comforts and genuine love among your kids, wife and parents."

"We are going strong because you don't tax yourself."

"I can imagine you are ignoring and..." I have resisted myself to inflict wordy injuries on them when I had invited them.

After a second I had said, "They are feeling your absence."

It had no visible effect on them.

The lunch was over.

*** *** ***

It was after about ten minutes when the table was cleared that Jaycee had remarked, "Nobody is really concerned about you so long you are not of some use. Your wealth and status, connections and confidence make you what you are."

I had read for long the agonized expressions on his face which showed that some deep scars were unsettling him mentally. I knew, Jaycee could never hide a lie from me.

But that afternoon, it was despair and distrust and nothing could save us from the imminent chaos in relations. I had been a careful watcher of their attitudes.

"Did my Mom said something?"

"She had been finding you absent."

"I am holding a responsible position. Here nation's security is involved. I am not using high blown-up words to impress. Perhaps, in fact, I do not count on my contribution. It is nil. I am worried about my safety. All of them too, in case it works out according to plans."

"..." I had asked a long wordless question which could be understood by him only.

"I follow the movements of your eyeballs. I know the meaning and the non-meaning." He had become more authentic and courageous, "It is all in the game. In the arena of files and papers, you ought to be realistic. No harm to be an idealist. No cause to worry even if we are bloody bastards. Here a stage comes after spending a decade or so, when you conclude that the so called purpose you wanted to achieve, was a non-existent thought. It was mirage. You suddenly realised that all those solemn words had no meaning whatsoever. If you did not suit the current, you were thrown out like a straw. It was ought to happen. I did not want to be a mad man. No. Like my mamma Rajshri, I soon found out that all those words of praise, eulogies and songs of glory were of no substance. You found out that she was exhausting her wealth in the false hope of getting something eternal or everlasting. I felt a sense of repugnance and antipathy. You don't know what happens when you are threatened with...oh, you are shuddered and destroyed internally. At such times, you want to recover with tremendous power of coolness."

And then he had gradually but reluctantly given account of the real intentions behind all those Yajnas, lavish dinners, donations and valuable gifts. Malkhan Dave, Madhav Wadia and Dhawan were not saints to run charitable institutions and donated huge amounts.

They were benefactors and their generosity knew no limits. I had known them all, because I had never believed in behind the back transaction. I always manoeuvred to remain outside their reach and at the same time I took care not to displease them. Under threats, mild and strong, all of them acquiesced in their evil designs. For them, there was no vice so long it didn't damage anyone. It was an individual struggle to survive, sacrificing a collective will in small particles. Then Harry Singh, Asif Khan, Patel and Jacob were individuals of powerful thoughts and extra constitutional authority. They were ruthless and calculative. They had the capacity to win over anyone with saintly spell or if that failed to impress, with the satanic power of money and muscles.

They could work on different alternatives to achieve their goal. To reach their specified destination, they never cared for the means. It was not an age of truth. It was a period of disintegration. No relations could hold sway over man. It was a curse these saints proclaimed that they wanted to avert. Then there were Soma Gandhi, Dawra, Samanta and Sonali. The argument was lengthy and full of riddles. Everybody was taking shelter under cover of lofty ideas.

"They have been paid for what they do and what they shall plan in future."

"You too..."

"Yes. It is the price you pay for..."

"Jaycee, I am deeply hurt. There is something that pricks me within. Blood oozing out. I feel the pain but there are no wounds. It is a conflict. I have been lost in my faith. Convictions that proved futile and suicidal. I have lost."

"No, in fact, you think too much. You think of past. Gone and dead. In fact, a man can never go back to his original birth. No. It is birth defying all logic. No rationale behind this. It is a stupid idea. To remain tied up with the past is to stilt your growth. It is killing and...past does not lead you anywhere except to a dark cell. To a burning hell. A man cannot live on memories and hopes. Past is dead. Forget it."

"Jaycee, you are justifying...I am sorry to have hurt your feelings. But now I realise the journey has been too long and tiring. You know the progress. I am a fence-seater. You have gone out of your...it is a treachery."

"You are harsh."

"I remember my old days."

"..."

"Jaycee, I want you to become Jayanta."

"..."

"I can read in your eyes the intensity of pains. An injured soul. An unfulfilled desire. I cannot say what precisely you feel and... Jaycee it is time to return. I find myself almost choked. I don't know why this relation has dragged on? But for the last ten years, I have realised that I am feeling forsaken...and you have been responsible. You lost yourself in...Dave and Madhav...they are noble souls...everybody says?" My irony had cast a long shadow of challenge.

"Yes, they are embodiment of purity...sainthood is the ultimate goal. They are nearing Godhood."

Jaycee had said as if he were knowing them fully.

"Godhood!" I had said sarcastically.

"Yes. It is the language of all noble souls...I am sure you understand."

"Yes, I get you. You are now unsympathetic. An absolute round-about, what could be a worst situation."

"You think too much."

Jaycee had called the waiter.

"Bring some drinks. Peter or sixty-nine. We'll not go anywhere. Let us enjoy friends." I was surprised. The hunger was still there.

We had all shifted to a corner. Drinks had been served in plenty. All of them had filled their glasses and orders had been placed for roasted chickens and all that."

"Tell Madhav...I mean his cronies...those bastards to make arrangement for the night. All of us...you should know...it is a modern man's desire to go higher and higher."

"You are blunt..."

"You should know, my dear friend, our women are tasteless and have lost their verve and appeal. What do we get from them? They concentrate on children and..." Jaycee was asking all of them "Now tell me, what about you? My Romi is a social worker...a woman, now more interested in her name than..."

"You are great crooks. You should be ashamed of such comments. All these ladies are God-fearing and graceful and...but you, all of you are..."

"I don't want to..."

Jaycee had become violent on that day. It had dazed and shocked me beyond patience. I had felt sorry for all of them. They had been never as shameless and ungraceful as they were on that day.

I had decided to walk out.

*** *** ***

17

Those were crucial days of crisis of faith and revenge. I had been obliquely humbled by Jaycee and others.

His last words while consuming a full glass of whisky were, "You just talk of sick values. I have never been attached to them. You are enamoured of Romi and Rajshri mom and...but they are all decrepit and disabled women. I don't want to align myself with them, I want freedom and mind you, you have also become a liability. We are not fond of individuals who stagnate and watch. We want constant movement. You can tell my parents...those old people. Known social workers. Bloody shit, they are selfish. They have also created a cell. Want name? I don't want ailing relations to follow me like shadows. And you too..."

"Jaycee..."

"I think time has come when we could withdraw from diseased relations...there is no fun in carrying on bonds which are proving a liability."

"You are out of senses." It was an interminable hot conversation.

And there was an unpleasant scuffle. He had rushed as if to slap and punch me and had probably quipped words about Romi which had infuriated me. I had seen a monster, a rogue peeping out of his eyes.

I had been seething with rage. The anger and passion rose very high but I had to control. Jaycee had been harsh, I could never believe. I had been thinking about relations but found them too cold and empty.

I had committed a mistake in not understanding them correctly. I believed on the face of it but otherwise something else was undergoing. They had been ahead without caring for anybody's emotions.

But I also knew their concern for a minimum value system. I always had contradictory options but had to admit their points of view. The living-standards had the touch of a class.

They had special and measured regards for Malkhan Dave and Madhav Wadia. Their saintly presence inspired them, they would always profess. Madhav Wadia was a powerful man who had access even to the bedrooms of many mighty politicians. He was reserved, brief, mild and commanding. His major concern was the welfare of people. He in his speeches and written words spoke about the faulty economic policy which was heavily tilted towards well-to-do houses. He also made a fervent appeal to discontinue with the practice of financial support in the shape of subsidies or incentives, for these, too, were cornered by the influential people. An unholy nexus between the favoured few who mattered in the government and the people with dubious characters could never be ruled out. They were men of dangerous dimensions.

Wadia often summoned policy makers and made suggestions to benefit poor citizens. He was apparently mild but when confronted he was hard and ruthless. His house, a large palace, was a temple for many. All those who wanted to achieve something in life required his blessings. Wadia whose image as a father-figure remained untainted was like a godfather to them. And then Malkhan Dave. He had numerous charitable institutions and was true social worker. In many business operations, he had a partnership with Wadia and others. Both had close contacts with those politicians and bureaucrats who were amenable, docile and easy to influence. They had an access to secrets and were the beneficiaries of new benefits and commercial projects. They also functioned as a strong conduit between the multinational companies and the Govt. and received the kickbacks. In this game my friends were enthusiastically involved. It was a period of money and matter.

Their method of operation was subtle and harmless. Earlier when any proposal was put across, all of them scrutinised it from all possible angles and gave fair, free and frank comments. Ratnam, Rama Raghunathan, Yadav and Jaycee invariably felt proud of themselves. Those were days of early sixties, years of youthful passions. It was a journey to a rosy future. They were worried about the man, society and the nation. In this passion of ideals, Jai Bhadra, Raji, Romi and Soma Gandhi strengthened them. It was the destiny of a country which was of supreme importance for them. They were all sincere, true and faithful. But when it was unacceptable they began to get indirect hints. Their inconvenient suggestions required polish and embellishment so that these could be agreed to. To them in the initial stages, this all appeared an abject submission, a kind of surrender to corrupt practices. They wanted to keep an upright image. Their testing hours were those when costly gifts started landing up at home with numerous invitations for dinners and parties. In an imperceptible approach they liked all this yet expressed reluctance. And slowly, they started feeling convinced.

"A weak man cannot help anyone."

Malkhan Dave had once told them during a dinner.

"Look at this greyhead. You ought to have..."

"It is an age of speed. Every work has to be done speedily. No time to think. All ideals and principles get strength out of money and muscle."

*** *** ***

His lingering laughter had surprised all. That day, we were on the second floor of his palatial house having dinner.

"I regret very much I had to issue a threat to some...but that should not be taken otherwise. In the functions of babus you people think that you are the custodians of all...you take upon yourselves that the nation looks at you, it is your word that is listened to, it is your act that is initiated. Similarly, I think we too have a wrong notion." Dave had by then stripped off his saintly image and gulped down a large peg, "This yellow attire and fragrance...make us adorable."

The glass had been emptied. I had found our culture and heritage in those culinary dishes and glasses. I was excited. In that single second was an experience of a life for everyone present there. It was shocking, stimulating and tantalizing. Dave's eyes spoke of an age. Those saintly clothes? All of us watched the great man with amazement and awe. He had come close to all by turn, a purposeful smile. Touching everybody's cheeks with satisfaction. In his movements there was an assurance, a fountain of confidence. Dave looked like a complete man. While moving around with us he patted us with Midas touch. This warm patting was blissful and full of godly benediction. He had laughed and laughed, and enquired about all of us. Favourite words that we made use of, talked to us about our wives, children and old parents.

It was a long and weary discourse on values and morals, man and nation. He was nakedly frank. He had not hidden anything and yet we felt he had said nothing. He had given details of many Peeths, Mosques and Churches. All sects and religions had come under incisive scrutiny. He had, in other words, while condemning lasciviousness of priests also attempted to justify them. This had bamboozled us. We had been immensely flabbergasted by his approach. In his discourse we discovered neither lies nor truth and still we believed there was sincerity in his outbursts.

Of all, I had been the worst hit.

Dave, an impressive personality, had, in no uncertain terms, torn himself apart. There were fragments all around and from each torn-off piece, it appeared he had been peeping out. Eyes bulging out with hands becoming bloody fangs. Mouth assuming the shape of a jaw from where blood and flesh in morsels appeared trickling. Dave had become an animal, a monster in a human form.

I had been perspiring with fear.

The next moment he had, with all the available sympathies and love, hugged me in his spreading arms. It was love but I had felt a sense of guilt, a kind of felonious conduct.

Our facial expressions showed furrows of doubts.

But he had dispelled all our suspicions in a single stroke by cursing everyone. For him, all were debauch, bastards and mere throbbing lumps of flesh. Nothing more. He had been disparagingly contemptuous. But throughout, he had been maintaining a lusciousness in voice, words and manners. When he saw that we had exhausted our drinks, a full bar stood opened before our eyes and without caring he had himself started pouring whisky into our individual glasses. We were simply aghast to see the various brands of drinks. Again he had come back to me and a full history of insidious business techniques was opening up. A gourmet concept of life contained a full book.

In his opinion, I was a dullard, a dunce. No knowledge of market pulse. The important intricacies of demand and supply. He had told me to make full use of connections, and in my ears he had whispered many words. It was his fatherly treatment. The next moment, he was as intimate as a friend, who stands by you through all your travails.

"You should know the age in which you are living. Be cruel and corrupt. Honest and upright."

He had with unsteady steps moved to talk to others in his gay mood.

I had raised the question of a mentally sick man. And Malkhan Dave had laughed ironically for a long time. I had felt suffocated.

Somewhere, I had been observing a thick sheet of darkness. It was a sheer torture.

I had felt an attack of severe bitterness.

There was no end. I had been hurt. I wanted to come out. But had decided otherwise. One thing that I had experienced was the irrevocable fact that all were untrue and insincere. Possibly, all had been scrambling to find a plausible reason to hide shortcomings.

*** *** ***

Dave was immensely vociferous in the expression of happiness and joy. I had never found him as open and frank as he had been that day. I had realised all of a sudden that all of us were searching for a sound and strong foundation but admitting not the implicit and terrible vacuum of misunderstanding.

Dave had at once taken another large peg and said, "I know all of them. All fools and dishonest. It is a talk only. No substance in fact. I know what I want. I wished to be rich. I tried. This was the only way. I don't think any one of you can suggest. I am frank with you. Now listen. It is a strange world. You are kind but also a heartless fellow. It is a question of tolerance. You are eliminated and you feel you are existing."

His philosophy was untenable. I had to listen. They had to listen. There was no escape. "Ask Jaycee, Swamy and Raghunathan...all of them. I know their bank balances. Their accounts where only fictitious names appear. Swamy and...would have been exterminated. Washed out. Would have banished had I been not saving them. They are immature. Even now, they exhibit utter lack of realism and practicality."

And Dave had vilified and condemned everybody including himself. Then had begun the interesting revelation of how he had managed foreign tours for all of them.

"These tours had no purpose. But papers never spoke so."

Facial expressions of everybody showed fears, doubts and sin. Jaycee had been feeling uncomfortable and tipsy. I wanted to run away but something had held me back. I had been feeling enraged and disillusioned.

It was a world of facts and fiction. I had recuperated from the earlier shock. Dave was laughing loudly and without shame. I found out that he was wilfully trying to humiliate us.

That Malkhan Dave could have been absurd at times, I had never thought of. He was cynical and appreciative though the truth remained that he was a man of authority and we had to accept what he said.

"It is truth that prevails."

He had declared, "Yes, truth."

And then at length had spoken about Asif Khan, Patel, Mahapatra, Mukherjee, Dhawan and Wadia. He had not hidden a word.

"No use to cut off yourself from the real world."

I wanted to leave but the manner in which he was picking up the threads was grand. He wished to tear apart each aspect so as to show the real face of truth. In his view there were countless faces of truth. A man had to agree to only one face. A relative interpretation always suited mankind.

Dave had said, "Violence is a theme, close to man's heart."

It was revolting to hear those strong vituperations. There was nothing soft or pleasant that day. Dave had told in clear words that existence was a major issue. For him Asif, Patel, Mahapatra and such like men were important for they always felt obliged when bending backwards. Kneeling down was one of their strong attributes. They know how to suggest, do and come out successful. Then the entire centre of discussion had been Asif. He had without mincing words given a long and verified list of persons who were always important and indispensable for carrying out unwritten orders. The art of state and politics was his strong point. Dave, in a nutshell, wanted to stress that when we agreed without much fuss with whatever they did, we would be happy.

"It is not an easy task to perform social welfare duties. We ought to have some power...these politicians depend upon us because we hold the strings of power that they enjoy."

"Mr. Dave," I had endeavoured to ask a straight question, "we could do whatever we wanted otherwise."

"No, it is not possible."

"..."

"Ask Ratnam and Rama? Know about Mahapatra and Mukherjee. What happened to his daughter, Radha?"

"What do you want to say?"

"Nothing. You are a petty shopkeeper." He had insulted me but I had kept my cool, "I am sorry. Business is a vast subject. Here you need to involve people."

"I am not interested in sermons."

I had poured a peg for myself for I had resolved to stand before a man who thought, he was very tall. Dave had watched my retaliation in an amused expression.

"Let me help you."

Without waiting for him to say, I had poured a large one in his glass, "A big man should be served in a royal fashion."

I know I had become tense and impudent. The limits of grace were possibly collapsing.

I had exploded into a roaring laughter without delay.

"I like it."

Dave had said with a suppressed voice and had come forward to put his arm on my left shoulder.

"You have been pitying us."

"No, no pity. It is not the question of my showing mercy. They want to be pitied on." He had said in a controlled voice, "This word pity is damaging but it is their inherent strength."

"I would like to go."

"Promise, I shall not give you sermons. I also considered you like my son. Like them. You know they are young...yes...still a long way to go. They are totally fused with the system."

"Yes, you need them."

"They also need us. You know, in fact, perhaps, Jaycee...and...they will bear me out that we derive energy from one another."

"Perhaps, you derive more."

I had looked into his eyes. Yes, I had found a very strong individual. His eyes were impressive, dangerous and meaningful. His lips, wide and black, instilled a kind of fear. All of a sudden, I found that his black complexion was turning into a brightness not seen earlier.

A terrible business tycoon, with explosive and violent eyes, had now started threatening me.

I had retraced my steps.

Dave was not so tall but he had looked so and now I was measuring his height. A short-statured man with broad forehead and beautiful face was really attractive.

I was undergoing tremendous inner pain. I had committed a mistake by challenging a person who pulled up even the strongest among the all powerful.

He had dragged me to a corner and said in a low, loving and casual voice, "You are right. You know, at this stage, we require many hands. Asif had to suffer and sacrifice and ultimately realised that to be earthly was not a defect. When you move with the world, you have to accept its ways. One has to..."

He had laughed again.

*** *** ***

18

A long speech on the practical ways of the world had started. There was truth, reality and a violent fact. It was a dream and yet nothing. The life histories of all those who ruled and controlled, were recounted. There were individuals, soft and weak. At the same time, they were the mighty. He had made his point and I had felt very small when Jaycee had said, "My friend is a...now forget sir, I know him. He is a good soul. Very noble and sincere."
"What do you mean? Are we rascals?"
"..."
There was a noisy clapping, "No, we are not."
"Jaycee, I am grateful."
"We are human beings. Your problems are your own creations."
"I would...you people don't care for emotions."
I had said many words and perhaps I had hurt him.
"Now come on, if these officers...I say all of us...including this tall man Malkhan...and people like Wadia...Asif and...Well I have the number, if we have achieved success, it has been at the cost of...Arey, you people with small...Well, I don't want to hurt."
Dave was suddenly quiet. His eyes had become dark and dull. Facial wrinkles had been more prominent now.
"Sir, Mr. Dave, I did not mean to injure your feelings. I know, all of you love me. I cannot be an ungrateful man."
There was an eerie silence engulfing all of us and I had been feeling restricted to unfavourable and hostile environment surrounded by strong and potent organs of the society. I had also an incorrigible sense of hope in man notwithstanding disintegrating relations.
Yes, I could not call Dave vicious as was my earlier assessment. They were inveterate individuals who could not be changed. Self-willed, determined and deeply habituated as they were, I was a

small fry for them and my moving out of the scene would not make much difference. I had known this and so making myself clear, I was suspiciously fluent but choosy about the words.

"Nothing can happen. Yes, really, nothing concrete will emerge. It is what we want that will happen."

"Yes, that is happening. Yes Sir, I am very sure. It is happening."

"Your views will determine the symptoms of age. Madhav, Malkhan, Soma Gandhi, Sonali, the Sadhvis, Dawras, all those Brahamcharis and..." He had given a queer look and then spread out a mischievous smile, "Yes all of us together will create history."

I had squeezed myself with an assault of scorn. I was out of place there. In order to avoid direct confrontation I was looking up here and there, searching nothing particularly but still throwing hints of a chronic search. The vast superbly carved-out ceiling, the huge, impressive and grand chandeliers and the hanging lights had attracted me. These spoke of the grandeur of the man who was standing just before me.

"You are..."

"These are fabulous."

"You are smart."

"No, I was...where is the great lady of the house? It is long, I saw her. I would like to pay my regards. Your two sons..." Perhaps to establish a more deep and lasting relationship, I had said all those words which had surprised all of them.

"Great lady of the house! Sons..." Malkhan's laughter had raised many eyebrows.

Dave's laconic descriptions and sometimes his trite habits had created suspicions in the minds of many others. There was something in him that made him a person worth millions of jewels.

"Am I wrong?" It was a simple question.

"When you reach a certain stage, you have to be indifferent. Lady of the house! Yes. A grand epithet, you can say. In fact, persons like you use honourable words." He had again laughed, "She was a burden. All ladies...when given status, assert and build up for themselves a different structure, durable and worth mentioning. One should not mind it. I too liked. Who does not want a reputation? But she was too bad a..."

Malkhan's words had lost voice.

"That elder son! Yes, he is in Australia. A vast business did not suit him. The profitable Shipping Company was too small. I told him he could rule this country. But that love for a white woman took him away. He does not want to return. The second son...that violent boy, it was the kindness of Madhav, Mukherjee and Patel that the young Don was saved. He killed...you know...yesterday's killer is today's saint. He is the conscience keeper. A true Sadhu. Soma and Sonali, such women are symbols of his strength."

His words were so casual and off the emotional content that I had felt awkward. Because of high connections he is running his trading empire. Those ordnance factories...and...anyway forget about it. All of them are on the pay roll.

He was looking into Jaycee's eyes, "He is a rich man. The great Jai Bhadra's son. But ask him. Was his present living possible because of me? Alone he stands. And still in the crowd. You are all my own people."

He had become normal now, "But, if I give you your due share, I am not bestowing on you special favours. It is an obligation I have to discharge. My son has to give some portion out of his profit to them. If a few crores of rupees are distributed to keep his profit and many skeletons in cupboard safe, it is not a bad bargain."

There was a hushed and dreadful silence.

"Jaycee talked to me about you. But I knew, you could not become a dependable partner."

"He is my best friend."

"Yeah, he loves you."

"Yes, that is why you ruled out the idea of partnership even before its birth. I like and admire a sharp nose."

"You can draw wanted conclusions."

"That was about sons. I think the younger son is the most able, practical and successful."

"Yes, you are right."

"And I can..."

"You don't know, it is through him that young boys and girls in the colleges and universities are directed to take the right path."

"I see."

"All parties, in order to keep in...well, I would not say. My argument is, young men and women must be kept on the right side or else we shall be writing our death warrants. We have young boys and girls on our side. We pay for them and use them when we need. It is the Chanakya and Plato all mixed up with a clean practical approach in the true and modern sense of the word."

"Well, that is very good."

"You must say."

He had taken hold of my arm and said meaningfully, "Come. I shall show you the real picture."

We had climbed a few stairs when he had called out, "Jaycee come here."

I was trying futilely to get rid of the strong grips of that statured man but to no avail.

"I am strong, my son."

"Yes, Sir." Jaycee was standing before us, "You have special arrangement for us, sir."

"It is your choice."

Dave had thrown a sinister smile.

"The younger son is coming under the so-called auspicious influence of Sonali Sadhvi and Soma Gandhi. You have to call somebody from Bombay. Those good people can spell disaster. Don't kill them. Just create moral problems. Ask somebody to invent stories. These women should know their bodies."

"They must know that their flesh can be...they are women of good figures."

"Sir..." Jaycee was giving a confused expression.

"Mr. Dave, you could be treacherous."

"No. You know in politics of power and money, relations don't matter. Value of man is of little concern."

"..."

"It changes from time to time."

"Yes, I can understand the cult of violence. The definition of truth changing everywhere. Yes, I can know the shift."

"One is happy when one lives in harmony."

"Mr. Malkhan Dave, I have seen too much."

"No, you have yet to see..." He had taken my hands in his and started climbing up, "Come."

I had unwillingly followed him.

Jaycee, with a glass in hand, had patted me and signalled me to obey, "We are all saints."

"Yes, it is a world of saints."

Dave had said softly.

I had kept scrupulously mum. They were talking too tall. It was not an exaggeration but still I had found out the latent truth.

"You are all saints."

I had admitted the untruth as truth.

There was again a big hall on the third floor. It was lavishly furnished and decorated. Its regal looks had cast a spell on me.

"Are you surprised?"

"No. I see the usual glitter."
"You are hiding something."
"No."
"Look there!" The big door stood opened, "Come."
Time was a big dilemma. And I thought we were marching on to another era of culture. A pure modern age indeed.

*** *** ***

• 19 •

Another large room almost a hall spread out before us with all the grandeur. A few girls were sitting and drinking there, unconcerned about the world outside.

"They are the trend-setters. Custodians of our culture and values about which you remain worked up."

He was dear Dave, Malkhan, darling, dearest darling, boss, sir and godfather for all of them. Dave had stood there with a bloated chest. His ego was inflated. I had observed my conscience was crowded with dark thought. The scintillating environment was too dazzling for the eyes.

I was happy and sad at the same time.

They had stood in front of the young damsels. They had been extremely garrulous and making an ear-rending noise.

"These girls are intelligent."

Dave had commented.

"..."

A question taking birth in the mind was still groping for words. I was constructing sentences but these could not find voice. I was making massive efforts to fix in my memory each and every one. Living and non-living, all. There was an uncanny noise. All those girls were busy in discussing welfare schemes, plans relating to women and achievements made in different fields.

I had been totally confounded by their intelligence. There was no formal introduction. Only a silent and smile-filled exchange of words, voiceless and unstirring. I had been surrounded by those who were apparently worried about society and its ailments. Something was cutting through the nerves and making me weary and aghast. I had understood the purpose and its extent, both of them wanted to convey. But, why? I was no threat to them.

"How do you like?"

A mild question had been whispered.

"It is dazzling. And these girls..."

"They are all in the university. Doing research. But permanent members of our party. Youth wings are controlled through them.

Dave had given detailed accounts of their functions. He had given an excellent description of those girls. I was fully convinced that those girls were really an asset to the society. Even nuns could not be so pious. At times, they looked an embodiment of purity. But then the drinks, the smoking and...I had found a certain laxity in their words. That had alerted and warned me.

"Don't you wish to participate?"

"..."

"You have a godown in Chandigarh, I learn." Dave had asked me and then directed his gaze at Jaycee, "You told me. I also know. He is known as the most honest, principled and upright businessman. None can ever doubt him."

"Yes nobody can. And then we are there."

"It is about cash and kind. A total of two-three hundred crores. I want a safe custody of the amount till elections. A few projects have to be taken in hand. And those projects and plants...are worth thousands of crores. And this money is..."

I had understood the terrible with the ulterior objectives.

"I may not be able to do."

I had conveyed my decision after a long persuasion. It had not made them happy.

"You know, we have to adjust in this world. It is a collective responsibility to run the show. We are morally bound to assist each other. You may not agree with us. You may also not approve of the intentions, with which...but you must appreciate. It is so common. A man cannot be perfect. I am not a saint. These girls, too, have not come to waste their youth. It is power and wealth. It is the prerogative of we people to govern..."

I had not agreed to their preposterous proposal and thus I was inadvertently incurring their wrath. Those girls were gabbing ceaselessly and at times, making meanings clear. It was now quite difficult for me to stay on, but looking around, I had found out that an early end to the dinner was not visible. Those girls were fabulous, intelligent and charming. After half-an-hour, it was a jungle law. No one was recognizing anyone. Jaycee after dancing with a girl for about fifteen minutes had settled by my side.

"Forget yaar, go and enjoy..."

"So this is how you keep busy?"

"Yes, real enjoyment. He is our godfather. We help him and she looks after us."

"Only he...?"

"No...there are a handful of...those who are close to...we have to keep our boss in good humour and that is why...why don't you agree? We shall give you..."

"You know what you are doing? Mom and Pop...Romi...kids... they are unhappy. You have started staying out...after all what is all this? You are belittling their feelings."

"When relations prove shackles..." He had picked up the glass, "You don't know. Such an attitude in close relations makes you sick. Romi is a social worker. My father and that mother...Rajshri. She behaves...I tell you she has lately started behaving as an empress. She is dominating and nauseating. I just hate..."

"She is never in a mood to..."

"That is what she is. You'll never know. I know how much money is wanted to carry on with the social work."

He had finished the last drop.

"This way..."

"It is not bad. You are mistaken. They want money. Vicky, Ashey and Rahul are grown up now. Romi is concentrating on social work. I am...they don't want me...and I am also occupied with tiring official work."

"All of you...?"

"Yes."

A young girl had sat beside him. She was saucy, sexy and devastating.

"You want to..."

"You are pushing yourself into a..."

"..." He had thrown a passionate glance.

"Jaycee, I have lost today...I thought, I was having a wrong impression. Romi, Vicky...pop-mom...all, yes all were incorrect. But today, I have seen, they were...it is a deep abyss of vices and look at this much-praised Saint, Malkhan Dave will...you will not be able to get out of the magic spell, nay, curse. It is a journey to perdition. An extinction untimely. The death of a heritage."

"You are unwell."

I don't remember how many words had been spoken without any positive result. There were heated exchanges.

They were many. Strong and rich, very powerful and famous. I was an insignificant man. A pigmy. A moment had come when I had wished to banish from the scene. I had a hint of an impending disaster. A premonition had taken birth somewhere to warn me of an imminent death. I don't recollect anything but this much I know that I had virtually run away as if I were protecting myself against some danger.

*** *** ***

I had decided to forget Jaycee. After having outrageous and humiliating experiences, I had concluded that Jaycee had been undependable. It was after more than a period of eight months that I had to go to Jaycee's place on the occasion of marriage of his son, Vicky. It was Nineteen Eighty-four, the year of colossal tragedies and upheavals.

That was the year of marriage, celebrations and deaths. I had gone because my wife desired and then Jai Bhadra, Raji and Romi had requested me not to undermine the relations. And after immense reasoning,...I had come to the conclusion that it was wrong to be adamant. I was finally persuaded by my wife and parents to attend the marriage. All my contentions bore no fruit. I had contended for long that Jaycee particularly must get a shock. That I was not going to tolerate his tantrums any more. He was a powerful and important figure but it never gave him the licence to run down old friends. Somehow I had the feeling that he wanted to downgrade me though indirectly. I would often go into each detail of words, meanings, incidents and relations to find out the background of his changed behaviour.

In my lonely hours, I realised that it was not his fault. He was in the system,...carrying out orders and doing nothing of his own.

When you are groomed up in a particular environment, you imbibe unpretendingly the air and attributes of the surroundings. I had gone into the depth of every year from birth to this date. There had been sincere protestations once which now stood ignored. Born in a period of political turmoil, when the country was under tremendous convulsions, we had not exactly known the pangs of freedom struggle. It was a terrific and uncertain war with an enemy of upredictable temperament. Those were grand and memorable days, we used to call, when during college and university years, there had been long discussions about the pre-independence era. There was surfeit of grace, cultured expression and sublimity of words, polished submissions and unassuming sophistication in actions and words. We had heard passionately many touching stories of freedom fighters. Their pangs and sufferings raised our heads in prayers. I had been much involved in those nostalgic memories. In fact, the credit must go to Jayanta who dragged me back and back to forty-seven and to the years prior to early forties when all patriots were immersed in planning and strategies.

I was usually wonder-struck by his remarkable memory. He had been fond of history. A kind of craze haunted him. To know more and more, about freedom struggle and about all those days. Because of him, I too had developed a taste for history. Also, we had always recalled stories, passionately related to us by teachers and old men. Many a time Jai Bhadra and my father too fell into reveries and told in bits and pieces the story untold and the sweetness of sufferings.

There was much to be known and learnt. We had felt proud of our history. It was a nation of great men. And we had a pious feeling and a prayer-like attitude before talking of Gandhi, Nehru and such like great men. A few other names too crowded us with reverence. Those were days of dedication, zeal and devotion.

It was a coincidence that many of us met in Delhi where invariably we had found the life-sized leaders, the towering and mighty public figures, statesmen, the politicians, philanthropists, social workers and the saints moving about delivering sermons, planning for a bright and prosperous future, opening up their minds and hearts, dreams and aspirations. This had helped us to a large extent in shaping up our thoughts.

There was no self-interest. It was a truthful concern for the people. Their country's future was uppermost in their minds. When fiddling, frolicking, jumping and dancing with new and contemporary thoughts, we had treaded the roads of Delhi and were filled with a spirit at once sacred and inspiring. Those leaders were saints.

Jayanta's habit was to read and re-read out the life-sketches of great men. There was the intensity and fervour in his voice and words.

*** *** ***

Yes, there I had realised my wife was not incorrect. My parents had not been unthoughtful. The long and warmly affectionate letters from Rajshri, Jai Bhadra and Romi were not out of context. Even dear Ashey had entreated lovingly and deeply. Vicky too wrote a letter and was quick to add that if elders could go to that extent how could they expect miracles from their children.

"You had been very close. Relations do not end up like this."

It was Raji's phone call.

"I think even today if we can nourish passions and warmth in human relationship, there shall be a..."

Jai Bhadra had rather emphatically asked me to come along with all the members of the family. Notwithstanding unwillingness and an element of detachment, I had finally made up my mind to attend the ceremony. In a long challenging and fruitful journey of about twenty-five years, they had changed for the worst. A full age had appeared before my eyes. Days of joys, pains and sorrows with no complaint. That was a period of prosperity and adversity. But I found them negotiating with the toughest personal suffering. They knew how to transform threats into a positive bargain. I had known the movement of files, the changing notes, an about-turn to opinion and views from negative to positive invariably to serve personal interests. The earlier unflinching fortitude and faith in man had been groaning under doubts and infidelity. I was thinking about vested interests. They were outwardly good, basically quite warm and lively. Those were the years of turbulence and peace. Many events taking place at the same time and we failed to take stock of the situation. There was a slow change in all of them. I had never been introduced to Malkhan Dave, Madhav Wadia, Patel, and such like strong people in the beginning, for my friends had hesitated, and when I was introduced, I had found them kind, generous, humane, large-hearted, mild and bright. But it was after years that I had discovered the real intentions. I, without comments and apparent expression of suspicions, had continued to read between the lines. Their words and voices, sighs and songs, joys and regrets...all had changed.

For the first few years, I had the privilege to visit them at their places. All of them had welcomed me. All had treated me with an openness.

I had come out and was standing alone in the middle of the verandah, a small ridge in Longwood. It had always fascinated me. Impressive state hospital and the tin-roofed military hospital. On the other side, the Great Ridge and then the Institute. On this side of Shimla, I had a modest bungalow, an old structure which was kept reserved for my friends and colleagues who wanted to spend their time in Shimla. That evening, I had come to supervise the arrangements for some delegates who were coming to attend a meeting of Confederation of Indian Industries. And now the big question. My parents and family had been staying at Bemloi. I was just tossing between two opposites. The next morning we were to proceed to Chandigarh. My father was a little worried, and at one point of time planned to dispense away with property in Chandigarh and Punjab, for the increasing incidence of terrorism had made him concerned about our safety.

But somehow the decision had been put off.

*** *** ***

"Sir, your phone!"

I remember something had happened. I had not been able to find out the reasons as to why I had started roaming about in the memory lanes of my own past. Father's apprehensions about spreading terrorism were not unfounded. There were deaths in the family at Jallandhur and Amritsar as if with a destined regularity. But business interests and fixed assets discouraged us from taking a drastic step. Jai Bhadra had advised at that time, "It is the loss of man. I tell you, Mr. Vijaya Chand." He had told my father. "We have travelled a long distance from Mundhra's Scandal. It has been a loss on all sides. Mr. Vijaya Chand, it is a good decision. Yes, I don't challenge your wisdom. May be good to dispose of property and land in Punjab and...but tell me Sri Vijaya, would you be able to forget? Where would you go? Will you be able to run away? No. You cannot. We are not only businessmen and landlords but also social animals. We cannot shirk our responsibility. The world moves on. We have to play the role."

"Mr. Jai Bhadra...it is an experience to meet you..."

"We have lost many things."

"Yes, we have lost. I think we are without basis. Religion had never been an enemy to this extent..."

And the conversation had become alive. Vijaya and Bhadra — those remotely sad faces had spoken the truth of life and their times.

"Yes, it is true. Man is losing interest in emotional life. Relations are at a discount. These are losing warmth. I felt as if an age had passed.

*** *** ***

20

These were persistent calls, echoes and re-echoes of my words. I was listening to my breathings and had been conscious of my own words. After a few seconds, I had entered the room and picked up the receiver, "Yes."

"Come immediately."

My father had asked me to get ready in no time. I had ultimately realised that relations could not be hurt in this way. Those elderly persons were, too, undergoing pangs of separation and loneliness, yet were brave enough to endure the infliction. While going to Delhi, I was recapturing their words.

"It is a temporary phase. You cannot play down your old associations."

"When I go back, each word and incident becomes alive. They had been intelligent. Always duped me. I thought they were busy people. But in reality it was different. They had an entirely new and fresh field to explore. In their living patterns I think, we have become irrelevant."

"No, my son, it is not so. You think what you...you...no, everyone cannot move according to...let them live and they shall learn."

"You don't know how Sri Bhadra and Raji are worried about? You choke."

"This phase will also pass away."

"I am concerned about Romi and kids. You know, I have seen them growing up. Those vacant eyes, suppressed anger and... something...inexpressible coming out throbbing and bubbling."

"When a man exclusively spares himself for the people, his relations suffer and suffocate."

"May be, they are doing so much for the people or..."

He had blown into smithereens of laughters.

His meaningful exposure had made him bright and my eyes had started sparkling.

"What is it?"

I had looked at my wife.

"Nothing, dad says when you spend time for others you feel stress on time."

"..."

"Don't you think I should have agreed to their proposals. Malkhan Dave and...lot of influence and wealth."

"They are mentally dissatisfied. I have seen into the eyes of those women. Glued to teevees and...not fair. It is an unhealthy dissipation of energy. You are businessman. Yes, earn money but confine to what you think is good for peace. Your heart and mind should lie in..."

"Now don't advise. This is too much."

She had smiled, "Cards, drinks, tambolas, kitties, functions and that undefined urge to serve roadside hawkers and beggars..." She had been unusually vocal and I with eyes wide open was penetrating deep to lay hand on the intended meaning but failed each time. She had patted the driver from behind, "Go slow. Not more than fifty."

"Could I smoke."

"..." She had thrown an unwilling glance, "Think about your grown-up children. If they become independent to take decisions ...it may hurt you."

"No, I don't like..."

"I also don't like. But it gives you unlimited joy and happiness when you learn that everyone in the family respects your feelings and ideas."

I had lit a cigarette while responding to her mundane opinion.

"Romi rang me up the other day, she was sad and anguished."

"Her words were truly intense and deep. I understand the pains she had been experiencing without letting me know. It is the suffering of richness and immense comforts. She forgets or perhaps tries to forget herself in the midst of small or big social programmes. Yes, I say arey, do it secretly. Why do you publicise? What for? Visiting dirty streets and unhygienic bastis. It is all done to attract people...to...the way things are...you are..."

"You also speak the language of..."

"Look, I don't want that our kids should also go on their ways. You cannot live in a big house alone and..."

"What do you say?"

"No, we have to care. Romi is feeling inner miseries. Totally her own. Nobody can participate in the mitigation. It has to happen. Now that Vicky has decided to marry a girl who...there is nothing Indian in that family. They have spread out their business operations all over the world. Do you think, they will live here and...?"

"You are painting a sad, depressing and...no I don't believe. Vicky is planning to establish his headquarters in Bombay."

"Your world is too small for him."

And she had been incessantly speaking. So many words but all authentic and born out of experience. She had been very practical. I had felt guilty within. I thought, I was paying full attention looking after my parents and members of the family but it was a fallacy.

At Kurukshetra, she had stayed back.

"What about the children and..."

"I have talked to dad. They will go straight. I have a commitment to fulfil."

There was nothing more to say. I had followed her without an argument. I had settled myself under a tree, she had dragged me to pay obeisance and say prayers.

"All these women too keep visiting temples and...it is a marvellous instinct. They worship, pray, count beads and..." While following her, I had been mumbling my words into her ears through whispers. She would turn back, cover her head, smile and soon fall into her uncommon chanting and incantation.

*** *** ***

Yes, here, I was a helpless child. She had been superb. I didn't know, but what had surprised me was my wife's intensity of glow in the eyes and face that stirred me with an unspoken threat. And the long discourse only culminated when we had reached Delhi. Before entering the compound, the car had stopped at the gate and she had hesitatingly opened, "Now look, don't say anything which hurts feelings. When you have no interest, it is also not your business to use bitter words. Everyone does what he wants and accomplishes what he attempts. There may be failures, but this world moves. Sometimes men of wealth are egocentric for they think they can control the world with money and they misconstrue themselves to be the major meeting point of all.

"Thank you."

I had resigned myself to her wishes.

"It is a morbid obsession. These people are intolerant. So we often sermonise."

"And you..."

"I want you to stay away from any unseemly controversy. It is their way of looking at relations. We must perform our duties. There should be no disagreement."

I had been carefully listening to the words of my wife. A patch of half an inch of grey hair made brown with the use of henna and then the application of dye had made all the difference. She was simply attractive at her age. I had tried to smile away her words of wisdom but my expression had probably made her shrug her shoulders.

"I know, you are non-serious. But don't create a scene."

"I have listened to each word and you are the wisest woman on earth. Very pretty and...I am proud of you."

I had spoken mildly though with full seriousness.

It was Romi, near the main entrance who had been waiting for us anxiously.

It was a day before the grand marriage.

She was vibrant and happy. With bright eyes and face, she had come forward to embrace my wife.

"Oh Devyani, it was a long wait." With arms spread out, she had enclosed my wife for about two minutes.

Devyani was looking visibly flattered. I stood admiring and speechless.

"I have to discuss...you know..." Romi's eyes twinkled as these appeared dewy. Immense love was shining dazingly in her dark watery eyes. I had felt overwhelmed by the emotions.

"How is everybody? Where is Jaycee Saab and..."

"Come. They are inside. Jaycee is away to Calcutta for an urgent official meeting. A fabulous negotiation. He is expected anytime, but positively by morning next."

Romi had given a manipulated account.

Devyani had pierced her eyes to find the real intention and looked at me.

"He is an officer whom everybody wants." I had said yet was unable to understand the hidden implications.

"Yes, Bhai Sahib, he is a very important person."

Romi's words were exceptionally forceful but lacked meaning.

I had not responded. Devyani's eyes had been examining the scene around.

"Yes, another bungalow. It was constructed recently."

Romi had started giving details of the second big multi-storeyed house with some old architectural designs.

"The old haveli-type construction is dear to Papa's heart. An old grand revival of tradition. The expression so eloquent."

"And what about Jaycee?"

My unblinking eyes had cautioned her.

"..." Romi had looked at the tall deodars, pines and willow trees with expectations. For a couple of minutes we all had stood quiet and dumb.

"I am sorry. But this is what exactly gave me torments." I had wanted to submit but Devyani with a flip of her eyes discouraged me. I had twisted my lips without resentment.

"Jaycee is a man of purpose. Files, pins, plans, projects and schemes. Budget and finance. Advice. Notings. Drafts. This is the workable vocabulary." Romi had burst in a fake and hollow laughter, "He is deeply involved. He is an obedient officer. Very true and faithful."

"Yes, all are like him."

"They should be. True and sincere." Devyani had said in all tranquillity and poise, "These officers perform onerous duties. No time for anything. We should be considerate."

"Dev, I understand. Service riddles? No one can know. I agree with you." Romi's words did not convey her agonies.

My wife had decided to keep silent.

"Yes, Govt. spends immense amount on them. After all, this is the ultimate result. Should we accept this as the outcome...in less than forty years...the standard of... They have become toothless, spineless and not even barking dogs. Mind you, dogs too discriminate but these..." I was bitter and had left many words unsaid.

"He has no time."

"But money..."

"Yes money and money. Shares. Partnership...business operations and now Vicky too is a mature guy who knows the vagaries of the world." Romi's words were taking birth out of a suppressed heart, "You know, I have to live in these two large... palatial houses should I say, alone...and with a sense of defeat."

She had laughed without passion, "Am I too much...You are tired. I think."

She had said with extra care and sensitivity, "Come I am happy now that Devyani had found time to come over to us."

"You are an eminent social worker."

"Yes, I am. I have sufficient time. Not only I, but women similarly placed. We spend time because there is no alternative. Our children have started showing signs of total independence. Vicky has already done it. It is only a formality. We had to acquiesce in. If we had disagreed, he would have revolted. Thank God, I am feeling relieved." She had not said any more though I had tried to ask in detail.

"They want to become lords of their fields. All of them want happiness on their terms. Do you really think relations have relevance in the present context?"

We had entered the main hall.

*** *** ***

21

The servants of the house were engaged in small household chores. The entire hall was being given a face-lift.

"Elder sisters and brothers have arrived. Everybody in his room."

"That is good."

"Yes from the village. They left to the servants and...you know it is all uncomfortable. But they are trying to adjust to the environs."

"Yes, they all did come earlier but each time...on some occasions. This living is..." Romi had laughed, "There is something, they always miss. They don't say but it is hidden in the words. They have brought a pandit with all those books. A bundle of leaves of different plants. For Yajna, they are making the material ready by mixing up ingredients. No packets."

Romi had been telling us about the old guests who had come from the village. She had offered a cup of tea, made us comfortable in the room and thereafter had taken us to the rooms of her old relations. They had asked us about everything. Each minute detail was their concern. I had found fountain of love in their eyes.

"Do you visit your village?"

A pertinent question had raised a host of issues. My answer had been vulnerable, they had appreciated me.

"You people remain in big towns. Good. We also like, as life here is comfortable and easy. You know, we too have those things inside the house but early morning stroll along the fields and small village streams has its own freshness..."

We had only listened. Before coming back to our rooms, we had touched their feet with profound regards. Great souls wishing a happy and bright future.

"It is going back to..."

"Yes, they like it. But the occupations here rarely give you time to go to..." Romi had tried to say which she never wanted to do otherwise.

"You are..."

"This ostentatious living. A luxurious expansion." She was perhaps looking out for some consoling words from Devyani, "Don't you see where have we reached?"

"..."

"I am fed up. Those old men...they come here but slowly the energy is dripping out. How long they shall continue to meet us? I feel I am guilty. Pop Bhadra and Mom Raji...! You know how grand those old men are and yours...it is a big festival. I feel I am getting a shower of love and benediction. All of them are around. It is a vital function. Mornings and evenings...I mean those days have been enriching. You see them around. Conversing. Walking, jogging many a time in the lawn and the small flower garden. It seems they talk to plants, trees and flowers. They water them, tend them delicately. You know, I simply watch the old men working...and it is extremely exhilarating."

She had become pensive.

"It is a glamorised living. What is the use of..."

"Romi, you are taking too many things to heart."

"No Devyani, not that. It is different. I am keeping track of my pains but I can't control. It is unfortunate. Those demanding eyes. Poor, sunken and half-clad or totally naked faces. Hungry and homeless. We had been planning for them. Many words of compassion and sympathies spoken and written for them but with what result?" She had been bluntly piercing, "I know the intentions of my husband. Jaycee, you know. If he...No, this is a bad thing when a wife discloses the sources of income. At our stage, we know, how gorgeous living standards are achieved?"

There were numerous explanations bubbling in her eyes. A sense of self-condemnation was also enveloping her.

"Romi, I think we have to live in such conditions."

"No, you have no experience so you are casual and uncaring. Look at Vicky. How he had forced us to agree with him? I don't know, where do they want to go with all the money? It is immense. No count. But still, there is no end. And Ashey, she is telling me the secrets of life and so is Rahul. And you know Jaycee? There is no end to the journey. I am also forgetting myself in that so-called social service but with what purpose? You see people waiting to cash on." There was a hint of extreme indignation and jealousy, "I hate them. I learnt the art from my mother-in-law, my pop is too ...but you know in the hand of Jayanta Chandra Chauhan, the great Jaycee...it has been reduced to a vote depositing scheme. He says, nobody serves people without interest. There is a definite method in the welfare programmes."

We had walked up to her bedroom, not that we desired but possibly her voice and softness had made us forget our fatigue.

"Here we will have those religious ceremonies, Yajna...old men want it and Vicky too has agreed. Then a reception to persons...who live around. But...some of the functions. I mean a part of..." She had laughed, "It is at Taj."

And she had given us the details of different ceremonies. At the dinner time excepting children we all had gathered, about fifteen in all, and we had talked and talked. I had heard those old men saying many things in a spirited voice. After finishing their meals, with pipes or cigarettes in hands, they had strolled and gone out and then retired to their respective rooms.

"They are full of life."

"Yes, among children..." Devyani had kept deaf-mute.

I had been thinking about all but without a solution to their emotional problems.

*** *** ***

It was very early when there was a knock at the door. Devyani had risen to open the door. It was Romi with a tray and three cups of tea.

"Oh, my God!"

I had comfortably settled myself on the bed with two pillows at the back.

"Good morning, I disturbed you." She was all smiling, in the wide eyes, I had observed spots of moroseness, "I thought, I should..."

"It is our duty to bail you out."

"No Devyani, they have gone out for a stroll and children are asleep, I thought I should spend a few minutes with you."

I had gone to brush my teeth hurriedly.

After five minutes, I had...had my first sip, "You are so...she always looked after me...but today...has he come?"

"No. He shall be coming today...late night call from him."

"Thank God. Does he know it is the marriage of his son?"

"Yes, he knows." There was an uproarious laughter.

Both had observed that Romi was mentally upset and physically exhausted.

"Romi, we feel cut off..." Devyani had tried to sympathise, "Yes, totally distraught and distressed when it is clear that our ideas are not taken care of or are stealthily ignored. But it is inevitable. Perhaps we also did the same. It is the age. Times are such as do not afford us sufficient scope to relax. I think we are at fault."

"At fault?"

"Yes, possibly we do not understand our compulsions, may be unknown frontiers. I have stopped forcing these points of view. Why should we? You expect and find a purposelessness."

"I am alone in these palatial structures."

I had been marking her words.

"I want to involve myself in various social activities yet the anguish within continues to remind me of the futility and inanity. Mom is happy, but she too...feels a kind of dichotomy. Somewhere. Whenever I feel perturbed, she takes me into her arms and assures."

"Mom is a sophisticated and graceful lady..." I had also participated many a time in their talks, "I understand them and know them closely."

"How do you stay..."

"It is simple. But I cannot tell you, how it happened. It is spontaneous and undemanding."

"Here, I had been...you know Bhai Sahib, I dont't know, what do they want? It is abrupt now. Earlier, there was a slow going away. I thought, it was pressure of time, work and colleagues. Jaycee had been apparently compassionate and obliging, then preoccupations with official functions started multiplying. His engagements mounted. I soon detected changes in his schedule. He began to skip his lunches on many occasions, then dinners. Earlier it was once or twice a week, then the frequency increased. In those years, yes, it was in the early seventies that his routine assumed complexity. We all thought, being a responsible and important man Jaycee was wanted by all alike. And in private and official circles, his eminent position became strong. At home, he started getting frequent and odd hour phone calls from senior bureaucrats and Cabinet ministers. Even the Chief Minister from the home state sought him too often, and I really felt proud of him. The most sought-after man he was."

She had poured tea in our cups from the silver kettle. It appeared to us that she had been collecting herself. None spoke for a few minutes.

"I think, it is not his failing. Under strains of work a man is exhausted and you know, in a democratic set-up a government servant cannot be funny. He has to work so that the Govt. is strong, progressive and has a socialist inclination."

I had been pacifying her in my own way though I was convinced within that it was in vain.

"Bhai Saab, you are smart. You have been watching him closely and now..."

Her sharp tongue had warned me against a baseless defence line.

"No, I understand these "Babus" in a democracy, as you said, bureaucrats are a necessary evil, a hangover of the English Rule."

"That was not my point."

She had said without a second thought.

"He is a diligent officer."

"Yes, that is why he is occupied in drafting agreements. Political and economic notings. Memorandum and then..."

She had given a hearty laughter.

"Romi Madam, you should believe him."

"Yes, I believe everyone. I should. Why not? He is a true Indian. You know it was the year...I would not say. He is your friend and you must defend him."

"No that is not the question. What is the use of bemoaning? Do you think any purpose will be served?"

"Yes, if truth comes out."

She had opened the window and was beholding those beds of laughing flowers. Lost was the hearing and whispering of breeze and the musical chirping of birds and butterflies.

"He is surviving on the strength of truth."

"No, Bhai Sahib."

Romi had rejected the facile argument.

"We have to accept him."

"That is the only alternative left with me. Perhaps I am condemned to live a lonely existence. Devyani, I want to share my sentiments...anyway...one should not...at certain moments, I feel, he'll need me...but look at Vicky, Ashey and Rahul. They had been...today, they feel monstrously independent. Vicky told me once that dad was so cool and indifferent. Everything we have but where is the fatherly hand? Mom, we shall live and tell you we are learning to live alone...it is a lonely existence. At that time Ashey had said dryly, "Mummy, daddy has no time. I can see in your eyes a wanting...Devyani, she had trembled and at that moment Rahul who was always considered a sympathetic individual had said, "Mamma, I hear so many things. Dad is...he does not require us. He says he has given us money, hefty bank balance, buildings, benami deals. What is the use? You ask us and when...?"

I had been stupefied and struck hard somewhere inside.

She had now been sipping tea without a word. "The judgement of two sons and a daughter had totally rendered me helpless, alone and dejected."

After a gap of some minutes she had added. A full song of a Hindi film had filled our silent moments. I was lookig at a forlorn woman who had everything sans peace of mind. We had spent about one hour, sharing her emotional turmoil. It was painfully clear to us that our sympathies had been of very little use. With downcast eyes we had decided to run away yet were unable to make an exit.

*** *** ***

22

Time was running out for us. The two women had been deeply involved in their own affairs that they had no concern for the outside world. I had been without interruption hearing them but now I was trying to concentrate on the newspaper. At times they thought they were responsible for the present mental disturbance. Then a thought would run that they were worried over non-issues. It was a persistent and deliberate search for peace, harmony and love.

"What did I achieve?"

Romi's question had not been attended to.

"You have lost nothing."

Devyani's words would echo and then everything was quiet and lost in oblivion.

In the meantime, Ashey and Rahul had come, enquired and disappeared. Vicky and our sons probably had gone to Birla Mandir for an urgent piece of work.

"They are dry."

"It is not their fault. I think, it is happening everywhere. If no proper attention is given, these young men and women want to have their own way. A genuine wish to feel free."

I had thought not to add confusion to a disturbed state of mind.

"Yes, may be right." Romi had said in a resigned spirit, "I think there had been glaring shortcoming somewhere otherwise it would have been entirely different."

In fact, I had been averse to all their depressing talks. These two women had been seriously concerned with family affairs and there was nothing else they could dream of.

"We will break up."

"Nobody will be able to save us."

It seemed both had agreed. In the ensuing dead silence, I was unintentionally shuffling through the newspapers when Jai Bhadra and Rajshri had made an entry. After exchanging formal greetings, they had ensconced in front of us and with bright faces and sweet words apprised us of the happening outside.

"Dev, did you tell something?"

"No, Romi is unreasonably panicky." She had been reluctant to commit frankly.

"Yes, that is what I say. You know, look at the old woman...I am fully busy. I keep fit by running from one place to another. Always forgetting my worries in the service of the poor people. That is the rub. I enjoy. Romi too is engaged in all these welfare deeds. Now, you know, time is changing. Many strains. In the present crowded and rash environs, a man finds himself completely done-up and purposeless. He takes care of moorings but fails. Why bother? We have to live with the times. I think in the years to come relations shall undergo shocking changes."

Rajshri had then directed her words to Romi, "Our friends are there...I think they are more keen to offer prayers and meditation."

"They shall be taken care of."

Jai Bhadra had taken out his pipe, "Now you are not the only person. The world is moving like that."

"Papa, you know me."

"Darling Romi, we come here because it is you. We are to meet children. When they were little ones...yes, it was a pleasure to play with them."

"Raji had not deeply realised. I too felt that to be among your dear ones has an advantage. Vicky...Ashey...Rahul and your kids I mean all of them. It is intensely warming. You know when you speak of relations, however unimportant these may be, these involve feelings of togetherness and unity. It is not a dodgy love and warmth. No, it cannot be. There is not only anger, hate, jealousy and condemnation but love and intensity of emotions also. All these feelings move in a circle. It is an experience beyond words and language. I can easily guess the emotional turmoil going on in the mind of Romi. She has been sensitive to outside surroundings. I say, don't care. Just gather up yourself and keep fit. We are living in a highly calculating society. Here we do not go by scruples but by expediency."

He had exploded into a resounding laughter, "Now, these old men have earned a cup of coffee."

Romi had pressed the bell and gone up to the main door to order coffee.

"Romi, your sufferings are your creations. Look at Raji, when she found Jayanta is occupied, she diverted her attention to social work and she was reconciled and for that matter, we too continued to live in a tranquil and even frame of mind without a slight pay-back in terms of love and affection. I know, how dexterous Jaycee is. I am an old man and my nature of functions is not demanding provided I am not attached. In old age, I mean above sixty, a man should find happiness within. Yes, now we find there is an inexhaustible fountain of joy and divine bliss. The miseries start when you are surrounded by ego and self-interest. You know, I don't spare anyone. I understand what goes on and for that matter nothing remains a secret. All your friends are practical and ruthless.

"I know. You too had a chance to become rich but you paid a deaf ear. That was good. I did comment but never forced. I left the decision to you. Now that you were never caught in the web it is for the better. I tell you and you too, Romi and Devyani...there is nothing radically wrong. You are absolutely upright and correct. You give credence and repose confidence in man's nature. When we start moving out of the emotional arena we come across a kind of barrenness. I don't say one should not move but then...one should also plan to come back. Jaycee is involved without knowing the gravity. His friends are no exceptions. And those leaders, to whom they are obliged for the present status, they don't mind even mortgaging their souls. I don't believe these leaders have any...compunction. All those lofty words of national and social service are nonsensical. It is their self-interest. A well designed and planned scheme to perpetuate their sick minds and bodies...I think Romi when she asked me to do whatever I wanted but without any hope or reward."

"And from that day, I have been feeling internal..."

The servant had brought coffee.

"Shall we go to Vijaya's room?"

And we had to obey.

I did not know the reasons of my staying over. There were endless discussions. Bhadra and my father had remained closeted throughout the day. Smoking, strolling, taking tea or coffee or playing with small children. The trees around were tall, wide and ancient. In these two big bungalows, grandchildren and great-grandchildren played and chattered without a stop.

*** *** ***

It was only in the afternoon that invitees had begun to land up in groups. There was an animated and noisy hustle and bustle. I still remember the huge and unmanageable crowd.

"Hey uncle, how are you?"
That was the brief meeting. I had with Vicky.
"Fine my son. How is your business!"
"It is superb."
And he had given a summary of his business operations. I had found him highly practical and earthly. There was nothing that could have thrown a hint that he was even remotely respectful towards emotions.
"You are flying to..."
"Yes, uncle what to do in India? Nothing worthwhile to achieve. The atmosphere here is contaminated and polluted. It is because of immature and ever changing political thought. Yes, indefinite because politicians blow hot and cold at the same time. Economic policies do not give lasting support to commercial ventures. Here nothing is really firm. I find individuals bending policies of national interest to their advantage. It is the nation that suffers."
"Vicky, you are so..."
"You have not asked Rahul, he is far ahead so far as business is concerned and your..."
I had been unnerved by the strong words.
"You have to care for the old men, I mean now I am growing old and your father too. I know Jayanta, you should be here and not in a foreign country. I tell you, Jai Bhadra and Raji Mom, these old men only pray for you. You must get their blessings."
He had not said a word but I had witnessed expressions disapproving indirectly my suggestions.
"When you are stuck up, you don't grow." Vicky had given a frank opinion, "Our father has given us all that he wanted. We had no difficulty. It was a life of glitters. He had never asked us what we spent, how much we squandered and why? It was money in abundance. Though our mother did ask questions as usual. On the other hand, our grandma is a powerful woman. She also enters into the how and why of affairs and that makes many things uneasy and irritating for us."
"How! She is so generous."
"Yes, elderly people are, I agree, kind and loving."
Vicky had tried to dispel my doubts in an ironic reaction.
"Can't you look into the affairs without running away?"
"No. She is also a specialist in designing and fashion. Now we want to establish an international agency. In the world of computer and fashion, we want to be trend-setter without insulting the finer sensibilities."

He had started indulging in nuances, music and rhapsody of the moment. I had found him passive to emotions.

"If you go abroad, there people will feel...you are the..."

"Uncle, I agree. It is a different story with your..." He wanted to name my sons and daughters. But then perhaps to avoid he had decided to change the thrust of talks.

"Nursing relations enriches men."

"Uncle, I have the best of drinks and choicest wines. Rahul will serve you."

"You don't bother, we shall look after ourselves." His audacity and impudence had shocked me.

I had in a split second recollected childhood days of the kids.

"I didn't mean..."

"Jaycee and Romi have hopes. Those old waiting eyes pray and bless." I wanted to remain inexplicit.

"Uncle, modern education and liberal-minded society. We are ever grateful to parents for giving us the best of opportunities. But the living trends of modern times are different. In an age of cut-throat competition no time to show mercy. You cannot tarry a second or else you shall perish. That is the crux. I don't want to be caught unawares. Uncle, I understand..."

"Vicky, I think you are to keep the flame of family traditions burning. We can discuss all these things..."

"Sure, uncle I want but tell me uncle you are family's close friend..." He was standing still with numerous questions which had alerted me for a minute, "Three of them have come. He has not returned from Calcutta. I don't know if he shall come even today."

Vicky was sad now and his voice had shown signs of disappointment and facial expressions exhibited deep helplessness. If had really hurt me.

"He is one of the finest officers. Rarest and the most wanted. He is brilliant and you should be proud of Jaycee. In most of the policies, whether economic, political or foreign, his stamp is apparent. His shrewdness is unparallel. Your state chief runs the state with his consent and counselling."

"I know."

Vicky's voice was low and without enthusiasm.

"You are...? Where is he? Should I talk to Patel or Mukherjee? They must be knowing."

"No, no use. If my father is to come, he'll be here. If he is devising a strategy, nothing can bring him back. I know my father. Seventy or seventy-five birth days or even more such like occasions have been celebrated without our dad. I may be harsh but the game of numbers weighs heavily against him."

"There must be reasons."

"..." Vicky had peeped into my eyes. "Yes, he had been engaged too much. No, it was indulgence. He was to do so much that he had very little time for us and I think we too have exhausted our time."

He had pulled up his nose and walked out in desperation.

*** *** ***

23

Jaycee had been suffering from work mania. Hard-pressed and besieged so immensely that he had no time for any other member of the family. The oft-repeated points of discord continued to be drummed up. I had been quite conscious of the simmering discontent. When the children were in the schools, they devoted much time to studies and playing. And of course, his parents and Romi visited them and made them feel great and secure. But when they had settled down in Delhi after the completion of school education, they noted rather violently the absence of their father and the disgusting engagements he was involved in.

The world was unintendedly opening up as it happens. The realism and the romance had come up with all the brightness and at times showed the ugly side. The seamy scenario had discouraged them but the youthful spirits had kept the enthusiasm alive. With fabulous richness around, they had no scarcity. It was a world of plenty and pelf. There was fulfilment and an atmosphere of total abandon. Simultaneously, they underlined the absence of their father. Too many phone-calls at the residence bewildered them.

Numerous files at home, shuffling and burning of papers, dictation and frequent rather disturbing visits of private secretaries and women subordinates. It was an untiring period of drafting and re-drafting. Those were days of closed door meetings. And slowly the venues shifted to unknown places. Now the evenings were spent outside with notice and sometimes even without informing. At dinner time they would watch T.V. or listen to songs or absent-mindedly concentrate on studies though they knew it was a futile exercise. Romi was the only consoling factor. She was a world for them. Her warm and cozy arms, a sweet kiss, a loving pat and an unexpected embrace would assure them of a comfortable and secure life. Romi had her world in their eyes, smiling faces and wordy duels of her children. Then Raji and Jai Bhadra made regular visits, stayed and played.

I had been a silent and non-commenting spectator of the growing age and maturing minds. It was during those days I had nearly full or I can claim total knowledge of Jayanta and his affairs and the complex and mysterious world of human behaviour had without a voice begun to spread out its magical curtain.

Jaycee had mostly met me in the office. Whenever I had gone he would not be found. My wife along with children paid regular visits. Romi and her children made it a point to stay with us or sometimes I had spent a night in a hotel. It was an innocuous behaviour and we had recognised each other's areas of freedom and limitations. And finally when he had decided to stay in Delhi, we would visit them at least once a year. We also visited all of them dividing our time meticulously. We did stay in hotels when we thought it would make us convenient.

And during those years I had found out the change in Jaycee's attitude. The idealism and morality were the words which found least acceptance. It was with the age. The system in which Jaycee was operating had been woefully contaminated. He had often recalled with a remorseful heart.

It was not that he spared little time for his close relations and friends. He did. I was taken to a hotel whenever he had no time or wanted to share secretly his mental and intellectual predicaments. I do realise now that he was relentlessly struggling within but all in vain.

"You know, it is a world you cannot fight. I have found my colleagues suffering. If you don't submit, the vicious caucus, the deadly liaison between bureaucrats, businessmen and politicians makes you wreathe with excruciating pain. I had undergone the pains of such moments. My lineage did not help me. It was a threat. It is also a misfortune to have pretty, graceful and attractive wives. It is the world where..." That evening we were sitting at Oberoy. He had drunk heavily.

"It is a beautiful world when you accept it. When you are strong you are wise and pure also."

I had been listening to such words off and on whenever I had met him.

"But still these are people..."

It was fruitless to argue. The world of richness, enjoyment and money making was very much dominating and vast. Jaycee had been expanding his areas of influence. I had been watching him. There was a regular expansion. Jaycee, Ratnam, Raghunathan, all, I had found all of them tough in official matters. They were rapacious and ruthless too. It was an unending journey to the land of pleasures and principles, a daily death and birth. It was revival of values which had no substance for them.

I would often analyse and face defeat.

*** *** ***

"Yes, I was astonished." These were the words which I could speak to express my disgust and despair. Whenever I visited them they showed indifference to Jaycee.

"Uncle, he is indispensable. Very important. When at home it is the phone. Bundle of papers and files. We take pity on him. He has immense responsibilities. So many dependent on him. We cannot pressurise him. He gets irritated. You know, uncle, you are a businessman, don't you know the ways of government? Many decisions take shape during luxurious dinners and those drinking bouts and...rest is all a formality."

And Vicky had given hints of how Jayanta was spending his evenings in the posh hotels. Those frequent seminars, conferences, meetings and negotiations were nothing but waste of energy and time. Vicky would say rather agitatingly. At that time I had thought he was inexperienced and immature.

But, perhaps I was wrong. He had given observations of a man of the world and maturity. Without falling into the trap of inconclusive dialogue, I had thrown a congenial smile and patted him.

"You should not think. Affairs of the Govt. are guided by..."

"Uncle, I am a man of commerce. I go into the details of each and every thing. In human affairs sentiments matter when it is a question of..." He had laughed rather shyly and said, "No, uncle, I will not say. It would constitute discourtesy. But I tell you I have a different attitude. I like mamma's social work. Yes, I like her discourse on...she is not only my mother but my teacher also. I know her eyes. She always speaks silently. Uncle, I have seen her vacant eyes on the dining table and the breakfast time...her eyes give sidelong glances at a seat...she does not say but she feels the absence. When grandpa comes, he occupies the chair, yet she misses...it is the absence of a man."

Vicky had forgotten that he was to attend to some other important engagements and I, on the other hand, had been looking into his eyes.

The hidden anger and an extreme sense of revolt? But his lips had been marvellously shining with smiles.

"I can't do anything. Mamma's lips tremble but the words do not come out. She keeps laughing. Her sweet and soft words continuously ring in our ears yet the pain and agony also give me cause to worry. I simply can't..."

"You are talking about her or..."

"Possibly all of us feel."

And he had gone out. There was a dreadful dumbness. I had seen the total emptiness.

It was a day of celebration as also of illusions and despair. Romi had been restless, uncomfortable. At moments, we saw a layer of water appearing in her eyes.

"They are living in their own world of satisfaction. It is with all of them. Have you seen...those eyes...hundreds of eyes? Squinting. Wide open. Small. Big and moving without purpose. I have heard their words. High-flown and loud. The fragrance...should I call it fragrance or the smell...talcum? You know...look around...that jostling and whistling. It is intentional and with purpose. But their..."

Devyani had stood before me and in broken words conveyed her assessment.

"Where is Romi?"

"She is with the Pandits. I think religious ceremonies are in progress."

"Oh, I see. Vicky was depressed and pensive but outwardly kept up a brave face.

"Yes, that is what I am finding around. Even papa and mamma are concerned about."

I had said, "Yes, Jaycee should have been here."

"What could be the reasons?"

"A tough and sensitive work has been assigned to him." I had said in a nonchalant voice, "That is what they tell me."

"Yes, your friend is always..."

That was the end of the conversation. We had been moving among the guests.

Devyani had commented in a serious tone, "They are rootless, I suppose."

I had penetrated deep into her eyes.

"Romi's agony is unbearable. This enormous wealth. Fat bank balance, name and fame?"
"Did she tell you about Jaycee?"
"No."
Jaycee had not reached on time.

*** *** ***

24

It was next morning when the marriage party had come back. It was at that time that Jaycee had returned from Calcutta and in an unusual informal manner regretted and apologised. Malkhan Dave and Jacob were with him and they had not for a second hesitated praising him. They were in fact justifying Jaycee's unwanted prolonged absence.

His children had not shown displeasure. It was only Romi, who had said, "Mr. Jaycee, you are playing a dangerous game. I am exhausted. Totally tired. Look into these eyes and wrinkles."

She had mingled with the guests and was entertaining them. We had settled ourselves in one of the corners on a white sofa in front of a small bar. There were drinks, dances and music. I had been drinking my favourite brand of dry gin with lime cordial. Devyani was sitting beside me. Exactly at that moment Jaycee had appeared before us, laughing and laughing excitedly. There was no trace of regret on his face. He was stretching across and chattering as if nothing had happened.

I had also observed that he had taken drinks quite oblivious of his condition. His intoxication was apparent in his steps and his trembling voice made it clear to us that he had consumed too much.

"Yaar Vicky..." He had addressed his son, "I am sorry, my son. But today, I am a proud father."

Vicky had mixed up with the guests exchanging greetings and I had observed in the small balcony on the second storey Romi standing with the new bride. There was terrific noise all over.

"Jaycee, should it happen?"

"What...?"

"Vicky was unhappy. At least on those days you should have been here."

"Yaar, you too are sick. What is the problem? We should not suffer from any hunch. Look all are enjoying themselves. They are dancing, singing...and have gone to the hall where dinner is being served."

I had been looking at my empty glass. He had come forward and called out.

There was another large peg in my hands, "It was Jai Bhadra's and Mom Raji's desire. You know, they still carry those ancestral remnants with them. The majestic exhibition. The grand celebrations. What else do you need?"

"Madam Devyani, these women are excessively possessive and domineering. I told Romi many a time that she should change herself. Now that she is involved in social work...these extra welfare activities provide you a launching pad to..."

He had been talking of politics and democracy, "I want her to join politics. She has already made a sound ground. With this wealth, don't count on social service, it should be translated to actual benefits. This is happening. All these politicians are doing it. I am not an exception. It is also a tradition. Those who wield power are men of little virtues. They are also perfect saints, full of evils and piety with modern sense of adjustment and compromise. It is a simple equation. I am living. I have known the other face of virtues. I am not worried about the infamous and the scandalous."

His voice had been astoundingly balanced. I had been dumbstruck by the amazing choice of words he was making.

"Romi is hostile, I know."

"You have other duties as a father and..." I had whispered unwantingly. "Jaycee, you have not behaved in a responsible manner. The first big occasions and you..."

"..." He had not answered but gone to the other side.

Ramanathan and Swamy Ratnam were now closeted with Jaycee. Asif Khan, Patel and Raghunathan were vociferously discussing the role of opposition parties and declaring them as irresponsible and unscrupulous. "Oh, Mr. Jaycee's friend..."

I had stood up with a bow. They had paid their respects to my wife.

"Yes, a new wave of militancy and terrorism...this country can progress in a spell of discipline. There is shameful anarchy and violence among...you know when you work, you contribute. It is peace when there is growth."

"We should think of the country."

Devyani had with Ashey and Patel's wife gone upstairs.

"Where are..."

"Ministers and others are in the adjacent bungalow. They have some time to discuss problems of the states. There is a political uncertainty in many states..." Asif had said, "People are becoming violent."

"Yes, they are made so." Rajput had commented, "If a common man is violent, I think you...we...are responsible."

Pandit and Yadav were in the centre of the hall engaged in a lively discussion with petty politicians and other well-known citizens. And there the old men Vijaya Chand and Jai Bhadra were rubbing shoulders with pipes in their mouths and the old ladies were in amiable disposition. They were the centre of attraction.

"We have to take care of people like Soma Gandhi, Dawra, Sonali, Malkhan Dave and..."

It was Mahapatra, who had joined us.

"These businessmen and social workers..." Perhaps Patel was unable to contribute to different strands of his thought process.

"Yaar, we should take care of criminal minds?"

It was a dangerous statement.

"We may not give rise to doubts in...our conduct is subject to intense scrutiny." Harry Singh had commented in a dreary tone.

At that time Rajput had added, "Sir, you will not retire. This nation needs you. Even after fifty-eight you shall...and then our Jaycee...will be an expert on economic and foreign affairs."

"What do you suggest?" Ratnam was suppressing his rancour and displeasure, "Rajput, I must tell you, things move only when there is a will."

"I know." Rajput had come closer to him, "You people are...I am proud of you. Docile and humble. You must praise what is happening? People like me are irrelevant."

"Rajput, you have been harsh."

"I know what has gone wrong with you? Nothing is hidden from me. I am a mute spectator."

"What do you want to proclaim."

"You are a rich man."

He had without arguing further left the scene.

"He has always been a hot-headed man."

"But never untrue." Pandit had remarked, "Actually we need such babus."

He was meaningfully looking at Asif Khan and Patel.

"Pandit, we honour your words but what did you get?"

"Nothing. I can never boast of any achievement. A babu, however big he may be, cannot live lavishly in case he is to survive on his own income."

"..."

"I like Yadav because he hides nothing, I remember all these... Mohan Khanna, Sadhvi Sonali, Soma Gandhi, Dawra, Samanta. I know the subtle methods they employ to protect their positions."

Pandit had been emotional, "But tell me, Ratnam, are you happy? Have you forgotten old days? You succumbed to pressures of pleasure and...it is simply ridiculous when one sees around the orgy in drunkenness. Disgusting, I tell you. I know, you find real happiness in hotels. No it is carnal pleasures. What do you get in the end? Nothing. And your wife and kids? Have you thought of them?"

There was no immediate reaction.

Pandit had been, I had observed, inciting and provoking them and I feared somewhere that an unpleasant scene will spoil the show.

I had put my arms on his shoulder. He had not touched me, "Panditji, you are forsaken and angry."

"Jaycee's son...it is a marriage. You know, he had come to us and today we found out, he was still to..."

"He has been considerate, I know."

"You know nothing. All of them. They have contacts with big and powerful people. They call these contacts relations. Blatant hypocrisy. And then they wanted to mould us."

"You are levelling false allegations!"

Ramanathan had said.

"Rama, Pandit...I...this Pandit, I know him."

"Jaycee, you have been scathingly indifferent." I had said when Jaycee with a glass in hand stood in front of me.

"Those who are mindful of emotions, ultimately fail. I am not averse to any new thought. But I cannot prolong. It is not a negative attitude but a practical approach. I had been a tireless worker, obeying seniors. No questions. You talk of conscience. What conscience? My virtue is in complete submission. I remain indefatigable. I have never been insincere to anyone."

"Jaycee, nobody doubts you."

"Vicky...Romi I know all of them. They have been always cold and passionless feeling the absence. You are the centre of their lives. They want you with them. They miss you throughout. Look deep into their eyes. See the thin layer of moisture. Those tears which now stand frozen are reminders of their long unproductive wait. You are mortgaging their happiness for all the pleasures."

Jaycee had placed his glass on the tray a waiter was holding and had taken another.

Taking a small hesitant sip, he had said, "You are right." There was sincerity in the voice, perhaps full of anguish.

"Jaycee, you have been callous."

"No, I have been living in my own way."

"You should devote time to them."

"I shall keep note of your words."

"Jaycee!"

He was fixing up his eyes on the glass as if in deep deliberation. He looked at me and then gave a soft laugh, "All of us...with a few exceptions have gone too far. We are down-to-earth."

I had kept quiet.

"Come." Without having concern for others he had dragged me, "Come, I shall introduce you to ..."

Beyond the glass-wall, he had made me settle down among Madhav Wadia, Malkhan, Jacob and such like prominent people. There were Soma Gandhi, Sonali, Samanta, Asif Khan, Patel, Mahapatra and Mukherjee. I had been simply aghast. I had seen beyond the wall. It was a noisy scene. Three-four ministers and their cronies with moistened lips and hungry looks were pouncing upon plates and bottles.

"They run the show."

Jaycee had been emphatic.

"..." With folded hands all were greeting one another without wanting. It was an unwilling expression of courtesy.

"I know, he is a difficult businessman." Someone had commented.

"Here, we have contacts. Purely functional relations."

"Relations?"

My voice had not risen. It was becoming impossible for me even to listen to my own words but Jaycee had no problem in understanding me.

"Why worry? We cannot stop here. Another relation has been added to the family. It happens. Nothing new."

"You should think of them."

"Think of whom? They are concerned about me." Jaycee had thrown his curious glance at them, "They are the generals. I am their leader. It is an understanding of mental faith."

All of them had roared and ogled.

I had been feeling uncomfortable in the company. For a minute or so, I saw darkness enveloping me. A state of delirium seemed sweeping over me. They were too big for me. Dominating and dangerously calculative.

"Hey, what man? You are stunned?"

"No. It is a state of mental imbalance and neurosis, I think."

"He has not anything in life." It was Madhav Wadia who had directed wordy arrows at me.

"Mr. Wadia, I am not an ambitious man. I am simple and not very rich yet I am satisfied."

"What do you want?"

"Nothing. I favour clean dealings."

"You think, we who are gathered here, are..."

"I have nothing to say."

"You want to embarrass us."

"I would like to take leave of you."

"We don't want to hurt your feelings. However, you should know, in a world of economic activity, we have to take care of..."

"I know."

"People like Vijaya Chand and Jai Bhadra, Raji, Romi and Devyani are not many and they are hardly listened to."

"They are warm and understanding, soulful and conscious. It is enriching and meaningful to live in their company."

They had looked at him with grim faces. Before going out I had stood in a defiant mood, "You are not happy. You say, you are happy but the glass walls and the drinks, the dance and goings-on are not your glory but indicate a furious end. I shall call you back Jaycee. They say, in Delhi, it is the masters. I feel all of them are slaves. You are...I am sorry...you are alone. Nobody is there to console you."

"You are teaching us."

"No, I am warning myself for I don't want to live in isolation like you."

"We cannot help you."

Madhav Wadia had given a sinister laugh.

'Wadia Saab you are insulting me."

"No, you have not understood us rightly."

"I know all of you. Wadia, Malkhan, Dawra and..."

"Cool down."

"Let us take our dinner."

We had come out.

I had observed latent bitterness and enmity taking roots somewhere in the inner recesses of our hearts. That was a horrible moment of my life. Before the end of celebrations, I had not been able to meet Jaycee. I had, of course, long and serious talk with Jai Bhadra, Rajshri, Vijaya Chand and Romi. Devyani too had participated in the discussions. Jaycee could never get sufficient time to sit with us.

On the fourth day, we had decided to return home. Perhaps, Jaycee had felt some kind of inner pain. He must have been repentant because of his behaviour. Before we were to get into the car, Jaycee had come to give us a send-off.

It was a casual, cold and formal send-off. I did not have the feeling at that time that those moments would prove fatal. I had felt as if I had been wounded.

"Could you spare some time when coming to..."
"Really, but you are busy."
"I have to speak to you."
"Jaycee, it would be far better if you could talk to Romi and kids."
"I know what you wish to..."
"I think you had too much of richness. It is playing havoc with all of us. A strange cankerous growth in relations shall be suicidal. I think we have lost our future."
"Nothing. We shall recover. It is your unfounded surmise. It is a world, we have made it and we are to live."

He had assured us with renewed love and warmth.

*** *** ***

25

Many years had passed without a whisper, it appeared. There were no questions. I often visited Delhi in connection with my business operations. I did not know what had come about among us but there were growing signs of bitterness. Vicky's marriage had left many scars and emotional setbacks. I had experienced on that day that in spite of having intimate and warm relations with Jaycee and others, those eminent persons possessed a sniffing nose. Their urbanity was untampered and the often quoted words of sympathies and equality were empty of meaning. I had realised that when it hit them severally they could wipe you out irrespective of the weapons.

A man of substance he was, Jaycee often called and declared himself, a person on whom depended many important matters. He was always vocal and specific. Persons, policies and plans took birth in his mind. Those were the years of progress. I had seen him growing with the fast changing concepts of governance. He could read the gravity of coming events in the velocity of air. He had the knack to understand people. Those days were full of sincere declarations. I had felt hurt on the occasion of Vicky's marriage. After five days, he had contacted me at Shimla, "Yaar, I don't know, something terrible is happening and I don't understand. It is a sense of madness."

I had not said anything.

"You come. Romi...all of them, they are behaving as if I were an unknown person. This never happened earlier."

I had tried to pacify him. It was after two years when there was an atmosphere of comparative peace around but we were yet to come out of the irreparable loss we had suffered after the death of the Iron Lady. Her own bodyguards were behind the conspiracy and death. It was not only shocking but also dreadfully disgusting. Yes, during those two years I had not intentionally met Jaycee.

I was recollecting each detail of those days when wintry cold winds had started blowing.

Today, I was sitting near the window of his palatial bungalow. Jaycee had attained a position of unrivalled stature, earned an immense amount and now on the verge of retirement was expecting a rewarding posting.

It was an absolute silence. There was no noise in that hill station of the state. It appeared to me as if two shadows were lengthening out and physically marking my presence. I had been aware of the surroundings.

It was Suraiya who had come back again and virtually dragged Jaycee, and he like a little complaining and unwilling child had followed her. I was still gauging the unparallel strength of her eyes, wet moving lips and the softly confident words. She had cast a magic-shadow on him, it was evidently clear. I was at a loss to know what exactly was happening to me. It was the first long and intimate meeting in a period of twelve years. When in eighty-four, during winter I had gone to Delhi, he had said, "I am finished. This unmeasured power and authority...these do not provide happiness, an iota of joy...nothing."

I had not been able to sleep comfortably. Jaycee had been silent and lonely, that had truly infused deep mental anguish. I had emerged out, strolled about in the finely kept grassy ground. It was after hours that I had thought of my precarious intellectual indecision and returned as a tired man.

It was at seven in the morning that there was a gentle knock. Zeera stood before me, "Sir, tea."

He had gone back. I wanted to ask a few questions yet held back my temptations. After half an hour, I had again felt a desire to have tea...it was not strange. I got up, and after brushing, refreshing and washings went leisurely to the kitchen.

Zeera was cleansing the kitchen.

"Saab!"

"A cup of tea!"

"Where is Jaycee and...?"

"They will get up at eight."

I came back to my room. After five minutes, Zeera turned up with a cup of tea when I was playing with a pack of cigarettes.

"Zeera!"

"Saab!" He had opened the window.

"Saab, your eyes...I know you drank, those butt-ends...half-burnt matches and ashtray full of..."

"Yes, Jaycee Saab and I sat for a long time."

"Saab, he is..., take him to Delhi..." Zeera had offered an opinion for which I was not prepared. It was sudden and from an unexpected quarters but there was hidden a truth about vacuity of man.

It was not a fleeting viewpoint. A small-time servant could give vent to thoughts was an indication of a chronic disease which would be mental and physical taking away happiness of my old friend who had always been a man of substance. My subsequent reactions were restricted and under utmost restraint.

I had clearly visualized that tacit and unobtrusive transformation taking shape during all those years but never for a single day expressed my feelings of vexation.

"How happened? What about them?"

"He was in Delhi. Routine wanderings. No time for home. Vicky...they say has left for ever. He is in some other country. Ashey...a daughter."

"Yes..."

"All of them went on their way. Very bad and angry those little kids were. You saab. Romi mem was there. When I come she looks poor and disappointed. Today also living in memories...and saab father and mother...lived and died."

I could see enormous pool of water in his eyes.

Zeera had tried to connect the loose strands without denigrating anyone. No aspersion on anyone. He was bearing melancholic looks and was visibly upset.

"Where do you live?"

"I am man of the hills. Those very rocky and high."

"Where is Memsaab?"

"She does not come."

"Why?"

"Saab...comes late and reads files. They say."

"Who is that girl."

"Good woman. She comes here. Kuchh khusi deti. Bahut Achha (She gives some happiness. It is very good.).

His eyes had brightened up. I had not asked anything more. Perhaps it was not proper. With a cup in hand I had lit a cigarette. I was thinking of the old age which was very near. I think it was there! How could an old man live alone? Many questions had crowded the mind. It was an eternal quest without the ultimate. Was it that all were living in an unreliable and delusory world. I had felt many needles piercing my body from all sides. I was drearily reminded of the dust and files. There had been a metamorphosis in Jaycee. I had found him a sad and lonely man. A man who stood vanquished and profusely bleeding without a fight. A forlorn and dejected man who still exuberated joy and life. And then suddenly expressed unhappiness.

*** *** ***

I had never foreseen this sickly face. I had known the humiliation and rising convulsions in the eyes of Jaycee, a day before while he evaded direct questions about his family. Those were days of fierce race and dangerous relations. It was a tortuous journey from sixty. An age of development, unwanted but expanding. I had not been able to find solutions to many of my questions when Jaycee had entered my room.

He looked composed and relaxed. Those agonised tensions of last evening had vanished. His face was smooth and brilliant.

I was penetrating but failing in my accurate analysis. Jaycee was definitely a man of substance. I had put a constraint.

He ensconced himself in front of me.

"I have ordered coffee."

I placed the empty cup on the peg table.

"It was after many years I called you otherwise I knew, you would not have cared."

"..." I thought to keep mum. For, there was no use to dig up past and justify the present.

I knew the secret and unexplicable joy and satisfaction one has after a relation is resurrected and initiated into an emotional warmth. His emotionally surcharged words made me think and regret. I have been adamant and foolish. I was addressing myself.

I had pushed the cigarette pack towards him.

"It is ominous."

"..."

"I have decided to go back to Delhi. It is very small and narrow. I thought Shimla would provide mental peace. But here the originals are so shallow and hollow. A cultural drawback."

"It is a peaceful hill town."

"You are right." He had resigned himself to his present fate it looked, for, he remained puffing off incessantly.

He had come out with a contact question.

"What about your bungalow here?"

"I have rented out to Govt. No one wants to come. Yes, during summer we stay at Upper Dharamshala in Kangra. And sometimes we go to other beautiful places but not to Shimla."

"I think, you are also nourishing such thoughts."

"Nothing special. But it is inhabited by halftorn people. Naked and dirty. Roads crowded and busy. Water is dirty. Drains stinking with packed garbage. Polythene galore. No more freshness. At least, I don't find. Unplanned and haphazard growth. No trees. You know, here people are...perhaps no one thinks, in fact, there is no serious thinking. No vision. And then the politics." He had been examining with a curious eye.

"You are irascible and hot."

"No, not at all. But I am interested in a stationary life. My family loves Chandigarh. They do go to Delhi, but it is different with me and Devyani. After a considerable pondering, we think we should plan to spend the last few years of life...quite unknown and away."

"You are poetic and philosophic."

He had exploded into a faded laughter.

"I know...what is it that you are facing dilemmas?"

"No."

"You were with your children. Always chummy, warm and kindly."

"Yes."

"But now...your concern about bygone years or...you were never pessimistic. You had been loving and...".

"Yes, Jaycee, I have lived my time. Playing and singing. Now, I like when they come to me. We celebrate the occasions. When children come to us we feel extra energy, you know Devyani herself cooks for the children. She is very happy...she spends most of her time in the kitchen. When she is not in the kitchen, she is with the children jumping and playing children's game, dancing and telling stories. That reminds me of youth. At mornings and evenings, she is with her sons and daughters-in-law."

I was lost in my thoughts.

When there was no interruption, I felt, I have been disturbed.

"What happened?"

"I was burdening you with my..."

"No, I was listening. I thought, it was I who had been playing."

Jaycee threw a faint smile, "Devyani is great."

There was a quaint depth in his eyes.

Zeera placed two cups of coffee before us.

"Has Suraiya got up?"

"...No, I shall..."

Zeera disappeared.

"Where is Romi?"

I had re-opened the old subject. Perhaps, I tried to analyse the answer to the question and thought it could offer clues to the inner conflicts of Jaycee.

"In an Ashram. She operates from there. She does not come. She was more worried about social welfare programmes. That remarkable flow of genial and generous sympathies, gentle and assuring words, vigorous nature in helping out others, the unlimited warmth and exultation. I knew her intrinsic human compassion. I understood her sweetness."

"I am..."

"Romi is a woman of exalted virtues and ideals. I don't know what made me discourage her. She is a fountain of love. An intrepid crusader. I do not find appropriate words to describe her."

"Jaycee, I was asking you to..."

"It is my own destiny. This richness and frightening clout in the...I move with each and everybody who matters or matters not. It is all mixed up. I have observed and learnt many tricks. There has been change of policies and Govts. Politicians don't think beyond their nose. You level allegations and they acquire strength. She perhaps did not like liaison with them. But an officer is insignificant. No existence. You are killed. You face extinction. I have seen officers choking and suffocating. No respite. If they submit, they are on the top. I have seen paupers among bureaucrats becoming rich overnight and street urchins and goons, petty local toughs becoming powerful politicians and they run the affairs. This is the culture. I had to change. There was no escape. I knew the fatigue of work. I knew the sin.

"I knew what is conspired in those lavish dinners? The wordless submission and defiant postures. I was to save everyone. Yes, I am reminded of those charming times — the Chinese aggression, the collective national uprising and the patriotic fervour. I am an eager student who pledged and forgot. Who protected leaders of straightforward character and truth? I also have interaction with leaders of towering statures who are an embodiment of virtue, truth and a composite culture and also those who are hungry and...I know them who make history and who are murderers. I know babus of strong principles and moral strength. There are and were babus who thought of a nation and its people and are still worried. They knew the aspirations and sufferings of a growing and developing country."

"Jaycee, you are propounding a philosophy of..."

"I am approaching the present."

He was lost as if in the appendix of memories. I slowly crushed my cigarette in the ashtray out of visible peevishness and discomfort.

"You have misunderstood me."

"I am resigned to fate. I have become a fatalist. You see these white-clad roving...they all fall prey to these pandits and astrologers. Even the food they eat, clothes they wear and rituals they perform are all on the dictates of these pandits. In the hill station this disease is very strong. I am my own enemy."

He had started laughing in a loud and mischievous haughtiness. It was irritating but I was silent, for there was no escape. The room was filled with smoke. I had got up and opened the window.

"It is a clear day."

"Yes, these days are refreshing."

"Why did you want to..." I had turned back and asked a different question, "No office, I suppose."

"I shall be here."

"I would like to go to the Ashram."

"It is a six hours journey. Forget. I want to see, how long Romi can continue with this kind of life."

"Your kids?"

"Vicky left in eighty-five. In Los Angeles, he is running his business. A top man. Ashey has married a Muslim, a citizen of England now, so away to London. He is heading an advertising agency and publishes a widely circulated yellow magazine. Abdul Rehman is a lord in his own way. Interferes in Muslim affairs. A fanatic but liberal when in England. Rahul has settled in America. So I am alone."

He heaved a deep pensive sigh and fixed his wide eyes on the ceiling with an exquisite carving. After a while, he stretched his legs, yawned and looked at me, hiding his inner grief. In a second, he closed his lips, pressed them hard under white teeth, moved his tongue in the mouth in an apparent disgust and said, "It happens."

There was no need to intervene.

I knew he wanted to share his miseries and agonies with me and it was my duty to give a patient hearing.

"Madhav Wadia once commented." He opened his mouth and said, "I remember his words uttered with confidence. Jaycee, to show moral and social concern about life and people, is a fundamental duty of those who run the country. It is not my worry. But I too, as I am engaged in social welfare programmes, it becomes my bounden duty to conduct myself in a dignified manner. I am a rich man. When you expand horizons, you squeeze somewhere. You don't know the change which is there without voice. It is a religion of all those who are rich. However, it is also the moral duty of the wealthy and the famous to discharge their duties..."

"..."

"To society and the country..."

"It is a usual intellectual hypocrisy. The rich and the intelligent are cunning and clever and can impress innocent people. This is what we do, you do and so the social cycle revolves around."

Jayanta Chandra Chauhan was sitting confused and in complete helplessness. A fierce feeling of desolation was haunting him, I realised.

*** *** ***

26

I could observe for the first time those moments. Loneliness and vacuity born out of lost relations are more devastating and self-destructive.

"Yes Jaycee, what else did he want to say?"

"Madhav Wadia is a man of few words."

"Wadia is a good person. A noble soul. Knows the reality of life also. Always donating money, helping charitable institutions. Many hospitals, asylums and orphanages enjoy his patronage. He controls youth wings of different parties so that in case of change in Govt. he can have an easy sway over the ruling party. Then anti-social elements in almost all parties are on his pay-roll. To remain a social worker and a benefactor one has to keep lumpens and goondas to protect himself. That is the secret."

"Yes Wadia is a man who keeps a perfect image."

"Yes. I have also known the other side of his personality. Wadia is a saint, an imperturable man in crisis. He hits and demolishes yet restrains. He runs about and yet stands like a rock."

"I have heard so about him."

"I have to live with them. In a civilized society such strong men control the reins. They determine policies, plans and choose the masters."

"You are painting a dark picture. The scenario is not as dull as we make out. In a country of gods and goddesses, whose gods lived in human forms and more recently where gods walked in the form of Viveka and Gandhi and...could there be such a..."

I had given a valued and reserved opinion.

"You were not concerned about such aspects of life. The seamy side too is a reality."

"I know but it is certainly not dark or dreaded. You are justifying a wrong cause."

"..."

Jaycee was feeling a kind of uneasiness, "I think we should get up. Am I playing on your nerves? Are you interested in whatever I am trying to say about."

"Yes, I want to know what is going on in your mind."

"You are very considerate."

I had another cigarette.

"You smoke heavily!"

"No, Jaycee, I don't smoke much. It is only when I am with somebody that a queer feeling arises, a prickling temptation to enjoy and forget in the process so that I may reach heights or depth of your emotions."

He had felt embarrassed.

"I don't know whether I am exact or lacking...but the fact remains...?

"Where is Romi Madam?"

"Yes, she has left me. I don't know how to bring her back. My children have settled elsewhere. And they never write a word. It is their mother, who gets the news. I am cut off. Those big bungalows, multi-storeyed buildings, benami commercial interests and...bank balances...these are now redundant and waste. Rahul and Vicky refused to own anything and that darling Ashey finds happiness with a Muslim who has four wives. She is not more than a concubine yet still she prefers to stay with Rehman who is a man of dubious character. I live here in the halo of glory. Alone. In a capital of mafias."

Jaycee's heart seemed to be increasing each moment, "Jaycee, you were talking of Romi and suddenly Madhav Wadia attracted your attention. I am worried about you. I don't say that you did some mistakes. No, you were part of the world. I was part of the system."

"She was ever patient. I know, I could not devote time to them. However, it was the period to learn and earn. Everybody was busy in filling his coffers. You know, my mental frame. Those days, I thought to be an ideal officer. But nothing could be done. They were against me. It was only in name and words that concept of good life was propounded. We were rogues. Tigers. Creating our own Senas and Dals to propitiate our self-made gods."

"..."

"Today, look at my face. Wrinkles have started appearing. A baldness also scares me and then grey hair. This richness has been my worst enemy. Yes, it is killing me every moment. I don't know that after thirty-two years this would be my plight. Bureaucracy...this babudom is so wretched, impotent yet strident. I never knew. But I don't condemn anyone. Madhav, Jacob and Malkhan Dave are not three only. They are more than three lacs. They are dangerous people. They can kill you. It is an excitement in evil that fascinates now-a-days."

"They are inhuman, but you..."

"No, you cannot condemn anyone."

"Jaycee...?"

"Now Vicky does not write to me. His grandparents died in eighty-six...I informed him. But a telegram was received. A son consoles his father...by sending a telegram. Three words. There ended the relation. After that he never wrote to me. I rang him up a few times but when I found him indifferent and casual, I stopped. Once he told me, "Papa, you told me, world is running. You should live in your own way. He says I must learn to live alone. That is life."

His voice was devoid of warmth. Had I peered straight into his eyes, he would have wept. So I avoided a situation which would have proved us emotionally weak.

"Vicky could not be emotionless."

"No, he is. I am getting what I..." Jaycee called up Zeera again, "Suraiya...she has not yet got up."

He had gone up to the door.

*** *** ***

27

It was apparent to me that Jaycee was under agonising strains. He wanted to avert an ugly situation but was regretfully incapable of doing so. I saw grave concern in his eyes about happenings around. His lips at times fumbled for words and voice. The half-burnt cigarette would continue to emit smoke almost scorching fingers. Yes, I would then examine palm and hand. It was a spontaneous reaction. I would look around, breathe heavily, feel fresh, close my eyes. For a while in deep thoughts as if in prayers and then fix eyes at his serious face. To my surprise I would find many rainbows making numerous layers on his temple and then disappear. I wanted to stand up yet something weakened me, and I remained glued to the chair.

"Vicky is a strong man."

I had been disturbed.

"I presume he has a technique to run business."

"He is a millionaire. Even in-laws commercial operations are being looked after by him."

"What was the cause? He went away that far."

"May be marriage or it is possible I might also have hastened the departure. Or it cannot be denied that he wanted to invent reasons to leave India."

Jaycee had been extra careful in observations. He was patiently narrating tales of success and failure. A man of ardent zeal and initiative today lamented before me as a vanquished and forlorn individual. It was not difficult for me to comprehend the grave mental upsets. He was frank and to a large extent self-condemning. An abrupt transformation had come over him. The earlier right attitude had given way to remorse and diffidence, "It was not Vicky's fault." He would repeat these words time and again. At certain moments I realised that he was cleaning his choking throat but the eyes betrayed him.

I watched as if in a trance at times for he was emotional. I experienced a current of unhappy events leaving nothing to reason. He was regretful and sad without a minute's respite.

But sometimes he would also show unhappiness over indifference of members of the family. It was not true that he was unmindful or unaware of the sentiments of worldly relations. He too wished to live among them, however, Jayanta's misfortunes were the continuous occupations with onerous obligations.

He was also a man of files. As far as his parents were concerned, they also felt though they forgot all worries while involved in various social welfare plans and thereby established cozy, selfless rapport with the downtrodden. They thus wanted to dive deep into known and unknown social acquaintances.

He would forget himself in nostalgic memories many a time, and I could see mental imbroglios and downfalls.

"I am not alone who is in crisis. It is the class which is suffering irredeemably."

He had raised a harsh voice.

I had been told that Vicky was fascinated towards the materialistic aspect of life. Unheard changes taking place in technology had influenced him. The terrific speed with which media was making inroads into the private affairs of man was a matter not to be ignored lightly. Electronics and computer science were attracting attention. He was ambitious and volatile. He was a darling of Romi. For that purpose, it was sufficiently explicit that four of them always remained together and shared warm emotions, thoughts and experiences when he was away on tours. Jayanta was caustic and accurate in self-appraisal.

I was all praise for him since he had not hesitated to tell me that with the passing of time there had percolated symptoms of laxity in conduct and behaviour.

"You know, you are alone in tours even when you are surrounded by a crowd."

I silently watched with quivering and twisting lips the facial expressions. It was an unblinking gaze. His words sometimes flowed out with great intensity. He was visibly avoiding the orgies and rendezvous of tours intentionally and with great circumspection and it did not escape my attention. I also thought it proper to permit him to speak out his mind voluntarily. At that moment, Suraiya had appeared and wished us well with a disarming smile.

"You have been reminding of..."

She was beholding us with meaningful expectations.

"Did you have tea?"

"Yes, many times."

"I enquired Zeera about you. Yes, I knew old friends should share certain private experiences." She was graceful, soft and charming and involuntarily compelled me to delve deep into her wide eyes. I found a strange aura of divine innocence on her smooth face.

"Uncle, Mr. Jayanta is enamoured of you."

Her pronouncing the name struck me with a warning. I was recalling every word, sidelong glances and movements of eyeballs but was unable to comprehend the hidden motif.

"I am sure I did not disturb you."

She had laughed away. Zeera had emerged out with a tray and a plate of biscuits. We sat dumb and blank. I was diverting uncertain attention to cigarettes.

*** *** ***

Three of us took tea quietly. Suraiya was looking fresh and informal.

In a few minutes she developed an intimacy with me to such a degree as if we were known to each other for many years. She was a woman of intellect and beauty. An ideal woman she was, and possibly this was a single cause which to my mind might have fascinated Jaycee. I was just imagining the probable impact and fall-out of the relationship. A dangerous game Jaycee was playing, I thought.

She was loquacious, vibrant and engaging.

"Uncle, he remembers you quite often."

I did not react to her comments. I could follow that she was giving expression to a harmless truth. I concluded without going into the ifs and buts that she was a woman of word on whom Jaycee could depend and seek shelter. That made me nervous also. This could be emotionally disastrous, and it was already showing signs.

"Uncle, it is not easy to maintain yourself in such challenging and selfish times."

"I have not accomplished a special feat."

"Nobody does, uncle, but in the modern age, I mean in our times man to man relationships are irrelevant. A man in love with rash, wealthy, unscrupulous life destroys intensity in relations."

"At your age you have given a verdict which no doubt should have some bearing on..."

"It is what I have learnt in a life of glamour, fashion and fastness."

She had not allowed me to speak. Suraiya's confidence was nerve-shattering.

"I am the product of this age. Yes, I have learnt to live fast."

"Yes, I agree with you. I don't want to argue but is it proper to live dangerously when you have sufficient time to look around? Where is the necessity to run? And the manner in which you have been relaxing since last evening, I can say if life can be lived like that, I mean with relaxed working schedule, a sweet exchange of words, a few moments confined to yourself, I think it is enough. You are wise..."

"Arey Uncle, I am a simple person. Nothing to hide."

She was serious now.

While taking a few sips, she observed me, "Uncle, I don't know how one comes close? It is abrupt and immediate. Look at me, I found Jaycee at a hotel in Bombay...Yes, I found I would say. He was in his room. The door was opened. I heard loud voices." She had looked at Jaycee.

There was a long expectant pause.

"He is a man who has been much misunderstood."

I was wondering as to why she was defending him. It was a relation of just a few years and I who had known him since childhood was not in a position to declare like this. This is what she wanted to tell me, I was thinking.

"How do you say he has been misunderstood?"

"Don't you know?" She had shot back a question. I pulled out a cigarette.

"I will lit it for you." She had taken out another cigarette from the packet and without hesitation put that in the mouth of Jaycee and the next moment had lit the cigarettes for us.

"You...were telling me that Jaycee."

"Yes, his problems and limitations have not been appreciated. Why do we become excessively possessive?"

"She is your fan!" I had looked at Jaycee with a mischievous glance.

"..."

"When we become possessive, we deprive a person of individual identity."

"You are raising a different question."

"No, I am making a realistic proposition." She placed the cup on the table, "I shall make arrangements for breakfast. Would you like to take bath first?"

"We don't mind." Jaycee said, "We shall talk and talk. Experiences to share. I wanted him. Suraiya, I think I have blundered somewhere. I want to go back. No retracing of steps but finding solid moorings, Suraiya, I feel my age is not in my favour. Now on the verge of retirement, I feel alone and rejected."

I was overwhelmed with a sense of disgust and loss. Jaycee was unnaturally frank and incisive and Suraiya was exceptionally mild and intelligent. The difference in age did not create chinks, I realised.

But I found chaos and disorder somewhere when an articulate acceptance was present. I found a graceous sweep over my entire body for I felt within that some injustice might have been done. Suraiya was affecting my thoughts. But the premature run of my feelings halted and again the next second an emotional upsurge seemed imminent. There was an atmosphere of pathos and poignance. I realised I was nibbling a half-consumed cigarette.

She said, "It is an age of fulfilment."

"..."

"One should make life interesting. I am making it. I enjoy myself among..." She was quieter now. I read her facial expressions. Her calm countenance appeared to have been disturbed. She took out a cigarette, played with it for a few seconds and added, "There is an element of decay. Jaycee, you have to control yourself. It is life. Nobody has time. You know, how do you expect them to come back from Los Angeles, Australia...and London? It is a long journey. They are all busy." She was defending them, "I know Vicky and Rahul! A traditional outlook would not benefit them."

"Suraiya, you are..."

"I am not going out to a questionable background. But I think, the sins of age stick to those who..."

She again smiled in a prolonged uneasiness. However, It was difficult to find the enormity of pain. Her heartbeats were clear, discernible and loud. It was a reckless push to an unpleasant past. A soft wilderness was overreacting to stir us. It was infusing faith and truth also when revival of the past gave an assurance.

With them, I too thought that I belonged to some distant past.

"Uncle, there is nothing wrong." She said confidently, "I do not repent. Should one regret? Jaycee is not unaware of what he did. He was fully conscious. It is unethical when we justify mistakes by invoking the spirit of time."

She laughed and suddenly put her fingers on the dangling cigarette more firmly.

"I could not have drinks."

She unwillingly pegged the cigarette in between her lips, "We fear and that is the tragedy."

I observed that she wanted to smoke but was probably reluctant and felt ashamed. But no, it was not so, for immediately she said, "Not now."

She took out the cigarette.

"You are tense!"

"No uncle, I am all right. When you think of past, it gives you unwanted pain." She looked at me with deep dark eyes, "I shall ask Zeera to..."

She walked out without finishing the inconvenient sentence.

"She is not revealing."

"But she is not secretive either." He said, "It is her pain. You know, perhaps all of us in one way or the other have an unknown injury. Some of us may be knowing. Yes, may be. But to tell you, we know the area of inaction also. Even the effect and range of thoughts which never get an expression yet infiltrate and cause damage irreparably. Yes, I am witness to this. It has been happening to me."

"She is forthright and exact in her words."

"She tells me not to curse loneliness for that handicaps a man. This world likes to dominate."

"What is her problem?"

"She never points out rightly. She does not want to disclose her mind."

"..." I conveyed through my eyes that I was not convinced. He started looking in a different direction.

"I am impressed."

"..."

"What happened in that hotel?"

"..."

"Jaycee, she was referring to a hotel incident. Don't you wish to tell me?"

"Yes, that was the first meeting. Important negotiations were taking place. But I found that it was a sheer blackmail. It was a contract and here relations of Dave and Patel were at stake. Some eminent persons too had their interests..."

He sensing some danger changed the subject. He told me that there was nothing worthwhile to mention. Those persons had been loud and emphatic and under the influence of heavy drinking had become angry and imbalanced. Perhaps, it was clash of interests and egos.

But I kept my thoughts and feelings contained. It was fruitless to condemn also. Jaycee was repentant for his deeds, I observed. And the young lady! She was an enigma. A woman of grace and mysteries.

"What happened?"

"If I tell, it will hurt me and humiliate you. I don't know...they had taken me for granted. But those..." He threw an obliged and uncertain glance, and added, "Yes, we were drunk and had inner poise. Those words which we never wanted to bring on lips had been spoken. Everybody wanted considerable share of profit and active participation in the project which ran into fifteen hundred crores in the first stage. I think the party was also to be funded and then...you are aware of the great untiring fund-raiser Besariram."

It was Patel who had said, "We never thought of these gains and now...if tomorrow I come to power, then..."

It was a threat.

"Your son and wife? They have been very urbane and unkind."

It was Kaka Kharbanda who had said without show of courtesy.

"What do you mean?"

"You can ask Khan and Mahapatra. What they have been..."

Kharbanda had opened another bottle, "We have been working on an understanding. This time I felt, you babus...have been behaving more like businessmen and politicians."

"Who is he?"

"He is running a film studio and controls a shipping company. Kaka is a known figure who operates in the air too."

"..."

"We fear him."

"Jaycee, you are..."

"You know, these leaders and babus are just pawns. I felt very small that day. Kaka's glowing eyes and rage made me shut up." He was trembling with the thought of Kaka.

After a brief interval he recollected his thoughts, "Kaka is the strongest of all. Nobody can disagree with him. His writ prevails and we babus, masters and social workers unquestioningly pay obeisance. It is a feeling of persecution that holds us in lease. Madhav and Malkhan are all his hands. He operates through them and you should know he is great. After him, they move. Kaka is a person who is difficult to understand. Nobody can subdue him. He is a brute. A killer though looks a saint. And that was the mistake. I had dissociated and after heated exchange of words all had walked out. You know, I had kept sitting without any concern about the outside world. The waiter had come with the food and disappeared. I had probably taken a few more pegs. I don't know what happened after that. I had washed my hands and after that...it was all darkness before my eyes. I had fallen unconscious on the bed."

*** *** ***

28

It was Suraiya who had entered the room, witnessed the disturbed papers and other documents.

Jaycee sighed deeply and looked relieved as if a massive burden were off his shoulders.

"When I had regained consciousness early in the morning, I had found police personnel outside my suites. She was there sitting by my side. Bright and soothing. I was in a state of emotional fixation. A kind of speechlessness was...I was incapable of uttering a word. Her magic and charm were unique and assuring it appeared. It is not an exaggeration. I tell you those moments were full of bliss. I cannot commit but I was relatively finding myself safe. Nevertheless, I must say you should bear in mind...but it is a fact that she was casting a deadly spell on me."

He was describing the beauty and grace of Suraiya in many words as if in a trance. I was listening without interrupting the thought process. He did not appear supercilious, still I found there was something which could be called hyperbolic. Jaycee stood up and went up to the window, "Come look...I came intentionally to this state, an allottee state to find peace. I could have refused but I was much disturbed. The huge property and those two bungalows more than havelis...had no value or attraction for me."

He was lost in the dark charm of Dhaudhar and I could see a new horizon taking shape in his vacant eyes.

"This hill...is no more calm. You cannot believe those rascals. A spineless collection of babus...following like puppies."

"I was forced to cling to his side. I also wanted. It was the only solution. Jacob and Kaka Kharbanda were brutes, animals, powerful and politically well-connected. They operated through anti-social elements. A goonda kind of people. It was known to me but they...could spell disaster and go inhuman...was not known to me.

They could cross any limit of decency. In fact, Ashey's decision to marry a Muslim tycoon was to strengthen their influence and roots. I was a silent spectator. I could do nothing. Nothing, I tell you.

"When I had objected to, Jacob had said, "If you are attached to relations then forget. You will repent. God does not show mercy."

"Dave had also advised me, "Relations make you sick and pigmy. You subdue your energies and restrict growth. It is in the interest of all of you that we want you to enjoy. Moral notions and obstacles could prove fatal."

"I thought they were just accustomed to these pranks to make you surrender to them but no, I was mistaken. They had damaged career-wise both Rajput and Yadav. Pandit was totally castrated. And Patel, Mahapatra, Singh, Mukherjee and Ratnam...you know their sufferings and the ultimate subjugation. Swamy Ratnam could heave a sigh of relief only when he dittoed them. A pet dog he has become now. And I, perhaps, I was allowed to exit honourably because of my parents Jai Bhadra and Raji. Yes, today I feel..." A few tears rolled down his cheeks, "Look, what I did to my old parents. I threw them out...literally into a life of humiliation when they needed me."

He was soaking up his incessant tears.

"Suraiya must be waiting for us. We should get ready..." I also stood up and moved towards him.

He turned back with Herculean efforts to look calm and composed.

"You would be wondering that one of the strongest men of the state is weak. Yet it is a fact. This is the humiliation, the terrible moral defeat. And I think babus of today have to die a slow death because they want to live, live a life that is borrowed. I don't claim an exception. Not really living, it is a living death. There are emotions you want to show but in actual fact you deceive yourself. I am living, I know...an idea strikes me that I am not living. It is in reality a daily death that I am surviving."

He laughed and grinned at the same time.

I was quiet.

I heard Suraiya calling up Zeera. Jaycee also heard, I suppose.

"She is great. It is she who had saved my life."

*** *** ***

He had passionately told me how she, when all of them had walked out of the room, after the heated and violent argument, just entered to look up for the waiter. She had stood there breathless and a little flabbergasted.

"He is playing a deadly game."

"It is too much. We invested money and now it is a question of fifteen thousand crores."

"It is better he is..." She had heard their poisonous words.

Suraiya had trembled with fear. When she returned to the room, she had found my door open. Out of curiosity and fearful excitement she had entered with presentiment and doubts. When she had found me in a state of unconsciousness possibly in order to find out my identity searched for something in the room.

"I don't know what was the background of her sympathies. She had rung up the police through the manager. Suraiya, a fashion designer, was an individual in her own right. She on enquiry told me that she was daughter of one of the most famous curators and painters, Ritu Rai who is now married to Akbar Hussain, and later it was found that Ritu Rai was a collegemate of Romi. You know, man is never alone and links are always established. Anyway, a few photographs...all those papers...she had really..."

"Why they wanted to..."

"You know, I have been a bit indifferent to the business operations lately. I wanted to build up an empire, but when I sensed that my children and parents were no longer interested, I started growing restless and angry."

It is a destined outcome."

It was another long dry story. He was pretty outspoken and blunt about himself and I painfully felt that I was sitting with a totally disillusioned man.

"You were already rich."

"Yes, I was wealthy and powerful yet not contented. Jai Bhadra and Ma Rajshri were not wrong. Even Romi's comments were relevant. No, my kids loved me but..." He was stiff and it appeared he was squeezing his face.

We took another cigarette.

At that time, Zeera stood before us, "Saab, get ready. Breakfast is waiting." He had collected the cups, "Mem Saab is now in the kitchen."

He was gone.

"Suraiya...she is a woman of fine taste. Obviously, she should be. But her mind and heart are also transparent. She is an intellectual beauty full of grace and womanly charm."

I split into a sad forced smile, "Yes, I know."

I was amused at the way he was showering praise on her, though the questions which raised their heads before me could not find appropriate words.

I was given to understand that Jaycee's present status in the Government had forced the Bombay police to act speedily and effectively. He was given full protection and more so when Suraiya had started evincing interest in him. Jaycee was under a strong security umbrella, though he also had told me that many politicians, bureaucrats and businessmen had grown skeptical about his intentions. He was in a reminiscent disposition. "Once, Soma Gandhi, Jaycee confided in me, had warned me. Gandhi's outlook and perspective, parents' selfless devotion to social service also attracted her. You will be surprised to learn that she wanted me to walk cautiously. She now averred that these people are going away from the basic human instincts. Who can better tell you about the plans and schemes of mischievous minds? We are all dedicated to social work. Yes, that is our religious duty. But you know these devils. I know the people who move at the top. They are naked yet look fully clothed. They look soft, sweet and gentle but possess tough interiors. I find them comic and empty...Jaycee, I am a social worker what threw me into this? Do you know the background? What that sickening wealth did to me? My husband Vimal! Anyway, but now immersed in selfless social work, I find, I am satisfied. I don't say, I was not to be blamed. I must also be at fault. I chose this path. Had I been a little considerate I would not have reached this level of recognition in my life-time. But I don't repent."

Jaycee looked at me with a questioning eye, "She had on that day opened up her heart."

There was a pause.

I was experiencing a unique pain. It was sweet and yet I found sharp knives being thrust into my heart. Soma, Jaycee and Suraiya had created upheavals in my thoughts, visions and imagination.

They were open and still I felt they were clandestine and cryptic, hard to understand.

"What was her opinion?"

"That this life was nothing. No meaning or interest. It is a world where selfishness is a permanent virtue and this alone inspires man to go up."

"You agreed?"

"Yes. I too with many years of struggles and sufferings concluded ...yes, it was a difficult proposition...Nobody assuages your hurt feelings."

He was evasive and in a fit of restless outburst I released a sheet of smoke from my mouth.

"She was practical."
He was silent again. The atmosphere was oppressive and intolerable. It was unusual to be loaded with gloomy side of life. I also discovered a thin sensitivity in his words which showed worries for relations though he looked cool and frigid.

*** *** ***

29

Jaycee talked of loneliness and the pangs of a man who was deserted and ignored by his own people. Soma was a victim of emotional blackmail. Her husband Vimal could not grant her moments of love which she eagerly desired. Soma Gandhi was a true Indian woman and that was the reason of her being docile and obedient. She suffered and endured the pains till it was unbearable to withstand any more. Soma Gandhi turned a great social worker with powerful links.

"I have heard that she is also having unethical connections with those in Government and an important leader...your political Guru is enamoured of her charms or was her paramour. I am not painting a negative picture but the fact remains that you people who claim themselves to be the custodians of people's aspirations are insincere to a large extent. So long as it serves your purpose, you talk high and pious, not always."

I saw wrinkles of disappointment appearing on his face. The intense undulations of thoughts remained infinite and kept measuring up the dimensions of my presence. It was a delightful confusion. Soma Gandhi had affected him, no doubt. So was Sonali the Sadhvi who had no future but only darkness and social service in which she had decided to forget her present.

"Sadhvi once told me that in Indian society woman has all the good words reserved for her so long as it is a collective judgement...when analysed in isolation, she is considered an object of pleasure, of no value. In such circumstances what happens to a young woman who is...a widow, young and pretty. Sonali belongs to an age forgetting its culture and ethics."

"Jaycee was frolicking, I thought, without adhering to a particular stream of thought. He was uncertain of himself. We felt disturbed exactly at that moment when a woman's voice stirred the calmness of the bungalow.

"She is gentle and caring."
"You thought her an intellectual beauty."
I was left with no words.
"Yes, I like her. I love her." The unequivocal admission was sudden and unexpected. I felt like withdrawing from the scene.
"..." I threw a suspicious glance.
"Yes, I feel, I love her. It was a feeling that took birth long ago in that Bombay hotel where she had nursed me. Yes, she was a true saviour. I would have been killed and thrown out in the vast sea, yes, I tell you, for the next day, Kaka had rung up to say that had a fashion designer not come to rescue me, I would have perished."
"You have not completed..."
"Yes, yes, I forgot to tell you." He felt sorry and then added as if nothing had happened, "There is a confusion in the mind. I am mad, I must confess. Suraiya had acted wisely and timely. She had informed the police, sought the help of the Mayor and introduced me to him. Jaycee...I, a powerful man and an officer of integrity for public consumption, a man with a clout...a vastly rich man...should be a weak man it surprises me. Suraiya is my goddess."

Jaycee was now a man of no consequence, an innocent man with no ambitions.

I smashed my cigarette beneath the left foot. I neither exhibited anger nor satisfaction. Jaycee, at his stage of life, could use words to the extent of worshipping someone, rendered me speechless. He appeared mad and blind. It also raised countless suspicions in my mind. I wondered whether these outpourings could be called sincere declarations or simply to beguile me into believing that he meant no offence. But his double entendre irked me. Jaycee was vague and yet exposed a definite thinking. His flaccid comments cautioned me about his relations with the young woman. To dispel increasing ambiguities, Jaycee raised his voice a little and peeped direct into my eyes, "I don't know time makes a deep scar on your heart. I am experiencing the terrible pain. It cannot be explained at all. I cannot share it. Romi, too, did not understand me. You can imagine the social position of a man, a man of substance to use an old cliche, whose wife moves in saffron-colour with all that chanting and incantations. I am facing a dreadful dilemma."

I was wanting to get up.

"Suraiya had heard them saying that they wanted to eliminate me. They had found me dangerous. I could never know about the gravity of the issues involved. It was a plain business. No scope for lenient attitude."

"Suraiya I think was possessed of a godly instinct which persuaded her to lavish love on me. She was a woman who wanted to save life."

He thus related to me the entire episode. The next evening Jaycee told me when he had recovered from the initial shock, he had been rung up by Kaka and Patel. They had rushed to the hotel suite without a moment's delay. However, Suraiya's presence made them circumspect and prudent while probing into the ugly incident.

Kaka had said, "It is a heinous crime. You must not worry. I shall speak to the Police Commissioner and the Home Secretary. It could happen with anyone."

"Suraiya, you must have made a..."

"I listened."

"Kaka and Patel had been looking aghast and I had read into contours of expressions indicating an unwanted failure of words. But they along with others had consoled in so many words that I had felt convinced that they could never manipulate to liquidate me physically. That evening, I had told them to leave me alone and I had seen in their eyes a ray of disagreement. They had been very sympathetic and considerate, for the scene created that night had sent terrific warning signals to all and it was crystal clear that any threat to me could prove devastating for them too."

The next few days were hectic, and decision-oriented. I had also seen exhibition of paintings of Suraiya, organised and sponsored by the Cultural Affairs ministry in collaboration with various associations of artists.

It had been a thundering success and Suraiya had entered into an agreement with a few foreign multinationals to visit European and American countries. Even the fashion extravaganzas were a spontaneous success. Jaycee had been exposed to a world of art and culture. A new sensitivity had crept in, he admitted. Jaycee was animated and thrilled when he talked of Suraiya and that left me simply wonder-struck. He talked of his meetings and reconciliation.

"At that time, it was different."

He stretched his arms towards the sky.

"We should talk...she must be ready with the breakfast."

He looked at me and smiled, "Yes, we should go."

We walked to the main room without a word. At that time, Zeera announced that the warm water was ready.

*** *** ***

I didn't take much time. I took bath, changed myself and was out in the verandah. It was a bright day and I settled on the cane chair. Suraiya appeared before me with a fresh and genial smile.

"He will take time, what would you like to have?"

"Nothing. Already consumed enough tea and cigarettes."

She was attentively watching the flower plants and picking up the dry leaves.

"He is your sincere admirer. He told me of the night...that dark and chilling night."

She looked up with an anxiety, "Yes. That was an important day. They were clever people. All retracted."

"How did you assess the situation?"

"I don't know. Had his room been closed or say had a waiter would have appeared earlier, I would not have entered his suite. It is God's will. I still try to imagine. That particular hour was unique. I used to visit many places along with my troupe. Large number of visitors, I attended to. Aspiring models and fashion designers. Artists. Interviewers and press people. That day, nobody was to come. I was free. Absolutely relaxed. It was the noise. The loud words. I had emerged out and then those words that the man was not a fit person to be believed."

Suraiya related to me the entire sequence of events.

"It is all mixed up."

"Do you think they wanted to do away with him."

"I suppose, yes."

"Those three or four days...he says there were shows...exhibitions and..."

"Yes, he attended almost all the fashion shows and..." She was thinking something else, I observed.

Without much formality, she perched herself on a stool in front of me, "Zeera."

Zeera was popping out of the door.

"Coffee!"

"It has been too much."

"Mr. Jaycee takes half-an-hour or something more."

I did not comment.

"Suraiya..." I intentionally pronounced her name in a bit raised voice

"..."

"We do not know the ferocity of an unknown force that draws us closer and closer. Emotions of love continue to find roots. It is a sentiment for a relation that is alive and virile. It knows no bounds.

I think this unique power of feeling existed between us. Jaycee and I grew up...I still remember those days. It was a warmth that kept us together. Jaycee was a man who once espoused the cause of..." I realised, I have been going out of the track, so I controlled myself and added, "Madam, nobody knows what would happen. I shall not recall years of romantic enthusiasm when he used to talk of society and nation. We could not avoid the excitement of those days."

I, out of zeal, told Suraiya too the story of our youth. We had dreams and ideals. Everything that came to mind was divulged. With direct reference, I even told that Jaycee had been gradually drifting away. I even rejected Jaycee's pleas that he was not compromising with principles. I told her without any hesitation so many things.

At last with a restrained voice, I said, "Madam, Jaycee's march towards opulence has been slow yet steady. He has been condemning the system all along. All of them...they are calculating and cunning. Self-interest is their main consideration."

Suraiya stood up and said, "You are prejudiced. They work under immense strain."

We did not speak for a few minutes.

I was astonished at her observation. Was she trying to play with me? Zeera appeared with a tray...we were so engaged in our talks that we didn't notice. It was only when he physically handed over the cups to us.

"Very hot."

He laughed and went to the kitchen.

"He has been serving Jayanta for many years. Such servants are rare."

"Yes. I find him overconscious. He tells me so vividly about the growing difference between Romi and Jaycee. The ever-existing points of contention between Rajshri and...the son and mother could never see eye to eye. She a renowned social worker had different plans for the son. Zeera knew the inside story."

She was silent.

*** *** ***

I also knew that Rajshri and Jaycee could never get on well, particularly when Jayanta started involving himself in outside shady activities. Rajshri was a woman of courage and confidence. She took steps only when she was convinced about the genuineness of a cause.

"I know my son. These people are playing havoc with his life."

She had once told me. Probably at that time, she had meant his alienation from man's basic nature. She was piqued and Jaycee was angry with her style of indoctrination. I had attempted to bring about rapprochement between them but it proved a farce. Even graceful but forceful piece of advice of Jai Bhadra had not worked. No doubt, we were aware of the deeply felt acrimony growing between the two. One day, on a dinner table, Rajshri had said, "This babu, your son, is becoming stronger and stronger and going out of the track. This family has a tradition and I would not like him to undermine the glorious heritage."

Jaycee had ridiculed and said, "We are living in a different world. Values and morals are undergoing a sea-change. Mom, it is good to serve people, you need power and strength to serve them."

Jaycee had walked out. That was the beginning of an open war. I, even today, suspect that Raji Mom had got definite inkling of Jayanta's furtive dealings and unethical methods. Wine and woman in bureaucracy and politics were assuming power. This attrition continued for many years and ultimately it resulted in a break-up, silent and wordless.

*** *** ***

● 30 ●

"You were talking of Zeera." It was after a long uncomfortable moment that I violated the silence of verandah.

"I mean, he knew the genesis of ill-feeling."

"Yes, he was a quiet watcher."

Suraiya then told me in immaculate details the sudden and unfortunate break-up between the son and the mother. In his innocent assessment came into focus all his friends who had often visited them. Ratnam, Raghunathan, Ramanathan, besides others were subject of enquiry. There was also a frequent incoming of high profile politicians and business magnates. Raji had often disapproved of her son's growing friendliness with them.

In those days, Malkhan Dave and Wadia were spreading their deadly tentacles everywhere. They had a powerful influence on all politicians and senior officers. In fact, they operated behind the scene and dictated terms. Asif Khan, Patel, Singh, Mahapatra and Dhawan along with numerous other so-called benefactors and philanthropists were apparently very kind and benevolent. They were God-fearing and staunch devotees. They used to visit churches, mosques and temples. Still, they keep the practice I remembered. There was nothing new which Zeera had told her. In his simple words, Zeera possibly had described the gambit of all actions. Suraiya while giving a graphic picture of traditions of the family had avoided details about herself. I was satisfied with whatever was known to me. I did not think proper to work on further.

She was also giving me unconfirmed information because I also knew she did not have any knowledge of Rajshri and Jai Bhadra, a family of landlords who had cared more for their honour than anything else. "I also don't blame her," she said.

I looked at her with a feeling of doubt and surprise.

"Yes, who can know better the mind of a woman?" She took a few sips and placed the cup on the table. At that time, I was unintentionally thrusting my hand in the pocket of Kurta as if searching for something.

"No, wait. Let me help you."

Without waste of time she with suppleness and soft steps walked to the bedroom and in a minute was back with a pack of cigarettes.

"Oh, thanks." I was admiring her silently.

I took out a cigarette.

"It is the limit. Whenever I have time, I come to spend it with him. It is a time to freely consume and exhaust yourself." I laughed at her words without inhibitions.

"Yes, Jaycee has not changed his morning schedule. He spends enough time in the toilet. That is his old habit."

I sent out a thick sheet of smoke.

"You know, Madam..."

"I am Suraiya or..."

"Oh, yes Suraiya nothing has changed. Yes, not much. You know when you move with the times, take on the modern speed and essence, you feel you are the same. I don't know. I am not a preacher. No. Not a man who could claim authority over goodness. Suraiya, I have seen all these people visiting temples, organising Yajnas and similar functions. I stand apart. I have not dissociated. I like to move, worship and pray. It is a purely private sentiment. Yes, confined to heart. I am not inclined to express my religious faith to an outsider. Yes, but I also don't dislike any creed either. Yet I changed to the extent it was proper. I am a businessman. No hassles about conduct. Absolutely no. I keep carrying..."

I did not want to elaborate.

"You like to..."

She did not take the pack.

"You can, why worry?"

I thought, I was extra soft and gentle with her.

"It is all right."

She continued with her cup of coffee.

"Those were days of undiluted enjoyment. We spent time and words."

"Yes, he tells me."

"I don't have any taboos. No, whatsoever."

" ..."

"Zeera told you correctly. He is innocent and simple. But Suraiya, time affects a man. I came to enquire about their welfare. I would stay either for lunch or dinner. Romi, the gentle soul, yes, I called her either by name or as Bhabhiji. She is a woman of grace and intellect and freely talks to all. So affectionate and attentive to little needs and comforts. Vicky, Ashey and Rahul concentrated on her and found solace in moving around her. Mom Raji and Pop Jai Bhadra did come to meet wherever they were posted. Romiji is also a woman of large heart. Never heard soft voice beyond a distance of two feet. She never raised her eyebrows. I cannot forget her brilliantly shining eyes.

"We sometimes turned up to spend vacations with them. She had developed special regards for my wife, Devyani and kids. Yes, we did not meet too often, but whenever a happy occasion arose it was a celebration. They also, when time allowed, stayed in our bungalows or three-roomed modest cottages at Dharamshala and Shimla. I remember pleasantly warm days when we fished leisurely for hours together at Ohal in Barot. Those curious soul-filling visits to Dev Hurang, Narayan and Pashakot, "Gods of the tribal Belt.""

"Uncle, you are great."

"When you are in a painful present, you go back, even when you don't wish, to past to find happiness and joy. You know it was after intense and consistent persuasion that I came yesterday. When you were...we spent those dry hours together. I saw his bedroom, camp office, bundles of files gathering dirt and...an entirely different scenario. It is a feeling of loneliness but I admire his courage."

There was an uncomfortable silence between us.

"Suraiya, I remember and I feel the thrill and warmth of those days. It is unforgettable. Yes, totally engraved within. We never went out...spent time at home among relations. Romiji looking after us, sharing pleasant moments. At times when Jaycee was not there, I took the children out for a picnic. I played with them. I was comfortable. But moment by moment, I started getting pulsations that something indescribable was happening inside. There were unknown scratches of anguish."

I was looking towards the door. Jaycee was still to arrive. A long halt in the toilet, I thought. I fixed my eyes at the door and inadvertently laughed.

"It seemed all were trying to protect themselves. A sense of insecurity had crept in, I think. Jaycee's too frequent jaunts to foreign countries and within the country were disturbing, which I did not know in the beginning. He had started staying out or wasting out. Dining and drinking till late nights were a passion with him."

"He is alone."

Suraiya's voice was putting up a deeply disconsolate appearance.

"I think he is responsible."

"Mona was considerate." She was sure of her comments.

"But he took none into confidence."

"He is an important officer and the family should have known this."

I was uncommitted and quiet, unable to give an opinion on her raw reaction.

"Suraiya," I said in a measured tone, "Jaycee was uncommonly involved in official rut. I believe money and power assumed importance for him. Yes, he was a personality much talked about and praised. I don't envy him. I like when he is eulogised. I am sure even today he is likely to occupy an exalted position after retirement. Suraiya, perhaps you know that he has immense political halo. Nobody can sidetrack him. It is not without a purpose that he is here. You know how richly Patel and Asif Khan have been rewarded ...honoured and given covetous positions."

I saw Jaycee coming out of the room.

"What are you doing!"

"Nothing, we were waiting for you."

"I take time in the bathroom."

"..."

"I shall prepare for the breakfast." She said, "Would you like to sit in the verandah or..."

"It is okay here."

When she disappeared he added, "She has been a source of renewed energy. I feel rejuvenated in her presence."

"I know."

"What do you know? I think you met her for the first time."

"Yes, but it appears we have known each other for many years. She is a powerful brain. Mature and intelligent. Very graceful. But how you..."

"That hotel incident. I was feeling abandoned. You don't know when you are endangered you strive for a sympathising relation."

Jaycee fell into reveries. I could see in his eyes an overflowing stream of love. It was Suraiya who was visible.

"How long will you continue to live in..."

"I am destined to live a lonely life."

He lit a cigarette and looked at a distance. He was now neither sad nor happy.

"Why do you think so? Everybody wants you."

"Nobody loves me. All left me without affording an opportunity to explain. I had not committed a crime. What was I doing? Is it a sin to earn for the family? Vicky...Look how I was insulted. Ashey, she almost refused my existence and married a Muslim. What has happened to us? Apparently it looks dignified, beneath we are all hollow and the vast richness..., land and property that I collected... for whom do you think, I have done? If·I went on tours within or outside the country, it was for them. Even parents failed to appreciate and understand. Romi, Vicky, Rahul and Ashey shrank away when I needed emotional protection. I know, when they hear about my death they will come back. They will count each and everything. Today, they arraign and condemn me for my avariciousness. I know they call me a greedy leech. A man of low taste. Yes, I am an officer in their eyes who has unholy alliances and links with anti-social elements. I know, they want me to die."

He was suddenly breathing rapidly and with huge efforts, "When I think, I become mad. I feel I should commit suicide. A man of pelf and power, a person who has a potential of being one of the strongest men and who thinks he runs the government now...I am a man who is bereft of an identity in their eyes..."

Jaycee's words were clear and emphatic. I found it difficult to stop him. He continued to give expressions to his injured feelings.

Zeera had placed a small table in between us in the meantime and we did not know.

"It is a wishful thinking in which I am living. I have a hope, I shall live with them like those initial years of service before Rahul was born. I think we were not handling important jobs. It was as insignificant as the work of receipt and despatch. That profound and deep sense of relation is nowhere. I am horribly alone. You often spoke to me about the ailments. Yes, you made a judgement that babus have lost their duties and obligations to the society. You did not have much faith in them. And now? You feel your friend is doing nothing worthwhile. That belittles a cause and humiliates a class as such. All your friends are...and then in business I don't think you can claim the piousness of the Ganges."

I laughed without ill-will. He also spoke to me at length with derision and outrageousness about others. I realised that he had taken an offence to my views.

"No, I did not mean. I am a businessman and I know the intentions of shopkeepers. I have to sell out and certain unholy alignments cannot be ruled out. Yes, in an age of...anyway leave it. If something is not pressed into pockets and hungry mouths. Let me be frank. These big clerks and leaders do not move. It is with majority. I have seen the hands and eyes...Jaycee, living in this kind of world is a vexed puzzle and an uphill task. You people...as a class have miserably no regard for tradition and heritage. It is sinful. Polluted thinking has taken roots. I am visiting all places, historical and religious. I know, Jaycee, I do not deny that I could have built up a strong and vast empire. Yes, you were there. Ratnam, Ramanathan...all those friends even now nurse a grudge against me. You cannot disclaim. I know, I did not extract benefit from your resources and...I am the most linked man. Who could have been better situated?

"Jaycee, I am satisfied and take pride in Vasya's functions. You know I owe these relations to Pop Jai Bhadra and Mom Rajshri. They were great, well known and highly respected. Then Vijaya Chand. Even connections with Soma Gandhi and Sonali remain warm. Dave and Wadia speak to me with utmost humility. Jaycee, I am not ungrateful. It is because of my strong links, I too get love. But tell me did I derive even an iota of benefit from...you all advised and encouraged us but there the net result was a big zero. A punishing review."

"It means whatever we did...it was a void."

"No, I don't mean."

"Today, I called up not that I am repentant. No, why should the idea of regret upset me?" He raised his voice, "But what happened? Was it the finality? Everyone marching out in different directions."

"..."

"I didn't wish it. I was not dishonest. I never had a fear about the calamitous future for the close relations, the shocking and ill-timed dismal passing away of parents with a startling history."

I did not mean to insult. I wanted to calm down him. It did not prove an effective instrument. A life of emotions deluding him.

"I know, when one is bound unnecessarily to family and relations, one reaches nowhere. Why is it that persons like you anxiously project a relation?" Jaycee thought long and after a few seconds added, "That you are honest. Is it that you want confirmation?"

The wide eyes looked frightening, then with a gruff he said, "Everybody tells others."

The observation was incomplete.

"I understand." I peeped into his frosty eyes, "I don't claim that I am a saint. No, I am also not honest. A shopkeeper can never claim that he is upright."

He smiled at my admission.

"Jaycee, I have been dishonest to an extent. I thought I am not exploiting. A reasonable profit, I take. But...yes, I have also ambitions to gather richness. I feared also for there I would have been lost and forgotten in the Gobi-like desert of emotionlessness."

"Do you think...?"

Suraiya and Zeera were standing with breakfast.

"Suraiya, there is a confusion in values and thoughts. I don't know why a man thinks he lives in a crowd and is still alone. Jaycee is an institution in himself. A wealthy man who added greatly to ancestral land and property..."

She did not react.

"There comes a stage in life when one is totally vacant."

"..."

"I also feel. I know them. Too much power and fame makes a man forget human relations. The public acclaim makes him blind. In the initial years I had to rush about. You were helpful. You all stood by me. Even Dave and Wadia came forward with plans to exhort me to expand business. Why? Do you know? It was because of you, they came forward to guide and encourage."

"..."

I took two slices and spread a spoonful of butter.

"No, I will do it," Suraiya said.

"Jaycee, I know the respect I get around. All of you are holding important positions in the Govt. Our continuing associations have been beneficial, I know."

They did not interrupt me.

"I am not thankless. Jaycee, all know me and...but I wanted to keep the relations. You know what my father and mother told me when I could not get through the civil services...they advised me to do whatever I wanted but probity and candour have to be maintained and a man has to be valued. Man's relations are supreme."

I was lost in old memories. For a couple of minutes I did not stop. I said whatever flashed across the mind. But it was not offending. I know for certain.

"I never did anything against them."

"But I feel you were careless."

"All my friends...you know, it was a cut-throat competition. Had I not followed the general stream, I would not have been able to reach such heights of glory."

"To whom do you owe this position?"

"I didn't get you."

"Jaycee, think for a minute. You had been indifferent to children and sister-in-law who waited and cursed themselves. It was a painful experience. Not a question of one day. It was a habit with you. Those hotel adventures and escapades! Frequent touring. Purposeful and yet without an objective. Do you think we are really a success?"

"Oh, my God, you are serious. I don't want."

Suraiya was obviously nervous and embarrassed. She was marking each of my words but hesitated to intervene in emotionally surcharged conversation.

"It is a journey, not the ultimate."

"I am aware of the obligations."

"You know what you did? Today, you have time when others are madly occupied."

"If I didn't have time at least they should have responded positively. Agreed I did nothing. I did not worry. I devoted very little time. I shall not boast of an all-pervading influence. No. Romi was everything to them. I accept I wasted emotions and time then they also have hit me back. For all the comforts that I managed all that money and land...assets precious and lasting, for whom did I collect? I thought man can safeguard others sentiments when a right opportunity comes."

"Take your breakfast. Please don't..."

We silently took our breakfast.

Jaycee was making feeble efforts to justify his sins. His sad voice conveyed depth of emotions.

"The punishment is severe."

A half-burnt cigarette was dangling in between the fingers. "Forget now," Suraiya said in a sympathetic voice, "you don't have to say that whatever you did was wrong. It will humiliate you. If a man condemns himself he can't recuperate or rise above. What you did and whatever you said, was pressing demand of a particular moment. Mr. Jaycee, your attitude was positive and energising. It was a right understanding of time and you could not go against. Uncle, when one is tied up with relations one is confined and restricted. I think they were fondling high hopes and were irrational."

Suraiya's argument did not finish there. She was conscientious and miserly in the use of her words. She showed audacity and yet she was mild. She told us in no uncertain words that Jaycee had selected the right direction and that at the crucial fag end of the twentieth century, man required a discrete dispersal. A philosophic undertone did not impress me.

"Suraiya, family ties are sacred."

"I, too, thought on similar lines. I have held my family in high esteem and..."

She collected cups, plates and left-overs in the trays and called out Zeera to take them away.

Zeera said immediately after he picked up the tray, "Saab, a few officers and visitors are wanting meeting with you."

"Nobody should disturb me today. No phones. No callers. Just tell them politely to stay away."

Jaycee stretched his legs and looked leisurely at us.

"I got nothing. I am a total bankrupt."

The words carried force and a truth for me. I wanted silence to establish a contact among us.

*** *** ***

31

Suraiya a young lady of tantalizing grace and intriguing words, undoubtedly authoritative and insistent. It affected me deeply. She was wielding a terrific influence in the house. And she walked softly and unintendedly into an unnamed but controversial relationship with a tinge of immorality. I was mesmerised, I would not hesitate to admit. I was recollecting each and every word she had uttered so casually. She was emphatic and complex in vocalising thoughts.

"Jaycee."

We looked into each other's eyes to find a lost relation. I also thought for a while that I was alone and vulnerable. I picked up a leaf and started nibbling in a contemplative mood.

"Did you read my letters, diaries...?"

"Yes, I leafed them through."

He handed over a cigarette.

"I don't know, if a prosperous life can be questionably desolate." He heaved a deep cheerless smiling sigh, "I pass through intense internal turmoil!"

I said nothing.

We stood on the edge of a flower-bed.

"It was an unchallenged choice. But here too, people around you professing high ideals don't look beyond a hill top. It is a frog-like living and jumping and I thought we'll advance but no...there is nothing to achieve. We are selling dreams. Perhaps...I feel a musical strain. I listen to cautioning words. Together..."

"I am not concerned about the dreams."

"Did you visit Hardwar and Dehradoon?"

"No."

"Romi is looking after those Ashrams like a mother. That house for the forsaken old men. It was not our tradition...culture to allow old people to live in a deplorable condition. Don't you think there are crevices in the human mind? Romi could not be ungenerous with me. Do you also dream? She was a source of courage and love. A fountainhead of immense power. Where is that vision? There is some loss somewhere."

He forgot himself in contemplating whirlpool. I was still fumbling for appropriate words.

"Romi could take such a step. I never expected. How could she think without me? Everybody left me. It is story of a sinking ship! Is it? Now I feel tense and alone. It is all an outward joy that you find here."

"All...all for that emptiness. You don't know how to kill empty feeling."

"Those who stretch hands and legs a certain limit, experience the pains."

"..."

"Jaycee, you are your own enemy. A man is a devil when he is in love with himself. I think your tragedy is that you are..."

"No, we have been performing our duties."

"You...have failed."

"You'll also condemn me." It was a question raised without a feeling of rancour and annoyance.

"I am nobody to belittle you." I was as calm as I could be.

"At this stage, when you want emotional shelter and a loving care, you are left alone. Do you think Romi is happy? You didn't tell me about her. You know what could be more tragic for a man like me, who achieved what could have been a Herculean task for any normal man?"

"But you were abnormal and insensitive."

I raised my voice.

"..."

"Terrible ambitions and a paranoic desire to..."

Suddenly I saw, Jaycee's fast changing facial expressions exuded strange layers of tranquillity. He was placid and sedate.

"I have suffered."

"..."

We smoked, I think, unwillingly. Jaycee was not angry or excited now. There was a relaxation in the air. I felt the earlier bitterness disappearing slowly. After a few minutes, he began to open up his heart. He was now without hiding anything coming to terms with facts. The struggle was calm and the poised countenance impressed me. He, in a few words, gave voice to inner conflicts and agonies. In the process personal lives of other friends also attracted our attention. It was about emotions, relations and man. In fact, this class, with a fat bank balance, was tired and unhappy. It squandered wealth and displayed the power of money. But what was the end? "Yes, I was sad today. All want to be rich. Pandits, Yadavs and Rajputs will not be happy for they are always open and frank. I am earning..."

I silently went inside while he was faithfully grappling with his internal pains and sufferings. I wanted a few pages of the diary which I had left on the table.

"Yes, those are still lying on the table." I said to myself and the voice echoed in the room it appeared. This was an immediate reaction and even I, in the heat of emotions, remained uncontrolled when I thought, I was in command of the situation.

*** *** ***

I collected all those scattered papers and emerged out of the room.
"What happened?"
Jaycee asked me.
"Nothing."
"I have not written anything wrong. These are just scribblings. True and factual."
"I can trust."
"You have been knowing all of them and now don't you find there is a deep conspiracy? Nobody tolerates a successful man. What is this? I thought I should take notes...and then write a life story, but...I shall. Let them go..."
"You are unrepentant."
"Yes, I did whatever I wanted. In this age to regret is not a virtue.

The verandah of the big bungalow appeared engulfing itself in darkness.

"Romi wanted me to be present. Those children also played on my nerves." He had fixed his eyes on the flower pots. Those were rare and sincere words. He did not deny that a kind of laxity and indifference affected the relations. His pleasure tours, dining out plans, jaunts to foreign countries and increasing number of seminars and meetings. It was an important switch-over that young and old, politicians and bureaucrats, policemen and businessmen paid visits to him. He was a guide to them. It was not a policy or a long term statesman-like words of wisdom to influence men and their affairs.

To be true and down to earth it was a deep-rooted plan to get entrenched and strongly oppose anyone who stood in their way. He was an emblem of sustained growth, hatching conspiracies...seniors like Patel, Mahapatra and Mukherjee and with the goodwill and blessings of social workers and philanthropists like Dave, Wadia, Sonali, Soma and Dhawan...he was expanding areas of operation and influence. Ramanathan and Swamy Ratnam were an added strength. Then Jacob and Asif Khan. The miserable and condemned destiny of Pandit. The defiant stance of Yadav and the all-rejecting characteristics of Rajput. Jaycee's words announced rebellion. His voice showed a defeat and his eyes still expectant, awaited some miracle to happen. No one was happy. His pains were numerous and insurmountable. At other times he thought that morals and virtues proved baseless and devoid of meaning in the present lifestyles. The minds were flying high. In that murky environment, Jai Bhadra, Rajshri, Vijaya Chand, Devyani, Romi and Zeera could never fit in. Jaycee was not unconscious of this. When he wished, he observed a stoic indifference, yes, that too in a state of pleasant craziness and coma so that he could relish the flavour and comforts of money. His tenderness and cravings warned him of an imminent sickness. Jaycee was scrupulous and immorally trustworthy. He did not disguise the genuine analysis of relations. He had been warned of an impending catastrophe, we remembered without loss of words.

The ever-growing enchantment with wealth and power did not afford private moments to think and visualise the man in man. The dining, waltzing, rolling and singing in the hotels were much more enthusing and pleasure-giving.

He had no time for Romi.

He found that Vicky, Ashey and Rahul needed money and he was capable of displaying the glint in plenty. They had acquired imported cars to move about, overflowing bank balances to squander and undefined power edicts. Vicky was rapidly growing and developing into a man and was imbibing attributes of his father, Jaycee, and he knew this.

He had lately found a renewed love for the nation. He was instrumental in the conceptualising and drafting of many programmes and plans. In the corridors of power he wanted to take strides with his head high. His personal charm and attitude were widely supported by well-known personalities. He suited politicians and his docile and humbly silent contribution during the years from seventy-one to seventy-five impressed them. Those were years of rejuvenation of youthful spirits. An Indian youth was realising aspirations and his dreams were coming true.

Yes, the Indian young man was now twenty-five...anywhere between twenty and twenty-seven. He had become animatedly strong. He was now awakened to the needs of the nation. Everyone was astonished and dazzled at the stupendous emotional outbursts for the poor, wretched, miserable and downtrodden. Yes; those four words were large-heartedly circulated in speeches and newspapers and were quoted. It was also a time when people liked or were forced to appreciate Rag Darbari. Songs of praise began to find place in Radio and media. It was a period of resurrection. It was time to demolish and construct, to praise and condemn. To give life and kill man. It was also a time when the civil servant by and large willingly offered himself for castration. He sang songs of glory when stood thoroughly emasculated. His eyes were symbols of that strength, weakness, glory and contamination. Jaycee liked a babu who admired eunuch. He liked proselytisation in ample measures but he also hated evangelists. Jaycee was frank and I occasionally showered words of praise. I, briefly speaking, was soft to Jaycee. His agonies were much more than I could imagine.

"I was the lord."

Jaycee would exclaim with satisfaction and joy.

"I was a sinner. I think now."

He said and threw a prolonged famished laugh at me. His words were deeply etched in my mind and I was in a dilemma to convey my reaction. It was a meeting with the true face and words which required courage to withstand. His self-condemnation was disturbing.

"I was a sinner. I think now."

He repeated those words quite often.

He reluctantly acquiesced in my earlier observations. There was enough weight in his justification. I was arguing within. His years after seventy-four were not only important but these transformed his routine. It resulted in mammoth change in thoughts and ideals. He thought that whatever makes you famous and notable is worth emulating. Patel, Mahapatra and Asif Khan were going out of the way to placate authorities. It was time to bid goodbye to values and morals. Mukherjee was getting thick with politicians. There were humiliations yet those white-collared men showed fortitude and perseverance. Jaycee had been so surcharged that he was sticking to truth, "These politicians and babus have no qualms of conscience when self-interest overtakes them." He was neither uncharitable nor ungraceful towards friends.

But that was a transitory phase. If there were ideals and patriotic fervour, these were only temporary gusto. He was ruthless. And he had accepted the tragic truth as to how he was thrown into a world of sex, scandals and conspiracies. There were women, wines and drugs. There were social workers and great men running the affairs of the country. There was no looking back.

"I tell you, soul, yes the conscience pricks, warns and awakens you in lonely hours. But when you don't pay proper attention, it suffocates. And you know, one finds pleasure in a crowd. In the din and noise, you fail to listen to the inner voice."

He had been astoundingly blunt and carping.

I was speechless. In order to make him understand what crimes he had committed, I took a few hurried puffs yet could not put up a brave face.

Jaycee's eyes sparkled when he went back to his past. The memories of those years were sprinkled with treachery, faithlessness and violence. I was shocked when he told me about the involvement of families in the vicious circle of scandals and sexual exploitation. He admitted the depravity to which he had descended. Jaycee was regretting the manner in which he had conducted himself. But he bravely defended himself in the name of family and society. It could not be said that they were insincere.

"A system of new values had taken birth. New trends had set in. It was a culture of violence and easy virtues. Youths were ambitious but not hard working. They wanted wealth through easy methods. They were fond of morals and high ideals but in words only. They formed the so-called youth wings of the parties. No leader worth his salt could stop the wholesome onslaught.

"Youth of the country of late seventies and early eighties were also rash and vibrant, simple and patriotic. Innocent and intelligent yet misguided and ill-advised. They were also sincere. But the politics played havoc with them. They made them instruments of their own sinister designs. National plans were all right. But majority of them had been so bad."

His words created a massive deluge within. He also unmasked Dave and Wadia and all those who claimed proximity to powers that be. He apprised me of the murky background. I was simply listening and nodding my head.

"So many drastic changes took place in the field of politics and economy. It was a policy of a moment. Today was important to everyone. There was nothing like patriotism, honesty or values. We spoke words of no substance. It was a frivolous excursion to find consolation."

He said in a low voice.

"Are you sincere?"

"Yes, I am telling you what I feel. Those years...full ten years...perhaps a little more have been painful. More than...I tell you.

"I touched heights of glory. But it was a lonely battle. After the marriage of Vicky...I could not keep pace with the turn of events. Nothing was under my control."

In his voice there was a fantastic poise. I found in him a man of punctured intellect. Jaycee looked calm and quiet. I was marking his words carefully.

"You could have saved yourself."

"How?"

"Don't you think, Romi was right? Your parents had a right. It was your mistake. Jai Bhadra...was a man of traditions and values. Don't you know how much he was concerned about us? Mom Raji was always worried about social welfare programmes. She had been sincere. And then you..."

He was greeting me with a persuasive smile, it appeared.

"What happened?"

"..."

"They died and you..."

"You also did not wish to come closer after Vicky's marriage."

"Yes, there was no one!" I said with a load of guilt.

"She was adamant. Romi, in order to belittle me, made fun of me and diversified her activities. It was a farce. She visited all those dirty bastis and...you know these officers' wives are clever. It is a way to...to be noticed. Romi too was hungry for publicity. Donations to orphanages, hospitals and charitable institutions. Why? An intelligent way to become important."

I thought he was jealous of Romi, and I noticed that he was unnecessarily tense. Perhaps his trouble was not unfounded. I did not know but I realised Jaycee was passing through stormy and testing days.

"Vicky was callous."

He wanted to protect himself. At that time he was reminded of merriment and joy in which he indulged. I told him of his irritating schedule. Always occupied in papers and files. Meetings and tours. Dancing and dinners in posh hotels. Then involvement of...I was slow but persistent. He listened to me carefully, and gradually a smooth face developed wrinkles. I could fathom depths of despondence. He was standing before me and hearing without a show of agitation.

"What do you think I was responsible for all this?"

"Perhaps all."

"You mean?"

"You are living a lonely life. You don't have hopes."

I was slightly rough and harsh.

He was a statue now. Almost dumb and calm. I penetrated into his eyes for a few seconds.

"How do you say?"

"I have read and followed all. When a man does not attain inner happiness, there are reasons."

"..."

"You never saw the reality. You never listened to the inner voice. Ratnam...Raghunathan...Patel..."

I was counting names on my fingers. The list was long and inexhaustible. It concluded with the names of important personalities, living and dead. There was authenticity in the voice. I wanted to warn him. It was a challenge to his existence. He was double-crossing and I wished to extricate him out of that predicament.

"Why do you remind me of these...I know them. All of them are my well-wishers. Not only my friends but more than that. They have been confidants and sharers in intense grief. All my relations deserted me...it was at that time...that these friends, from Ratnam to Yadav, came out to console me. They gave everything. They taught me one thing, and it was that a man is down and diseased when he speaks of...what did I achieve? I gave them immense happiness. I purchased luxuries and joys for them. For all my friends. From Dave to Sonali. I have met many. When you move in higher circles, you have to reach high. Those who rule, if kind and gentle, create a feeling of respect but they do not provide sensible protective umbrella.

"I moved among politicians and senior civil servants. It is a collective wisdom. If I had not obeyed their commandments, I would have suffered irreparable loss. It is violence of the age, the criminal instinct and pitiless mind that govern contemporary intellectual and emotional lives. Nobody can escape. I, notwithstanding words of caution from Pop, Mom and Romi, could not unshackle the powerful grips. Do you know how many babus, businessmen and politicians suffer? No, you don't understand." Jaycee drew me near and laughed.

"You asked me to come. I knew the dilemma and the anguish. Those dark pages of diaries. I understand the gravity of problems, worries and concerns about nation, society and family. You are living in a shell."

I was now restless and ironical though I never wanted to embarrass him.

"I am hypocrite you suggest?"

"..."

"We are also living in a world of dangerous equations in relations."

"You are blind and ambitious."

"Is there no redemption?"

"From what?"

"This life appears fatally burdensome. As usual, when under a spell of depression, one feels totally cut off. What do you achieve in the end? Romi spoke of generosity and pity. She was for the poor. All those sickening words about poverty...I shall not recount the social and individual ills we Indians are suffering. Theirs are the contaminated minds. When achieved freedom, self-governance promised an era of prosperity. What happened? These babus and Co...a private limited company that protects and enhances the image of anti-social elements and criminals among politicians and clerks."

Jaycee was again lost in thoughts.

*** *** ***

• 32 •

Suraiya, after taking bath and changing herself into plain green Salwar-Kameez, appeared before us.

"You are really old! You have not moved an inch."

"Yes, I think old men do not move."

"Mr. Jaycee, you have to live in the present. Your past is not that happy. You are pinning hopes on those who are not bothering to help you."

She was drying up her hair with the towel.

We stood without a word.

"Would you like something?"

"No."

"I want coffee."

We looked at the sky, confused and puzzled.

"You have no artistic instinct to live on. Dry, dull and barren thoughts about earthly existence do not provide inspiration. You have lived your life, earned money, served the society and the nation ...now why should you pester yourself?"

She was gentle and loud.

"Suraiya, you are brilliant."

I was provoked to praise her.

"Thanks."

She laughed away my light remarks, "He shall not go. No social or other engagements. No phone calls. Well, I shall be preparing something special for the lunch."

"No, let Zeera get ready with it. You have come after many days. I shall not allow you to go to the kitchen."

Jaycee was emphatic.

"But in case you continue with the sullen talk of days..."

"He knows me. This man has been intimate. Has also been rude and unkind towards the white-collared class. You people are sensitive. But we too do not live in a vacuum."

You are damaging none. It is your loss."

She sat in front of us, "I shall make..."

"Not now..." Jaycee said with a disinterested voice.

"..." She got up and asked for a cigarette, "Oh, let me have a puff. I am sure, you won't mind."

I, in heart, was admiring her. Suraiya was courageous without inhibitions and outspoken.

"If you re-build past it will not give peace."

"She is an artist." Jaycee was ironical.

"Yes, I am an artist. I am here to suggest that the more you think deeply the more you would suffer. How long can you carry the body of dead memories? Don't exhaust and live now."

She lit the cigarette, continued to watch the flame till it touched her fingers and then spread out her hair at the back over a large white towel.

She was a reminder to old relations, for I believed Suraiya was a force to awaken them to the harsh realities of life. Jaycee's tragic experience was born out of total rejection by members of his family. He quite often thought that as head of the family it was a sacred duty to amass wealth though it was a wearisome process. His efforts were sustained and the outcome prodigious. Unending ambitions motivated him to have a fat bank balance at different places. With the initial connections and importance of job he was aware of his strong position. The indirect and continuous drifting away from human ties and emotional relations was the major cause of driving a wedge among themselves. When he did not attend Vicky's marriage, it was not intentional but an inadvertent action. He was held up because of certain urgent State affairs. But the explanation was too fragile to elicit sympathies. His close friends had also not found anything wrong in his behaviour. It was an age devoid of convictions and passion. A ruthless vacuity was devouring Jaycee but he did not know.

Today, I was passing through a wonderful experience. I cannot forget her. She was full of life. She had opened up new vistas. A life of newly found joy and pleasures. It is warm and emotional. Life cannot be restricted to the four walls of the big palatial havelis. I am not confident but these were some of the words of his diary. I was trying to find out the page. After some time, I read out the lines to him. He looked at me with suspicious eyes and did not answer.

"You don't find a moment at home to release your pent-up and tension-ridden mind. A man needs to relax without control. They ought to have some freedom."

"It is not in your case, I too feel some unmitigated strain. At home they are too demanding, very much possessive and unreasonably advising. I don't like. After all we have to see what is expected of us."

"Had I stuck to my earlier stance they would have caused headache. My family would have suffered."

"Once you are in the company, you have to be watchful of your interests. In the government nothing is demoralising and corrupt so long you are together. You have to strike a gainful bargain. You cannot operate only with ideals and morals. These are sick and dead. In a democracy or whatever you may call, you have to be responsive to the aspirations of the people."

"Today, Swamy Ratnam met me. He consoled me for my loss. A few days ago Romi had left me forever. Her meaningful letter read, "You have been feeling suffocated. I felt you were disliking, rather abhorring the emotional needs of your family and parents. Now all are gone. Nobody is here. Vicky asked me to go over to Los Angeles. Rahul also asked me to reach Australia. They, it appeared, were genuinely concerned about the health. Pop and Mom probably wanted to live with you but...you have been cool and frigid. I don't know what has happened. They also asked me to reconsider my decision. But I found there is nothing to which I could attach to and find sympathy. I shall not hold you responsible for the rebellious unconventional behaviour of children. But probably they chose their share of happiness in their own way. Yes, Vicky wanted to go. He also requested me. He remained tense and unstable but never really made it public. Three of them had only one complaint. And you know what they wanted? Perhaps we are lacking in warmth. And I am aware of what conspires in the half-lit corridors of power. You people are busy. The burden of nation. Your people talk of progress and reconstruction. I know. I don't know but I moved among the big and the small. You bosses. I looked into their eyes. Well, I could not mingle the way they wished, you understand the hint. Today when I go out, finally from your life I am left with a question. It is answered and still I find the wide and long words remain gazing with a threatening posture. We were in hotel Taj. It happened. We were at Ashoka, it again occurred. Yes, I noticed you dancing with a glass in hand and peeping into the eyes of a woman. And there were frequent repetitions. I don't know the motif. To touch posterior, slight casual punching and tongues lisping at a distance with eyes ready to devour. That was the scene. And yes I know the purpose and the intentions.

"No I shall not speak of your friends and colleagues. Those lecherous and immoral politicians, senior babus and violent uniform walas. All hungry. I found it was only physical presence that was appreciated. The charm, the flesh and the beauty. It was a show of animals laying bare their bottoms and desiring to be kicked. Mr. Jaycee, I would congratulate you. You did not think of us. I spoke not a word. I lodged no complaint. You ignored us, I still tried to give all love to children. It was their love and affection. Those mild caring words which kept me living and moving around. Ashey went out in defiance. Rahul left India not that he wanted but because they didn't find anything worth the time at home. Yes, they regularly ring up. Ask about you and then with a low sad voice, talk to me for ten to fifteen minutes. I experience the pain and tension. Jaycee is a busy dad, I tell them and still convince them that you really like them — you are not a free man. Jaycee, I don't know but it gives me ominous inklings. Yet I am deciding to run my orphanages and Ashrams. I don't know...I shall be missing you.

"There is no purpose to argue. I think we should be realistic. In social sphere, I found extra impetus to love life. Who knows the reasons? I tried to fulfil all obligations. Pop and Mom were also not very happy and still they wanted to live with you. I don't know what goes on in their minds? But do you know, the great Rajshri's 'how' and 'why' were not without substance. She is a probing mind. She devotes her time and energies on a deprived lot. Her elegant conduct cannot be questioned. Pop and Mom cannot be doubted. I have lived with them. When they came to meet children, I saw a quaint stimulant in their eyes. In their company, I felt, as if I were fully protected and secure. You don't know how I spent those lonely days. Just consider Jaycee. How many days you have spent at home?

"I have the full account. Since nineteen seventy-seven...upto eighty-five...it is a period of full eight years. And eight years is not a small span. It changes the spectrum of life. It affected warm relations and family. You have not seen those vacant and waiting eyes of Vicky, Rahul and Ashey. You have also not heard voices of parents. I knew why Mom Rajshri and Jai Bhadra moved around in the bungalows. Both tiptoed from one room to another. It was an endless search. I saw them dusting off family photographs. They would touch and smell books. They spoke to me about your childhood habits. You were pretty touchy about words. It was difficult to convince you. Mom Raji explained to me the meaning of "how and why". In her opinion if a man understands the inner substance of "how and why" he can follow what is it to be a sensitive man? Your mother and father were always blessing me. To share a secret with you. I must admit if I stayed in these bungalows it was because those two noble souls showered immense love on me. Mom always lavished unlimited affection. She was more than a mother. She was a Goddess. Jai Bhadraji was my guide. How could I say anything which could hurt them. They played with children for hours. She was awfully engaged in social services. Her contribution to women's emancipation and rights cannot be undermined. She was a source of inspiration. She initiated me to adopt social welfare programmes and yes, I did it and there was excellent serenity and harmony.

"And you know, in Vicky, Ashey and Rahul, they found a unique contentment. It was your childhood they were reviving. In lonely moments they spoke about you endearingly. They did not express but I found in their silent eyes the unspoken wish to see their son."

"He is busy. God bless him."

"They prayed for your well-being, and I...I shall not mince words, I felt pity for you. It was not pain and anguish of a day or two. It started from late sixties and continued to...with each day you assumed toughness, indifference and the distance widened. The unfortunate gap could not be filled up. I could not bear the sight of those two noble souls who are seriously involved in the saintly social service to the community. They don't make use of the influence they create. Impervious to fame they were. Not greedy. It is your politicians who benefited from them and I don't know what is happening to the world? Nothing moves without self-interest. It is evident.

"All those who rule have become profane, sinful and violent. This militant environment is the outcome of their thinking. We thought we shall live happily but the devils did not allow. Father and mother simply could not endure such a dangerous change in thinking. That is why they withdrew. They had hopes on you but now seem to have reconciled to the present fate. They don't make complaints, speak no words...live under terrific emotional vacuum. I don't say they are demanding yet must admit that parents cannot tolerate the separation. I know the existing value-system and aspirations do not integrate but even then unspoken attempts are made.

"I feel, I am breaking up. Something is tearing me apart. There is a constant struggle. It is burning. I am exhausted and impoverished. It is all a false show. Nothing remains in act. Yes, I resolved to live a life of enrichment. I wanted to draw emotional strength from you. I aspired to live an intimate life. Wasn't I your wife? I think. Yes, in the eyes of the public.

"But where was the sanctity? I think I am a crazy woman in search of an identity. It was a marriage of convenience and physical necessity. A man is an animal. Totally lacking in human spirit. Don't you think that at a certain stage the relationship between man and woman living together becomes rusty and burdensome. It does torture you, I say. We are not an exception. I never thought it could affect relations. There was no visible acceptance but slow moving away sent sufficient signals that all is not well. Perhaps, I too remained a silent and inoffensive spectator and then I feel no, it was not there for I had been seeking comforting and satisfying presence at home. I asked you to come, live here and play with us. I was radically wrong and mistaken. Yes, when I see in the mirror I find wrinkles sending a warning. Yes, that glow has faded away. Something is missing. But I also found that the same changes were reflected on your face. With the spending of each day, I felt I should go closer to you. Was it the same with you?

"I remember these words, Mr. Jaycee. I am worried, no, it is not my nature to bemoan. No repentance. The only fears which keep lurking and injuring are the unknown crevices that must have appeared without sending cautioning signals. In your job you could not withstand the initial shocks. So it was with Swamy and others. The present set of things takes full advantage of human emotions and weaknesses. The enfeebled soul, the bleeding heart and the wounded intellect, I am carrying, are all rudderless. No courage to fight back. Yes, I am here alone and destitute. My husband has no time. He had never had, I think. Was I living a life of dreams? Yes, I think I was selling dreams. Together and alone.

"There was no evasion which even I wanted. I shall not allege that you intentionally wished to opt out. But subsequent tours and jaunts revealed that you were developing disinterestedness. You did not find time to be with those who were praying for your well-being. At the physical level all was smooth and good. I agree that you earned a lot yet I never for a single moment approved of the ways and means. It was not an instinctive disagreement but deeply thought of. There was, I am confident, no need to acquire wealth by unscrupulous means. It hurt me whenever you did something which was against morality. We had sufficient resources. Pop and Mom rightly regretted that you kept company with men of doubtful integrity and character. I told you to be watchful but you developed cold feet. We wanted a relation who should be close, intimate and sincere.

Today I feel I was dreaming of a life which was not in my destiny. May be I misunderstood you. It is possible. I failed to measure up to your ambitions. You are powerful and strong. Your area of operation is wide and indistinct. It cannot be fathomed. But I want to live in a well-defined field. Mom Rajshri's "how" and "why" which gave you moments of uneasiness were in fact sources of caution and inspiration to me.

"Vicky's marriage was the last straw. You could not make it. How it happened I don't know. You never intended. I convinced them of your commitment to duties but they refused to appreciate. Now it was not a question of sentiment and relations. It was an intellectual debate. Vicky had said in a melancholic voice that Pop was a man whom...anyway no desires would be fulfilled since our existence is meaningless for you.

"I am harsh today. It cannot be denied that my observations might also be exaggerated. Yes, when I feel emotionally disturbed I can fall. I am a woman who is also a wife and a mother. Your Romi had also been feeling the torture and agonies of an ignored woman. It was Pop and Mom who stood by me in my secluded and testing moments. They taught me the sanctity of relations. But I am firm. I failed to sustain relations. I have been regretting my sense of indecision—one day this was to happen.

"It was a total revolt. Vicky was adamant and so was Ashey and Rahul, and without showing resentment openly, took a decision to depart.

"Do you know what Vicky had told me? After ten days, he said, "Mom, I am cut off. I want to live an independent life. No need any more to cultivate relations though these make life easier, happy and rich. In our case it has been dreary and without substance. It is a perpetual headache...I want to liberate myself."

"Ashey was more emphatic, "He is a Muslim boy, but we have agreed to live like ideal human beings. No religion will hereafter restrict us. Our lives would be dictated by love, affection and friendship. And if that means disowning our respective religions, we won't mind. Thanks for whatever you gave us."

"And Rahul in a calm and quiet manner had said, "I think I have to translate a dream into reality. So I go. It is happening to all. When for years he didn't have time for us, why should we waste ourselves?"

"They were never disrespectful. They keep ringing me up. Talk of home-coming. It looks strange but I know they will not return. It is no use to expect them. And now after many months, I am forgetting to cherish and sympathise.

"Have you thought of those eight years? It was a period of glory and downfall. I wanted to collect everything. I tried hard but was a total failure. Your journey to reach zenith of a glorious career remained alive and unending. It was not your handicap. It was the age. Babus could be heartless, I never imagined. Why they all stand up against the fragile, sensitive and tender human feelings in the name of progress and nation? This question agitates my mind. I often asked you...you were non-serious and casual. Your occasional smiles did not carry warmth, for these were feigned and mechanical. I always lived in a fool's paradise because I believed you'll come back from a life of hurry and storm."

"You never turned back."

"I have kept account of my miseries. Inner pains never permitted me to sleep peacefully."

"You hardly stayed with us during those years. I can say with confidence that a total period of three months was our destined time. You could easily find out from the tour programmes. At home we waited for you and you took flights from one country to another. It was irrevocable, father Jai Bhadra told me. Perhaps both had some kind of presentiment. It was a period pregnant with thoughts and emotions. There was immense disquiet. Anxiety disturbed us now and then. I thought myself a crazy and wild woman. Children stopped talking about you. Vicky's observations were pertinent, "Those people have nothing to offer to the family. No time for them. They have a queer sense of delusions. Think they are the greatest. This alienation is a product of their own actions. Why to be obsessed and..."

"I am responsible for all that went wrong. I could not waste myself in activities which were fake and without roots. I could not go to clubs and dinners too often. Today, I realise why these women liked to spend time in shopping or clubs. High society has a diseased mind. I have found there is nothing within. They are maniacal and sprightly mad. They want to forget themselves in frantic words about growth. They even bring out tears in impulsive moments to show a weighty attachment to the poor. When in mental turmoil, born out of personal vacuum, they are lost in dry gin and wine, in cards and in gossips. Or if the frenzied mind is a bit puzzled, they go to sweep streets. Their false wailings and fomentations elicit words of sympathies. I found those tears in the eyes of Patel, Ramanathan, Swamy and Asif Khan. These women, in secret, confided in me. You will not come back. The glitter and grandeur of service will not guide you to the right path. I shall not live in despair. So finally I have made up my mind to spend my last days in peace. I want to live in a serene environment. This wealth is not giving me happiness. Who knows when a hidden enemy hits what will happen? You can think. Earlier you had a feeling that someone must be waiting at home. Now that possibility is over.

"I don't know if you remember words which you uttered casually.

"In this race you are far ahead. I am also aware of the tragic fate of those who lived enrichingly. It was a life of loneliness. Don't you think I am obsessed with relations. But man needs. When I with children and parents visited temples and ashrams, I saw hundreds of old men and women, suffering and moaning human beings stretching their arms. It was an entreaty for pity, mercy and alms. We gave them something. Their eyes brightened up. What was it?

"Those handicapped children! No one to share their mental or physical infirmities. I always thought of human nature. It puzzled and injured me. I remember each word Pop and Mom spoke. The community lunch they had with those in front of temples, invariably impressed me. Rajshri and Jai Bhadra were known names. Very popular and talked about. Rajshri then had looked into my eyes and said, "Don't forget them. Perhaps there was exploitation. If you can put in a sparkle of joy in their sad eyes, think you have achieved something."

"Raji, a woman of grace she was. I think she always missed me yet it is she who had initiated me to serve the cause. Mom Raji was a woman who knew the mind and heart of a woman. Once she had said, "Romi, look I have always been with your Pop. It is soothing and assuring to live with your husband. It is a togetherness that keeps us happy. He shares my little good things and I in return participate in his hobbies. We don't know if we require company. But, yes, after a few days we feel a tinge of pain rushes back to you. To these children. We always liked to play with them. We don't know...their little pranks, chatterings and acts of mischief always instilled in us a feeling of fulfilment. Those were moments when we thought we were grateful to...yes...God has always blessed us. We know relations are changing. In this age I feel, a man has no time. He is busy in himself."

"Raji Mom was intimate, intensely emotional, and for the first time I realised that behind those smiles and visible bright face, there were multi-layers of disillusionment.

"When warmth among human beings is lost, you know the futility and meaninglessness of a life. It is in closeness that one feels secure."

"Mom, you have been..."

"I remember those days when struggle for Independence was in its fierce form. If many sacrificed it was because of the purity of love and warmth for relations and motherland. You ought to have something to depend upon. Love gives a feeling of pride. Now, I find people are running away from one another. Yes, we are going away...away and...it is neither hate nor affection, it is a kind of dispassion and detachment. Man is just disinterested."

She was feeling dejected and her voice had been low and remorseful.

"You can guess my mental tensions. I did not want to create a scene. I could only lodge a protest. I did so sincerely. I have been telling you always but it was a futile exercise. I deliberately wanted to avoid a show-down and why should there be any bitterness between husband and a wife. I did not develop personal ethics for that matter...I only desired that man and wife's feelings should remain alive and bubbling. However, this was not acceptable. Do you think that I had for that reason a female centric approach to life? You have always been hinting at? No, I never wished so. it was not my habit. I lived a life of self-effacement in the light of relations.

"Now, all are gone. No one is there who can give me what I want. You tough-talked, moved without a thought and quietened me. Our children could not live in a void in spite of the love I showered on them. I think we were living together without being ever getting the feeling of the much-wanted togetherness. You were inaccessible. Today, I am alone. Terribly in a depressed state of mind. I have sought loving blessing from mother and Pop Jai Bhadra is also not averse to my line of action. I am feeling relieved.

"So I decide to live a life of my own. It is possible you may feel upset...there is no other way. I can hardly bear with an acquisitive culture. I don't require your money for Pop has given me enough. And you know the truth.

"I am sorry for my children. You had opened joint accounts and so they have decamped with the entire money. Yes I would term it as a demeaning adventure. It is learnt that this had your tacit approval.

"Vicky told me, "It is not his money, so nothing will be given to him." Whatever bank balance is in our name I am leaving it as it is. With this letter, I am sending you a few keys, code numbers and other important papers. A separate packet contains...shares and certificates have been kept in the locker. I don't think I should write any detail.

"It is surprising that with these papers and bank balances, I lived for such a long time. It requires a good amount of courage to live with material which does not belong to you.

"I can only pray for your soul. I am fully awake to the feelings that I am committing a sin...there is no solution.

"Last words: Dear, if you can still decide to live a life away from the present one, I am there. Nothing is lost and we have time to redeem ourselves."

Romi's letter had created a void and both wanted to fill it with all the warmth.

*** *** ***

• 33 •

We still heard the echoes of each word. Romi was forthright and true to her spirit, it was apparent to us. After heaving a rueful sigh, Jaycee said, "Look, how she has defended herself."

Nobody spoke for a few minutes.

He took the letter and counted the leaves. Threw a cursory glance at us and grieved, "I wanted you to read. This is my story, heart-breaking and avoidable. She was right. Always correct. An embodiment of virtue and uprightness..."

And he was using sombrely all the soft words for his wife. Suraiya sat in a stoic posture. It was difficult to make out anything from her mysterious face.

"Yes, I was immoral. Whatever I did, it was a sin." He suddenly split into a blighted laughter, grim and threatening. I felt guilty but could do nothing.

"You were sceptic too." He directed his assault towards me, "Romi could be harsh and cruel, I never imagined. They took out everything for it was a vice. What a funny and violating thought?"

Nobody spoke.

Jaycee added, "My earnings were full of pleasures. When they knew that I had collected money by foul means, they should not have touched it. I would have given the entire wealth to some charitable institution and made a name among philanthropists. It means they did what suited them."

I could see his eyes burning with rage.

"This was the longest letter she ever wrote to me. It was her decision. First and irrevocable. Who suffered? I am the victim. I am the sinner. A criminal could I be called. That is the world. Everybody abuses the world. Condemns the world. There are speeches, lectures and discourses on morals and ethics. Yes, I too listened. I liked. Even a priest...does so. But no one is serious about doing what is expected. Babus, leaders, rulers and all such big people...what do you think, they practise what they preach? I think they don't mean this. Only one in hundred is perhaps sincere and faithful. Most of them are rogues. They don't want it. They booze, carouse and expend themselves. That is life at our level."

Two of us threw questioning looks at him.

"Yes, nobody worth his salt at the top wants to do what he says, otherwise there would not have been such a chaos. So many scandals...kickbacks and...what not? You see...these people govern otherwise who would have..." He laughed, "I am a corrupt man. Yes, I am a criminal. You can call me by any name, it fits into my personality. From a saint to a Satan. There is nothing to worry about. We have not learnt by experience. Our old man was the only person who was honest. This is what I have known. No one else has been able to attain those heights. Our motive has been to have a fabulous bank balance."

Zeera was standing before us.

"Lunch! What should you..."

"I shall come..." Suraiya intercepted him, "I will help you." Then she turned to us and said, "Would you like to have coffee?"

"Oh, sure..." Jaycee said loudly, "Suraiya, just bring another pack of cigarettes. Box of cigars."

Suraiya got up to say, "Alright, I shall also bring coffee..."

"That is fine."

"She is brave."

"Intelligent too." I said, rather whispered.

"It was my destiny."

"You did..."

"No, listen..."

"Jaycee, you have been your own undoing."

"Everybody says I am responsible."

"Accept and forget. That is spiritually satisfying."

"It is difficult."

"Not exactly. The soul and spirit require..." I gathered up my words and added.

"It is. You should go back to Romi. She is waiting for you."

"I am a man who is thrown out."

"Nothing is lost."

"I am a man who does not like to be pitied upon."

"..."

"Jaycee, Romi will forget. She is a goddess."

"Keep quiet yaar, she is a woman of strong will."

"..."
"That great woman. You know, that famous woman Rajshri...wife of Jai Bhadra, the landlords...social workers..."
He was satirical, foreboding and threatening.
"Jaycee, you are..."
"I have felt the pains. I agree I did. I committed such blunders. I was haughty and apathetic about their feelings."
"When you sincerely realise, why don't you accept?"
"They should have warned me. Romi could use...but she also learnt the art of life from her snobbish mother-in-law. Very dominating and ordering about."
"You misunderstood."
"No."
"Jaycee, you can still improve."
"..."
"You are alone."
"I am."
"Jaycee, forgiveness can be effective."
"..."
"You are...I mean you have done so much for the country."
"You can flatter me."
There was no noise around.
"I...tell you...Jaycee, after all there must be some solution to such sensitive issues. It affects personal relations."
"Why do you say so? It was a deliberately nursed ruckus. An estrangement carefully cultivated over the years. You have seen her letter. Mildly virulent and full of critical comments. The wrath so bitter."
"You don't see any hope?"
"..."
"You have been a man behind many economic and political decisions. You are among those few...an integrated part of the caucus. If I am allowed to use the cliche, who have solved many tedious problems. You have a knack to command and have always been intimate to those who are important. I believe your own problem should not be that grave."
"Because it is a personal problem."
"..."
"You can solve emotional tangles but when your relations become enemies, you are lost. What can I do to them? She is filled with so much anger and aversion and children...all have deserted me. They

took everything I don't mind. What is the use? I feel and firmly believe that they have been unreasonable."

"You are..." I wanted to tell him that all his emotions and thoughts about them were misconceived but could not open my mouth.

"You have been very kind to me, I know. A family friend."

"You should bring her. This life will not lead you to a comforting old age."

"What...?"

"Jaycee, why do you move from one question to another? Don't avoid facts. There is nothing. You should not have been adamant."

"Were you not meeting her? Even Vicky, Ashey and Rahul came to India. They lived with her. There was a Yajna...but I was alone in Delhi..."

"They invited you, I suppose."

"..."

"You should have gone. That was an opportunity."

"This was no way. Couldn't Vicky...or Romi could have made it possible."

I knew his grudge and terrible avoidance at Yajna. Romi had organised a Yajna on a large scale for peace and prosperity. It was for general welfare. But when I had gone for a day along with my family, I had found life-size photographs of Jai Bhadra and Raji in her simple room. And Jaycee was also there. So were children. With Devyani, she had shared her emotions. I was surprised the way Vicky, Ashey and Rahul had welcomed and looked after us. This was unusual. But another stunning and bitter truth was their utter indifference to Jaycee.

Romi had said, "It is blissful. I think when you have too much, you run to...such life. Here I have no future plans. When You don't function with self-interest, you are in harmony and peace with the world."

On my asking them that they should have gone to him, Vicky with a touch of melancholy had averred, "Uncle, I have observed, these people live a lonely life. It is fated. Very few live a life of fulfilment and happiness."

He had not agreed, "Uncle, when there were days he was after name and fame. A false living it was. When you live for others it is good. A generous act. But when you hurt feelings..."

I still remember his words, glowing eyes, faces, the vast Yajna scene and the ensuing tragic incidents. The vacant eyes of his parents and the accident.

I felt deep agony within. There was complete darkness before my eyes I had felt.

*** *** ***

Zeera turned up with a box of cigars and a pack of cigarettes. No one spoke. Perhaps both were passing through tormenting moments.

"Forget. I am happy. I know. It is all a show. She wants to tell the world..."

"No, I don't agree. I had been there."

"Vicky should have come here. After all, I had not..."

He stopped and took out a cigarette.

"..."

The tantalising face of Suraiya appeared before my eyes. Truth was poisonous.

"Jaycee, you fail to recognise realities."

"..."

"You could have acted with a large heart."

"They call me...agreed so many cases of corruption were there. I accept. What was the need? All big people are involved in such cases. Crores of rupees exchange hands. You know people are free to level allegations. Who can stop them? I have a list of about hundred scandals right from late sixties. Then what? We have gone far ahead. Those who move fast, do fast. They also sacrifice their interests. If they give their lives to society and nation, forget their own...and lead the nation to progress and prosperity then what...? I don't consider it an act of corruption. Wine and women are integral part. All of us, objects of usage at one point of time..."

I was surprised at the changed stance but kept silent.

"Yes, I feel I am right. All of us faced enquiries. Commissions. Parliamentary Committees. All grilled us...these also filled their bellies. I am witness to many historical events. If I have become rich, I also have contributed to the progress and growth of the nation. Everybody extracts a price. Nobody is a saint. If there are, they are very few. Sonali, Soma Gandhi... all of them. To become a successful man you have to...Now think of those, Asif Khan and Patel...they are men of crores. After serving the Govt. they are holding giant public undertakings and the process has not halted. Malkhan Dave and Wadia and the kind of people are keeping their tribe fit and alive. Papers speak of corruption, sex...it is all nonsense. Bunkum. Nothing concrete will materialise. Enquiries. Investigations. All these will continue. Police and investigative structure is for the weak and the helpless. It is for those who cannot defend themselves. I know the system. Do you know all those enquiries that I faced...or the ministers face...it was ultimately the poor section officer or a clerk or...Yes apparently accused persons, those who committed crimes, were defended and protected."

He kept quiet for a minute and said, "Because they took upon themselves our acts of...I mean they admitted... so they were to be protected. Lacs of rupees were spent on them also. We had good, intimate and firm relations. We benefited and protected one another. That is the spirit and the religion."

As if a great mind had propounded his creed and philosophy.

"You are back to..."

"There is no alternative."

We lit a cigar each. It was a coincidence but a fact that both coughed and coughed loudly. When after a couple of minutes we penetrated into each other's eyes, there were thin layers of water. I experienced exhaustion. I felt a tearing pain travelling in my veins. Clouts of cold blood collecting and stopping the flow of blood. It was, as if, I had become ice and stone.

"This brand is adulterated."

"We were restless and impatient, I think."

Jaycee with wide and frustrating eyes continued to stare into my face. I also could not keep away the suspectful eyes.

"Should I admire you for the immoral defence?"

"There is no way out."

"Where shall we reach?"

"A modern man is mad and crazy. Rational, and if emotions disturb him these are just appendages. No meaning is attached to them. I am a man who walks on earth. Here we do everything for our own kith and kin and sell dreams. All of us are followers of those who laid down their lives for the country, who wanted us to establish a divine kingdom. A Ramrajya. Who has not been benefited? From top to...if I did some unethical exercises and minted money..."

He was startlingly frozen.

"He had been my teacher. Dave. And also Asif, Patel, Dhawan and Jacob were my guides. So many brains. It was difficult to escape."

He was slow, consistent and confident. For about five minutes, he spoke with fervour. It was only the puffing sound that was slightly perturbing. Suppressed and controlled breathings disturbed the voiceless inner conflicts. It was a floating sheet of smoke which stood apparently still between us. A man who had been powerful, was today trying to put up a brave face. The internal weakness had made permanent chinks on his face.

He was defensive and covertly violent.

He took a prolonged puff, grumbled a few unclear words, squeezed black lips and stretched legs to yawn noisily.

There was helplessness and failure in spite of the immense courage shown earlier. He looked at the ashtray and then at his cigar. He was now impatient.

He picked up the ashtray and kept it back on the table and spread out an unwilling depressed smile and closed his weary eyes. I thought it improper to needle him.

And there was Suraiya, fresh and beaming, with a tray in hands.

"Jaycee!"

He opened his eyes with a deep whistling breathing. Without a word, he took the cup and looked passionately at her.

"He is reminding me of my..."

The meaning was sufficiently clear and rude. I was caught up in a whirlpool of emotional distrust. It was doubting a friend and at the same time reposing unqualified faith.

"Suraiya, my friend was in a reminiscent mood. Memories were so many. It is pleasant but bitter also. Who has contributed to progress? This growth. Prosperity all around. Have you heard anybody starving to death? It is rare. Don't you call it a success? If in the process some...I believe morality and ethics are something personal and relative. I am perfectly honest. No hanky panky. I worked day and night. My friends...I told him of sex scandals, kidnapping, robberies, kickbacks in projects and purchases whether of food, fodder or weapons. Yes, these are inseparable from the system. Yes, system of which all of us are components. Had we been saints, we would have been slaves. Only clever, ruthless, violent and dishonest rule the world now-a-days. We have developed such a cultural ethos. You have to kill people if they are inconvenient even if saints or innocent. I have seen, for power, a man can kill, eliminate or poison to death his or her relations, however close one may be. Here no religion is an exception. There are squabbles for the control of maths, mosques and churches. It is sheer greed and violence that help you to exist in the world. I did it."

He took a few sips of coffee.

"I never meant to..."

"No, my dear friend, I shall be untrue to myself if I refuse to lay bare my heart and mind. It is all well-managed. I told you the result of those enquiries, commissions and...it is an endless process of crime and sin. If I had tried, I would have been killed or subjected to torture. I am in the system, I have to follow. I don't hesitate to accept. I knew they didn't like it. But see all over and then tell me. These civil servants when in service remain slaves and spineless, and that is what they produce. In the system slavery and weakness prove a blessing. They bow. They eat. They touch feet and without making a noise become rich by unfair methods. This is the culture. Now it is the competition to excel. Yes, there is the RAW and CBI. Numerous agencies. All enquire and the victims are those who can be dangerous or who are no longer required or who are weak. Dangerous and unwanted are made victims in well-planned air accidents or bomb blasts or...are burnt alive. That shall be my end when a stronger man takes over. So we have to keep all happy. I also obliged them for they..."

He was recovering himself.

"Yes, coffee is hot and tasty."

His compliments were lost in the thick jungle of memories.

"I am sorry for the poor subordinates who suffered for us...I feel we are not at fault. We compensated them with money which will feed seven generations and even then it will not finish."

"..."

"I remember them. It was the closeness. Intimate relations. Those were the relations which were mutually enriching and beneficial."

"Jaycee, you are understanding and still..." I said, paused and when I found both were listening to me, I added, "One should find a solution. I think we lacked in those qualities...we lived together and when approached...Jaycee, it is now at this age that we want warmth and togetherness."

"Yes, you are right."

"There is nothing which cannot be set right."

"Yes, I want it."

"They want you, too. Show generosity and..."

"..." He burst into an exhausting and disgusting voiceless laughter, "Yes, you are right." He said after a few seconds.

"..." I lit another cigarette and said, "A man's life is not to be wasted."

"Now I feel it is already wasted and finished so far as they are concerned. They don't figure anywhere in my future plans. If they return, most welcome but I think all should live on their own terms."

"Is that possible?"

"At least under one roof you would have the consolation."

"That is your answer to loneliness."

"Now what is left? I wanted to count my fingers. Size and strength. But I found them unequal and small."

"..."

"I think people will suffer. No escape. Those who rule shall remain victims of tenderness with a few exceptions. Perhaps lack of warmth in relations is everywhere. It is with those who..."

"No, wrong...Pandit, Yadav and Rajput and..." I was putting up a poor defence, "They are happy. Live among their relations. Joys and sorrows are shared."

"They are living in their cocoons. Self-centred and self-satisfied."

"Yadav is not so!"

"..."

"He is dangerous."

"Yes, he can kill."

"What do you mean? Is it a fact?"

"Yes, he would have strangulated his boss..." He put a stop to unmanageable flow of unrestrained expressions, "But then he is..."

"Jaycee, loneliness shall poison you to death."

Suraiya, who was quietly sitting intervened, "Uncle, you are right."

The word 'uncle' struck me hard. A relation was under a close scrutiny again. In the meantime she took a cigar and lit it, "I can guess the restrictions within which you are trying to find a solution."

Her hurried puffing made us mute spectators.

"I don't know what makes us mighty and also outlandish that ultimately results in inflated egos. We try to find justification in different directions. It is a living at multiple levels without being useful. When effectively convincing it sanctions even the worst and most vehement comments. That is exactly we have been propagating. I was lost in the world of fashion and art. I thought a free life would infuse meaning and rhythm. The world of glamour and richness makes a man weak and...Yes I agree there appear unintended crevices in morals and virtues. Relations also suffer. A respectable distance and correct appreciation of human emotions also undergo changes for the worst. You become a functional relation. Yes, a performing machine. You call relations by names and pronounce their non-entity.

"I too soon found out that I was a mere object of pleasure. A pulsating and charming mound of flesh. Yes, those artists, dancers, painters...and all sorts of so-called art-loving people, including authors of no consequence were found shallow. It was a harrowing experience."

She was blurting out rather pantingly, "You see this figure. A curvaceous body. White and hard. Shining oily and smooth like a sheet of marble. Those sheets that you fix up in kitchens or bathrooms. That is the mentality. It is the consumeristic mind. Yes I had passed through those hands and eyes. Hungry and pale."

She shrugged, laughed heartily and resumed in a hateful tone, "Here relations come under pressure."

"Suraiya, you are pricking my conscience and belief."

"No, when we expose ourselves in the name of progress, modernism and broadmindedness, we contaminate ourselves. We believe in swapping." She controlled herself and then said, "It is despairing."

She, out of womanlike modesty, hesitated in disclosing a terrible truth.

"..."

"I am sorry. When we...I too feel that it is really unhealthy to tolerate an amputated thinking and living. It pushes into an ugly world of loneliness."

"But relations are not forthcoming."

"They are. But not functional or self-centred relations. Openness and frankness do play a synthesising role in the affairs of men." I was again wrong. I thought there was no purpose to repeat.

"I regret very much." It was a naked declaration of a man who had been through a hellish experience.

Jaycee understood the purport of those three words, I suppose. He said in mild words, "Look my friend, we have gone too far. When I spoke of living under a single roof even if differing and quarrelling, I only wanted a nearness."

"I know."

"Romi cheated me. She left me even before my parents. Look at the colossal tragedy. What happened to a man who once thought would become another apostle of..." Jaycee smiled rather faintly, "But nothing positive happened. All were harsh. I am a murderer. A man who poisoned relations. A frenzied man who brought downfall and disintegration. I was selfish and also an animal. I felt and wept in solitary hours. They were coming to me from Chandigarh in a car.

I was waiting for them. I knew they were with Romi, the saint and Sadhvi of Hardwar and Kashi. Her own calculations she has. Sonali and Soma Gandhi are her regular visitors. What a funny situation! Not mocking even but provocative and violent. That day I was crestfallen. I was soulless. Heartless and brute."

*** *** ***

34

Jaycee finished his coffee and fixed his eyes on a dry tree. A huge dry deodar tree at the next hilltop appeared to be participating in our painful dialogue. For a few seconds, his lips quivered. Then seized of the situation he said to me, "I was an animal. I am. Do you know what I thought?"

"..." I took a long puff indifferently.

"Jaycee please don't disturb."

These were the words of Suraiya. The imploring touched me deeply.

"..." I stared at him questioningly.

"I was a devil. I wished their death."

It was a fatal stroke. There was darkness before my eyes.

"Yes, I was hard and unkind. I was an animal. A Satan. It was a wish no child would ever nourish. But I thought so. I was not prepared to welcome them. I was a monster."

"Jaycee cool down."

Suraiya dragged her chair towards him. Then stood up, consoled him and put her arms around his neck.

"Suraiya, what is heard and seen, everybody speaks about. Those words were mine. It was neither prayer nor a deathwish but it proved right. Exactly at that time...perhaps...my devil had hit them. The car collided headlong with a speeding truck near Sonepat and there ended the great story. They were injured grievously. When the news reached me, I was shocked but it was not a question of repentance. I was frozen beyond imagination. For three days they remained unconscious, struggling for life. Then was a crowd...huge crowd outside the hospital. Host of political leaders, senior bureaucrats, social workers and philanthropists made a bee-line to the hospital. Everyone sympathised. Truck load of bouquets. It was not because of me. It was their assiduous earning. Three days kept me occupied.

There were words of consolation and encouragement to bear the tragedy. And to be true, I must admit I never thought of them. Their legs were totally crushed. Amputated from above the thighs. The first question that had struck my head was, "What shall I do with my parents? And now without?"

There were tears in his eyes. He trembled for a few minutes and then said with a choked voice, "Yes, it was a shameful experience. I did not want to take them home. And see the drama Romi enacted. She would visit hospital when I was not there. Those sanyasins, nuns, saints, sadhus and dhoti-clad social workers crowded the hospital's corridors.

And I wanted their death and that was a demon's heart. Death of those who gave precious life. A man could be a murderer to that extent. I never believed. But I was there. And today I am standing and sitting before you. I am a sinner. A criminal."

He related to us each and every detail. He was emotionally surcharged, feeling the heavy weight of guilt. The vices and sins of years back were alive in those eyes. Romi and children visited them in the hospital yet were conscious and scrupulous to avoid him.

"You don't know, how much they wounded me?"

"I knew the pangs and agonies. True I killed them...but that was a solution."

"My parents on wheel chairs expressed stoical detachment. And at that time entered Suraiya in my life."

"You know I could not avert fatal crisis in life. Parents lived in those two bungalows. Moved on the wheel chairs. Silent and disgusted at times. People visited them and slowly they lost the desire to meet people. They just listened with blank eyes. When they were alone they simply looked at each other. I knew my acts. Parties. Dancing. Singing, those jaunts and orgies. Perhaps I was becoming more and more involved. I was intensely engaged in a few negotiations on important projects. Crores of rupees were at stake. It was nation's prestige. I was to do it. Confidence had been reposed in me. I was to go abroad. Then Bombay took about two months. You know Patel and Asif Khan, the most powerful dreaded chairmen were to assist me. Don't you think I was a potential policy-maker? Or was it my wrong belief or overestimation? Yes I was unduly pampered, inflated and flattered."

He stood up in a huff, went inside and did not return for about ten minutes.

"What happened?"

"He is upset. He is punishing himself."

"Suraiya, what does he want? I was finding out but he is self-contradictory. He wants and still refuses to accept relations. And now..."

"He is naked and true."

"Yes, that is the fortitude of the man."

We took another cigarette.

A calamitous dullness was sweeping over us and possibly we wanted to look comfortable in those monstrous strains.

"How do you...?" My question was incomplete.

"..." Suraiya did not probe into doubtful procrastinations.

"Have you met these people?"

"..."

"I mean Patel, Asif, Harry and..."

"Yes, many times. They have visited exhibitions and fashion shows. They are pretty jolly old fellows. Want to expose and open up. I need courtesy and patronage of such vulnerable individuals. They are enamoured of me. A few smiles and twinkles in the eyes can seduce them or slyly movements of lips with words soft, whispering and..." She was innocently satanic in her smiles, "I admire those rogues and condemn too."

She looked relaxed.

"You can be..."

"Patel has promised to organise ten grand shows for me. He has found out sponsors. Similarly Asif Khan. And Mahapatra who retired five years back, now a politician, is very intimate. All of them. I know their weaknesses. They are crooked, cunning and lascivious old men now but sufficiently virile and..."

I did not want to comment or else I would have invited her humiliating observations.

"Jaycee is entrapped. He feels the burden of sins and vices yet is totally emasculated to fight back. The tribe of Dave, Wadia, Dhawan... forget, why to repeat names? It is a flourishing class with no love for oft-preached principles. Rajputs and Pandits would keep struggling, create fears yet prove ineffective in the contemporary outfit. Suraiya is known to them. I have professional and evil designs. Jaycee somehow appeared to me honest. He is a poor victim of circumstances. He needs warmth...there is nobody who can bestow moments of joy. He is empty and there I fill his vacant moments."

She was giving emotional and intellectual dimensions to the conflicts of Jaycee and also disclosed her relations with him. She assured me that in case there is a reconciliation, she will walk out without much fuss. She did not hesitate to open her heart. In a manner wrapped in mystery she told me of a past not so happy. A woman of beauty and brain when rebelled proved strong. But I found in her words streaks of blighted hopes, chagrin and bitterness. I observed as if she were passing through a period of penance. I, after listening to her words, developed utmost compassion, but it also astonished me.

She crushed her cigarette in the ashtray and said, "When I come to this place I stay with him. The life of a hill station has not given him peace. He is required in Delhi. He bears the pain. He realises the depth of sufferings that come out of separation. But that grants him strength also."

"Are you happy?" My words were incisive, clear and loud, "Suraiya, I want an honest answer. If you want to...only then."

" ..."

"Have human relations any meaning?"

"..." She penetrated into my eyes with an uneasy glance, "This huge palace-like bungalow has only two souls. What a joke? When such a living begins to consume a man, it raises many eyebrows."

She was evasive and deliberately trying to mark time when Jaycee was absent I concluded.

"Those two big bungalows in Delhi are majestic and spacious. But when we go, these tear you apart. Those buildings devour you."

"Uncle." After a while the word pierced my ears, "I think large space requires..."

An emptiness seemed permeating into our bodies and minds.

"I wanted you to..."

"Don't say. It would push me into a state of dilemma. It is not always that words give substance."

There was a long silent shadow engulfing us.

*** *** ***

Zeera was coming out with two glasses, bottles of soda water, a bottle of whisky and a full plate of dry fruits. In a moment Jaycee also turned up with a glass. I felt embarrassed and angry. It was time for drinks...yet I kept mum. Zeera placed the material on the table and returned.

"I thought we could sit and talk."

" ..."

"Come on, have at least one. I know it is not a good time. However, when you realise the desires, it is okay. I have refused to meet anyone, not even the big boss will be attended to. No phones..."

I could know that he was repeating each word. He had said this so many times earlier. His babbling and chattering appeared irrelevant but he continued to grumble and groan alternatively. I was simply reading his expression, trying to make out what he precisely conveyed. It was a futile chase. I did not want to drink, for yesterday's hangover was still making me uncomfortable.

"It is a culture of drinks and spending away. I am splitting up myself to join a cosmic vision."

Jaycee's confused and philosophic outpourings did not impress me. He knew how to justify past actions. Aware of my doubtful expressions, he made an addition, "When you are unable to find a cogent explanation for your words and deeds, you co-relate yourself to cliche and general perceptions. It was silly on my part to commit so."

He gulped down the entire glass, "Nobody appreciated mental agonies. There was none to sympathise with me. Even my parents on wheel chairs did not ventilate their grievances. They endured the sufferings alone and without words. I, in my lonely hours, wished to repent and I wanted to open my heart. But they did not afford me an opportunity. It was a clash of giant egos and self-esteem."

"Jaycee, you relax. There is no necessity to return to past." Suraiya said in an emotionally surcharged voice, "Look I have forgotten everything of the world of art and fashion. I too confronted emotional turmoil."

"But look what has happened? Nothing is giving peace."

"It is the inner will and determination that will guide you to the right path."

I said nonchalantly.

"What do you want?"

"You called me Jaycee."

"Yes, I was upset. I wanted to share my heartfelt pains. From Jacob to Madhav Wadia and Malkhan Dave, from Soma Gandhi to Sonali and Romi, it was not a convenient journey. Everybody craved for my company. The great Mom Rajshri and father Jai Bhadra were before me. I knew they never agreed. They wanted to live in the past and dragged rather stretched past to the present. Who would have accepted such a situation? There is a wide gap in years and age. Twentieth century is an age of vacuity where time has lost purpose. It is the cheapest."

"Is it not the case even today?"

"I say yes. I am also not reconciled to the past. I lived in the present and am still living. It was full and satisfying. Rich and total."

"Jaycee, I think you are unwell. Better take leave and go to a doctor for check-up. You are mentally sick." In a gruff voice, I exclaimed.

"Suraiya, I don't know yet I am tempted to say. Both of you are firm and..." I stopped, picked up the glass and brought it near my lips, smelt and placed it back on the table, "Jaycee, you live in a world where it is your edict that operates."

"What for did I do all this?"

"Nothing is stable, permanent. You are also sentimentally going back to past. Isn't it? Why do you refuse to admit facts."

"..."

"My fault was that I remained away from them."

"Yes. You wished to live...well, no fun to repeat."

"I have shown you my diaries, letters and..."

"..."

"Suraiya tell him, we can survive even if he leaves me."

"I am your friend, not a blood relation. That is the question."

"Do you make a difference?"

"At personal level I would not agree. But if I look into the present puzzling set-up, your relations do count for mutual benefit and self-aggrandisement."

"You sincerely mean it?"

"Yes, that is the culture today. You live, eat, collect and gather rudiments of life that come your way. It is a collective approach to legalise scandals, if you permit me to argue."

"Yes, you are right to some extent."

"Now, you are after peace and happiness!"

"..."

"I am torn within when I remember the plight of those two souls. Helpless and invalid. Always waiting with wide vacant eyes for somebody. Was it not a vacuum that killed them? Lives of enrichment and meaning now stand wasted. Did you ever think of sharing a few solitary moments with them? Without notice and complaints they finished off their hopes. And what was their destiny? A room at the back. Did they retire of their own or were made to squeeze themselves? Either way it was a withdrawal to death."

"Why does it happen? You ask even Patel and Mahapatra...or any one...I have found them putting up a brave face and laughing, without meaning it. A life of sophistication and education could be a liability I never knew."

"Education!"

There was no rejoinder. The atmosphere was becoming heavy and grim. Jaycee got up and picked up my glass. He moved close to me and handed it over, "Why not? Take this one."

I did not resist. While sipping unwillingly I was observing them. The silence seemed soothing and compassionate. Jaycee after a great deal of effort said in a suppressed voice, "I must go back to Delhi. Tranquil environs of hill station have not given me inner joy."

He looked at Suraiya with expectant and beseeching eyes. I guessed it was neither failure nor victory. It was an expression of a vanquished man. I failed to collect right words that could have conveyed what I wished, yet I exploded into a soft laughter and said, "It is because you have learnt to live in a noisy crowd with a feeling of loneliness."

"But do you contribute?"

"Yes, I agree."

Suraiya, it was evident, did not want to disclose what went inside her mind. She was reticent and quiet.

I don't know what was happening within. I experienced an extremely strong current of nervousness and pain running through my veins...a voiceless anxiety and anguish beyond physical boundaries.

*** *** ***

35

Another half an hour passed in the jungle of words and words.

Suraiya in her usual innocent countenance stood up, threw a careful comment, "You forgot something."

She picked up a bottle of whisky and made one peg each for both of us, "You look sad and exhausted. When caught up in quagmire of relations, nobody can find a solution. You have to allow freedom. Yes, freedom to yourself."

"Freedom!"

"We are not free. All are slaves. To duty, to ideals or to emotions." She laughed pensively, "To relations, we owe our existence and for the relations we reach a stage of no-return."

"You are right. I was a cynic. I never thought for a moment that I was free at anytime. It was a freedom born out of donations. Yes, I have lived on borrowed patronage."

Jaycee said in a flat bitter voice. For a minute he was not the same Jaycee it was observed. I found him pale, thin, haggard with his eyes deep-sunk. His face was turning ashy. It was an extreme decay that warned him, I presumed. "Nothing is worth-believing." His throat was choking. He made tremendous efforts and controlled his voice. Perhaps he wanted to look undaunted.

"Yes, I know. It is the end! No, I shall not surrender. Why should I accept what you said. I can easily read the contemptuous looks of people. The utter disdain and the mournful faces that see darkness only."

He took another large peg, "I shall not measure the depth of dreariness that surrounds me."

I was absolutely silent. Jaycee, it appeared, was recuperating and gaining confidence.

"I think the world has to move on. It is a process."

Zeera, meanwhile, informed that Asif Khan wanted to speak to him.

"But he is in...Italy on some important job."

"Must be a long distant call. He must be somebody else."

He got up to attend to the phone.

"Suraiya, he is unsure of himself."

"Not exactly."

"What has become of him, that is the problem? Nobody wanted this. This rejection! He should be forgiving."

"They have been censuring him severely...in an indirect way he usually tells me."

"May be, they must be feeling emotionally infused. Romi and...I know them, they were self-abnegating. Always trying to remain in the background. They looked unabashed. It was a triumphant simulation."

"Are you..."

"I meet my familiar relations. Yes. No, restriction."

"You didn't..."

"I don't want. It is a jaded...insipid tale of defeat and coarse impropriety. Now it is free living. An artist's life is also not..."

She was deeply wounded within.

"I wanted you to..." She resumed after a painful pause, "It is his destiny. When he retires, he will occupy Patel's position or even may go higher. Yes, once when gone to a minister's house I was to get a fashion show inaugurated..."

It was a long-winding argument that defended Jaycee.

"He may be a Governor one day or...a strong political nexus is protecting him. Here too his writ runs. He is the boss but he is...his own wife, children and parents..." She took a cigarette, "I smoke, drink. But that is not a fault. I had also passed through..."

She thought and changed the topic, "Uncle."

Her voice was sharp and raised.

I found there was an inherent resentment. When the word "Uncle" struck me, I penetrated into her deep eyes.

"..." I wished to say many words of love or consolation, softly and tenderly, yet some unknown power discouraged me.

"We have lost but still not disheartened."

Her head was wilting down like a dead and dry branch and I saw she was in a deep trance. The door at the back opened where we were sitting. We turned back and saw Jaycee standing with a few letters and three albums.

"Wants my consent. Yes I will go."
He handed over the albums to me, "See the smiles and the closeness."
"What was he saying?"
"He sought clearance for my visit to Italy. A great assignment. Some business matters. A few multinationals interested in establishing their units. Crores of foreign investment in India. It is prestigious."
"You are all in favour of foreign collaboration?" I said and started looking into the coloured photographs.
"I think we can move ahead. We should. There is brightness and future."
He was in a brooding demeanour and looked quite stately.
"These are beautiful photographs."
It was a ritual, I thought, I performed. There was no elation or joy.
"Are you going?"
"Yes, I should." Jaycee said and added in a commanding voice.
"You will also go." He was addressing Suraiya.
"..."
"Yes, I have told him to make suitable arrangements for exhibitions and fashion shows." Jaycee was subdued and patient now.
"I shall be..."
"No argument."
Suraiya took a cigarette and lit it with an expression of satisfaction.
"For how many months?"
"I want to get rid of these pigmies. To Italy with love."
I watched and listened to the few lines, indicating enrichment and fulfilment of a long-cherished desire. They were lost for a few minutes in their own plans.
"That old man has high hopes."
I could find brilliant sparkles in their eyes. At that time her presence was significant. Jaycee said to me while handing over a letter, "These snaps, letters and diaries are my valuable possessions."
He looked beyond the horizon, it appeared, for in his eyes, I found hundreds of rainbows. There was an unusual and blustery power in his words when he slowly unfolded his future plans with renewed hopes, "My friend, there is a future beyond this life. Those soaring heights are calling me. I think whatever has happened, it was a predetermined plan."
"I shall feel for them. However for a greater cause one has to suffer. This country has given me life and purpose...Now I would like to move. Why cling to past? It is over. Time has always been on

our side. Today the idea to go to Italy and then...A man lives here and expands with petty human feelings. I too feel the same. If they wanted to go, yes, it is fine. I am here. Suraiya is there. I think life is purposeful, when you widen and broaden your outlook. There are other horizons. New relations and a far more bright cosmos. A new search positively gives you inspiration to live differently and so I am here. How long can you carry the burden of dead relations? It gives you pain. Let the time act. Man lives in time and finishes off."

I was struck by the sheer force of his poetic explosion. He was candid and true to himself. The change could be transitory, I thought.

"She was right."

"Suraiya is never wrong. At this age, she has enormous pulling strength. An artist par excellence."

"I was thinking of Romi."

"Romi, Oh yes." He spoke in a detached manner, "It was a journey, very long and tiring. But now, I think, a man has to move and complete his assigned duty. I am sorry for my parents who died in tragic circumstances. I also regret that my wife...decided to go about in different directions. But you will find, all of us have a right to live in our own way. It is an individual who is important. A man's identity is far more sacred than a mere attachment which stifles and sickens."

"..." I thought I was groping in the dark. There was a massive thrust within and I experienced I was being driven virtually to a dark tunnel without an end.

I closed my eyes in desperation.

There was a mild split of laughter. I opened my eyes and saw Suraiya throwing a purposeful smile disarmingly but voicelessly. There was pure grace and a pious charm.

Jaycee said again in a convincing manner, "Let me put it in different words. There is nothing unwanted or untoward. You open this heart. Numerous wounds and scars. I have listened to all. I have also closed my ears to some but there has been a continuous search. If a man loses here he gains somewhere else. I faded away. Yes, I lost them but I also progressed. I blossomed. She has been with me. You have been hinting at sufferings but I find it is a mental condition. At the physical level, you never really suffer. It is a transitory phase. Your miseries are linked with your mental and spiritual state. And to this I say it is futile.

"Freedom is very important. It enlarges and expands you. I think I have yet to finish my work. Don't you ever think that limits of the land restrict a man? A true man goes beyond the visible world. It is

the world of joy. Here a man lives and laughs and so the long and uncertain journey to Italy is imminent. We ought to unlock our minds. I must agree though reluctantly that there is still a hope."
   He exploded violently into a laughter.
   I made a movement to stand up. I found my body was stiff, heavy and icy-cold. With stupendous efforts, I leaped forward and lost myself in the flower-beds. The roaring, boisterous and blustering laughter still chasing me. Suraiya, after a few minutes, approached me with soft steps, held my hand and implored to forget. I laughed and laughed without an end and realised that a new world full of hopes and brightness waited for us at a distance.

*** *** ***